T0209136

Long Way to the Horizon

A Bridge on the Prairie

ROBERT HUNTER

LONG WAY TO THE HORIZON
A BRIDGE ON THE PRAIRIE

iUniverse books may be ordered through booksellers or by contacting:

iUniverse
1663 Liberty Drive
Bloomington, IN 47403
www.iuniverse.com
844-349-9409

ISBN: 978-1-6632-1217-7 (sc)
ISBN: 978-1-6632-1218-4 (e)

Library of Congress Control Number: 2020921067

Print information available on the last page.

iUniverse rev. date: 11/04/2020

Dedicated to

My Grandchildren and Greatgrandchild
that sadly I could not see grow and thrive

Alexandra Hunter/ Paquin and Max
Chaz Hunter Laroche
Dexter Hunter Laroche
Rhys Gittens
Gwynn Gittens
River Hunter
Rocket Hunter
Phoenix Hunter

And to my wife
Bobbi Hunter
who walked to the horizon and beyond with me

FOREWORD

Bob Hunter, first President and visionary behind the Greenpeace Foundation, had been commissioned in 1977 by Holt Rinehart Winston to write the early history of the Greenpeace movement. The book was swiftly brought to print in January of 1979. His well received book "**Warriors of the Rainbow**" pleased the editors and management at Holt Rinehart Winston, so much so that they subsequently asked Bob to write another book.

The *Thorn Birds*, a 1977 best-selling novel by the Australian author Colleen McCullough was making the best sellers lists internationally and the strategists at Holt Rinehart Winston thought Bob would be the ideal candidate to write a multi-generational Canadian saga. Bob had a very graphic and insightfully emotive style of writing similar to that of Colleen McCullough.

Bob settled in to writing this book in the early 80s. We lived on a small hobby farm near the outskirts of Vancouver. At the back of our three acres there was a meandering creek. Overlooking the creek, we had a funky little structure built that looked like a sharecropper's cabin complete with the rocking chair on the front porch.

Each morning he would head to his writing cabin and I would head off to my work and drop our little son off at daycare. We were full of hope and responsibilities. It was the best of times.

About a year into the writing of the book we received sad news that his much-admired editor had just had a heart attack and died. Bob had been working with this same editor through his earlier book "**Warriors of the Rainbow**" The editor and agent of his earlier successful book had been instrumental in getting Bob signed on to complete this new Canadian saga which he was tentatively calling "**Long Way to the Horizon**" It was very disconcerting and painful news. Soon after the publisher let Bob know they had assigned a new person as editor. This new editor was a woman and needed the time to read the book in its current state of three quarters finished. She took a long time to read the manuscript which put Bob off his stride. When she replied she basically wanted Bob to toss his work out and start it over with a strong feminist angle. Bob was depressed and, in a rage, but after a few cathartic drunken sessions he succumbed to our financial realities of needing the payments and with heavy heart started the rewrite. He was halfway finished with the new and less improved version of the book when they fired the second editor and brought in another editor. They had paid the advance money at this point, so, when the third editor wanted his complete rewrite, Bob gave up. At this point Bob had written approximately one thousand pages.

Life went on, but life throws you unexpected ups and downs. Bob had proudly been the driving force in the birth of the Greenpeace Foundation and now suddenly after his departure all his work in setting down the principals of Greenpeace was being destroyed by the new regime of people who were in the midst of vicious internal fighting. The degeneration of Greenpeace on top of the huge disappointment in his hopes of writing the great Canadian novel having been crushed, caused Bob to become very depressed. He was adrift with no horizon in sight.

By the end of the 80s, I pushed and won the struggle to move our family to Toronto for greater opportunities. Bob, ever optimistic and resilient, soon was hired on at City TV and became a local celebrity with three shows airing on various slots. He once again became the voice of the environmental movement and continued to inspire many people through his writing and his on-air work. We happily settled into our new life with our two children Will and Emily.

Bob and I always shared a passion for the book, "**Long Way to the Horizon**", that had not gotten published. Over the years we tried to condense it, re-edit it, and tailor it to the times. We tried a few times to get it published, but we never found the right timing for its emergence. We often laughed at the title for indeed it did seem like a long way to the horizon.

Tragically we lost Bob early from cancer in 2005

Through the years Bob wrote about eighteen books. Thirteen of these books were published. He won several prestigious awards for his writing and his book "**Warriors of the Rainbow** "has been turned into an award-winning documentary called "**How to Change the World**".

I have now taken it upon myself to try to get some of Bob's unpublished works published. I want to honour Bob's art and the time and energy that he put into some of these books, so that they do not just remain with us but are instead shared.

This version of the saga is a modification of the original book. All of Bob's works are at the University of Toronto Library Archives. I cannot access them at the present time due to Covid. I found this version of the "**Long Way to the Horizon**" at home in hard copy. I transcribed this book and I am now getting it self-published. It will be available for any Bob Hunter friends, family and fans to purchase.

Many of the people in the story are modelled from Bob's French-Canadian family and many of the scenes are places Bob remembered experiencing as a child. This is a fictional book but as with most of Bob's life work it contains some very real truths about the human condition. We do not have to look back far in our history to see the racial and religious fears and injustices that are perpetrated on innocent people and how this affects their whole lives.

Look around at the times we live in and see the same heart

wrenching inequalities being forced on the innocents. See the power structures not listening to the weaker sectors of our society. See the twisted religious indifference to moral rights.

It seems like we never learn from the past.

Bobbi Hunter
September 2020

PART ONE

DEPARTURE - PRINCE RUPERT, B. C.

1979

Like a camera lens folding shut but never quite actually closing, the breakers swept against the hunched stone shoulder of Vancouver Island. Plumes of spray erupted over the rocks. Along speckled beaches. Waves heaved themselves forward, hissing greedily as they sucked tons of sand down into the foamy chaos. Lengths of ribbon kelp lay snagged among the colonies of starfish and razor clams. Through the binoculars, having to wipe the lens with her precious Japanese silk scarf, Bernadette Wilding caught glimpses, despite the clouds blurring jerkily across the lens of the old packer heaved toward the northeastern lee of the island, of fragile fingers of coral clinging to rocks where the surf pounded most adamantly. It seemed impossible they could survive without being snapped. Here and there a blue crab emerged out of the sizzling whorls, claws wagging in defiance, only to vanish in the next green lime avalanche. The pockmarked zone of barnacles and scallops was scoured free again of all creatures save those which could cling with a grip of iron. In rims of saliva, the water left its imprint, depositing the chemicals that ate at the island's shell. The wind at the stern, coming from around Cape Scott, had the fir and hemlock writhing as though dancing, while the arbutus trees along the shore cowered stiffly like old men on their knees, twisted into supplication. There was something more marvellously exultant about that first shout of the gales of winter.

Out of slanting grey sky, wet gobs began to fall, clicking on the water. In the mouth of the Sound, the whole horizon was in motion, thrusting forward, drawing away, tossing as those straining to escape to the sky. Leaping up *after* something! A line of squall obliterated the thousands of fragments of rocks awaiting the unwary helmsman. From out here, just before the *Mary Boehm* reached shelter, the silver veins of the continents wall appeared to be engulfed by waves, and the sea seemed to have conquered the whole world. The black water steamed, and sizzled foam spread like flat little bombs. Gulls pin wheeled and shouted.

KYKYKYKYKYKY

The boat made a chulgh chulgh chug noise with another noise within it, chit chit chit, and with that yet another sound chut chut chut. Reflections of scuttling clouds ran across the puddles on the deck, worked into mandalas by the vibrations from the big Atlas diesel. In the late afternoon light, scattered fish scales were half ignited as tiny rainbow petals.

For a moment, the old, familiar thrill of being out on the water glowed its way through her limbs, vanquishing the bone deep, nearly ever-present ache of arthritis. David and Linda kept telling her she was crazy not to move to Vancouver, get away from the infernal rain and damp and fog, how could you stay up there? Besides, she was missing out on the Granny trip, as David called it. Little Paul was getting un-little fast. Bernadette smiled at the thought of her daughter and son-in-law and grandson who would soon enough be in her arms. It would be good to be closer to them for sure and that was always possible, but then she'd lose the independence which had changed in the last few years from loneliness to surprising un-false sense of freedom—at last. Why struggle with others? If they want to do something their way, let them. She quite enjoyed no bigger a task than caring for herself and her own life. She was still quite capable, nobody challenged that. She did not need anyone, after all. God, if she had only known *that* from the beginning, but, after all, maybe she *had* known, and somehow hadn't allowed herself to accept it, because she had too many responsibilities to be able to let go. She had not asked to be alone, but now that she was, she found herself hugely relieved. Of course, she loved everybody, but she had never experienced being by herself in her life that she could remember except for a few precious hours stolen here and there, like after fainting in church, or taking care of chickens. Even before, when she played the piano, there was almost always someone within hearing range, and she was always affected by it. It was only now, with the house John built overlooking the Bay all to herself, and two widows pensions to sustain her, her nearest neighbor a mile down the trail, could Bernadette play to her heart's content, the cruel part being the arthritis, of course, coming now. If it could have held off for a few more years... In any event, it was good therapy: keep the fingers moving, until it started to hurt too much, even for her, and she was good solid French-Canadian prairie stock. There I go again, she sighed, sounding like *him*. And anyway, if she moved to Vancouver, she would not have any excuse to be out *here* anymore, would she? Also, face it, there was a pleading tone in the kids' voices. Maybe at least a *little* bit of babysitting duty, eh? Yeh, yeh. They love you most when they want something. Once they have gotten the habit, and they all get it as bebes they never lose it. Help me, help me.

Bernadette refocused on the not so distant shoreline. The shock of how close they seemed to be, for a second gave her heart a small thump, despite her utter confidence in Jim Boehm. He had asked her twice, since Mary had died, to marry him, and he had taken both no's like a gentleman. She knew he would never allow anything to happen to her, especially on a boat *he* was running. There was nothing to worry about -- well, to the extent you could say that about the coast, when hundreds of brigs, schooners, steam collier's, sloops, cannery tenders, salvage scows, mission boats, barges and fish packers lay on the bottom, mostly just skeletons with cedar ribs. While it was only the magnification of the binocular lens that had made it seem to Bernadette that they were just about up on the rocks, Jim was in a businesslike mood today, as always a respecter of weather, which they all knew was coming, so he wasn't wasting time. His headings were straight-line from marker to marker, and that did bring them in closer than usual to the shore. With the tide and the wind up, and a following sea, the boat *seemed* to be sliding toward one particular pile of mountain wreckage thrusting out from the beach, it's purple and orange stratum of starfish and barnacles revealed like gums supporting crumbling teeth as the surf drew slavering back, preparing another massive slapping assault. Knowing that Jim would welcome a chance to reassure her, Bernadette looked up to the wheelhouse and pointed toward the approaching rocks. She'd been around too long to take anyone else's brains for granted. After losing two of her men to the sea, she was *allowed* to express any tiny little anxiety she had.

Jim waved and nodded and climbed out on the deck, unfortunately leaving the wheel to fend for itself, and yelled. "No problem, Bern! Deep here. Half a cable easy."

"Half a cable, my ass! Just get your butt back to the wheel!" She shouted in a joking tone, she was expected to, but meaning it.

Jim chuckled and slouched back inside, dropping his big paws on the wheel and cranking her over a few notches. On his own, a seasoned skipper like Jim Boehm would have cut through the gap there. Couple of feet clearance. Long as you know what you're doing. But we'll go round, just to make the poor old gal happy. After all, she's probably thinking Frank Stein and John Wilding figured they knew what they were doing too. Then there was that husband of hers, sad story as well, truck crash out on the prairies, something like that. Never really asked her about it much. Mind you, a-sure can't tell from looking at her or listening to her, always cheery, not a moaner that one. Think she didn't have a regret in the world, but she sure ain't been lucky. No wonder she wouldn't …

Unhappily, he let it fade.

Bernadette was, indeed, thinking about Frank Stein at that moment. And, strangely enough, almost fondly.

Even in his final years, no matter how drunk, he would have loved to be here, like this, she realized, with the late afternoon light burnishing the swells, the clouds fleeing from whatever was building up out there on the open water. Despite his awful failings, Frank loved the sea. She had confused that love for a kind of intelligence that turned out not to be there. She had overrated him, assumed he was more than he was. It was their mutual admiration for the sea, indeed, even their hunger for it, that eased the pain of not being able to *reach* him for a long time after communications had been lost. It was something that overwhelmed them both, and at least they could be overwhelmed together. Otherwise, Mon Dieu, what a waste of precious years! The familiar anger flared up. Was it ever possible to get over it? Still a …twinge. A love between them *had* existed. It had been real, it had stirred her deeply, it had changed her. She had lost an old version of herself, and it was gone for good, as good as dead after that. That is what love was about. Even just a few minutes of true sacredness, a sanctified state, she had gone through it. It had not been hormones or drinks. There was nothing wrong with her memory, and she could still recreate those high emotional moments. Maybe once or twice a year was all she would allow herself, though, because it left her weeping and aching. And worst of all, longing. She knew whose fault it was that it got all torn apart. So clumsily and for such stupid banal reasons! They said it was a disease, the booze, but she did not believe that. It was a choice he made, damn it. It was equally possible he might have grown. Given more time he might have actually begun to mature, although she had an extremely hard time imagining Frank as a mature male. He would have to change into a different species, nearly. Although, obviously, at one goofy, delusional time in her life she certainly *thought* she had some sort of chance of bringing him *up*, literally. There was that one obscure line of poetry he managed to hang onto no matter how much the alcohol consumed him: "You never enjoy the world aright, till the Sea itself flows in your veins."

Had he seen it coming? Had he in fact willed it? This was what she secretly believed, although she had never said it to anyone. That wouldn't be fair. After all, he hadn't really been evil -- at least not until near the end. The thought of Frank, in the rare context of a moment of tenderness, flushed -- perhaps in defense -- loving images of John to mind, John, who had possessed all the strength Frank had lacked, but which hadn't been enough to save him in the end, either. Two husbands lost to the sea.

One lost in flames on a Dead Sea bottom -- his own fault, too, really. Laverne McLeod shouldn't have been out on that road in the middle of February just to get to a bonspiel.

By now those pains -- like violin strokes, she often thought -- merely tickled and shivered through, their worst effect being to inevitably bring to life the most debilitating, unhealable wound of all: a clear-as-a-bell sighting of her beloved Stephen, the self-tortured young man who would have been slouched against the wheelhouse in this setting, hands deep in his pockets, shoulders hunkered to block out anyone around him, staring, haunted by things he had no control over, at the westerly sky, seeing some sort of apocalypse, his mind a billion, maybe a trillion miles away. She'd never seen such a dreamer in her life as that boy of hers had been, but then her sisters all said he got it from her, just because she could talk a blue streak. She knew, in truth, where it really came from: that lost-in-space listening-to-the-angels, out-of-touch-with-anyone-except-themselves, half-here, have-not personality, it had been Mon Pere, of course. It was him who passed the demons along, not herself, and certainly not Laverne, whose brain was in his pants. She never made that case, though. She was amazed that none of the others saw it, but then they were such blockheads, all of them. And *she* certainly was not going to be the one to stigmatize her only son by saying that he was the very incarnation of his grandfather, although thankfully soft rather than hard as a brick, or cruel. Stephen didn't have a cruel bone in him, he was like Laverne that way, whereas Joe the Mouth went out of his way to hurt people. He had a gift for it, a real talent. Mon Dieu, she could almost picture the old bastarde himself here on the deck, and wouldn't that be a sight? Prairie dog that he was, he never saw an ocean in his life, so far as she knew. She savored the idea of him seasick. But why waste time on make believe? Her moment of revenge was coming. She would be striking him on his deathbed, and what could be a better time? It would be like driving a stake into his feeble heart. She hoped she would have the satisfaction of seeing it kill him.

She *knew* he was not dead yet, even though Lorene's voice had been full of urgency over the phone from Montreal. He *could* die, it was true, in the time it was taking her to make her way down the coast by serving as a cook on Jim Boehm's packer as he deadheaded down to Steveston yards to put the old boat up on the ways for the winter. It was just herself, Jim, old Doug Moore acting as an engineer, that silver flask of his hanging as precariously as ever from his hip coverall pocket, and a deckhand, a boy, probably Haida, she thought she'd seen before, but couldn't place him. When she asked his name, he muttered the answer so shyly she missed it, and decided to let him off the hook. He would get over the shyness soon enough once she got a meal in him. Probably running, but then again more probably not. Jim wouldn't want to go getting himself in trouble over a runaway. Anyway, the boy knew his lines and knots, and kept to himself. Jim was no talker, either. Easy passage! Three meals, sandwiches, a heap of eggs, toast, bacon and beans in the morning. As for herself, she just picked as she cooked. Grazing, she called it. One good thing about getting older, you don't waste so much time eating.

It would only have been a day and a half faster taking the ferry, and, besides, she was used to earning her way rather than throwing money overboard. The cost of the train to Montreal, Linda and the baby's fares, meals probably some taxis: all that would have taken too big a bite out of her modest budget, but John, bless him, had bought a few bits of land here and there, and phoning up that young couple who had been begging to buy the three acre waterfront on Desolation Sound, and saying "Okay," had been easy. Although Linda would whine to heaven if she knew. Bernadette would tell her the money was coming out of a stock dividend, or something. But the main reason she was travelling by boat -- there being no road -- was a grimly learned coastwise bias. There was no way Bernadette was going to climb, at her age, on board one of those deathtrap, bucket of bolts China Clippers just to get from Prince Rupert to Vancouver, en-route to face a father on the other side of the country, whom she hadn't talked to in years -- not, damn it, since that night, the night before her wedding to Laverne, when Mon Pere, mustered all his bitterness and pettiness and poison, fully employing that instinct he seemed to have to try to ruin her life at every turn, had announced that he was refusing to attend the marriage of his oldest daughter to a goddamned Protestant.

Even a careening memory-flash of that night was like a bruise being elbowed. But then, there were so many things, so many hurts and grievances and wounds and festering sores, and, one thing was for sure, he had certainly succeeded in leaving an emotional legacy. Somehow, he had sunk his bitterness into her, like a fishhook. She had spent her whole life fighting that nagging, itching, loose tooth undercurrent of rage and frustration, the horrible certainty that so much of what could have been beautiful and joyful had been wrecked, botched, soiled, trampled. And all because she had been given the worst possible father she could have had, under the circumstances, and the last moron in the world whom she would have chosen to hold her faith in his hands. *Everything* was his fault, from the disappearance of the piano that would have given her a *career*, instead of a lifetime in the shadows, to that first disastrous marriage to Laverne, whom she only married, she had quickly but belatedly realized, to spite Mon Pere. Frank caught her on the rebound, and that proved to be even more disastrous a relationship.

And, of course, ultimately, there was the death of Ma Mere that he had to answer for.

Bernadette twitched suddenly, lowered the binoculars, tingling for a moment with the feeling that she was not alone on deck. This feeling happened more often with the passing years. It was not so much alarm; it was more like a reflex. But, of course, a quick look around told her, she was absolutely alone-- unless there were ghosts out here with her, the spray hissing through them without leaving even an outline. She had prided herself, ever since leaving the church, on her stern rationality. But there were times when she was almost sure the ghost--spirits, essences, shades, lost souls -- existed, reason notwithstanding. At times she could see them all. Laverne and Frank and John, but mainly Frank, probably because he brought his death on himself. Sometimes, when she looked down into the water, she swore for an instant here and an instant there, she saw him floating amid the kelp or in the shadows along the cliff-face. Was it because her first, overwhelming reaction when she heard he had drowned was: Thank you, Mon Dieu! She was free.

It was late in the season, and only a few boats were out, tugs and ferries, the mattress- loving yachting fools, who tied their boats together on log booms and drank all night through every weekend of the summer were mercifully gone. The whole way down Grenville channel, Bernadette had counted only three other fish boats, all of them long liners heading the other way, hoping to make it across the open mouth of Hecate Strait to the Alaska stretch of the Inside Passage before the Gulf got too sloppy. She glimpsed a school boat slicing through the rain off Klemtu, and the back end of a tanker disappearing around China Hat. Otherwise, just the slish of the *Mary Boehm*'s bow through the water, the chugh- chit- chut of the engine, the twanging of the guy-lines, the flopping of a rubber tire that somebody forgot to bring in against the hull, and the distant oddly metallic, echoing sound of falling boulders.

The paint of the old eighty footer's hull had been gouged away, revealing flesh colored naked fir. Her rigging was frayed. Broken lines had been slashed with wire. The deckhouse was white, like the hull, but the paint had flaked away in huge scabs and one of its portholes was cracked. Rust stains ran down from the pipe railing around the upper deck. The insides of the bulwarks were a fluorescent aquamarine green, peeled and streaked with free-flowing rust. At the starboard stern sat an ancient Clinker-built lifeboat, mounted on pitted chocks.

The Haida boy was sitting back there, she suddenly realized. Had he been there all along? He looked like a Space Bunny with big green plastic headphones hooked up to a tape recorder, his whole-body jingling to the music. Feeling playful, Bernadette turned, hoisted the binoculars, even though he was just forty feet away, and focused on his face. He was staring down into the cauldron boiling whitely in the black water out from the stern. A good-looking boy, although not your classical Haida of features. Dimly at first, she realized he could not be Haida, after all. Some mix. You saw all kinds up here. Despite the icy nor-westerly blast, he was clad in only jeans, a jean jacket and gumboots, even more reason to suspect he was running away. Long black hair ... His face: so much like...Oh, Mon Dieu, what was his name? *Another* full-force memory rush, up from the deep inside! What was going on today? He had been a mix, too. Part Cree -- or was he Assiniboine? Part French, anyway, which was why he had been in the Catholic school in Agassiz. This boy wasn't much older than that other Indian kid had been in Manitoba the summer the grasshoppers were so bad.

Bernadette lowered the binoculars abruptly, a new wound seeming to open in her chest. This was crazy. What was going on? All these memories are getting stirred up. She hadn't thought of *him* for years and years! And how could that have happened? To have buried him so deeply you forgot. Was this what it was like, losing your mind. She had seen it in others, for sure. Knew it could happen. But losing her heart too? Losing those emotions? And with them, even the name? It was horrifying. The boy, the Indian boy who was her first true, pure love, and, who, in a natural, just world, a world in a state of *Grace*, as they used to talk about in the church, she would have run off with, and they would have lived a *whole different life*, a life as completely different as the life of a concert pianist would have been, compared to what happened instead. It made her almost sick to her stomach, an unpleasant, vertiginous flush of weakness, each time the thought hit her. *It could have all been so beautiful.* There were so many points -- well, perhaps not that many, but key ones -- where people could have simply done some other little thing than they did, and they would still be alive. Laverne could have stayed home that night instead of going to meet the boys (but then why did that little floozy know about it before me?) Frank could have decided to ride out the weather on the boat and not give in to his cowardice (or was he, just possibly, really trying for the first time in his life?), and John had others to save (given his character, no choice), so perhaps it didn't always apply. Storms and politics had a way of intruding, making things turn horribly for the worst whether it was your own damned, stupid fault or not. The war certainly was not Laverne's fault, and it messed him up, even though he did not take a scratch. Frank, of course stuck hating himself for being a Kraut. That damned, godawful war. Yes, it ruined things too. It was not just Mon Pere. She had been *born* at the wrong time -- although, she reminded herself sharply, Mon Pere had done all his damage *before* the war. Her life was already squashed by the time Hitler came around. Couldn't blame him for *that!*

Besides, there was nothing she could ever have done against a monster over in Europe -- whereas there was something awfully specific she could do to that other horrible little fascist over here. That was the word for him, what he had always been, even though she had never read the word -- even if she couldn't help *hearing* it often enough -- until just before the war broke out. She was selective, even then, in her reading. She had not wanted to know *anything* about politics. She had had enough of it when her father was mayor of Saint Boniface, and for years, enough before and after that. She had seen politics up close, around the family dinner table, and in the smoking room, their harsh drunken laughter. It sickened her. The plotting. The indifference to how much they hurt others. The savagery. The glee. The arrogance. Above all, the hatred that motivated them. She recognized what the word fascist, meant, at least in terms of behavior, immediately upon seeing the word in print. That is what he had been, alright. Her own father, Joseph Labouchere, had been a fascist in his heart, at home, at work, in politics. He deserved everything he got -- except that there was only one more astonishing, unexpected pain that could be inflicted on him. And this she swore she could do. It was within her reach.

For a moment, she felt her heart rate speed up. Must watch that. She took a deep breath, wrapping the scarf around the wool turtleneck that hid the cancer scar on her neck. Enough of the binoculars. She slipped her sunglasses on. Ever since the operation, back in the early 50s, her eyes had not been able to take the outside light for long periods and she certainly did not want to go blind again. Three months had been enough of that -- and here, suddenly, was another memory welling up, the image of herself sitting at a table while Stephen, barely five, groped his way through the headlines, forcing himself to learn to read so he could be "Mommy's eyes". Phew! Didn't *that* bring up a lump of broken, bloody emotion? Bernadette faked wind in her eyes, took the sunglasses off to wipe the tears away with the scarf, took another deep breath, readjusted the glasses, and decided, needing relief from her volatile memories, it was time the skipper had some coffee.

As she moved across the deck to the galley, folding the binoculars back into their pouch, the boy sang out from the Clinker:

"You OK, Granny?"

"Watch who you call, "Granny", sonny," she answered, nevertheless letting herself sound like somebody's grandmother.

It was her habit to camouflage herself. It was much easier, she'd learned long ago, not to let them know you see right through them. Might as well act out what they expect, or they get confused and uncomfortable. True of all men, from old farts like Jim Boehm to this little cutie. Mind he was used to manipulating his old aunts, and probably females in general, around something fierce, this one.

When he started to follow her into the galley, she stopped him.

"Before you start begging for treats, sonny, better fetch that loose bumper from the other side. Old Jim won't be happy if he sees it."

She smiled briefly as he hopped to it, a stricken look on his face, immediately understanding the enormity of the failure. He has got a chance, thought Bernadette darkly, not quite able to shake the resurging feeling of loss eating at her: he is insecure. That's good. You need to be.

It was with a bleak eye that she viewed galley. At least the boy had done his job, which was to wash the dishes and put them away. Jim wasn't going to have the still-marriable, much widowed Mrs. Wilding doing the dishes when there was a thirty-three-pound slacker sitting around, twiddling his thumbs, meaning the kid. Too bad he'd hung the mugs the wrong way – Kids! All they do is watch TV.

It was a small space, as galleys on boats this size went. A ceiling to floor fridge occupied the area between the door leading to the aft deck and the stove. The handle of the fridge was just tied together with wire, and during the crossing of the Johnstone Sound, it had torn apart, whacking the side of the table and spilling milk cartons, boxes of ice cream, lumps of frozen meat and tubes of frozen juice all over the place. Luckily, nobody had been sitting there. Several times, cupboards had popped open, sending jars of jam, packages of beans, pancake mix and cans of sardines flying everywhere. The stove itself hadn't been properly scoured for years. And grey-blue flecks of metal kept coming up on her flipper. It only had one temperature: blast furnace. Bachelor boats! They were all alike. From the day Mary died, this boat had started going downhill and so had poor Jim. Jim and the old boat, she mused, were exactly as weathered as each other. Every gouge in the boat's side matched some injury of Jim's, like the three missing fingers and the squinty eye and the scar across his cheek. She *had* thought of marrying him, just to help him back on his feet. But it was *helping* again, and she didn't have the compassion left, or maybe she just plain didn't care as much anymore about all these damaged human beings staggering around in the world, and how much they all needed so much help. Possibly she did not care about *anybody* as much as she used to anymore.

Although, she had to amend that. She had to admit to a weak spot. The one and only time she had so far held little Paul in her arms (stubborn, independent cuss of a grandmother who will not move down to Vancouver) Bernadette had felt something she had never felt before. There was a hush, almost, through her entire being, and then a wave of relief and joy and pure triumph. She felt so moved, her whole body and mind, no thoughts, just pure bliss, that tears filled her eyes. It was a letting go, somehow, as though an invisible tide had surged back and forth between them, passing through the molecules. Linda got all flighty and possessive, the hormonal birth-convulsions not having quite settled, and tried to take the baby away. With a feral growl, Bernadette turned her back to her daughter, holding her grandson in a grip of wrought iron: the most fragile, precious, beautiful, warm, perfect smelling thing that could ever have been created (all of time in this moment!), holding him and feeling his little heart pulsating like a rabbits through both their bodies, calling up that long lost nimbus like glow she used to experience around rosaries and crucifixes and altars and Holy Bread and when the organ played. A grandchild. Miracle compounded. A second stepping of something from out of herself. A new, independent limb, an extension, out *there*, but still a part of herself. In the infant's utterly black, fully dilated pupils (it was immediately after the delivery), she had seen -- space. She staggered; afraid she would faint. A void as big as the night sky without any trace of stars or a moon. It was like she was looking *into* the universe and somehow seeing through some amazing hourglass type of mirror *out* into it. She had been so struck by the experience it had left her feeling exhausted but oddly peaceful, contemplative, slightly serene for days, thinking she had glimpsed some Great Truth. In the end, she could not figure out what to make of it. Not even now, she groaned. After all these years. She *was* supposed to find out before she passed on, surely? But then, that was a baseless idea, as zany in its own way as the Catholic brainwashing it had taken so long to rid herself of. The last time in Vancouver, she must have spent too much time listening to David babbling all his new age, Buddhist, hippy dippy nonsense. Did she personally know anybody who looked like they had seen the Truth before they died? Not one. Not one. They all died ignorant as they were born.

The boy had slipped onto the bench by the table and was dragging some peanut butter out of the can with a spoon when Jim came in and his eyes fell upon the row of China mugs on the hook above the window sill, his face turned a dark purple colour.

"Yuh goddamn ninny!" he yelled at the boy, shaking his fist and kicking his foot in a rage at the bulwark.

Bernadette's eyes, too, jumped to the mugs. She winced, knowing what was happening. It seemed for a moment Jim was going to grab the kid and throw him overboard.

"Don't you know anything, yuh gaddamn farmer!" Yuh don't hang cups facing *outward*! They gotta be facin' *inwards*! Goddamn jerk!"

He whirled toward the sink, but Bernadette was already reaching for the offending mug, turning them around.

"Goddamn kid," Jim growled, glaring at him. The boy had the good sense to be cowering, looking thoroughly miserable, ashamed and scared. "Think an Indian kid'd know better!"

Jim lunged across the table and grabbed the boy by the upper arm. His big ham sized hand, the one with the fingers missing, bunched into a fist. As his elbow cocked back, the boy squirmed frantically, trying to tear himself loose.

That was when the blackened kettle came hurtling across the room, missing Jim's nose by inches and clanging against the fridge, the lid ricocheting off the bench, brown water and coffee grains splattering across the table. It had happened so quickly; Bernadette was already in full swing before she realized what she was doing. There was only the slightest hesitation -- and that was over whether to hit Jim right on the head or give him a warning shot over the bow. By the time the big lug turned in astonishment to look at her, "What the fu--?" she was grabbing for the frying pan, hoisting it off the stove with both hands, advancing on him with deadly serious intent. Released by the skipper, who was stepping back in shock, the kid scrambled to the end of the table and dived through the aft door.

"You damn well leave him alone, Jim Boehm," Bernadette snarled, "He didn't know!"

"Well, I'd a god-damned made sure he'd know in the future!" Jim bellows, a shudder going through him as he wrestles himself under control, studying - like an object he'd never seen before in his life-- the big iron frying pan in Bernadette's hand.

"Yuh ain't yourself, Bern. What the *hell* you think you're doin'?"

"I'm going to hammer somebody on the head is what!"

"Jesus Bern, you can't go gettin soft."

"Just leave him alone."

"Bern it, it's my ship! I'll run it my way!"

"Then you can get yourself another cook."

His voice went plaintiff. "Bern hangin' them mugs up wrong's the worst damn bad luck thing you can do! You know that."

Oh, he was stung, not just by her taking any old position she wanted, regardless of what her position had been previously. This was a theological debate now, even though it had a highly physical look: Jim's nose, smudged with grease, seems small and bearlike, his hands were curled like claws. She could almost feel his hackles coming up. Yet he was a wounded old priest, not an animal. She had shocked him more by her heresy than by throwing the kettle or waving the frying pan. Physical violence he could understand, he was on boats most of his life. But to deny what *every* fisherman knew to be the absolute truth! Boats that were sunk always had a cup hung up facing the wrong way. If any female on earth ought to know the truth of that, it should be this little French gal standing here threatening him with his own frying pan. And it was true. If there was anything Bernadette's two departed fishermen husbands would have agreed on, it was the Law of The Mugs. German, English, it didn't matter. Culture be hanged, this was something to do with the deadly mysteries of the sea, which took some, spared others. Amen. It was not something to mock, especially in the swells, with only that thin cedar or tin shell between you and the rocks, should your luck change. That's the difference between land and sea, she mused, on land sometimes you realize how lucky you are to be alive. At sea you realize it all the time. Hang the bloody mugs facing *inward*, for Christ sake. Even if just to keep the peace. Anyway, time to wind this down.

"It's *my* fault, Jim. I should have told him. It's just nobody said anything."

That always worked. Take the blame. Besides, she knew with absolute certainty, there was no way Jim Boehm was going to take a poke at *her*. Hell, he did jump overboard to save her carcass, even if he cannot swim ten strokes. Still, they had to pretend to really *glare* at each other for at least twenty seconds.

"*A lot* of boats have gone down because of ninnies like him," Jim declared solemnly, showing major disappointment that she might have forgotten this salient truth.

She didn't want to play the inevitable card, but it would move things along faster, repair the damage quicker.

"You don't have to remind me," she said softly. Where was the line between acting and real life drawn, she knew her part so well?

It was so easy. So effective. It was real, but how many times could it be real before it wasn't real any longer?

She clanged the frying pan back on the stove, the strength genuinely leaving her. Jim looked away, the fight knocked out of him too, shaking his heads, slowly righting himself.

"Yeah, well I seen boats go down that shouldn't have, he muttered doggedly, turning around with nothing further to say and clumping out through the door that fit his girth and height so perfectly, swinging heavily up the ladder to the wheelhouse.

Bernadette overheard Doug Moore saying, "What's up skipper?"

"Goddamn fool kid hung the goddamn cups facing *outward*."

Doug groaned, "No shit, no shit." And after a minute, asked innocently, "Did I hear something about gettin' throwed?"

"Shuddup."

In the galley, Bernadette had to sit down, abandoning the effort to clean up. She was more shaken than she thought at first. Surprised too. She knew where that outburst had come from and could understand perfectly *why* it had erupted at that moment, but the force of it was rather astonishing. She seemed to be opening up, with each surge of these moments, re-learning the feeling of even the most ancient, hardened-over pain. Maybe she *had* been a warrior in another lifetime, like David was trying to argue, she could have been, and in that case, right now, she would be -- what was it? -- pumping herself up, steeling herself, re-motivating herself, revisiting the memory-scenes of the crime, mentally focusing, witnessing it all again, playing it back like the eight track up in the wheelhouse. Her checklist of grievances. Psyching herself! That was it. After all, this was judgment time. She had never dreamed that It might be herself who would get to judge, to pass the judgment, and to administer the punishment. It was not something she was used to doing. It would be so easy to avoid the whole situation, spare everyone. Just keep her back to him until he was gone, ignore his pathetic, fading cries. For once in her life, she did not want to *help*. She wanted to hurt it.

It was as simple as that. She wanted to *add* to someone's pain. She wanted to increase it to the maximum. She wanted to torture him. But wanting to do it and doing it were two different things. She had never deliberately been cruel. Through stupidity and youthfulness, too many times to count. But there was no -- what did the lawyers call it? --malicious forethought. This was both malicious and completely thought out in advance. And she knew herself. It was so hard to maintain a clear beam of hatred aimed at somebody. Why not just forget about it all? Move on to a new life, enjoy the Granny Trip.

But non! Maybe there is a streak of him in me, after all, she thought, like the worst part of himself coming back to ruin his final hours. She *needed* to feel all these pains again. Each little flare up about forgotten outrage stiffened her resolve. Clearly, she could hear John saying; "Let's see how much will power you got." Rekindled sparks of anger; useful and necessary if she wanted to start having doubts about the wisdom of what she was doing. She *had* been off in La La Land since leaving Rupert, and while it had a lot to do with the motion of the boat in the water, the constant shifting of the deck and the walls and the ceiling, like you were being shaken sluggishly around in a box like a pet rat, there was much more to it, having everything to do with this almost miraculous chance to avenge herself on her father. Although, be practical. The motion of the waves always made her dream spectacularly, and possibly it was also just kind of *loosening up* her memory cells, the ones packed down there at the bottom. No sense getting all psychological on herself.

The boy slipped back into the galley and was towelling up the coffee grains.

She glared at him. "Didn't anybody *tell* you about how to hang cups? Don't you live around here?"

"Nope," he grinned, and she realized with a shock that the little rascal was giggling. Rather than being traumatized, as they said about everything these days, he seemed to think the whole scene had been one big joke, a white man's story he would get to tell the rest of his life. Time the crazy old white granny threw the kettle at the skipper and he backed down like a wet dog. That's how it would come out. Anything to put down the white man. She knew how native humor went.

"Quit laughing. It's not funny," she found. But it was infectious, and suddenly she found herself first giggling, then chortling, then laughing out loud. It was not until she heard a heavy thunk on the wheelhouse floor above -- like a toolbox being dropped -- and she realized Jim and Doug could hear even above the wind. She choked herself off and hushed the boy quiet. No sense poking Jim's bruised ego.

"Where do you come from then?" She asked, calming down. Mon Dieu! That felt good. Standing up to Jim. If she had only stood up to Frank like that right from the start -- ah well --

"Winnipeg. Well close to there, nearer to Portage the Prairie."

The Prairie diaspora. Bernadette's mind suddenly went still. She was completely *here* in the galley, watching the boy's lips move, savoring the sound the sweet sound of his voice. No other thoughts or images intruding. She had to fight hard to control the urge to grab his hand in both of hers. That would be silly. That would be a senile old woman thing to do. Her heart was racing faster than it should, but it seemed as remote as the diesel.

"What are you doing up this neck of the woods on your own?"

"Seeing my Mom. Cousins an' stuff."

"Going back to Portage?"

"Yeh."

"Live with your Dad?"

He nodded, carrying the dirty towel over to the garbage, dribbling coffee grains across the linoleum.

"You're not Haida, eh."

"Mom's Kitasoo. Dad's a Cree. Well, part. Mainly." This last said with pride.

If anything, Bernadette felt cold all over. Afraid.

"Do you have a -- it took her a moment to get the right words out -- a grandfather?

He laughed gleefully. "Looking for a date?"

That saved her from making a fool of herself. "Damn rights, sonny!" She played along." What's his name?"

He shrugged.

"You mean you don't know your own grandfathers name?" Mon Dieu, what was happening to the world?

He brightened, "Gramps?"

"And what's your name, do you happen to know?"

"Rene."

"Yeh, yeh?"

"Fontaine." said not so proudly.

No, that wasn't it, thank God. He had a French name too, that other long-ago Prairie Indian boy. But it was something else. A small gasp of air. My, hadn't she got tense quickly? That would have been too much coincidence to bear thinking about -- for the boy to have turned out to be *his* grandson, travelling on the same boat as Bernadette all these years later As she went back to get even with Mon Pere, on behalf of all the ones he wronged, that Indian boy foremost among them. Something to write home about, a coincidence like that. But not quite. Not quite. Thank goodness. In another world, another history, this little sweetheart could have been her grandson. Again, how different life would have been. Some other time she might have welcomed a chance to find out, from a possible family member, what had happened to someone she hadn't -- seen -- since the summer of, God, what was it? The late twenties, she guessed. She *should* want to know as much as to find out, but she was rattled enough by the past, today, thank you. She didn't want to know what had happened to the other boy, what's his name, because she couldn't imagine that it might have been happy, and well revelations of ruined lives would undoubtedly stoke the fire of her hatred for Mon Pere, she was exhausted and drained. Still, this boy was probably related through family to that other boy (the grasshoppers, trillions of them) and it might be worth drilling him a bit more intensely --when she felt up to it. Right now, she was enormously relieved that a possible major revelatory moment in her life had brushed by without dragging her off in its wake. She was sure that David, if she told him this story, would talk about karma. But a near miss wasn't karma, was it? And, anyway, there was enough big, "karmic" stuff going on in her life to keep her plenty occupied. The boy, Rene, and her were *not* connected.

Except -- somehow. But it was a pretty big, cosmic somehow. And she was not close to understanding it. Sensing that something was out there, some truth, was about as far as she had gotten since declaring herself open to all new non-Catholic religious or atheist or agnostic ideas, providing God was not involved. Nothing else had quite worked for her yet as an answer, and she had read, even if it was just in Reader's Digest, at least a little something about every religion there was --

Now, likely triggered by the Catholic association, the name she had been groping for suddenly surfaced in the middle of her mind, Marcel! Marcel -- yes, but what was his last name? Marcel -- it was French. That was all she could remember. Oh, bugger, her memory really was starting to go! At least she had that first name. The rest would come. Maybe.

Bernadette abruptly stood up, looking for something else to do. Getting busy, she told herself sternly, fighting a wave of yet *more* memory stirrings, as if something was disturbed way down in her subconscious and was sending bubbles from the past upward into her head -- bubbles with pictures in them that burst into little movies In which she saw herself playing the various roles with the various actors in her life -- but always, at the end of each episode, so to speak, there was that same scene of loss waiting.

Fix Jim and Doug some hot chocolate and cookies, she ordered herself. Smooth things over.

Fortunately, she had a philosophy for moments like this. You have to live in the present. It is too easy to drift. There is finally so much past out there, or rather, in here, inside this huge mysterious place inside her skull, but it can crowd out the present, and turn you into a zombie. She did *not* want that happening. It was so tempting to drift, as among seaweed. All those colorful pictures. Shifting, like mirrors reflecting into one another, so it was all mixed up, but still flowing, and all she had to do was float along in it, let it go –

PART TWO

AGASSIZ - MANITOBA

1928

God stirred the soil that drifted up by the road in the dry part of the summer, mostly dark topsoil the colour of German chocolate cake. It had got that way from being squeezed hard by the fist-sized roots of the tallgrass. God tossed it around, crumbling it, drying it out in the air, sprinkling it on the hard clay where the ruts left over from spring had been baked solid, and then had cracked like pieces of pie crust, revealing cold grey insides, the deeply frozen earth having taken until June to warm, first the soil broke down into damp powder, then became dust that stuck to the lee of the little stippled dunes that piled up in the ditches on either side of the road. By August, God had arranged patterns of dunes as if He were spelling out big, strange scrolls.

It was agonizing for Bernadette Labouchere's little Catholic soul. There, before her eyes, was a script, barely hidden, etched in the great parchment sheet of the land in a pepper spray of lost topsoil, mingled with sand, its message shaded and highlighted by the husks of insects and seeds, tiny round pebbles glinting like quartz, assaulting a brilliant, nearly invisible fragments of potash, the delicate tracing of tumbleweed addendum -- she could not read it!

Bernadette loved God. She loved God completely and purely, so much so that it ached, with nothing held back. No doubts. No hesitation. No confusion. Absolutely clearly, God was. God is. God always would be. And if she could not quite see Him directly, she was lucky enough to see His shadow everywhere, His artwork, His writings, and she was lucky enough to be able to *hear* Him.

It was as if He talked all the time, mostly slowly, although sometimes He shouted so loudly everything cringed and ducked and cowered. Other times He spoke with no more violence than eyelashes parting. She could hear Him before the sun came up. Speaking through the birds and insects. And, oh, what a song He sang. She was also, of course, so terrified of Him that if she thought about Him too hard, her bones turned to water, and it was all she could do to avoid collapsing completely, nothing left of her except a puddle.

Next to God, she loved the piano most.

At twelve, Bernadette Labouchere could play "The Blue Danube," "My Old Kentucky Home," "Mr. Johnson Song," "Sweet Rosie O'Grady," and the "Tannhauser Grand March," without making any mistakes at all.

She loved piano lessons more than anything else in life.

She would certainly never deliberately do anything to risk the incredible privilege of being taught to play, and especially by red-haired, blue eyed Mrs. Allenby, the most beautiful and sophisticated lady in the world, but she still couldn't control the urge every once in awhile to tinkle around down in the C minor notes, trying to imitate the way God's voice spoke through the robins and sparrows and the crickets: all trills and plinks and riffs, liquid and full of impossible to imitate crescendos.

Mrs. Allenby did not mind, as long as she was out of the room, but as soon as she got back, she would say "don't be lazy, dear." She was kind and gentle, and so well read and fashionably dressed, all the time -- unless Bernadette forgot herself and let her shoulders slouch or wiped her nose with her finger or picked her teeth.

And then Mrs. Allenby would say "Don't sit like an Indian, dear." Or: "What are you, a wild Indian?"

Joseph Labouchere (Joe the Mouth, les Anglaise called him) was just barely old enough to remember hearing the last of the Red River carts, pulled by cattle, that had been used by the half breeds moving through town along the Assiniboine, on their way to and from the states, via Winnipeg -- back when he was a boy, and they had just moved from Saint Boniface, the forward post of French civilization in the Lake of the Prairies, to Agassiz, 220 miles to the West, more than halfway to the Saskatchewan border.

After Agassiz, basically, there was nothing. Nothing for thousands of miles until the Rockies. Here, in the Assiniboine Valley, a few last patches of buffalo grass still grew, even though wheat had been overwhelmingly seeded, and taken root, everywhere else between there and the mountains.

Joseph heard an echo in his mind.

The noises those oak carts had made! With no grease at all on the axles, they had screeched hideously. There were several dozens piled up among the blueberries behind Sorenson's barn, hidden among the rusting threshing machines and tractors. The wood from the carts had been bleached by the sun and worn smooth from the crunching through so many hard-baked ruts in the trail, it looked more like great ribs, almost fossilized, than any man-made artifact.

Here and there in the fields around Agassiz, you still sometimes came across splintered cart hubs sticking up out of the ground like bones. Even more rarely, you might stumble upon bits of actual skeleton leftover from a buffalo. A finger bone sized chunk of rib cage, crackers of thigh bone, snake shapes of unattached vertebrae. Never a skull or whole pelvis or anything so unheard of as a hoof. Hides? No, forget it. Not since the turn of the century. The hides had all been sold far away. Nobody in these parts could ever hope to see one, even though, as everybody knew, the herds had once covered the grasslands as far as the eye could see, from horizon -- twist around completely! -- to horizon.

Along the train tracks, bones had been raked into three-foot high piles. Freight cars would arrive. Men would shovel the bones into the cars. The cars would depart, leaving little more than powder coating that ties, until the wind blew it away. Somewhere down in Minnesota, the bones would be turned into fertilizer.

As for the Red River carts. Nearly everyone in town had salvaged at least one old broken spoked five- foot high wheel and turned them into part of a fence or mounted it over a well as an ornament. In Joseph's fathers' day, there had been thousands of those carts squeaking and creaking awkwardly but sturdily down to the border and back, carrying buffalo hides one way and pots and pans back.

Joseph seemed to have a memory-- but surely it couldn't have been his memory, it must have been his remembrance of something his father had described (strange it was so clear) --- of seeing the carts filing in a long caravan on an old dirt trail along the river one morning, dim silhouettes in a cloud of golden dust, a lowering and clumping to be heard, as well as the din of grinding axles.

The half breeds had dressed like habitants in those days, with bright red sashes and toques, and they smoked the long stem clay pipes that he clearly remembered his own father puffing on, the odor of sweetgrass -- and they sang the old fashioned Quebecois songs. He could still, ever so faintly, hear those songs coming from the line of distant Red River carts as they bumped along the Valley Ridge. It was amazing that so many carts could have disappeared. There hadn't been any trains then, of course, just the Dakota paddle wheeler coming up the Red to the Forks. The Indians still using dogs with their travois. But this couldn't be his own memory, it had to be his Papa's, drilled into him by the retelling so often it seemed like part of his own personal life.

He saw it so clearly it almost hurt.

There wasn't a woman in Agassiz, or any place for hundreds of miles around, who didn't wish she had a parlor like Elizabeth

Allenby's : an Empire-styled grandfather clock, a slim hand painted Louis the XV chair, a flower vase on a bronze pedestal, a genuine candelabra and banquet lamp, with a cream colored open top baby Grand by the window. Elizabeth called the piano "my baby" hoping that people would realize she was being tastefully ironic, not bitter.

This morning, she let her fingers caress the keyboard, summoning her favorite piece of music, The Old Rose. She still practiced her beloved Beethoven, Chopin, Rachmaninoff and Rubenstein. Romance, Op 44 had lost none of its charm over the years. But she had found lately that it was mostly pop music she played. At parties, nobody wanted to listen to Mendelssohn. They wanted Peg of my Heart or Charmaine.

The one advantage of not having children, of course, was that between them, with Frank's work as a conductor on the Canadian Pacific, and her teaching piano, they lived elegantly by the standards of the prairies. Yet the women in town looked at her with ill disguised pity, and the men -- if there was one unspoken arrogant thought "If Frank can't do it for you." Worst of all, thoughts like that had crossed her mind often enough, what with Frank being away for weeks at a time. It was just too dangerous a game, and there was no one she could trust enough.

An urgent knock. It was Madame Labouchere and precious little Bernadette at the door. Elizabeth's heart went cold, because mother and daughter were both extremely distressed, which could only mean one thing; her worst fears realized. She let them in through the verandah screen door wordlessly and quickly, hoping to keep out any grasshoppers that might be leaping around out there.

Madame Labouchere was several months pregnant again -- these French! -- but her complexion was clear and vigorously healthy as her daughters. Whereas Madame Labouchere had dark oak eyes, Bernadette's were greener than brown, and finely speckled. They both had round faces, although Bernadette's was slightly more oval, and while the mother's hair was dark brunette, and tied back in a severe netted bun, Bernadette's curly flaxen colored tresses were allowed to spill down over her shoulders. She was dressed in her Sunday best: white lace dress, white stockings, white crinoline, white shoes, with a white ribbon in her hair. Madam Labouchere, by contrast, wore a plain grey shirtwaist dress. Bernadette had been crying. She would not look up into Elizabeth's eyes, and Madame Labouchere, normally a very solid, direct eye-contact sort of woman, was evasive and every bit as miserable as a girl.

In the small, hesitant voice she used when she attempted English, Madame Labouchere said. "My husband does not want Bernadette to carry on with her lessons. They cost too much money; he says."

It was all Elizabeth could do to contain the rage that flared up inside her. That goddamn peasouper ignoramus! She had known this would happen sooner or later. It was also all she could do to stop herself from dropping to her knees and throwing her arms around Bernadette, tenderly kissing her, to try to soothe away the pain radiating from deep inside the small, trembling body. How could that stupid fool of a man do this to his own daughter? How could he be so blind?

But Elizabeth had been anticipating something like this for a long time. She had a plan. And she knew she must appear strong, somebody who could not be argued with. Doing her best imitation of a completely calm woman, she said softly: "Madame Labouchere, please come in and have some tea." Bernadette was still too shaken and hurt to dare look up, but she sensed something in Mrs. Allenby's voice that gave her a flicker of hope.

It had been several years since Madame Labouchere had brought her daughter to Mrs. Allenby's house, and reached into her handbag made out of cucumber seeds -- a prize possession -- painstakingly counting out one dollar in pennies, nickels and dimes, the tuition fee for a month of lessons. "We do not have a piano," the woman had apologized, "but this is the present she wanted for her birthday instead of a doll."

And after that first afternoon's lesson, when the child's long, miraculous, almost unnatural fingers had reached out and found the keyboard and played her first chords with a seemingly automatic fluidity, Elizabeth Allenby elegant but empty life was suddenly transformed. There was something in it now -- Bernadette and her immense talent -- that was, in some sense, greater than motherhood itself. For now, Elizabeth had a mission. It was to bring Bernadette's great gift into focus, to channel latent genius into virtuosity.

And that pig-headed little dogan son-of-a-bitch of a father of hers was going to wreck everything!

No. She would not permit it. She led the unhappy Canadien-francaise mother and daughter into the music chamber and firmly directed Madame Labouchere to sit down on the Louis the XV. The woman tried to protest, but Elizabeth exerted all her force of will. She had been boiling water for herself when the knock had come, so it only took a minute to pour the tea.

"Bernadette," she said sharply, hoping to snap the child out of her despair, "Let us show your mother what you can do."

Bernadette started to shake her head, but Elizabeth cut her off. "Play!" she commanded.

Confused by the unaccustomed fierceness, Bernadette stuttered, "What should I play?"

"Your best!"

She had decided to trust the child's instincts, but when she saw which music sheets Bernadette was tugging out of the pile on the bench, she almost gasped aloud, wanting to shout. "No, that's too hard". But it would not do now to interfere, so she simply took a deep breath, secretly thrilled by Bernadette's audacity, even if she feared the outcome.

Such an abyss to try to cross. The girl had chosen the Second Symphony to the Eroica, Op 55. It was too dangerous! Too ambitious! She had practiced it before, of course, many times, but when it didn't work, the startling dissonance collapsed with a whine. The intense, passionate accents could so clearly become banal. Good Lord, Beethoven himself had had to pass through the hands of Mozart and Haydn before he could attempt this. Elizabeth remembered her own teacher, Mrs. Fraser, telling her you had to have suffered before you can understand this.

But, as Bernadette began to play, it was all there. The bold syncopation, the intensity, the sublimity, the incisive, full blown rhythms. The hair stood on the nape of Elizabeth's neck. There was something about the child's ability that suggested so much, something that was almost -- for lack of a better word, Elizabeth had to settle on: religious. No less.

Cautiously, she eyed Madame Labouchere. She probably could not identify Beethoven, but from the look of amazed, joyous surprise on her face, she could at least recognize the enormous beauty of the sounds her daughter was bringing to life.

At the end of it, Madame Labouchere broke into tears. "My husband – "she started to say.

Elizabeth interrupted. "Madame, your daughter is an extraordinarily talented girl. She has a great gift from the Lord. She can be a very great and famous concert pianist. She must not stop her lessons. It would be a sin against God, in my opinion."

"But –"

"It is not a matter of money, Madame. I consider myself to be privileged to be able to teach Bernadette. She is the best student I have ever had. I will not stand for her not getting the proper training. I insist, therefore, on not being paid any tuition fee any longer. Understood?"

"But I cannot take charity!"

"You are not being charitable to me, Madame. I consider it an honour and a duty, and I do it out of the greatest admiration. It is not a question of me being charitable to you, it is a question of you being kind and generous enough to let me continue to work with your daughter, whose gift is the greatest I have ever run into. It is as simple as that."

Later Elizabeth had cemented the triumph of having convinced Bernadette's mother by inviting the parish priest and the mother superior and two of the nuns over to hear Bernadette play. They were, of course, deeply impressed. The idea was to head off any further attempts by Bernadette's idiot of a father to pull her out of the lessons. So far, so good. But with that prickly little peasouper, you could never tell.

The wind!

Bernadette loved to lie in bed and listen as it made the doors of the chicken coop clack, so you would think at first a raccoon was trying to get in. It rustled the leaves of the cottonwoods Mon Pere had planted on the west side of the yard to break up the drifts in winter. It made the eaves rattle like someone was playing dominoes. And the swing in the backyard would sometimes squeak, as though someone was on it, but nobody was. It scratched branches against downstairs windows and sawed across the mosquito screen in summer. It plucked at the screen door on the veranda. The big prickly fronds of the rhubarb clacked on the pumpkin shells. Corn tassels would pitter-patter in the fields. The wicker chair left outside might fall over. Sometimes the wind would seem to get into the insulation, and there it would gasp, and pant as though trapped. In the attic, it caused things to shift and flutter. In the iron-bellied stove, there were puffing's and bumping's.

And all this when the wind was just teasing or being bored. When it got to blowing, it made so much noise it always amazed her that the little ones and Ma Mere and Mon Pere could sleep through it. The rose trellises being thrummed, sudden whistles coming from inside the walls, tapping on their traceried glass, long half sighing, half singing coming from the chimney, the very frame of the house abruptly being seized by the shoulders and shaken, so that the wind-vane squeaked out a complaint, and Bernadette thought for a moment the whole house might come loose, and fall over, and cave in like a deck of cards. In the gable on the roof, she picked up whisperings.

It was to this ceaseless background stirring that her ears were tuned, even when someone was talking. And, unfortunately, someone was talking almost all the time. It seemed. Or yelling. Or crying. Or droning on and on.

Was she the only one who listened?

The wind. The beautiful inexhaustible wind that drew pictures as it shushed across the tall grass. God almighty, invisible robe rushing this way and that as if sometimes He danced, sometimes He ran, sometimes He whirled in anger, and sometimes He seemed to lie down, the switch grass flattening for acres under Him, revealing His immense outline.

Long breathless minutes past before he got up, and the grass could try standing again too—

Grasshoppers were everywhere that summer. Windows rattled incessantly. Whitewashed walls and fences were smeared with yellow- green mucus. Verandah screens had clotted up with their bodies. The boardwalk in town was slippery with bug juice. At the stockyards, cattle twitched their muscles, using the lash of their tails nonstop, to no avail, and complained in low plaintive voices. Horses could be heard whinnying edgily, snorting and balking.

As much as they could, everyone tried to avoid the open fields where the grasshoppers were thickest. The sound of millions of tiny mouths crunching their way through the wheat and the Indian grass alike was a sustained background buzzing, although sometimes it was more like bracelets, more than could ever be counted, being shaken wildly.

While the hoppers never bit anyone, they smacked the flesh hard as they fell like spent bullet shells from the sky. At the end of a thirty-foot leap, a three-or-four-inch packet of armored grass-eating automaton would land like a fingernail snapped against the skin, enough to sometimes leave welts. The clicking, chirping toy monsters were everywhere. Just trying to get to the outhouse involved running a gauntlet. You had to walk holding your hands in front of your face, with a hat pulled down low, or wearing a shawl. For once, women could be happy about their crinolines and corsets, which shielded them when the clothes peg-shaped little dragons came ricocheting up under their dresses.

The birds seem to have gone mad, crashing into windows and screens in their frantic effort to enjoy the feast to the fullest. Scarcely a robin or sparrow could be seen without a part of a grasshopper sticking from its beak. Even the bats were moved to flit about blindly in the daylight, since all they had to do was fly with an open mouth until they got so bloated, they had to land.

In the wood frame, two-story, shingle-covered Labouchere home, with its trellises, veranda and single gable, only young Jean-Paul was enjoying himself.

For hours at a time he experimented with every possible combination of grasshopper dismemberment. Try yanking one hind leg off. Try another one. One wing off. Both wings off. Forelegs. Thorax. Antennae. He found, to his delight, that even when the head was pulled off, the rest of the body would twitch as though trying to escape. Some of the hoppers, with various parts missing, would make it several inches into the air before veering off to one side and crashing.

When no one was looking, Jean-Paul ate several of the hind legs. They were like tiny, delicate drumsticks, bitter tasting, but he could make himself chew them up and swallow them.

He was forbidden to stuff bugs down the backs of his sisters, and, of course, he would get strapped if he tormented the bebe in any way. So, he contented himself with sneaking up on Teresa, who, at ten, was the second oldest, after bossy Bernadette. She was sitting in the kitchen, mending socks. He smiled as innocently as he could, so she let him get near. When he was as close as he figured he could get, he popped open his mouth to reveal a live grasshopper perched on his tongue. Teresa wailed in horror as it leapt away, landing on her apron.

Jean-Paul savored his power.

Sissy-pants Teresa was so unnerved, after that, all Jean-Paul had to do was go near her with his mouth conspicuously closed, and she would frantically scuttle away, screaming for help. He couldn't scare Bernadette that way. He tried it once and she grabbed his ear and twisted it so hard he almost swallowed the hopper. "If you yell, I'll do it harder," she warned, without rancor.

Ma Mere was bent over the steel spring washing machine in the kitchen. Her sleeves were rolled up and there were beads of sweat on her forehead. Jean-Paul fled past on his way to the back door with Teresa, welding the big wooden soup spoon, on his heels.

"Ma Mere, he spat another bug at me!"

Ma Mere started to yell something, but the screen door clapped shut. Teresa stopped at the door, waving the spoon threateningly, but unwilling to go outside, where Jean-Paul was making faces at her, grasshoppers whizzing all around him.

"Teri is a sissy!"

"Petite couchon!" she screamed.

"Teresa," Ma Mere, straighten painfully over the wash, "you had better finish mending, eh?"

"Why doesn't he do anything?"

"Don't worry, his turn will come. Wait until this winter, and he will have to take out the ashes and fetch the coal."

"Still he does nothing," remarked Bernadette, peeling potatoes glumly.

"Well, I don't go off to music classes all the time like some fancy ladies I know," hissed Teresa.

Ignoring them, Ma Mere plunged her arms back into the suds, humming an old Habitant tune. She was scarcely five feet tall, but strongly built. When she was still a little girl, her father had entertained his guests by having her lift a grown man off the ground. Yet her hands and feet were unusually small for the size of her body, exactly the opposite of her long-fingered, gangling oldest daughter. Augustine Labouchere still curved nicely for her years, she knew, although the most obvious curve at the moment was the swelling of her womb. She was five months pregnant, due in November, and more than slightly annoyed with her body for having subjected her, once again, to a summer pregnancy, what Joe called "one in the oven."

It was in the kitchen, mainly, that Augustine lived, along with the copper-boiler, the cast-iron double decker stove, the wash bucket, the scrub board, the cream separator, butter churn, jam buckets and sausage funnels. In winter, when there were glistening crusts of frost on the storm windows, she enjoyed the delicious steamy smell of fresh wash clothes hung on twine lines the length of the ceiling, mixed with the odors of dumplings, boiled carrots, fried pork, pea soup, Johnny Cake and molasses.

In summer, her world expanded to include the back porch, where she kept her clothes baskets and pegs, and out into the vegetable garden, the orchard, and the chicken coop, although, since she was very young, maybe only five or six, Bernadette had taken care of the chickens. If anybody tried to help her, she got all moody and foot-dragging. Augustine was happy enough to leave the chickens to Bernadette. Nobody else wanted to do all the work, the cleaning, fresh hay, watering, getting rid of the dead ones, keeping the chicks alive. Bernadette, for some strange reason, liked it.

In autumn, Augustine spent the greater part of her days preserving, and storing the preserves in the root cellar, where the potatoes and carrots and onions were kept, buried in sand. Mostly, to her children, Ma Mere seemed happy. It took an awful lot to get her mad, although, when she got mad, everybody scattered. Even Mon Pere backed off, eh?

Bernadette could not stand being in the kitchen. She hated doing laundry, washing dishes, cooking, peeling, scrubbing, tending to the babies – well, the babies were alright for awhile, but then they turned into horrid little brats like Teresa and Jean-Paul. Neither did Bernadette have any desire to mop, to dust, to sweep, to the polish, to wipe or air things out. She often stared at her mother, trying to imagine what she was thinking. How come she did not just start screaming from the boringness of it all?

There was only one part of Ma Mere's life that was genuinely interesting to Bernadette, and that was the secret part: the life she lived alone with Mon Pere in the big chambre a couche. The only time Bernadette was allowed into her parent's bedroom was on Saturday mornings when she had to help with changing the linen. It was in this room that my mother had her babies, on the huge spool bed with its patchwork quilt. Except for the bed, the hot water pig, the curling tongs, Ma Mere's crocheted nightcap, and the large feathered boa, the room reminded Bernadette of church. There was a Holy Water font on the wall beside the bed, a statuette of Our Lady on the bureau, a Pilgrim's Rosary, a glossy reproduction of a painting of Jesus, his halo tinged with gold fleck, a nine inch high crucifix above the wash bowls, and a framed diploma from the Holy Family Society, to which Mon Pere belonged. It was somewhere in here that her parents said the special prayers that started babies happening.

"How many babies are you going to have, Ma Mere?" Bernadette asked suddenly.

Augustine laughed, noting that her oldest daughter was reacting to this pregnancy differently than the earlier ones, almost as though she resented it.

"I don't know, my lamb. It's up to God, eh?"

"How many babies can you have?"

"My mother had seventeen. Your father's mother had fifteen. Not all of them lived, of course, but that was God's will. Dominisco vobiscum."

Bernadette said nothing for a moment. Then almost to herself. "We'd have to get a bigger house."

"Not to worry my, my Angel. I didn't get married until I was in my late teens. They were worried I was going to be an Old Maid. Your grandmothers already had several babies by then. People used to marry much earlier. If you weren't married by the time you were fifteen, it was a big disaster. I started too late to have that many babies, but who knows? Only God knows, eh?"

Augustine eyed her oldest daughter contemplatively. Sometimes the girl worried her. Too distant. So, removed emotionally. She hardly ever reacted with anger to the other children, or to anyone, for that matter. But she hardly ever laughed, either. So gloomy. She will be a good-looking girl, but she takes everything so seriously. It is all so dramatic. She's like somebody in a play, always acting out a role, but not really being that person. I don't know about her. She always tries to get off by herself. The sisters say she is very devout, always praying, so I guess it doesn't matter. Maybe she will be a nun. Sure, that would be a good thing for her. She is not really all here. And the music. She plays so beautifully, but I don't know what she thinks she can do with music. She's a daydreamer, that one.

"Bernadette, attend to the dumplings. Where's your head today?"

"It's the grasshoppers, Ma Mere. I hate them."

Augustine looked nervously at the windowpane, upon which no less than a couple of dozen of the little beasts were perched. In a blink, one would vanish, replaced seconds later by another. They made a click as they landed. Click. Click. And another click. It went on all day. Sometimes they were so huge she was afraid they would break the glass. She shuddered. Since she was a child back in Saint Norbert, she could remember at least four times when the hoppers had come in such numbers that they swamped the land and forced everyone to hide indoors for days at a time. After they passed, there were so many dead, dried insect bodies on the ground that in some places they lay heaped up three feet deep. All around the horizon, fires had flickered briefly as bitter farmers burned the bodies in what was left of their fields. This particular batch seemed to have leveled off, but it was too early to tell if the main swarm had passed or whether a valley had simply opened up between the dense masses advancing from the southwest.

The smell of the old hen house almost always made her wrinkle her nose, but neither the thick gobs of manure on the garden nor the brown and white pudding of droppings in the chicken coop left her feeling nauseous at all. Except when she had to take the hoe, once every couple of months, and scrape away the deposits that had built up underneath the perches. Then, the gases would get strong enough to affect her. Otherwise, why was it that human poo smells so terrible, yet the cow pies and the chicken droppings almost smelled pleasant.

As always, Bernadette paused at the door to the outside pen, hoping to catch a glimpse of the rooster doing his dance before he spotted her and fled inside. From his cowardly retreat, the hens could tell that food was coming.

She was a bit early. One of the hens, at least, was still laying. The rooster, cowering in the far corner, had his feathers fluffed up, and was flapping his wings. She got halfway there, then his voice broke. He was a runt -- although far more beautiful to watch than the hens. She admired the luxuriousness of his wattle and comb, the tapered delicacy of his feathers, and, above all, his grace and bearing. He was constantly posing. He never stopped.

Realizing she had seen him, the rooster fluttered against the coop wall. The hens ignored his stupid panic entirely. They galloped, in their ungainly way, toward her, Pawk pawk pawk pawk. As she began scooping the feed out of her bucket, she noted that one of the hens had blood all over her neck feathers. The back of her head was raw, with the feathers all gone from around the comb. It had probably started with the rooster, as usual, but it had gotten worse than that. It was not uncommon for a bird to be pecked out until it bled. If this went on too long, more birds would join in. If the victim became too weak, you wound up with cannibalism. Bernadette hurriedly dished out the rest of the feed, then retreated to the tool shed where she unlocked Mon Pere's fishing net. There was no point charging around in the coop, trying to catch a chicken by hand. With the net, she had the wounded bird in a minute. The poor hen would have to be kept alone in the shed for a couple of weeks to give her neck and head time to heal and let the feathers grow back in.

It was so easy to think of chickens as just being stupid and cruel, and while Bernadette could not help feeling that way sometimes, she also definitely loved the chickens. They surprised her. They filled her with a sense of wonder, and pride. Out of the twenty-eight layers, she averaged two dozen eggs a day. Moreover, her hens kept laying through the winter, except for a single week when she educed molting by cutting off their water and food for two days. It forced them to molt all at once, speeding the process up, so that they could get back to laying as soon as possible. She also fed her birds warmed up feed during the winter months. She never missed a day without coming down to the coop with scraps, to collect the eggs, check the water, inspect the chicken wire, and make sure no animals had tried to tunnel under the fence overnight.

"There, there," Bernadette said to the injured hen. "You'll be alright."

The chicken's ruby eye gleamed. It was a single lens that seemed translucent. Bernadette had the impression she was looking into a small glass ball, as though the chicken's head was hollow; bottomless. She envied the chicken's ability to look at her out of one eye, while looking out the other at something completely different.

It took only a few minutes to set the bird up in the special place she had in the tool shed, complete with fresh scraps, corn, water and fresh straw.

"You'll be laying by tomorrow," Bernadette assured the hen.

Back in the coop, she scolded the other hens, and wagged a

finger at the still cringing rooster. "Bad girls! I ought to make you into stew. You too!" She threw leftover scraps at them. This brought even the rooster running. Bernadette felt slightly sad, watching them eat. They ate in a panic. When they got a decent morsel in their beak, they had to run for it while the other birds chased after them. Trying to snatch the food away. Often, the scraps got dunked in fresh poo, but the chickens didn't seem to care. Either that, or in the fiercely competitive arena, they had no choice. It was fending for yourself or die.

But there was another side to life in the chicken coop. When a shaft of light fell through a crack in the roof, and dust from the straw drifted slowly through it, and the hens were all on their nests or in their perches, mostly nodding off except the occasional sleepy "pawk", she felt as though she was half asleep herself, and only half in the physical world, even though she was still in her body. It was a place somewhere between dreams and reality. Very warm, very secure. Very always-as-it-must-have-been-since the beginning of the world. There were times when she felt such a sense of relief upon arriving in the simple, true, always world of the coop that she was as reverent, in some ways more reverent, than at High Mass. She not only treated the birds with respect, but she was also deferential. If a hen insisted on remaining on her nest, despite the temptation of the scraps and feed, Bernadette would leave her alone. She told herself there were two good reasons. First, hens taken off their eggs tend to get upset, and if they were upset, they didn't lay as well. Second, it gave her an excuse to come back to the coop again later in the day. But there was a third, secret reason. There was something almost holy about a hen on her eggs. Bernadette felt herself in the presence of a great, mysterious power. And she liked to think of herself as a servant in the face of it, certainly not the grand dame.

In the summer, she brought them cuttings from the lawn after Mon Pere had trimmed the grass. She always made a point of treating the birds as though they were small, harmless people who were her responsibility, and whose substitute mother she was.

Except for the rooster. If she could ever get close enough, she tried to hit him with a broom, or kick him, or sometimes throw snowballs or pebbles at him. Everybody said you had to have a rooster. She couldn't argue, but she wished it didn't have to be that way. Her flock was composed of three species, Comets, Bardrocks and Leghorns. The rooster was a Comet that Mon Pere had brought home for her one day, having taken it in payment for something at the store. It was a little rooster. At first, the scene was comical. He tried immediately to dominate the older ladies, but, to his astonishment, they pecked back at him, and held their ground. They even seem to assign one of the biggest hens to chase after him all day long, keeping him from bothering the others.

But after a couple of days the rooster got over his initial dismay. Small as he was, he was still bigger than any of the hens. In due course, he took them on in battle, one by one, and defeated them, leaping on their backs, seizing their combs in his beak, and forcing them into painful submission. Within a matter of days, the backs of Bernadette's hens were all tracked with mud from the rooster spending so much time astride them. Some of the weaker Comets looked half plucked. Bardrock feathers were everywhere. Several Leghorns were bleeding from the comb.

That was when she started throwing things at him. Whether that had anything to do with it or not, he eventually settled down, and was less violent when he jumped on a hen's backs. But she sensed that the real reason life became bearable again in the coop was that the hens finally truly and thoroughly gave up. It was their utter surrender that calmed him. That was all that could do it. Now, when he hopped onto a hen's back and seized her comb, she sank without a peep of complaint to the straw. He tugged her comb, flexed his slender claws into her back feathers, arched his wings, and looked exactly like a hawk when it was bent to kill. He twisted and yanked, seemed to bite as deep as he could, but the hens endured the ordeal in silence. When, suddenly, almost indifferently, he hopped off their backs and strode swaggeringly away, the hens fluffed their neck feathers, clucked resignedly, and carried on as though nothing had happened. The rooster lifted his own magnificent neck feathers in a fan, flapping his wings, and gave a triumphant ko ka ku, ko ka ku.

She had seen the face of the Virgin Mary ice-blasted in the blue shadows of snowdrifts, or in the hoar frost on window panes, so often now that she merely paused when she saw Her (if she could ever find a moment alone), and would compose herself for prayer.

It was normal for Bernadette to see the Virgin Mary.

It was just that she could hardly ever talk to Her directly, because of the shouting and wailing and banging of pots and pans.

Always she was surrounded by her squealing sisters and always-taunting Jean-Paul, almost always a new bebe, Ma Mere reeling out a steady stream of orders, Mon Pere always growling or shouting about something, the murmuring people at Mass, Father Patenaude calling out to God in Latin, the nuns reciting at Catechism class, high-pitched mean boys shouting insults at École, the ever whispering anglaise girls, Mademoiselle Lieumieux's shrill insistence on memorizing words and numbers, so much noise!

And everyone squeezing together as though they didn't know they had all the room in the world. In fact, practically holding onto each other, like bebes would hold onto your finger forever if they could. Hardly ever just one person all alone, except Mr. Todd, out with his horse in the field, like a tin toy in the middle of square mile upon square mile of goldenrod and blue stream and sunflowers and blazing star and liatris.

Sometimes Mr. Todd and his horse seemed to be waiting in the waters of the endless imaginary sea made by heat waves where the faraway floor of the land should have been meeting the ever further away ceiling of the sky, but dissolving into what looked like an ocean instead, only just ankle deep…

Mon Pere warned her, indicating his thick barbershop strap hanging from the wooden box telephone, never, ever talk to their solitary farmer neighbor. He was a Protestant, and he had cousins who were Metis.

Mon Pere had said the Metis were merde.

Ma Mere, in a rare display of fury, scolded him, and sent the children out of the parlor.

Mon Pere had had to go to confession that Sunday.

Bernadette and the girls who were old enough to understand watched, awestruck, out of the corner of their eyes, as Mon Pere meekly crawled into the Confessional Booth, on his knees even before he closed the door, Ma Mere glaring at him right up to that instant.

After, when he came out, she went back to her usual, bent forward self, and he went back to sitting ramrod erect in his pew, the clunk of his knees on the hard wooden prayer board being the signal for everyone in the family to get down on their own knees tout suite.

Once, when she was small, probably not more than six years old, there had been a tornado. It had come up from the States. She couldn't remember any particular sound that it made -- except at the very end, when it hit -- but the picture remained vivid for all her life of that purple blue, dark-golden vortex weaving hugely, uncertain, as if it may be drunk, still out there in a distant field, but already so horrendously huge that an entire faraway silo looked like a part of a train set with a grown man wobbling around, about to step on it.

It kept changing direction, as though it had hidden eyes that were scanning for her. Ma Mere had chased the animals into the small barn they still had then, (but wouldn't have after the tornado had gone by,) and ordered Bernadette to carry Teresa and Jean-Paul down into the root cellar where the preserves were kept. At the last minute, remembering she'd left her Raggedy Ann in the sandbox, Bernadette led her little howling sister and her brother into the cellar, and scrambled up the wooden steps, running as fast as she could across the yard. She got there in seconds, running effortlessly like a bird.

But when she turned, the wind was suddenly pushing her backwards. She almost stumbled over her heels into the sandbox. She bent forward, having to gasp for air because it was streaming past her so fast. She clung at first to her twitching, hopping raggedy Ann. She dug her toes into the crabgrass. But she was shocked into paralysis. The root cellar was amazingly far away as if such an awful thing were possible, it was shrinking.

Ma Mere emerged from the barn, the door crashing shut behind her, spotted Bernadette, and immediately started floundering slow motion towards her disastrously disobedient daughter. The bun of Ma Mere's hair broke open, her mouth working silently, as though she was yelling, but there was no sound except the great tunneling blast all around that absorbed all sound. Bernadette thought at first Ma Mere was looking at her, but no, Ma Mere was looking past her, above her, way over her head, at something else. And there was a look in Ma Mere's eyes that jolted Bernadette into an electric shock.

She started scrambling desperately forward. Everything was in flapping, streaming motion. Birds shot past. Stockings came loose from the clothesline, which gave in and settled on the ground, as if lying down. Leaves burst from the trees like slashed goose down. The nine-foot sunflowers bent their heavy heads as one, like people at Mass. A window shutter banged open and wagged at her reproachfully. The two of them moved with aching slowness in bodies that weighed hundreds of pounds.

Ma Mere finally reached the child and caught her so ferociously Bernadette thought her arm was going to be torn off. So sensibly terrified was the girl by then, she let go of Raggedy Ann and hung onto her mother with both hands. By the time Ma Mere clawed her way into the root cellar entranceway, Bernadette in tow, it was almost impossible to pull the wooden door down shut behind them. It flapped like a wing and seemed it would break off its hinges before it would bend.

Bernadette's last glimpse of the sky before Ma Mere brought the door whacking down shut was of a sullen mother of pearl torrent racing upward, illuminated by a cold light as though the moon was out in the daytime and the sun had gone blind. In the unfolding darkness of the cellar, Ma Mere squeezed her arm around her mewling infants. The blood veins on Bernadette's arms pounded where Ma Mere had grabbed hold of her out in the yard. The preserving jars tinkled on their shelves.

And the sound came. The memory of it would cause the hair to stand up on Bernadette's neck for years. This was the sound Satan would make when he came up from the crack in the earth to take your soul away.

A long time ago, that.

She felt so old sometimes it didn't seem possible anyone could have lived from such antiquity until now.

She also felt so small. That part was all right. She liked being small. She liked to walk out in the endless seeming expanse of grassland that spread out from their backyard to the northwest. Theirs was the newest and therefore last house on the road that ran out from town. None of that softly flowing Atlantis of tallgrass prairie was yet tilled, with Mr. Todd's fields of wheat splayed out to the east along the River.

She loved it especially in midsummer, when, before they got too tall, the thin pale bushes of the bluestem grew uniformly as high as her neck. She let her fingers, spread apart, glide through the silken filaments so that, with her eyes closed, she could imagine she was being caressed by silently swimming fairies. And because her head alone was sailing above the grass tops, casting a quivery wake, it seemed she was just a few inches tall, like her favorite character in the English story book she kept hidden out of Mon Peres sight at home.

"Poof, poof, Piffles," she'd quote, as she climbed between the barbwire to get out of the yard and onto the edge of the golden and purple flecked plain, "Make me just as small as sniffles."

Sometimes, she would imagine she was a duck, paddling across the biggest pond ever. She could turn sharply or move in languorous loops, go in any direction she wanted, without having to worry about bumping into anything. And if she wanted, she could drop suddenly to a crouching position, and there wouldn't be a trace of her to be seen by anybody. She was out in the open, in an openness that seemed to have no end, yet completely hidden. What she liked down in this forest of thin-stocked tall grass, down where it was almost dark and the lower stems were covered with a grey dying looking fuzz, was she could look up and see nothing but sky.

The sky, too, always moved.

Even when there wasn't a cloud insight, tiny spots danced in the eyes squinting luminescence. It was easy to imagine herself on the bottom side of the globe of the earth, looking down. She could convince herself she was about to fall off the ground she was stuck to and start tumbling through the air towards the blue nothingness beyond. If she did it right, she could make herself dizzy with terror.

And when there were clouds, she saw God's invisible hand at work again, painting with fluff and cotton baton and gauze and baby powder and talcum and shaving lather, throwing in shadows of every hue imaginable. Somehow, none of the colors ever clashed, even as the clouds changed before her eyes, reinventing themselves endlessly in gigantically as brand-new shapes never once repeating themselves, collapsing the instant they were formed.

It should be enough in life just to look at the clouds, she sometimes thought. How could you ever get bored?

The outhouse was at the back of the yard. All she had to do, when she wanted to get away, was pretend that she had "to go". She would take a schoolbook to make it seem like she was going to study at the same time, so if she took too long Ma Mere would just say "that Bernadette what a scholar!"

Trotting along the planks past the cabbage, the rows of corn, the potato patch, the stocked up tomatoes, the rhubarb, past her beloved chicken coop, with a nod and several reassuring pawks from the hens who immediately crowded against the wire, and who complained vociferously when she kept on going, moving gingerly past the beehives, holding her braids to avoid having them swing around, hitting a bee, she'd undo the outhouse latch, jerk open the creaking old door with its sawed half moon at the top, and step inside, always holding her nose.

There were air-holes drilled in the door, so she could look back out and spy on the house until she was sure no one was watching. In a flash, she'd be out, latching the door behind her, darting nimbly around the outhouse, until she was lost from view among the young crab-apple trees, and could clamber through the barbed wire, careful not to tear her gingham dress, and set out into --- forever.

What was really special about curling up on her knees on the hard-packed crust between the grass stalks, wasn't just that she was finally alone.

It was knowing that something would happen.

If she just sat still and waited long enough, she'd be sure to spot a field mouse, at least, or fluttering butterflies, or spiders, grasshoppers for sure, or maybe a garter snake -- which didn't scare her at all. She could pick them up by the tail, but she didn't like to, because the snake didn't want to be picked up. Sometimes she'd spot a prairie dog or a gopher or a groundhog or a grouse, which, as soon as it saw her, either shot away and popped into a mound, or leapt explosively for the sky, or pretended to have a broken wing, squawking and staggering.

If she sat long enough, a crow or fence hawk would bank overhead, making a tentative inspection for possible carrion.

When the grasshoppers were too bad, she resigned herself to finding what moments of privacy she could in the chicken coop. But, on this particular hot Saturday afternoon in August, the wave of grasshoppers seemed to have either passed by or settled down. There were still plenty of them around, but the chances of one striking her as it came down off its trajectory had dropped to nothing more than one every few minutes. She could endure that in exchange for getting away from the house, the bebe, the sisters, her brother, even Ma Mere, with her constant reminding of chores to be done.

Thus Bernadette passed nearly an hour of tranquility in an open wild grass field not far from the banks of the Assiniboine River, a couple of miles from the village of Agassiz, on the bottom of a dead and vanished sea, a small portion of which was now part of the province of Manitoba, in the Dominion of Canada.

Resting her head on her arithmetic textbook, she laid herself down, settling her body lightly, disturbing as little of the three-foot high grass as she could. The fresh smelling soil was still soft from the rain a few days ago. Breaking off a stem of grass to chew, she began rearranging the shapes of the clouds.

But, for a change, instead of conjuring the Virgin Mary's or various saints', or Jesus's or even God's face out of the swirling configurations of steam and dust, she found herself deeply distracted by the thought of the long lost inland ocean that Mademoiselle Lieumieux had told them once covered the entire Prairie from the forests of Ontario to the Rockies, North to the Arctic and South to Texas, and how it had been filled with creatures with a ticklish-sounding name, who had flippers instead of legs, and were as big as locomotives.

Almost effortlessly, Bernadette could make out their gigantic shapes among the clouds, their sail- sized flippers moving at a patient elephantine pace. She hardly needed to imagine that the shadows drifting across the Prairie were those of a whole swarm of drifting ichthyosaurus; they looked like that almost naturally. Merely as ordinary day-to-day clouds, the towering puff explosions cast a sense of brooding beneath them, as though they hovered, almost looking for prey.

As four o'clock came, shafts of light broke through and began to beam down on the tabletop land as those spokes were rotating across the face of the sun. A hint of coolness materialized in the breathless air. The hoppers seemed to have calmed almost completely down, except for a few of them zinging in arcs across the face of the sky. Mostly they clung to the stalks of grass, as though resting.

Suddenly, the world was too beautiful to look at! Too breathtaking to bear!

Too, too magnificent! Too brightly shining! Too overwhelming! Her heart seemed to go small and beat faster. She shivered and her nipples went lead-pellet hard. It wasn't any one thing, it was everything put together; the wind, the sound of the grass, dead grass and live grass, wrestling, scraping, the clicking and buzzing of insects, a far off cawing, a few ducks honking down by the river; the clouds shape now like an ichthyosaurus, now like angels, the hypnotising blinking of the light, it was actually starting to hurt. Physically hurt. Her heart had never beaten like this. She had to gulp hard, repeatedly, and smack her chest, and say "Mon Dieu! Mon Dieu!"

She had definitely not reported to anybody at home what she learned at École about dinosaurs, which were things that were not in the Bible, and therefore could not possibly have existed. She knew full well that Mon Pere would drive straight to École and yell at Mademoiselle Lieumieux again, and the other pupils would laugh at her and her sisters all the more because their father was the "crazy peasouper." She hoped that Jean-Paul would grow up fast so he could hit those boys for her.

Joseph detested speaking in English. One of the reasons les Anglaise called him Joe the Mouth was because he was so tight-lipped. "Oui, Monsieur – Non, Monsieur." The price, or inquiry whether a customer wanted his hair cropped short, Shaved, that was about it. Never mind the time of day or weather.

Yet he still had the use of English when he did business, he had to do it every day, all day, at his three establishments in town -- the Lobouchere Grocery store, the Labouchere Barbershop and the Labouchere Billiard Hall -- because all but a few of his regular customers spoke it, even the bohunks and the goddamned half breeds. He had no goddamned choice.

Except of course at home. And if any of his children said anything in English at home, they knew damn well what they were going to get. So that way, at home anyway, everything was still in Canadien-francaise as it could be. If any of the adults back in the Gaspe were ever to come out here and see what was going on with Joseph, they would be right at home. Everything would be the same as back in Québec. But in Agassiz, it was English, English, English, even though you heard people talking among themselves in Swedish, German, Norwegian, Finnish, Ukrainian, even Chinese. Not that Joseph could tell much difference between the tongues. It was like they were all farting through their noses. But when it came time to buy something, or talk about anything while he wielded the razor along their necks, or call out scores at the pool table, they all had to do it in English, otherwise nobody could get anything done.

The province, of course, was supposed to be bilingual. That was a deal when Canada took over, after The Rebellion failed. But it was a joke. Go ahead. Try to talk in francais to one of those bohunks or Chinks or those Swedish buggers. See how goddamn far you get.

Once a week after Mass, Joseph got to talk francais with the men from the other five French families living on farms around town, but none of them were businessmen. He bought in bulk from them, so of course they talked a lot about how things were growing and the grain and the flour freight rates, but when it came to politics, or the gold standard, or the nationaliste movement in Québec, Joseph always found himself the lone voice. His compatriots were sheep, thinking what the Church told them to think, that was all. He was in favor of Section 98, the Criminal Code change which had been brought in to crush the Bolsheviks during the Winnipeg strike. He believed that old age pensions would only reward laziness and break apart the family. He was interested in the new doctrine called Social Credit and would be happy to argue monetary politics for hours on end -- if he could find anyone to argue with. Certainly not Father Patenaude, the turd on a turd of an altar boy who should never have been made a priest. He was like all those people just out from Québec. They think they're from such a big, important place, eh?

And a man like me who has been out here all his life, and who makes a damn good living, and whose own father was here when that bastard Riel stirred up all the trouble with the half breeds, I don't get any respect. My own Father, this is Henri Labouchere I'm talking about, would have made a damn sight better leader of the French in Manitoba than that little half breed shit, but no one would listen to him when he told them they were crazy to take up arms. It was a hopeless, stupid thing.

Do I get any credit for being the oldest son of one of the true pioneers, a man of history, not these lazy farts who come out here on the train? Long before all these goddamned immigrants from Europe started pouring in, everything handed to them on a platter, the Labouchere's were around out on the Prairies building a civilization. My father came out by canoe, goddamnit. And I still say, you look at that River, and I say that's the way we get back home when It gets too bad here. Never mind all your goddamned train tracks, your bridges and your roads. The roads don't work worth a hill of beans in winter anyway. The bridges all get washed away in the spring. Someday we'll go back to the Gaspe by paddle. There is nothing to stop you. That's how it will be, by canoe, when I can't stand to eat the shit any longer from all these lazy turds who just got off the boat.

They took a little train ride. They get off here. They take the land that the government hands over to them. And they think they're so goddamned smart.

We've been here on this land since before it was part of Canada, when it was still just Rupert's Land, and yet I am treated by all these ignorant immigrants like a moron who has a hearing problem.

Sometimes they raise their voices when they talk to me, like the bohunks and the goddamned anglaise, and even the goddamn chinks, thinking because I don't speak the goddamn English anymore than I have to, I'm deaf as well as stupid, eh?

At least little Father Patenaude doesn't shout. Oh contraire, he is so soft-spoken it's like talking to an enfant or a goddamn nun. A Jesuit, wouldn't you know? And he always calls me mon fil. Can you believe that? I am seven years older than him, sacre bleu! I am not his son! I am old and ugly enough and experienced enough in the world to be his father, for God's sake. He has fuzz on his pink little cheeks.

And he tries to tell me who I should do business with just because the goddamned Sacred Cross Mission buys most of the potatoes and peas and turnips I sell.

For God sake, I am the only Catholic grocer in the whole goddamn miserable dried turd of a parish. He should buy everything from me. What the hell, us dogans have to stick together, eh?

Yet this little pink turd of a priest tries to treat us, the Labouchere's just like the goddamned half breeds because we're all Catholics, and the Savior loves us, no matter what, he says. Well, maybe we are all Catholics, but some of us are civilized, and take baths, but some of us don't. You can sprinkle all the goddamned Holy Water you want on an Indian, but he is still as crazy as ever. And the half breeds are just the same. You can't trust them as far as you could throw them.

Little Father Patenaude tells me I have to sell my produce to them, even if they can't pay right away like everybody else. I don't come right out and tell him to mind his own business. I can't do that. He is still a priest. But I have my own way of letting him know I'm the one to decide who I'll give credit to. That little turd doesn't know anything about business. Everybody else knows as soon as those half breeds get anything for free, that's the end you'll see of whatever it is they walked away with, eh?

And when they are drinking, they pull a knife on you just like that. If I think they have been drinking, they're out the door at my business in a god damn hurry.

Everybody knows they don't mess around with me. A lot of them, they come up this high over my head, but they don't know anything about how to fight. My father showed me a few punches. And I've got a bat I keep under the cash register at each place, eh? I've used it a couple of times. One good bonk on the head, eh? Those guys get out that door. If they know what's good for them.

Sometimes after Mass, I talk a little bit with the sisters, but what can you say to them? They just sit around and pray or read the Holy Book. Or maybe they play with broom handles when nobody's looking, eh?

There's that goddamn Lieumieux woman over at the separate school, and I wouldn't mind talking to her, but mon dieu Christ, obaines ce'oubeau la tabernac, she puts all sorts of goddamn lies into the heads of my little ones, but no matter how often I try to tell that Patenaude idiot he has to get rid of her, he says he can't do anything about it. Teachers who speak English and French are too hard to find out here, eh? And to keep them here, such a big deal. And of course, the children have to learn the goddamn English otherwise they're not going to be able to do anything much by the time they grow up, what with everybody coming in and learning English instead of French.

Well, I know that. What do you think I do all day? I talk to everybody in the goddamn English. You know what I think? I think that fuzzy headed little altar boy from Québec is putting the meat to that Lieumieux woman. That's what I think is going on.

Seldom, if ever, happy, Joseph was in an even bleaker mood than usual as he turned the knob on the front door of the Labouchere Billiard Hall, being forced to close early because of the warning about the goddamn grasshoppers. He had already shut down the Grocery store and the Barber shop. The Billiard Hall door was warped a bit and always squeaked the last inch before it was closed. He had to kick it. A flake of white paint fell from the windowsill. Mon Dieu Christ! He had just painted that last September. Twisting his key in the lock, Joseph ground his teeth together so that they squeaked audibly, like chalk.

This goddamn town!

Not much had changed in Agassiz since the turn of the century, except that now there was a monument to all the block-headed farmers' sons who went over to fight in the Great War and never came back, and of course the goddamn banks kept money tight to pay for all that craziness. Otherwise, the only new thing was the gas pump in front of the Red and White store, right next door to the blacksmiths.

You would see horses tied up to the roping post with either Joseph's or one of the half dozen other local automobiles parked just a few feet away, being filled up with gas. At first, the spectacle would attract a crowd. Now, nobody took any notice. A small fleet of a half dozen tin lizzies had been added to the town's population, rolling in one by one, making an unholy noise, and leaving a blue trail of petroleum fumes hovering in the air. The other autos were all owned by les Anglaise or bohunks, who loved to park together like a herd of cows whenever they could. Just after he'd gotten in his auto, he had tried to join them a couple of times, to show that he was every bit as good and rich is them -- but if I come up and park right beside them, first thing you know, somebody's got to go off and get something, and when they come back, they parked somewhere else eh? And then somebody else suddenly remembers something they forgot. And, after that, the next guys got to go get smokes. And somebody else decides it's time to go to the bootlegger. Somebody else must pick up the old lady. I've seen every last one of those anglaise bastards get up and move just to get away from being parked next to me at a ball game, eh? Even though they'll park with the bohunks. They all stick to each other like shit to an old blanket. So now I just parked where I want.

There had been talk about how life was going to change so much. Everybody was going to have a car of their own. Well, the truth was the arrival of the car didn't really seem to have made that much difference to life, not compared to the significance of the stockyards being built up, or the addition of a second grain elevator, or the baseball field getting bleachers -- bleachers that were already faded looking, even though they were built and painted just last summer.

Everything was faded. Corners sagged. Roof shingles were missing. Bone-grey wood showed through the tatters. Every building, from the courthouse to the hardware, had a frayed, splintering, sandblasted look. Joseph was one of the few merchants industrious enough or stubborn enough to repaint his premises every year, and still the protective coating was starting to flake apart by the middle of next summer. Paint was shed like skin. It practically molted, scabbing, peeling, surrendering to the digestive processes of icicles and hoarfrost.

Temperatures down to 60 degrees below, up to 120 above. Tree branches sometimes snapping without having been touched. Hearing a tremendous crunch when one of the rocks in the stone pile fence cracked apart from sheer cold, sparrows frozen solid to the clothesline, turned into fragile little pegs. And in the summer, heat that literally blistered the paint. It bubbled and popped. The winds that blew from every direction hurled grit like finely powdered broken glass, lashing the paint surfaces with bursts of hailstones and sheets of rain, a steady fingernail-worrying at ragged edges, and in a wind obsessed with flattening everything insight.

If they had any brains, these anglaise, and the bohunks too, they build with stone. There's plenty of good stone around here. Limestone. The best. They should have built like the French built right from the beginning, from Champlain, out of stone. Not this softwood that comes apart before your eyes. This goddamn half-baked turd of an excuse for a town isn't even fifty years old, almost brand new compared to how long the French have been building in Québec and look at it. Everything is coming apart at the seams, except for the railway station, the Post Office, the Court House, and the Mission, which were the only things made from stone, and the mission was here before the railway, that's why the railway came through, although God knows why.

Everything else is made of wood.

It would not last, Joseph knew with satisfaction. The whole town is worn down like a bone chewed over and over by a dog. A hundred years from now, the proud basilicas and fortified spires of Quebec City will hardly be polished by the passing of time, but Agassi will be nothing more than sticks. Life out here is like being crushed between grindstones, with the grindstone Prairie turning one way and the grindstone sky turning the other, slowly mincing everything between them down into powder.

And now this.

As he stepped across the boardwalk toward his proud, beautiful Model "T" tudor sedan, erect and haughty, the apple green polish showed through despite the layer of midday dust, Joseph cast an angry, apprehensive look down the long clay road heading west, it's journey towards the infinity point marked by the thin line of crucifix-shaped telegraph poles.

Usually the road and the poles alike vanished into the mirage of the lake on the horizon. But today, the illusory waters were gone. A dark cowl lay across the Prairie instead. It looked like a cloudbank coming in low, rolling visibly as it swallowed up the land over which it was skating, seeming to move and hold back at the same time, almost black but iridescent, as though there was a source of light inside the turbulence, a shifting, flickering illumination. Yet the approaching bank was as solid as a thunderhead, piling up as it slid forward. Goddamn grasshoppers!

It covered more than one hundred square miles, moving forward like the shield wall favored by ancient Celtic Chiefs, who would amass their horsemen behind the advancing iron barricade of foot soldiers. It was an immense plow, forty miles from tip to tip. A shadow. A fog. A cloud galloping along the ground. It came riding the prevailing winds of a cold front. Billowing upward into siege towers sometimes half a mile high.

Its one, desperate hope was to be swept eastward to greenness.

If the afternoon light was behind it, the incoming, ever breaking wave cast a gigantic shadow across the plain it was an engorging. Three miles wide at its slowly undulating gut, its shape was remarkably like that of an amoeba, which may be as close as one can come to comprehending it. It was a single organism, no matter that it was composed of billions of separate two inch long serrated, armored, short-horned, antennaed, spring-legged, four-winged, compound-eyed, starvation-avoiding, grass-digesting, leg-sawing, scissor-jawed, defoliating migrants.

Nobody knew how many exactly. It had been estimated that on each of the square miles occupied by such an entity, 200 million little mouths might be masticating like precision cutting instruments. In a day, all going well, the swarm would consume as much as a population of the distant cities of New York, London, Paris and Los Angeles combined.

Having begun this cycle as drab, shy nymphs, pursuing a lonely existence on hard baked ground, avoiding each other, the grasshoppers had one day found themselves under a low-pressure ridge that eventually brought rain. Overnight, a green carpet of vegetation was suddenly everywhere. The solitary nymphs began to feed. The females began ovipositing everywhere. Hatchings came in clusters. As the world filled up with others of their kind, the nymphs shed their independence, became wildly sociable, and began to court each other by rubbing their ridged hind legs on their forewings, producing irresistible vibrations.

The swarms that quickly formed began to move, and soon

collided with other swarms also on the move. A force like gravity was at work, drawing larger and larger super forms into ever more enormous constellations, so that, within weeks, the one group into which all the others had merged, acting now as one organism, had reached a total weight of tens of thousands of tons.

It had a motion utterly distinct from cell-glued-together organisms, which fly, swim, slithered, climb or run. The swarm moved like just the foot of an otherwise invisible creature so gargantuan it would fill up half the sky. Just the foot, one foot. But rather than being lifted into the air and directed back down to the ground, it moved in waves within waves, with the toes already touching and starting to take hold while the heel is still braced in the last landing place, and the arch is both airborne and firmly planted. It was the swarm's colour, in some ways, which was its most amazing feature. In the ecstasy of this tremendous violin-driven dance that they did together, the grey nymphs have donned glistening black and yellow spotted clown costumes, their textures somewhere between leather and marble, so that it glints in the sun.

And of course, its billions of wings blurring through the air form thin but brilliant films of rainbow.

Lost as she had been in the stately movement of ichthyosaurus across the imaginary sea above her, Bernadette had not bothered to look to the west. She was content to lie on her back, lost amid the giant grass stalks, until the moment came when she sensed an odd silence. A dusty burrowing owl which had stuck his head out of the groundhog hole it had taken over, had been looking around, squinting. Now, it froze.

Apart from the pink of a grasshopper arriving in the immediate vicinity every minute or so, there was a whole chorus of insect sounds that she became so used to. She did not even hear that anymore. Except that now they were gone. Out of the corner of her eye, almost hidden in the grass, Bernadette saw a prairie chicken shaking its waddle as they do when they are alarmed. Goosebumps suddenly popped out all over Bernadette's upper arm. She stood quickly, although something made her stop in a crouch before her head broke clear, giving her presence away. Cautiously, she straightened until she could see across the plain.

Instinct had brought her to her feet facing west.

At first, she thought, a thunderstorm. But it was so low. And it was not a cloud, really.

There was no lightning, no copper glow. And it did not roll, or turn on its axis, or keep re-puffing itself into different shapes. It was more like water.

It took a moment for her to realize that whatever it was, it was as huge as a mountain range, as though the faraway Rocky Mountains had gotten up and walked in shoulder to shoulder ranks across the entire prairies. What else could it be, coming up over the horizon? As far south as she could make out, the wall was there. And it extended as far to the north as she could see, covering the entire western rim of the world.

Her next wild thought was a flood! The great vanishing inland sea was coming back, spilling in a mighty tidal wave across its ancient floor, filling up the center of the continent itself. A flood like the flood in the Bible, only blurred rather than foaming or splashing. And silent. Horribly silent. There should be thunderous noise, but she could not hear a thing.

Mon Dieu, and no high place to climb anywhere!

Worst of all, the floodwall was moving fast. It had already drowned the telephone poles that told her where the road ran along the river. It was two, three times as high as the poles. But then it flowed backward and upward, so it was impossible to guess how high it might really be. It dissolved into the sky, and the sky into it. But, at the very least, it was already within half a mile of the house. And coming, she realized with a jolt of terror, about as fast as a horse might run.

The house had the shape of a bleached, half wrecked ship on an empty tidal flat, about to be crushed under the weight of the incoming surf.

She saw the back-verandah door slam open, and Ma Mere, Teresa and Jean-Paul crowd onto the porch, their hands cupped around their mouths, yelling her name. She tried to answer, but her voice would not work. Oh God, she could not make any sound, and her body did not know what to do. Her mind emptied itself, as suddenly and thoroughly as bowels voiding.

When the tornado had come, she had known fear and awe. But Ma Mere had been there.

Now, she knew panic. Already, Ma Mere, Teresa and Jean-Paul were retreating inside as the wave boiled toward them.

Bernadette could only manage a squeak of terror, then she was bolting toward the house, utterly forgetting something so minor as her arithmetic book. After a dozen frantic strides, she danced, however, to a halt, realizing it was hopeless. The flood wall loomed over the house already, inundating the furthest cottonwoods.

And then it started to hail. At least that is what she thought at first. A sudden, stinging deluge of hailstones. There was a loud, metallic clicking everywhere. The tall grass around her staggered. The yellow narrow leafed sunflowers went down as though blasted by a shotgun. She threw up her arms to ward off the pellets splitting down at her, only to have her hands immediately filled with big, heavy yellow polka-dotted grasshoppers. Their safety pin rear legs were as thick as her little fingers. Their antennae writhed like unconnected wires sprung from lidless eyes. Their mouths opened to reveal twig-like tendrils that came groping for food, as though there was another horrible little creature inside the shell of each of them, equipped with multi jointed arms like the clippers Mon Pere used in his barber shop.

Bernadette turned and ran, and almost immediately stepped on her textbook and skidded, crashing painfully to the ground, tearing the hem of her dress, and streaking it not only with grass stains but the juice of scores of grasshoppers she crushed as she's tumbled and slid. As she shook her hands wildly to get rid of them, ducking her face down, her hair and back caught the full incoming rain of hard-shell bugs. She could feel them, like clothes pegs, through the cotton of her dress. When they ricocheted off the ground and stuck to her infinitely tender inner thighs, the horror was like electric shock. To somehow make it even more obscene than she could have imagined, most of the grasshoppers were fused together in couples, as she imagined Mon Pere and Ma Mere must do, the one astride the other, catching a free ride and some kind of disgusting pleasure at the same time, and yet their segmented eyes were totally blank.

A fearful obligato broke out all around, causing her to thrash even more fanatically as she tried to regain her footing, clawing at the wig of grasshoppers that had formed in a cone around her head, finally, she could scream, along with the coyotes who exploded from hiding and plunged away in tawny streams in every direction. A prairie chicken, which must have been stalking, went delirious, leaping and hopping and beating her wings in ecstasy. The worst part was Bernadette's realization that the insect clattering everywhere around her and down on top of her, like a fuselage in a shooting gallery, were the equivalent of the first flakes of snow riding ahead of a complete white-out.

Like a gopher in a hole, she knew exactly where she was going -- but at the same time, she was totally blank. She lost track of herself. It was as if she was not there any longer. She disappeared. She might as well have been in the clouds or flying somewhere else. Terror had driven her out of herself. Into -- everything, it seemed. She just drifted. She was all over the fields. She was not in any place in particular. She floated. A long time seemed to pass. Peaceful. Like a leaf moving. She was the shadow of a flock of birds. She was smoke.

And then she was back on the open plain, running in a crouch, heart pounding, legs churning, hand swatting the air around her, battering at the insects pelleting down, coagulating into a fierce high-pressure shower of projectiles. But she seemed to step on another insect, or pair of insects, nearly every other step, and she kept slipping, and falling, hands and elbows first, into the writhing soup of broken, still twitching bugs.

It was as if she was being slapped by a hundred little hands at once.

There was only one place to go, the old water tank to the east, out towards the train tracks, right beside the windmill on Mr. Todd's side of the property line. From there, all the way down the river, stretched a low-slung web of barb wire, dangling between old fence post, where tumbleweeds and Russian thistles and cattail wool and popped open silver runner-beans had gotten matted, trailing a grey beard of plant husks. Astride a tiny cluster of poplar along the fence a squeaking old sheet metal windmill turned its rusting, bullet pocked petals to the wind. Even from where Bernadette was, she could hear its mournful rasping. Below it, she knew, there stood a cracked cement watering trough for cows and horses that hadn't held water for years. It was filled with broken glass from Mr. Todd being out there target practicing. The water tank itself was like a big keg, made from slightly curved wood planks, covered with tar and gravel on the top, mounted in an iron-work trestle a man's height above the ground. The grass barely tickled its rotted bottom.

The moment she could pick it out by eye, her entire being zeroed in on the hatch on the side of the tank. It was a round, metal thing, with slate green paint, and a heavy iron latch on the outside that had to be cranked in order to unscrew it from its casing. She had no idea of what it was supposed to do, but if the tank had somehow ever been filled with water, the hatch could easily be sealed tight enough so that it would not leak.

The hatch, she saw now, was closed. But there was nothing else to do except keep aiming for it. The thought of trying to ward off the whirlwind of bugs while climbing with one hand and trying to screw open the hatch with the other -- she didn't have enough hands; it would be impossible. But still her legs churned in the slush of insect guts, she charged straight forward to the one possible shelter.

The pain from the pelting was almost unbearable. She was crying and emitting shrill squeaks. But mainly she put all her strength into running, trying not to slip. Her dress got in the way. When her knee bone ripped through at the same time as a foot was stumbling on the hem, she gained a couple of precious inches for each subsequent lurch.

The worst moment was when she reached the matted old barbed-wire fence and had to decide whether to try jumping over or diving and squeezing through the hole the rabbits had already tunnelled in the weeds between the ground and the lowest wire. Either way, if she got snagged, the grasshoppers would be all over her. If she couldn't keep swiping them away, she was convinced they would start eating her, and the thought of being trapped, exactly as though in a spider web, while millions of these things sawed and tore and ripped and slashed and dug and drilled their way into her, forcing her mouth open so they could scuttled down her throat into her stomach, and, oh, God, they would push in from everywhere, her ears --- Oh no! Mon Dieu!

She dived for the tunnel, smacking her elbows and chin on the ground. Frantically, still crying so she was almost blinded, she writhed her way along as flat as she could, propelling herself with her toes. A shoulder blade heaved too high, however, and a twisted strand of wire neatly sliced open several inches of gingham, leaving a jagged claw mark on her back. Wailing now, she staggered to her feet on the other side. Her hem stayed hooked in the wire. There was no time to pause. She threw herself forward, temporarily slowed as the lower back half of the dress stretched out until it ripped, leaving her free to scramble across the last few yards to the foot of the ladder.

She had no idea how she would manage to open the hatch when she got up there but could think of no other course of action. She climbed desperately, trembling so badly from exhaustion and pain by now she could barely cling to the rungs, and her hands were slippery from snot and bug juice.

At last she was at the hatch, torn, bleeding, grasshopper innards smeared from head to toe. She tried frantically to budge the hatch. It would not move. She raised her head, eyes closed, head cast to the heavens, and cried a deep inner soul moaning cry "Please, Precious Mother of God, help me!"

Fearing no one was listening, she started to sob.

She opened her eyes and gasped, a Miracle.

The hatch swung open just as she was reaching the top rung. Swung open wide. And a familiar face appeared. Two strong young arms reached down to grab her hands and yanked her up inside. There were no words. Just grunts. The instant she had been hauled bumpily in through the opening, her rescuer let go of her and threw himself upon the task of getting the hatch closed. Just in the few seconds it was open, dozens of hoppers had plunged in through the breach, and, of course, there were dozens more still clinging to the frenzied girl. With an enormous, wrenching squeak, the hatch finally clanged shut.

Suddenly, apart from the hammering of Bernadette's heart, there was only echoing silence, the silence of being inside a huge, empty drum, with fingernails swishing on the outside all around, but the wood was too thick to even bother with a whisper in response. Yet her own voice echoed immediately. And so, did that of Marcel Dumas.

There were cracks in the planks that made up the walls of the water tank. It had not been caulked for years. They weren't big enough to let the insects in, these cracks, but they were wide enough so that the fine panes of light were lined up across the floor, all the way to the ceiling, as though the chamber had been sliced into separate sections, divided by dusty glass panels. When the grasshoppers that had gotten inside tried to fly away, they flashed through several of these screens, amazingly not shattering anything, before vanishing into the gloom, where she could hear them smacking like little pucks against the wall, and clinking almost like coins as they fell to the floor.

The horde outside cast a rippling tapestry of shadow down

through those smoked slivers of light, a bit like the stained glass at church when clouds whirled overhead.

It was this light that played across Marcel's face as he stood back, having done his duty by pulling her in here, but now apparently not having any idea what to do about her. The light made him look not quite real, and the thought entered her mind that she hadn't made it here at all, maybe she was just passed out in the field, dreaming this. But the bugs still hanging on to her hair and trying to walk down onto her face and along her neck and shoulders, were real. She gave a final convulsive shudder and pawed the last of them off onto the floor, stamping on them furiously! At the same time, she wiped her nose and face on her torn sleeve. What did it matter anyway? She was such a mess.

As soon as she could catch her breath and her sobbing abated enough for her to speak, she demanded in French: "What are you doing here?"

The boy stepped back, his face fading into the shadow, so she could not be sure if he were smirking or grimacing.

"Same thing as you, I guess."

Bernadette snuffled and finished wiping her face.

"Well don't stare!" she ordered; aware how awful she must look.

He shook his head. And stared.

He looked sorrowful, but in a detached way, like somebody would if they saw a dog lying dead in a ditch.

But then, he was always like that in Catechism class and at Mass. She remembered her Confirmation. Marcel Dumas had been one of the half-dozen children who had all gone up to the altar together to take Communion for the first time. A solemn boy. Skinny. A few years older than her.

Even outside on the grounds at the Mission, when most of the boys were running around screaming at the top of their lungs, Marcel always seemed to be studying. And there had been one particular day, when Sister Florence had asked questions about the Sacrament of Extreme Unction, and nobody, including Bernadette, knew the answer, when the sister had turned to Marcel, sitting at the back of the class, and asked him: "What is the most important thing, as you prepare yourself to die?"

"Say your beads," Bernadette would have answered.

But Marcel stood up, his eyes fixed on the Crucifix above the blackboard, and replied with absolute conviction: "We must be resigned to God's Holy Will."

Bernadette had shivered when he said that, not because of the words, which she, too, could have memorized --should have memorized -- but because she could tell he was talking directly to the Savior himself when he said that.

She wasn't the only one, then, who could actually see God!

But she had never been able to think of a single thing to say to the boy, to let him know that she knew he had been talking to our Lord Jesus as though he was right there in the classroom, standing behind Sister Florence. What bothered her was that Sister Florence seemed to be encouraging Marcel Dumas to talk the way he was talking, to go ahead and open his eyes and his heart and his mind to God, while Bernadette herself, a good French-Canadian girl, could expect no reward except a strapping if she ever revealed something like having seen the Holy Mother's face in the snow bank. Here was this Metis boy being treated by the nun as though he was already a priest. Someday, she realized with a surge of envy, he would be a Minister of the Sacraments. She could imagine him in his cassock. He would look splendid. But the thought of his triumph gave her no pleasure. She would just have to get on her knees in front of him; and close her eyes when he reached down to place the wafer on her waiting tongue.

All that she had suffered, the torn dress, the skinned knees and elbows, the swore chin, the cut from the barbed wire, the horror of all these little monsters all over her, and now this, being stared at by a stupid half breed boy who was Sister Florence's favorite pupil, abruptly overwhelmed Bernadette, and she screamed:

"What are you? A lump? Help me, for God's sake!"

The boy snapped out of it.

"Here," he said. Calmly, as though it was the most natural act in the world, he tugged off his white collarless shirt, and draped it over her shoulders. It was done as gently as if he had been lowering a veil. His skin, she saw, was drumstick tight. His ribs stuck out, and there were awful looking boils on his upper chest. She was struck, through her tears, by the smell of him. She knew the Metis were sometimes called the bois brule, the "scorched wood people," but somehow, she didn't expect it to be based on anything so tangible as a real smell. Yet, indeed, he had a smoky smell. What else could you call it. His clothes, she noticed, had a different smell entirely. It took her a few moments to recognize it as the smell of the wet clay down by the river, as though everything he wore was saturated in it. They said at school the Metis never got bit by mosquitoes, and maybe this had something to do with it. She liked both those smells. And something else. It was hot in here, and he must have run a fair distance to escape the bugs, just like her. He was sweaty, drops of sweat had beaded on his hairless chest. He was barefoot. Bernadette began to lick her fingers, dabbing the saliva against her scratches, calm enough now so that she merely sniffled and shivered. Outside, the swarm made a sizzling sound as it broke around the sturdy water tank walls. No better shelter, she realized, could have been hoped for.

She sat there in her torn dress, hugging herself, with her skinned knees showing, tugging the boy's shirt close around her. Marcel stood back awkwardly and leaned, hands in pockets, against the hatch, as though his shoulders might help keep the horde out. His hair, which came down several inches lower than his shoulders, was unevenly clipped in front into bangs that came down into his eyes, so he had to keep pushing it aside to see.

"We're OK here," Marcel said, his voice seemed to have deepened.

"I'm cold," Bernadette said.

"Is that right, eh?" He said hoarsely.

She saw him lick his lips nervously. She saw a worried look in his eyes. He gulped a couple of times. He was scared about something.

See him! He was practically turning inside out, not knowing what to do with his hands, looking all over the place except at her, especially not looking into her eyes. At least, at home, she was used to everyone looking each other in the eye, even if they were just glaring. Bernadette looked around for a few moments as well, wondering what to say.

"I hope we'll get out of this alive," She finally declared, as theatrically as she could. After all, this was a natural disaster, and they were in the middle of it.

When Marcel didn't say anything, she added, "Jesus will take care of us." And she lowered her head and whispered. "Amen."

"Amen," said Marcel, closing his eyes and bowing his head.

"My grandfather was the Cree who shot the priest at Batoche, eh?" Marcel suddenly bragged.

Batoche. She heard the name before, but it was like so many names she heard, she couldn't quite place it. Batoche. Ungava. Battleford. Duck Lake. Assiniboine. The Qu'Appelle Valley. Athabasca. Medicine Hat. Moose Jaw. Images of church spires. The famous Basilica of Saint Boniface. Fort Gary. The Red River settlement. Indians in teepees. Buffalo herds. Steam engines. Redcoats. Batoche -- wasn't that a place where a battle happened. The men Mon Pere hated so much, that Louis Riel who was hanged for making his own army or something, maybe he fought his last battle there and lost -- where they fired nails and stones when they ran out of bullets, and wasn't there a church that was profaned somehow by the traitors?

"That was bad," Bernadette declared sternly, not wanting to admit any ignorance. "Your grandfather must have gone to hell for that."

"The priest was working for the soldiers, eh!"

"You can't go around shooting priests!"

"My grandfather was a Cree. Cree don't believe in hell. They are not worried about going there. The bois brule do, but not the Cree. They are not Catholics."

"But you go to Communion. You're baptized."

"I'm mostly Cree, eh?"

Bernadette pondered for a moment. She did not like the way this was going. And then she spotted the flaw in his argument.

"Do you have a chief?"

Marcel stared at her for a long time. The lower part of his face screwed itself down into a hard, sad lump.

"No," he said.

Bernadette didn't hesitate before she replied with a smug grin. "Well then, you can't be an Indian."

Marcel turned his shoulder to her, so his face was in profile and he didn't have to look at her. He flushed.

"So, what do you think you are?"

"I'm French," Bernadette shrugged.

"Ha!" snorted Marcel.

"What do you mean, Ha!" I am French. My grandfather and grandmother both came from Québec."

Marcel turned his head slightly to watch her reaction when he said: "My father says the French only brought over soldiers at first, and they married Indians, eh? So, everybody who came over after married someone who was part Indian. All you French Quebecers are really mixed blood too; you just pretend you're not. That's why you won't fight along with Riel. That's what my father says. He says you're all crazy because you don't know who you are. You forgot."

Bernadette clambered to her feet angrily. Crazy peasouper! That's what he was saying, just like the others, calling Mon Pere and the rest of us names.

"I'll tell you who's crazy," she spat. "You're the crazy one! You're talking crazy. I'm going to tell Father Patenaude!"

"Tell him! What's he going to do, kick me out of the church. I only go because my mother makes me."

Bernadette gasped. There it was, out in the open. I only go because my mother makes me. He was not the reverent, scholarly young priest- in-waiting she thought. Mon Dieu, it sounded like he didn't even believe. He was a sinner.

She was so disappointed she wanted to cry. She turned her back on him completely, and sat down again, yanking his shirt from her shoulders and throwing it on the floor. After a moment, she did start to cry. This was so awful!

Jean de Pean was fifteen, a year older than his best only friend, Charlie Dufour. They both had proud, hard muscles from working in the fields during harvest and helping with the chores at home. Jean's face had been ravished by childhood smallpox. His eyes had a cornered look. He never relaxed. Charlie was a little bulkier, softer.

Jean's Mon Pere, Francois de Pean, owned the second biggest farm in all of Agassiz district. Jean had heard him, more than once, say, "That goddamn Joe Labouchere, he's a goddamn Tory."

That was the worst thing a Canadien -francaise in Manitoba could be, and still be French. Jean had even heard his Papa say, "That goddamned Joe Labouchere should be excommunicated!" No worse fate could await a Catholic. And, in town, there were signboards everywhere that said Labouchere this, and Labouchere that.

A big man, eh?

"Fermez la bouche," Antoine Dufoure, Charlie's Papa, had often said, repeating the line that the French-Canadians around Agassiz had all, at one time or another, whispered among themselves. For, as uncommunicative as Joe the Mouth was with les *Anglaise*, among the French, he pontificated endlessly, just like his father, some said, and was so set in his views that you'd think he was the goddamn Pope himself.

When there were just the two of them around, Jean and Charlie often talked about grabbing old man Labouchere's oldest daughter, as a way to gain glory in the eyes of their fathers. (We got even with that Labouchere for you, Papa!) by putting the meat to the little slut.

For years, they had slyly watched her at the church. They watched her in the classroom. They watched her in the school grounds. They nudged each other when they saw her walking off alone. She was a goofy girl, too. Always saying her beads. They had nicknamed her Hail Mary. Talking dirty about her had become a routine.

"Should we jump her now?" Charlie would ask, giggling.

"Not yet, wait until she begs," Jean would answer.

"Firsts!" Charlie would squeal with slobbering excitement, his heart starting to pump.

"You want first?" Jean would ask. "You can have the other end first."

And they both double over, howling and gasping with laughter.

They didn't talk about all the girls this way, only a chosen few. Most were too ugly, or too fat, or too skinny, or too bucktoothed, or they had glasses, or dandruff, bad breath, or big brothers, or they were Indians, or half breeds. Only a few had the right combination of features.

"And what, pray tell," Charlie would ask, "is the right combination of features?"

And Jean would answer: "Tits!" And they'd collapse against each other, hooting and shrieking. The little Labouchere bitch had just gotten hers, but they would do. And she was begging for it. The French bitches were the best, that's what they said, especially when they were ripe, and they hadn't been busted yet.

"When I pop her," Jean gritted through his teeth, "she's sure going to say Hail Mary, eh? She's going to say, "Hail Jean Le Pean!"

"How can she control herself?" Charlie wondered. "You can see it in her eyes. Can't wait, eh?"

Jean and Charlie were out at Dyson's Pond, one property past Todd's field, on the east side of the Labouchere spread, skinny-dipping and chucking rocks at frogs, when they looked up and saw that not-quite-cloud, not quite-wave on the horizon, rolling soundlessly in their direction. They splashed out of the water as fast as they could, frantically pulling on their coveralls, not bothering with the underwear, just sticking it in the back pocket, dry cloth sticking to wet skin, hopping around on one foot, their hearts pounding with fear. It was going to be a long run back to the nearest shelter, Mr. Dyson's barn. But they should make it before the main swarm hit -- when Jean, always the bright one, got a brain wave. Charlie didn't like it when Jean got brain waves. Sometimes they got into trouble.

We can make it over to Todd's windmill, Jean gasped, struggling to get his arms into his shirt. Already the hoppers were starting to pellet down on the pond like hail. "We'll hole up in the drum. Nobody will know where we are. They'll get really worried. Maybe a search party, eh? And then, when we show up, we will be big heroes."

"Why don't we just go to the barn?" Charlie's teeth were chattering.

"Come on, you piece of turd," Jean urged, automatically slapping his shoulder, "race you." Charlie moaned. But Jean was off running barefoot through the grass toward the distant windmill.

Charlie labored after him, knowing better than to waste breath yelling for Jean to slow down. The older boy always outran him, and loved outrunning him, so there was no way to talk him out of it. It was no use arguing with Jean de Pean. If he didn't like what Charlie was saying, Jean would whack him so hard on the shoulders it stung for hours. Every once in a while, he grabbed Charlie around the waist and rammed his knuckles deep into Charlie's kidneys, twisting until Charlie screamed. He learned to scream early and get it over with. Once, years ago, Jean had beat him up pretty bad. Black eye. Thick lip. But now they were friends, and Jean just kidded around, even if it did sting a bit.

Now, in fact, Charlie was stinging all over. The grasshopper cloud had gotten a lot closer. They were actually running along its flank, instead of away from it. For miles ahead, the telephone poles and clusters of bush were fading, as though being covered by a dust storm, but this wasn't just dark like dust when it whirled up into the sky, this was grey flecked with flashes of gold and silver, almost enough to make him want to stop and take a good look at it, like he did sometimes when it was storming and snowing. Kind of beautiful -- except being caught out in the open by this, hurt -- and seemed to be hurting more all the time. As he galloped miserably along, Charlie had to keep his mouth shut tight, with both hands in front of his squinting eyes, to have even a hope of knowing where he was going. Mainly, he could just see from the way the grass was wagging where Jean had passed. Grasshoppers began to pile up on his head and shoulders as if they had decided to take a rest and go for a ride on this huge, lumbering beast.

Uselessly, Charlie screamed. "Aidez moi! Aidez moi!" Then a grasshopper smacked down on his partially open lips and got its head and forearms into his mouth before he could spit it away. He nearly gagged. You could choke on those.

Finally, even Jean gave up and ducked into the shelter of a thick leaf maple stand along with a couple of willows about halfway to the still hopelessly distant wind vane. He started snapping young willow branches off, covering his head and shoulders, then cringed against the tree trunk with it between him and the swiftly advancing swarm. Charlie likewise tore off as many branches as he could and pressed himself up beside Jean, against the tree. The willow leaves did provide a canopy of small protection, and so did the tree trunk, so that when the main body of the swarm rolled over them, the torrent of bugs floated around their hiding spot like a river cascading around a rock.

There was nothing to do but crouch there, with the trunk shielding their bodies and the willow branches shielding their heads, until the worst was over, when -- out of the corner of his eye, Jean detected a flash of gingham -- somebody running! -- over by the water tank. Seconds later, everything was drifted over by a living dune of squirming, chittering insects. Both boys closed their eyes, pressed close to each other, and chanted through clenched lips. "Our Father, who art in Heaven, hallowed be thy name, thy Kingdom come, thy Will be done --. It seemed to help. If nothing else, they felt slightly calmer.

It was hard to tell how long they remained there, huddled together. It was the worst thing Charlie could ever remember happening to him. It was all he could do not to cry.

But for Jean le Pean, the passage of time was nothing. He had something to look forward to. That flash of gingham. He recognized it. He knew exactly where it must have been going. Exactly where it must be now. Bottled up, caged, snared. And it wouldn't be able to come out until the bugs let up. Jean's mouth was drier than he could ever remember, even though he had been drinking from the pond less than an hour ago. He felt a peculiar lightness, as though he might float up in the air any moment. His whole lower abdomen felt like water. God, they could do it. He could see it so clearly. She must have got caught out in the open too and ran for it. And she was in there. And nobody would be coming around here until the bugs settled down, and that might not be for hours.

The moment Jean thought he detected the slightest easing of the bug-cloud's forward rush, he decided to act. With all the noise of the grasshoppers clicking down around and on them and overlapping sonic vibrations from their legs as they sang madly to each other in their millions, he had to yell to be heard to his whimpering friend Charlie's ear.

"The Labouchere bitch! I saw her heading for the water drum. She's in there!"

Charlie was afraid he was suddenly going to have the runs. Everything below his heart went empty. It was like an explosion had gone off inside him, an explosion of feathers, tickling him into numbness. He saw the picture right away, with no more prompting than that.

Automatically, he turned his head and peeked out through his wreath of willows to try to make out the old water tank, a quarter mile away. At first it was impossible to see anything through the drifting mass of insects, then he caught a glimpse of old sheet metal wind vanes above the drum, pocked with bullet holes, as if the tank itself was the King of Insects, struggling to get off the ground, fluttering his torn, rotted wings, not moving.

"We've got her," Jean said softly.

Charlie started to speak but was afraid to mouth his thoughts. He knew what he should be saying. He should be telling Jean, before it was too late, hey, it's OK to talk about it, but we could get into big trouble with this. Big trouble. But Jean would not listen, because Mon Dieu Christ, this is too good to be true. We'll just go and have some fun, that's all, Charlie thought. Maybe she'll like it. Sure, she'll like it.

"She was probably looking for us, eh Charlie?" Jean yelled.

"I-I-I was just thinking that."

"Well, come on, let's go!" Jean stood slowly, straightening his cramped leg muscles, rearranging the shield of willows over his head to protect his back as well, and trotted out into the fuselage. He seemed to be skipping through a hailstorm that was flattening the grass, except that this particular downpour came in at an angle, as though driven by a mighty wind. Yet there was no wind, only a draft from all around. Feeling afraid but giddy with the thrill of the hunt, Charlie rearranged his own willow umbrella and lifted himself into the open, offering his body as a target, not bothering to stifle the squeaks of "ow, ow, ow." Hoping Jean Le Pean might feel guilty for causing his best friend all this grief but knowing Le Pean wouldn't give a shit.

They ran. The grass whipped by. The grasshoppers bounced off, sometimes flopping in their wake, other times springing away in a new direction, although never against the tide of their cousins. While the galloping boys took bruises, their skin proved to be a tougher armor than that of the bugs. They were unstoppable once in motion, loping, hunched over, through the exoskeletal squall -- Jean let out what he imagined to be an Indian war-whoop, covering and uncovering his lips:

"Woo, woo, woo, woo, woo, woo, woo, woo, woo, woo, woo!"

Charlie tried a few whoops of his own, but only out of the side of his mouth, for fear of swallowing bugs, and, besides, he was too desperate to get out of this Jesus puking plague to concentrate on anything except Jean's bare heels flashing through the tall grass ahead. Suddenly, Jean stopped. They had reached the water tank. Glancing up, Charlie saw the steel legs of the windmill disappearing into the underbelly of the insect wave breaking over them. He crashed straight into Jean, who elbowed him hard, then started climbing straight up, as agile as a squirrel. Before Charlie could firmly planted his foot on the first rung, Jean was up to the top of the ladder and pulling at the big steel crossbar mounted on the hatch. He twirled it, it cried out rustically. The hatch swung open.

Jean scrambled inside, his eyes taking a moment to adjust to the gloom: blank shadow spaces broken only by the shafts of light falling through the cracks.

In one of those shafts, Bernadette sat frozen in her torn dress, with her bruised chin, crying. In another shaft a few feet away, as though performing under a different set of stage lights, little Marcel Dumas was pulling his shirt down over his head as fast as he could.

"Well, well," said Jean.

Marcel Dumas, of all people. Sister Florence's pet. The little holier-than-holy Catechism class know-it-all half breed who was still frantically stuffing his shirt into his pants when Charlie clambered in, blinking.

"Get this," said Jean.

It took Charlie a few seconds to make things out. When it registered, he was as genuinely shocked as he could be. "Mon Dieu Christ la Tabernac!"

"Somebody else with the same idea, eh." Jean chuckled.

"Hey, Dumas!" yelled Charlie, "what the hell you think you're doing?"

"It ain't what you think," Marcel said through gritted teeth.

He stepped back, bunching his fists and coiling into a boxing stance.

"Oh yeh!" barked Charlie, clenching his own fists and starting forward.

Ignoring this, Jean was looking at Bernadette. He could see her legs where the dress was torn. Her lower lip looks swollen. Her hair was bunched in a knot. Her face was streaked with tears. She was barefoot. He'd never seen her looking so helpless. She was suffering, she was so sad looking, so hurt. He loved seeing her suffer. It made him feel ecstatic. If he could make her suffer more, it would make him feel even more excited, he knew with absolute certainty.

"What are you staring at, goof-face?" Bernadette demanded.

"Let's beat him up," said Charlie, squinting from Jean to Marcel." Look what he did! You're going to get your face changed around, you little turd!"

"No, no," said Jean, standing up in front of Charlie to block him. "Don't be an idiot. This is perfect, for Christ's sake."

To Marcel, he said with a little grin: "We know what you've been doing."

"Ain't done nothing, frog shit!" snarled Marcel.

"What are you talking about, you filthy boy?" Bernadette yelled at Jean. "I'll tell your mother!" she warned indignantly. "We've been hiding from the bugs, same as you." Under his rude, unwavering stare, she found herself touching her lip and looking down at her clothes, "I fell running. I hurt myself."

"Sure," sneered Jean.

"I did, you box-head! Oh, how can you be so stupid?"

"We'll let you go," Jean said to Marcel. Charlie started to object but stopped -- he had never heard that tone in Jean's voice. The muscles in his throat must have all caught tight. He was squishing the words as they came out, so that they almost squeaked. "We won't tell anybody," Jean continued.

"There's nothing to tell, eh!" Marcel said.

"You're crazy!" Bernadette shouted at Jean, getting angrily to her feet.

"Otherwise, Dumas, we're going to tell everybody what you were doing to her," Jean went on, enjoying himself hugely. "We caught you.!"

"Nothing to catch, frog-boy!"

"Her father is going to kick your ass," said Jean.

Getting the drift, Charlie joined in. "Mon Dieu Christ, he's going to take it out on you. You're finished, Dumas!"

Marcel looked at the two French boys. Jean was six inches taller than him, and sinewy. The fat kid was at least thirty pounds heavier. When they played hockey, Jean Le Pean was known to be the kind of player who'd check as hard as he could from behind and wouldn't hesitate to trip you with his stick. Once, Marcel had seen him get a player from another parish down and keep kicking him with his skates until the referee got there. Afterwards, Father Patenaude gave them all a lecture about playing fair, but didn't take Le Pean off the team, eh? He was too big and mean for any eleven-year-old to fight. Against the two of them, there wasn't a hope in hell.

And what did he owe this Labouchere girl anyway? She just finished telling him he wasn't even an Indian, for Christ sake. Nothing was going to happen here, anyway, and if it did, what did he care. What business of his was it?

How often had his father said, "The whites will never treat you like a human being!"

Sure, sometimes it seemed like some of the Sisters did treat him as though he really was just another kid, but mostly they looked down at him like he was partially an animal who might bite or have lice. And when he did have lice, he was mortified into speechlessness. And he could see the disgust in their faces.

It was only because he was Metis, of course, that he got to go with the white kids to the separate school. The public school was strictly for whites, and the Indian kids had all been taken away to the boarding schools out in the countryside run by the priests, where a lot of them died of TB.

He was lucky. If his mother had not been Metis, he'd have been full bred Cree, and he'd be out in one of those Indian schools, where you couldn't even talk in your own language, otherwise they'd whip you. His cousins who got to come back for the summer holidays wouldn't talk about what it was like. They would never look you back in the eye, either. A lot of Indian people were like that, but the kids who had to go to the boarding schools for most of the year, starting when they were six, were bad that way. They would look everywhere except at you. They giggle amongst themselves sometimes, but mostly they just seemed sad. Of course, none of them wanted to go away to boarding school. It was just that if their parents tried to hide them, the Mounties came and carried them away. There was no escaping. Marcel didn't like being around them. He tried to feel sorry for them, but they called him a name in Cree, meaning he was an inferior crossbreed of a dog, and he thought: "The Indians don't treat me like a human either." But he couldn't say that to his father.

This business of two dumb French boys and the smart-alecky French girl, it was white people's business not his.

"Piss off now, while you can," Jean Le Pean warned.

"While you can walk, eh!" added Charlie, straining to get past Jean, who was still holding him back.

Bernadette could not believe what she was hearing and seeing. Until now, she knew Jean and Charlie as noisy, stupid bigger boys from school, Church and Catechism, always falling down laughing about nothing, throwing snowballs, spitting, shooting at birds and prairie dogs with slingshots and bows and arrows, irritating and ugly, both of them, but it had never occurred to her to be afraid of them. They were buffoons, as ever, but she suddenly realized they were getting to be almost as big as men. There was fuzz all over Jean Le Pean's pockmarked face, and even some black hairs on his bare chest. They were only wearing their trousers.

Bernadette felt everything speed up around her, igniting a flare of anger.

To Marcel, she ground out an order, "You stay right where you are!"

To Jean Le Pean, a fierce warning, "I'll tell my Mon Pere!"

But the answer was not what she expected. It was insolent, dangerously lazy. "If you do, we'll say the half breed did it."

Charlie squealed and swore. It was so perfect.

"He won't believe you," Bernadette shot back, secretly shocked at the sense of desperation mounting in her.

"Oh no?"

Jean laughed as though he had said the funniest thing in ages. Charlie turned red cackling. Marcel was frozen in his boxing crouch, his eyes urgently gauging the distance to the hatch past the French boys. Everybody, even Bernadette, knew Joe the Mouth was a famous half breed-hater. Would he believe two boys of good Québec stock over just his daughter and bois brule? Really, was there any chance he wouldn't.

Although she suspected it was hopeless, she tried: "I'll tell Father Patenaude.".

"Hah!" sneered Jean. "He needs me."

Bernadette thought of Ma Mere and Mrs. Allenby. She would be able to tell them, but what good was that right now. These two bullies weren't going to be very worried about what a couple of women would say or do, that was for sure.

"I'm going," said Marcel.

"What?" squeaked Bernadette, starting to shake now with alarm.

Grinning, Jean and Charlie stepped aside from the hatch. Marcel kept his eyes warily on them, especially their hands and feet, ready to deflect a kick or a punch, if he could. He darted toward the escape route.

"Marcel Dumas! I'm ordering you to stay here!" cried Bernadette.

He stopped for a second. Then, looking at the floor, he said solemnly. "I'm not your servant, eh?"

With that, he skittered the rest of the way to the hatch, and gave the crossbar a single, violent spin. The hatch swung open, and, without a backward glance, Marcel leapt out into the grasshopper storm. Charlie pulled the hatch shut behind him, and spun the bar in the opposite direction, twisting it at the end with all his strength to screw it in tight. As though a down pillow had exploded, a plume of insects rattled in through the opening and were pinging and clicking around inside. Bernadette could not help but let out a shriek when one landed on her injured shoulder.

Jean reached out and deftly snagged a grasshopper in his cupped hand. He advanced on her, holding up his prize.

"How would you like this up your hole?"

Bernadette lost all semblance of control. She screamed, covering her face in her hands, and, when Jean let the grasshopper crawl over onto her hair, she screamed again, clawing it away.

Marcel ran south toward the river, not sure how long he could stay out in the open before the pain of being pelted constantly got to be too much to bear. He ran along the old cow trail beside the overgrown barb wire fence, not once looking back. He heard the French girl scream the moment he left, but as he managed to put distance between himself and the water tower, the screams faded, shut out by the pounding of his heart, his panting, the thumping of his bare feet, the swish of the tall grass, and something that was not quite a sound that seemed to saw at his ear drums, a maddening vibration that came from the grasshoppers rubbing their ridged hind legs on their forewings, as though a giant violin was groaning through the air.

He ran with his right arm over his head to ward off the pallets. Each hopper that hit him stung. And before the sting could ease, there were more stings. Even with his eyes shielded, he dared do nothing more than squint at the ground below and just slightly ahead. It would be crazy to stop. He didn't think he could, even if he wanted. It would hurt too much to stand still, or even to curl into a ball.

And so, he ran because he had to.

But even if there had been no grasshoppers, he would have had to run as hard as he could. For, while he had felt a thrill of pleasure at the sound of Bernadette's scream, the joy of getting even had only lasted for a couple of dozen strides before he began to feel something terrible closing in on him as relentlessly as the grasshoppers, but closing in on the inside. A slipping feeling, so unpleasant he felt a gush of nausea. It was as though he was being pushed from below, so that his balance was suddenly doubtful, as though he was being disconnected from the ground, and might float away. He ran faster, just to avoid falling face forward on his hands.

And it all had to do with the girl, the goddamn little nun, even though what she was getting, served her goddamned right. It did! What the goddamn French did to each other they all deserved. He knew this from his father, Albert. He knew exactly how the French had come in and pushed everyone who was already here out of the way. He knew that the French priests were the best liars in the world, and that they secretly worked for the devil, trying to capture the souls of Indian kids. He had heard Albert laugh bitterly about how good it was to see the French being pushed aside by the Orangemen and bohunks and fish-breath Scandinavians. They didn't like it, the Dogan's, when it came to be their turn to be shoved out of the way, to have the land grabbed all around them. And, even then, what did they have to complain about? At least they got to hang onto a piece of what they took from the Cree and Assiniboine and Metis.

Yes! Marcel had shivered with excitement at the sound of Bernadette The Mouth screaming. She had been so smart, eh? So bossy. Her Mon Pere, the big man in town. The great Frenchman! He should see what was happening to his daughter now.

At the sudden, explosive thought of what Jean la Pean and Charlie Dufour were doing back at that tower to Bernadette

Labouchere, Marcel suddenly convulsed and started throwing up, his stomach squeezed and twisted by utterly contradictory emotions. He stumbled onto the hard-packed clay, knocking tall grass aside, paralyzed, a puddle of vomit forming between his hands, fingers trying to get a grip on the earth.

Bleakly, he realized he could not just leave her there like that -- but wait, this was the right thing to do. Run and get help! But by the time he got anywhere or got anyone to come back with him in the middle of all the grasshoppers, it would be too late. They would have done what they were gonna do, and it would have been done for good. You would not be able to undo it. And he would have to spend the rest of his life knowing he was the guy who did not lift a finger to help. Why? Because he was chickenshit, eh?

But it was French stuff! Not his!

Agonized, Marcel lurched to his feet and turned, throwing up his right arm to protect his face. His right rib cage was suddenly entirely exposed, and somehow much more tender than the side which had been getting pelted, which was one entire bruise now. He could make out the tower as a dim turret like shape in the fog of tumbling insect bodies. It would, by now, involve several minutes worth of running back along the trail, being lashed at by the bugs like this all the way. And then what?

He would rush in and beat Jean la Pean and Charlie Dufour up before either one of them could do anything to him. He would save Bernadette, and Father Patenaude would bless them, and they'd get married, and they'd go live like the old Cree did in teepees, and hunt buffalo, and he'd be a great elected Chief Of The Hunt, stronger and a better rider than everyone? Yeh!

With exquisitely detailed clarity, he could see himself being knocked down and kicked and stomped on and maybe hit with two-by- fours until he was hurt bad. He would not be the first Metis or Indian kid to be beat up bad by white guys. Just the winter before, his father's retarded kid brother, Uncle Miles, had been found all chewed up by coyotes and birds so it looked like he'd just falling down drunk and froze to death, except a lot of guys, including Albert, say Uncle Miles had been all cut up by somebody's knife, and beat up real bad, before being dumped in the bush. Word was, there had been a live cigar stuck up his ass.

Big mean white kids. Be crazy to tangle with them out here with nobody around.

Marcel Dumas whined in confusion and physical pain. Unable to make up his mind to move one way or another, he danced wildly on the spot, his shoulders casting around like compass points. Unable to fix on any pole.

This was gonna hurt either way. If he did something, it wasn't just that he'd get beat up, he'd have La Pean and Dufour after him for the rest of his life, and all their friends, and he didn't have many friends to counter them with, because the Indian kids kept to themselves, and the rest of the Metis had gone west.

To keep running was easier. It never crossed his mind that whatever happened to Bernadette, the adult world would never know about it, he could just play dumb. Only the girl and those French assholes would know, and none of them would dare say anything either. The girl would not say anything because she would be too ashamed. This was just between the four of them. It would be so much easier to just carry on as if nothing had happened -- keep running. Run fast. But, if he just kept running, he could see himself running forever. A voice inside his head said clearly: Run now, you might as well keep going, boy.

His eyes welled up with tears at the thought of the physical pain he was going to have to suffer. And then the Fourteen Stations of the Cross sprang to mind. Christ, in his white loin cloth with his cracked white parchment skin and rose-red whip marks and grey face and streaks of blood from the thorns, suffering and even dying, and rising up to heaven, with Angels opening the clouds, and beams of light coming down on the hard rocks and blood-stained crucifixes....

Jesus, Marcel thought, be real. Do magic.

One step. A falling sensation in his stomach. Panic. He let out a sob but made himself focus on the tower. Judging. Aiming. Another step, skittish. Freezing. As though there was a wall. Frantically, he racked through his thoughts for a key. He found himself gasping. "Our Father, hallowed be Thy name, thy Kingdom come, thy Will be done ..." at the word "Will," he dug his toes in and charged, head down, whispering "Our Father, Our Father, Our Father," reverting, in a moment of crisis, to what the Jesuits had wanted all along, blind faith, but too scared and adrenaline-charged to take time to notice; although, for a moment, flinging himself with clenched fists through the grasshopper maelstrom across the field, he saw himself in full Cree warrior regalia with war paint and feathers. And even though he made no sound because he wanted to preserve the element of surprise, in his mind he let out a war-whoop like his Father did sometimes when he was drinking.

It was only at the top of the ladder, as he clamped a hand on the crossbar and prepared to twist, that his fear swooped back and kept his hand muscles, for a moment, from working. He didn't want to be hurt. For a kid who didn't belong to any tribe, he didn't get hurt that often. He could just slide away in most situations. Keep his eyes down, lay low. Drift. Not really get mad. Stupid to get mad. Albert got mad all the time. Dumb. Don't do no good.

Running looked good. But maybe he just couldn't stand the grasshoppers anymore. He was being riddled and drilled. Something had to give. He wanted to go back, but where to. It was a fog cloud of bugs in every direction.

He twisted and pushed the hatch open, and launched himself inside, more scared than he could ever remember being. Maybe he could get them to chase him. Poised to start swinging right away, he had to catch himself in full flight, skidded onto one knee, catching Jean Le Pean yelling, ---"If you say a single goddamn word, I'll---!"

Bernadette was on the floor behind him, completely limp, lying on her back with her arms thrown out, legs together and eyes closed, like she was nailed to a cross on the floor, with thank you Lord Jesus, all her clothes, torn as they were, still on.

Jean le Pean was pummeling Charlie Dufour on the shoulder with one hard fist, while the fat kid cringed away.

The instant Marcel landed inside, Jean le Pean swung to meet him, giving Dufour a savage shove sideways so Charlie blundered against the wall of the tank, whimpering.

There was no sound or movement from the girl. Her face was --- grey. There was blood in her hair and on her forehead, just like from the thorns in the Fourteen Stations of the Cross, and scratches on her arms, like whip marks. These had all been there before, but now her skin seemed parchment white, and the blood was rose bright.

Trembling with fury, Jean le Pean snarled down at him. "You're gonna get it now, you little half breed shit! I told you not to come back here!"

"You killed her?" Marcell asked in shock, overwhelmed by the enormity of what he saw. This wasn't kid stuff anymore. A nightmare was easy compared to this. All the fight went out of him. He was simply scared. He should not be near here. That was the one thing he knew for sure.

Christ, they would blame him, for sure. And get away with it because she wouldn't be around to tell the truth. "Nobody killed her!" Charlie wailed. "She just dropped dead like that. She did it to herself. We were just having fun!"

"Shut your mouth, Dufour! We weren't even here!" He jumped forward and caught Marcel by the shoulder of his shirt. "And if you're smart, you'll forget you were ever here either or ever saw any of us. Got that, you little turd?"

Seeing Marcel looking at her, Jean le Pean let go. He turned and dropped to his knees beside the girl. He grabbed Bernadette's body and lifted her head several inches above the floor, and then, looking to make sure both Marcel and Charlie were watching, he let the head go like a melon. It bonked on the wood and rolled sideways. The girl's eyelids didn't so much as quiver.

Oh Jesus!

The same voice from inside, which just a few moments ago had warned Marcel about the danger of having to run forever, suddenly cried. Run!

He moved at twice the speed of Jean, who lurched for him the instant he realized the Metis was making a break for it but couldn't get himself in motion fast enough.

"I'll get you!" he grated, flailing.

Marcel back-scuttled through the hatch and took the rungs of the ladder three bounds at a time, in reverse, on the way down until he got within five feet of the ground, and then jumped for it, spinning around in mid-air, landing in mid-stride, feet churning, body leaning forward like a hound, arms pumping harder than they had ever pumped.

It didn't matter where he ran, he just wanted away. He shot through the hail of hoppers, almost oblivious in his desire to escape to the little whacking blows being landed on him as he sped across the plain. The image of the dead girl was large like a fish bone in his memory. Tugging at him as he ran, torturing him.

If he had gone back sooner!

Oh, Mother of God, he was in trouble now!

He only looked back over his shoulder once, and it was to see Jean Le Pean clamoring down the ladder, with Charlie Dufour squeezing out of the hatch, the two of them yelling something at each other. Le Pean looking around, seeing nothing, and lumbering off toward the river, quickly disappearing into this swarm. Leaving the hatch open behind him, Charlie half fell to the ground, then limped off, hands over his head to ward off the hoppers, looking like someone surrendering, running away toward Todd's field.

Marcel threw himself flat in the grass, and lay perfectly still, ignoring the deluge of insects, while he listened to his heart drumming wildly against the hard clay.

A mighty hail of little skeletons. The clicking of millions of spoon and fork mouths. Violin limbs playing. Everything in the sky was grasshoppers, and all the grasshoppers were moving, but for an instant when Marcel squinted with one eye upward, it seemed the grey sky was not moving at all. It was suspended. The tall grass was flapping madly because the earth itself was spinning. He pressed his face into the cracked soil and hung onto the grass stems where they became the roots to stop himself from being thrown into the air.

The picture of the dead girl was still in front of him, as vivid as ever.

Run! Get away!

His toes churned, but, despite his panic, a part of him suddenly felt safe enough to pause to think. The French boys were gone, lost. They would never find him now. And it would be a while before anyone ventured out here. Who were Le Pean and Dufour going to run to anyway? The Mounties? Their daddies? Father Patenaude? Well, maybe him, eventually…

By this time, he hurt so much from the grasshopper bombardment that he stung all over. The only good thing was that it had turned into near numbness. He could imagine a point where he would not feel anything at all.

With Le Pean and Dufour gone from the water tower, what was to stop him from going back there again. It was by far the closest shelter. What? And be found by searchers beside the girl's body? Craziness? Yep, where else was he gonna go.? He couldn't just stay put any longer, and the French boys had gone off in the two best directions for getting to a house.

The horror of being out in the open in the middle of the grasshopper storm began to tear at him. It was like being in something's mouth. By now, he hated the hoppers.

He had been squashing as many as he could as he ran, altering his steps just enough to get extra kills without slowing down too much. Lying on the ground like this, he was helpless except when they landed within inches of his hands. He snapped at them with his teeth.

Anything, even being alone with the corpse, was better than this!

So, he put everything into one last beeline spurt back along the track he'd already broken through the grass. It was the third time he'd rushed to the tower for shelter in just the last half hour, he realized, pushing his feet against the ground as hard as he could, straining to make each stride a leap, leaning into it, running a gauntlet of a hundred million tiny torturers that it seemed he had been running forever.

He leapt at the ladder and hauled and pushed himself swiftly to the top, only to discover the hatch was closed, and when he tugged at the crossbar, it didn't give at all. Marcel was starting to get seriously afraid. The insects were getting to him. The thought of having to run across the field again was devastating. He didn't think he could face it. He started screaming and hammering at the hatch, straining at the cross bar, which, after a moment, gave slightly, enough for Marcel to collect himself and yell.

"Who's in there?"

There was no answer. Marcel heaved at the door. It gave again. It could not be either Le Pean or Dufour, they would hold it harder. It had to be her. She must have just passed out, after all. Or maybe she was faking it. But no kid could fake that good, not in his experience anyway.

"Bernadette Labouchere, if it's you, let me in. It's Marcel Dumas."

"Why should I help you?" came back the girl's voice, weakly.

Realizing it was just her in there, Marcel got his shoulder under the cross and hoisted. The bar lurched. Before it could swing back, he caught it in his hands and brought all his wiry muscles to bear, driven by fury at being left out in the open like this.

"Let me in!" was all he grunted before the bar swung free. As he pulled the hatch open, Bernadette tried in vain for a few seconds to keep it shut, but then let go and retreated to the centre of the tank. Marcel hauled the hatch shut behind him, cranking over the bar wearily. It took a moment before he could get his wind, and several minutes before he could stop shuddering and pawing at his body to rid it of any residual bugs. Only then did he look sideways at Bernadette.

"You left me," she scolded.

"I went for help."

"I didn't want you to go for help. I wanted you to stay."

"It was smarter to go for help."

"Where are they?" Bernadette asked. "They were hurting me. I'm telling."

"I came back," he said.

"I thought you said you went to get help?"

"I changed my mind. I came back."

Bernadette was dubious: "What did you do then, monsieur?"

Marcel thought fast: "I made them chase me."

"How do you do that?"

"I told him I was gonna run and tell everybody."

"Tell them what?"

"That you were dead, eh? That they killed you."

Bernadette stared at him. "Why would you think I was dead?"

"Because you were passed out. They thought you dropped dead."

"What did you say? To them."

"Them? I told them. I'm gonna tell everyone you killed her. I figured they'd chase after me and leave you alone, eh?"

"Did you think I was dead?"

"Uh uh, not for a minute, eh?"

She paused to stare reflectively at Marcel, then reached a decision: "You came back. You really came back."

Marcel gulped, nodded, and tried looking right at her, but could only maintain the contact for a few seconds. Still, it was the longest since Bernadette had known him. She was impressed.

"You came back to save me. You knew I wasn't dead, and you lured them away before they could do anything."

Marcel blushed, and had to turn away entirely. Basically, it was the truth, wasn't it? Just a few details…

Bernadette took the blushing as proof positive of his sincerity.

"My hero!" She declared, stepping briskly to his side, and kissing him, formally, on both cheeks. "I salute you. You may take my hand."

Awkwardly, still blushing, Marcel decided to shake hands with her.

"Not like that, silly," she said, and took his other hand, and held it entwined palm to palm while slipping into a position at his side. She did it so naturally, she was there, as though she had always been there before she realized what had happened. "Listen," she said, cocking an ear, "it's ending."

It was true. Outside, there were not quite as many grasshoppers as before. The main wave might have peaked, although it was too early to do anything so foolish as opening the hatch.

Marcel glowed, dazed. Bernadette smiled, even though she was sore all over, especially the back of her head, where there was an egg sized lump.

"How did I get this?" she asked.

Marcel shrugged. "When you fell, I guess."

When Marcel did finally open the hatch, and they stuck their heads out together, it was to see that the wheat field across which they had fled from the grasshoppers had vanished.

"Mon Dieu Christ," gasped Bernadette, frightened.

In its place, all the way to the horizon, was a broken, chewed down plain, stripped, almost skinned. Trees were miraculously unaffected, but there were few of these, and their shadows fell on ruined crops. The golden tabletop of grain and barley, speckled with blue-stem goldenrod and alfalfa and flax and great blooms of tallgrass, were gone.

While the grasslands had always at least rustled, disturbed by the passage of invisible creatures even when there was no wind, now they could hear nothing. An eerie stillness had fallen over the world. The stems of most of the grass were snapped, crushed under the weight of the passing swarm. The seeds of every single plant for hundreds of miles had been removed entirely, sheared away. Transformation was as dramatic as after a threshing machine had gone through a field, except this was the work of thousands of threshing machines all lined up in a row, having rumbled across the billowing prairie and left this flat and, clipped world of stubble and powder in their wake. But then it was also as though a fire had swept past, destroying everything to the roots, except doing it so cleanly nothing was left charred or blackened, a fire without soot or ash or fumes.

It was only after the climb down the ladder, Marcel leading the way, helping Bernadette down the last few steps, that they could look eastward, where the great cowl of grasshoppers was moving away from them like something hunched over, shuffling, all the more horrible for being noiseless. Dragging itself away.

"Is this the end of the world?" Bernadette asked. "It looks like it."

"It grows back, eh?" Marcel ventured, although he wondered too. What was anybody gonna eat? What would the animals eat? How would you make bannock?

Bernadette began shivering. Without hesitation, Marcel unbuttoned his shirt, slipped it off, and draped it over her shoulder.

"Merci," she said softly, looking quickly at him, then quickly away. The material was coarse and it smelled, indeed, of burned wood. But it covered the tears in her dress, and made her feel somehow proud, rather than ashamed. She reached out and took his hand. He started to pull away, but she held on.

They picked their way, hands tightly gripped together, toward the road by the river. It was a mile, at least. Grasshoppers which had collided with their own kind had been knocked down, stirred back to consciousness and took off in fits and starts, often heading in the wrong direction. A few stragglers came bounding in from the west, frantic to catch up with the swiftly distancing swarm. In the air, hawks circled in confusion. On the ground, prairie chickens fluff their feathers and sparrows tweeted querulously. They could hear dogs barking, and, somewhere, an automobile engine coughed. And the ducks along the river were making noises again. Slowly, everything was coming back to life.

Bernadette had never had a boyfriend before. This was quite exciting. He had come to her rescue. It didn't matter that he only went to church because his mother made him. Bernadette would teach him to love Jesus and Mary properly. She'd get him to accept the Catechism with all his heart, instead of just pretending to. As for Mon Pere, well, he would be so grateful to Marcel for saving his oldest daughter that he would stop hating Metis people, and they would all go to Mass together.

Very much against his will, Joe had had to stop the Model T in the middle of the double-rutted road to ride out the passing of the swarm. He sat there, trembling with anger because he might as well sell everything and move, everybody was going to want credit, this was the final straw, how in God's name could anyone expect to make a living in this turd of a prairie anyway? He kept the engine running, expecting the wave to pass over any minute. At first it was. Splt, splt, splt, splt! And then as though a shotgun was pelting the car all over. And then the windows were suddenly splashed with bits of green shell and yellow guts running together in a sickly yolk. As she idled, the tin lizzy's hood rattled, a sound that was normally so loud, Joe had to raise his voice to be heard over it, but which suddenly he couldn't hear any longer as the hoppers went from rat- tap- tapping on the steel and clattering on the windows and making a drumming sound on the tires, like leaden hail, to blasting the side of the car so hard he thought a couple of times the glass would break. He was lucky, the wave came at him from slightly behind, so the radiator didn't plug up immediately, and as long as he kept cranking the wipers he could see ahead into a flashing, flickering greyness. Everything in the background --- the telegraph poles, the farm on the corner, the windbreak of the cottonwoods --- vanished. He could barely make out the silver hood ornament. Joe felt no Fear, just disgust with the mess, how hard it was going to be to clean the car, how much these goddamn bugs are going to cost in lost business.

It was not until the tidal wave had swept by and he climbed out of the car to clean the windows that he could fully comprehend the transformation that had been wrought in the fields all around. Not only were the young sprouts of grain all gone, chewed to their roots as far as he could see in every direction, but even the cottonwoods were stripped to winter nakedness. Joseph Labouchere felt a sudden emptiness in his bowels. The phrase, "fear of God," sprang to mind.

"Mon Dieu," he whispered, crossing himself.

By the time he had climbed back behind the wheel, his pants and shoes and waistcoat and shirt smeared with insect entrails, Joe's mood had returned to simply hating everyone and everything. Unable to get the windshield as clean as he wanted, he rolled down his window and was squinting into the wind as he reached the top of the little hill leading down to the cantilevered wooden bridge at the edge of old man Todd's property, were two figures, a boy and a girl, the boy with his shirt off, were climbing over the fence into the ditch beside the road. At a glance, from the brownness of the boy's skin, Joe could tell it was a mixed blood or an Indian. And the girl ---

Bernadette heard it coming before it topped the rise, but when it did appear, the Model T, it's skeleton on the outside too, its body so splotched with shattered insect that it had acquired a green scaled quality, the windshield still smeared even where the wipers have been at work, like huge blank eyes, was, at first glimpse, more like a giant insect, the King of the Grasshoppers, than a machine --- except, of course, for the din of the engine, the rattling hood, and the popping of stones under the hard rubber tires. With all the bug guts on the glass, she could not see inside to read her father's expression. Marcel stiffened wearily and started to pull away, but Bernadette held him firmly.

"Don't worry." she said. "I'll tell him." She started running toward the car, tugging the boy reluctantly along.

The Ford stopped with a jerk. Later, when she thought about it, Bernadette realized bitterly she should have had the sense to send Marcel running, not deliver him into her father's hands. But in her mind at that moment she so vividly saw them riding home in the car, her and Marcel in the back seat, Mon Pere shaking Marcel's hand, and Ma Mere giving him apple pie and ice cream in the parlor while Jean-Paul and her sisters all stood around admiringly, and Marcel would be invited to come to Mass with them ---

They reached the door on the driver's side just as Joe pushed it open and came out of the car in a boxer's crouch. Bernadette started to speak but the words, whatever they might have been, died in her throat when she saw his face. The blood had all drained away except for a twisting blue vein on his temple which stood out against the skin like a worm climbing down from under his grey fedora. His cheek was twitching. His teeth showed. He made a gurgling sound as he lurched at them, catching Marcel by one hand. Bernadette by the other.

She felt herself being hurled against the Tin Lizzy so hard her elbow exploded in white pain. For a moment, Marcel's shirt obscured her view, but she clearly heard the sound of Mon Pere's fist landing with a loud clap on Marcel's body and several boney thunks on his head. The boy gasped and grunted but did not cry out. Mon Pere also grunted but was otherwise silent, too intent on inflicting as much damage as he could to even swear. Tearing the shirt away, Bernadette howled. "Mon Pere! Mon Pear! Don't! You don't understand! He helped me!" But Joe paid no attention. Still hanging onto the boy's arm, he battled at him as hard as he could with his right fist, like a man hammering at a nail. The boy's cheek cracked open, welts bubbled up on his shoulders and face, blood spurted from his nose and left ear, one eye all but disappeared amid swollen tissue, and a tooth flew away onto the road.

Whether it was brute defiance or simply that he could not catch his breath, Marcel made no attempt to speak or yell. He cringed beneath the rain of blows, but only half struggled to escape. There was something awful in his surrender. Bernadette remembered watching a sheep attacked by three dogs. It had just *stared* impassively as a beast tore into its belly and hind quarter, as though this was as much a part of the cycle of life's grazing as dropping little black pellets on the ground. It had been as if the sheep couldn't feel the shredding that was happening to its flesh.

When Marcel fell it was because Joe let him go. The boy collapsed so limply on the gravel, his skull making a sound like a squash being dropped, that Bernadette was certain he had been killed. Although numb from having smashed against the car so hard, she started to reach for him, but Joe grabbed her again, clawing Marcel's shirt from her hands and throwing it at the doubled-up boy on the ground.

"Filth!" Joe gasps. "Filth!" His wire-rimmed glasses had been shaken loose by the ferocity of his attack, so they hung from one ear, delicately swaying. As he groped with a trembling hand to fit the glasses back in place, Bernadette saw that the skin of his knuckles was split and oozing blood.

All Marcel could do, curled in on himself, clutching his head, blood coagulating in the dust all around, was whimper. Bernadette made much more noise, wailing in horrified disbelief. Joe's swollen hand came down in her hair, seized the handful, and yanked her like a dog on a leash toward the open car door. He heaved her inside, giving her such a shove on her shoulder blades that her head whacked against the door handle on the other side and she skinned her knee on the floorboards. She heard her father's snarl "Filth!" one last time. Then he clambered heavily into the car, panting, found the gears, ground them fiercely as he pulled the door shut with a crash, and then lumbered jerkily away down the road. Struggling upright on shaking arms, Bernadette looked desperately over the back seat, through the oval rear window, where she could just barely catch a glimpse of Marcel through the residue of splattered grasshopper parts on the glass. He was convulsing half in the ditch, half on the roadside, bleeding.

PART THREE

INSIDE PASSAGE COAST
OF BRITISH COLUMBIA

1979

Just a few miles around the lee of Vancouver Island, safely into Queen Charlotte Strait, the leftover swells of the Gulf of Alaska finally settled down into a rocking cradle motion. Above the spine of mountains rising up on the starboard to throw a shield between the *Mary Boehm* and the open North Pacific, the shout of winter was like some creature that had almost caught you, a frustrated moan thankfully muted by solid, thousand foot high rocks. It was hard, Bernadette reflected, not to think of weather as alive. Or the ocean. Or boats, for that matter.

There were places along the inside passage --- hugely, cathedral-piled-on-cathedral interior silences ---where the sea seemed disassociated entirely from the cauldron that surged against the island's outside rim. Here, as they knifed along in the middle of the channel, it was as though one had entered a narrow gorge, except that the scale had changed shockingly from out in the open. It felt like the boat had been shrunk to the size of a shoe. A ceiling of clouds closed between the steep walls of the mountains on either side, creating the impression that they were crawling along the floor of a giant's corridor.

As they chulgh, chut, chitted by, Bernadette could hear the water slapping gently against the rickety legs of the wharf beside an abandoned cannery near Sointula, its hundreds of little windows all pitted like the surface of satellites. Salmonberry bushes grew along the rotting wooden rails. Cormorant Island soon after passed on the port, maybe one hundred fish boats tied up behind the beak-water. While they were too far away to be make out by the naked eye --- at least not her damaged, fading eyes -- using the binoculars deftly she could plainly see for a few moments, little chest piece figures leaning at all angles except straight up in the old graveyard above the white beach just past downtown Alert Bay. How often she had stood there over the years, off a boat tied up at the government dock, and just stared at those old, broken poles. The totems were worm riddled, snapped, cracked, fractured, split, fallen, with the paint mostly weathered away. Wings and tails and arms had eroded, like stumps. On one particular pole only one eye remained, looking out desperately like somebody drowning. The faces and bodies, of demons and animals, were being moved back into the driftwood shapes, into something as weird as what Emily Carr had seen. And what did they mean. Nobody really knew. Something to do with clans and pedigrees. Although the explanation she personally liked the best was the one that had never found its way into Canadian history books, but which, as a subscriber to The Midden, the mimeographed paper put out by the Archaeological Division of the British Columbia Provincial Museum, she knew all about, or at least had followed the debate avidly. It stemmed from the theory, well, not a theory, really, since it was based on ancient Chinese court records that nobody disputed -- according to which, a Chinese Buddhist monk named Hui Shin had sailed a junk over to this shore 1400 years ago, and left behind the idea of reincarnation, Transmigration of Souls; *that's* what the totems were really all about, one species of creature turning into another, some of them into humans, humans into ravens or otters or salmon. They were not built as monuments to some indigenous aboriginal religion at all, but to something originating in Asia. What was the Buddhist fellow's name? The awakened one? Sid- something ---she was charmed by the idea of a millennium and half passing gently here in the mist with the only outside influence having been that of a fat, beaming Buddha somewhere in Tibet or India. Hui Shin, the sailor-monk, had called this stretch of the North American coastline Wan Shan, "Land of the Painted Bodies," after a presumed native style. She liked the sound of that. They were all Wan Shanians, then, or Whan Shaners. She could hear temple bells ringing, but, of course, there were no markers or statues bearing Hui Shin's name, no island named after him, and the capes and points and straits all had English or Spanish names.

Had anything changed since his time? Anything fundamental? There were still river mouths where heron stood daintily, their beaks poised like surgical instruments, to pluck a lingcod from the silver tray. A beam of golden light left between two peaks, flowing into the dark turquoise depths of the canyons between the cliffs, forming a tunnel of clear nothingness through which algae could be seen drifting, along with the occasional pulsating ghost of a jellyfish. From eight thousand feet, the mountains on either side of the passage plunge straight into the ocean waters --- the soundings on all the charts being marked in hundred fathoms, affixed with the "n- bottom" mark.

She watched through the binoculars as they passed an abandoned church, and shrivelled planks turned grey white, with lichen taking hold in silver and emerald patterns on the walls, the broken Russian Orthodox cross flapping in the wind, like the arm of a dead Jesus suddenly lifting -- weaving. Enough to stop your heart. Dirt drifted in through the church's open door.

Down through the inlet came millions of seeds, loosed by the approach of the equinox, embarked on an almost hopeless search for a patch of soil above the high tide mark, which was not already claimed by some other, tougher plant form.

At the Yuculta Rapids, gulls yokked and dived in their thousands, maddened by the feast below.

KY KY KY KY KY KY KY

Eagles plunged like javelins from the branches of overhanging hemlock. The only sound they made was the gunshots slap as they hit the water, claws hooking a slow-moving salmon, dazed from having been bashed against the rocks as the current swept at fifty knots through the Gorge. The water cannonaded down. It tunneled, it constricted, it back eddied, it coiled like a serpent, creating whirlpools and reversal whirlpools. And sometimes it formed a fist, smashing upward in a definition of what is known as a haystack.

The roar! It got into the middle of bodies and minds, making you want to howl with excitement as well as terror. There was a surprise to be found in the experience of this tremendous single vibration. In the very midst of the rapids, where the water was churned to lather and the thunder caused the ears to ring, there was a feeling of calm exultancy, a kind of white sound effect to go with the white water. Even at slack tide, when boats and Blackfish alike preferred to make their nervous run through the narrows, a mouth -- or was it more like a blowhole? -- was liable to open in the wash, as if the water was indeed alive, the mightiest beast ever, and had just decided to feed.

Whirlpools in the Yucultas had been known to achieve a diameter of seventy feet. One such monstrous orifice had pulled down the union steamship *S. S. Catala* with eighty-seven people aboard. No one knew how many anonymous trappers and fishermen and whalers and sealers and hunters -- and for that matter foolish whales or seals or bears -- had disappeared into those vortexes. The same mouth never opened twice, and no trace was ever found of the victims.

The chill of early winter swept down the passage. Cold sea-witch breath fogged the portholes and steamed the deck. Early dust came like smoke from the steaming, hissing black waters.

They had barely cleared the rapids when the pod of Blackfish came up from the starboard bow, just a stone's throw away. Jim and Doug were out on the flying bridge. The kid, Rene, had come bounding out of the bunkhouse at the cry, "Whales!" And even she, "Granny" Wilding, veteran of the coast, was out on the foredeck without bothering to stop for her jacket – silly bean--binocular in hand, not having to scan because there they were, coming up as one, all those strange openings on their backs spewing at the same time, or within seconds of each other. From the sound of it, they had been doing a bit of overtime getting through the rapids, too. Ordinarily, they were more leisurely as they surfaced, like stately submarines, gliding along through the still gurgling waters. The kid was acting like a farmer, of course, waving his plastic headphones at them, with some kind of rock'n'roll squawking out, barely audible above the massive *HISSS* of the upwelling water and the ominous, hushed cleaving of clear glass currents over the nearby barnacled rock. Still narrow in here, comparatively, Bernadette judged, flicking a glance upward to make sure Jim was on the job at the outside wheel.

It was a distracting view, a last-minute beam of sunlight, radiating out from under the belly of the storm and between the peaks of the island, had set the channel ablaze. The Blackfish rose and sounded in silhouette, their plumes of breath exploding slowly in the halos of salt diamonds hovering in the light, becoming fireworks displays, edging to purple mist as they faded, forming fragile, short-lived, collapsing rainbows that glowed against the shadowed mountain slopes. Bernadette caught the smell of their breath, slightly damper than the autumn salt air, a hint of fish, of guts, but clean -- a good jolt, like the beach at low tide.

"Will they come over?" the boy yelled to Jim.

"Don't be a goofball. They ain't dumb. They go to school."

Bernadette wouldn't have been entirely surprised --- had the boy not been along as witnessed --- if Jim hadn't gone and fetched his shotgun. The kids in the city like Linda and David could yatter on all they wanted about singing whales, and all that nonsense, but she knew as well as Jim and Doug, that for weeks after the passing of these big, hungry predators on their annual sweep down the inside passage, nearby inlets were cleared of salmon and halibut and tuna, even dog fish and smelt. Whatever life was left in these waters, apart from crabs and mollusks, would either have had the sense to flee or be eaten. A lot of dumb seals and sea lions often stayed too long too, she knew.

Still, what a sight! She wished she bought a camera back in Rupert, but she was going to save the money by waiting until she got to a big drug store in Vancouver, and now she was missing this. The kids would have loved it. And so close. This was about as close as she had ever been -- or wanted to be, thank you!

It had been Frank who first pointed out to her that the Blackfish all breathed together, as a pod. If one's breathing sped up, for some reason, the others would all start breathing faster, too, to catch up, and then they had all settled back into the calmer pattern. Or if the breathing of one got too slow, the rest would slow down to its pace and get it going up to normal again. "They help each other," Frank had said, "They're families." And added (she would never forget) "Makes 'em' more dangerous than fish."

And they were like an enemy to fishermen. They came from out of the depths. They raided. They tore through nets. They gulped down fish that men with families to feed had slaved to catch. Big, bullying thieves. They were like those Marlon Brando characters, bikers, sheathed in black, like a gang, roaring in and taking what they felt like. Well, that is, until the fishermen started aiming shotguns at them, or one time --- so the story went --- a machine gun. Fella up in Knight's Inlet killed a whole pod. Even if it was a long time ago, these Blackfish off the starboard *knew*. They didn't seem afraid but kept their distance. Probably just outside of gunshot range. Mon Dieu, they were magnifique to look at. The way they came up out of the water, charcoal fins waving like swords being plunged upward from under the surface, the curling of their backs like slowly churning rubber wheels, the fins like sails which she half expected to tilt the whales over on their sides. With the light like this, it was a magic show with special effects. Real, but not like ordinary reality. Unexpectedly, she felt a rush of goodwill toward the fish-stealers. They were a family, after all -- that's what a pod meant. Like a little tribe. All breathing in unison. Well she wished them luck. If they could keep their families together, they were not doing so bad, were they? The pang she felt was genuine, but after a moment she scolded herself for self pity. Maybe she was getting soft? Certainly, she was getting cold. Lost in her own thoughts and shivering, she moved into the warmth of the galley -- leaving the Blackfish to vanish in the dusk.

They were out in the Georgia Strait now. It was Bernadette, bringing coffee up to the wheelhouse, who noticed that Lasqueti Island, which lay dead ahead in the afterglow, had been erased by an advancing line of squaw. Suddenly they were pelted by small wet but distinct clumps of snow. The nor-westerly wind sheared down off Vancouver Island, which must have been taking a horrible beating on the other side. Soon it had stirred a little chop. The *Mary Bohem*, her hull empty, began to roll uncomfortably. Within minutes, it seemed, the normally laconic Jim was crouched at the wheel, squinting intensely, fiddling with the depth sounder, pounding it when it went dead, reaching over, whacking the radar, which would come on for a moment, then fade. The wipers strained to keep the soggy snow off the glass, but between the streaks left behind and the advancing veil of rain, visibility dropped to not much past the bow. The windows began to steam up, and it turned out the blower wasn't working. Wouldn't you know? This is a bad dream, Bernadette told herself as she wiped the inside glass with paper towels, which helped a bit, but not much. Doug and the kid hung out in the radio room. To everyone --except maybe the kids -- astonishment, Jim got the marker light at Lasqueti mixed up, and the next thing, they were among large rocks. The waves heaved around in long, slow motion, like corkscrewing bronco bucks. The gumwood hull slammed a glancing but heart-stopping blow against the side of a rock before Bernadette quite realized the seriousness of the situation, but she knew better than to say anything to Jim. He was flustered enough, as well as he might be. How had the old pro like him gotten into such a fix? Losing his edge. Instead of berating him, her instinct was to slip into the radio room and gestured urgently at Doug's hip pocket, where the silver flask was. He figured out right away what she was after and looked dumbfounded – because it was *her* -- as well as dismayed, because it was anyone. Asking for *his* flask!

"Not for me," she snapped, snatching it. A moment later, she was holding the open flask to Jim's lips. Although he spilled some over his grizzled chin, he gulped a good flaming mouthful of scotch down, and shuddered with relief.

"We could still make a great team, Bern," he grunted, slamming his ample belly against the wheel to steady it.

"Hope those aren't famous last words," she grunted back, gravity pinning her against the wall, hoping she was showing less fear than she felt. Not now! Surely not now! But then, another voice in her head said. "Why not?" Maybe now is when you deserve it for what you are thinking of doing. She shook the thought --- guilt, always goddamned guilt --- anyway, and decided on a quick shot herself before returning the flask to Doug's clutching hand. The boy tried to grab it, but Doug yanked the precious object adroitly out of reach.

"Hold her steady.!" Jim rasped, dragging Bernadette by the shoulder over to the wheel. Damn! It should have been Doug, but he was probably too pissed, and what would the kid know? No point arguing. The idea was to live to tell the tale. The wooden handles felt warm. The chain was tugging hard from below on the port side, as if there was something down there trying to pull them over. *Oh no you don't!* She thought furiously, experiencing a surge of strength. She took the spoke on the far portside of the wheel in both hands and heaved upward, hearing the chunk of the chain grudgingly coming up one notch. The bow steadied a fraction. She was happy to know she wasn't feeling panicky, despite her pounding heart. Mon Dieu, she had taken the wheel in bad weather before -- although she could not remember any circumstances *quite* this screwed-up. (Maybe once, with Frank, when the anchor tore loose one night during a blow.)

Jim meanwhile popped up in the wheelhouse door and pushed himself into the gale, struggling out onto the flying bridge, grabbing the outside wheel, allowing Bernadette to relinquish the spoke she'd been grappling with. Once out on the deck, visibility improved enormously, even though Jim had to cup his hand over his eyes to protect them from the stinging snow. He could see all around, except for where the smoke from the chimney was being blown straight ahead, billowing murkily in the beam of the deck light, rendering the deadly zone directly in front of him invisible. Couldn't take a chance going ahead. Yet there were rocks on all sides, and they did look like teeth coming up, ugly broken part-grinding teeth, part-tearing teeth, park-crushing teeth. They were so black against the water he could only see the phosphorescence around their roots, the outline like a negative of their shape as a foam surged upward. Behind? Well, they got in this far only touching once. The one way out of this mess was to *back* out. Whether the old boat, riding high like she was, with the engine on its last legs, has the power to march in reverse against the wind, tide and waves, holding steady against the sea that was surging through the rock passage he'd blundered so stupidly into, whether he could steer this sucker in reverse under these conditions, or whether they weren't at any second going to crunch against an unseen rock directly below, it all depended on acting *now*! There was no depth sounder out here, but he didn't need it to know they were too close, too shallow. The only thing to do was to go straight into reverse and crank her right up hoping the goddamn carburetor didn't flood.

Agonizingly, with much ponderous thrashing of the *Mary Boehm*'s stern, enough water poured over the back roller-bar, so the clinker came half loose and flipped on its side, the lifejackets washed away, the old packer inched backwards. When her square end smashed downward between waves, there was a paddle effect, the whole bottom hitting, sending plumes of spray washing back against the fo'c'sle, leaving the scuppers backed up, the deck a swirl. Once, the wheelhouse chain slipped, and the entire precarious elephant on-one-leg balance quavered. The boat began to wobble to the port, which meant the poop-deck would be scooping up water like a bucket when the next wave came. But Jim put his muscles to it and gained back those couple of inches, and the props -- half the time flapping in the air -- continued to claw and pull their unwieldy barge-like load into the worst of it: big-ghost-lit-from-below, white-topped breakers on the edge of the shelf they'd inadvertently crossed. Ah shit --worst case! -- they were hoisted, then dropped -- like riding an elevator down -- the hull just an arm's length from steep, barnacled, glistening black rock.

Bernadette stared through the wheelhouse window at the

cliff-face speeding by, expecting to hear the bone popping sound of the hull breaking against rock any second, but found that, aside from prudently hanging on to the radar handlebar, she wasn't having the right oh-my-God-I'm-going-to-die reflexes. She felt almost -- although not quite -- outside of herself. As though she was watching somebody else standing there calmly, watching the equivalent of a freight train whipping by mere feet away. Was she already so enormously exhausted that one more "life or death experience" did not have the power to register on her? Or was this what they called serene indifference? Probably just shock.

Jim was finally able to tuck the stern in, swing the bow out into the oncoming waves, and move straight into the gale, the *Mary Boehm*'s bow happily chopping water. When they were clear, he brought them around completely, got his bearings on the Lasqueti light right this time, and they jounced southward again. Bernadette brought him a hot chocolate with marshmallows, but Jim was not going to come out of it just like that. She remembered seeing her beloved John finally beaten at arm wrestling by some punk nephew. Sure, John was getting on, and the kid did all the weightlifting stuff. Natural. Sooner or later, when you get older, you are going to lose. But John took it hard. It was like he lost something more than a stupid arm-wrestling match with a nearly professional athlete. He lost some picture of himself that had always matched up with who he thought he was, and he was not him any longer. Because he'd been defeated, Jim was like that now, ashamed of himself for screwing up like an amateur, after all these goddamn years, and in front of *her*. Embarrassed. Couldn't look her in the eye. And it was too soon to try to talk him out of it. Maybe in the morning, before they docked. It was no help that Doug was up in the radio room, singing depression era songs -- *Hallelujah I'm a bum, Hallelujah bum again, Hallelujah give us a hand out to revive us again* -- and the damn kid was giggling wildly, more Crazy White Men stories to tell.

Getting to sleep was easier than she expected. The Yucultas sluiced and thundered on the screen of her eyelids and the Blackfish surfaced, exhaling together, sending little rainbows flying like parachutes. She frowned away terrifying incoming images of the black rocks spearing upward all around, blocking them off by returning to the Blackfish, the soft explosions of their teeth, then the rapids, the *roar* ---

Shortly before 400 hours, Bernadette was awoken by an unfamiliar noise. She staggered into the galley and found Doug Moore slumped in a little canvas fold out chair, with his Cowichan wool cap pulled down over his eyes. The boat was rolling maybe ten degrees. An empty bottle of rum was clunking from one end of the galley floor to the other, like a glass rat trying to get away. Everything was in motion. Somehow, Doug remained balanced, head tilted on one shoulder, his entire gravity just low enough so the whole galley, the whole boat, the whole world went swinging and lurching around him.

Sitting at the table, rolling with the boat, dawn coming through the window over the sink, a pale blue light rising across the pane of glass, then fading, rising, fading, as though the sun was having doubts about coming up. Only the sound of the engine, the hiss of water through the half open Dutch door, and Doug's snoring. Bernadette felt totally empty and fatalistic, the way she got when the Ferris wheel stopped with her in the seat at the top, and she wished bitterly she had never gotten on the darn thing in the first place, but now that she had, and there was no way of getting off it for awhile, no way to stop the seat from swinging, no matter how much it scared her, she get very clear headed, it was the only way to deal with terror. That was how she felt now.

The sun finally made up its mind and hurled into view between the mountains. She could hear the skipper clumping around in the wheelhouse. Doug snored torturously. The glass rat clanked and scuttled. The distant buzz of the boy's headphones still playing even though he was passed out in his bunk.

She was so tired already. Amazingly tired. And the journey had just begun.

PART FOUR

ST BONIFACE - MANITOBA

1928 - 1929

The clouds came from the North with the breath of distant glaciers. So far as the land was concerned it was as if a switch had been thrown. In a stunning display of perfect timing, the last of the surviving leaves fell trembling to the ground and less than a day later the air currents from the Arctic arrived too. The fields lay broken and stiff. The earth had turned into hard glue. It was like a muscular contraction in anticipation of some tremendous blow, as though the vulnerable soil could faintly recall the horror of burial under miles of ice not so long ago in the past. The gophers and groundhogs and prairie dogs and coyotes and foxes and even the rare squirrels had blended away into the landscape, motivated by some similar ancestral memory of a terrible time. Of the insects that had dominated the air since spring there remained only the rare slow-moving butterfly like an autumn leaf that had learned to flutter aimlessly, very much alone. Of the birds, only the owls and the sparrows and a few crows remained. The geese and ducks had swept away across the sky in tremendous honking. Smaller birds had vanished one by one -- furtively, without a peep.

The Laboucheres left Agassi no less quietly. Like the birds and animals, they hurried nervously before the deadly breath of winter. At the station there were only the immediate relatives to wave goodbye to Augustine and the girls. Joseph and Jean-Paul remained on the station platform with the rest, waving as billows of steam burst from under the coaches and the train began its long arrow-straight run along tracks that never seemed to bend. Joseph had noticed that his three daughters were crying. The baby was crying, his wife was crying, yet he and his son were grinning wildly. It was not just that they stood on the platform watching the women go, waiting until they were safely underway before turning to the motor car to begin their drive. It was also that Joseph felt enormously relieved to be escaping at last, and the boy imitated his father's feelings almost flawlessly.

No one else in town showed up to wave farewell to the Laboucheres. Nine years of my life I give to this excuse of a civilization and not one person will shake my hand as I go, thought Joseph indignantly. Are they afraid I'll bite them? I don't care what they think, Joseph declared to himself. I'm getting outta here. They can eat my shit.

Clifford Allenby, the stationmaster, was the only person beside the relatives at the platform. He nodded, smiled mildly at Joseph, and seemed to want to say something, but when Joseph barely managed to a curt nod in exchange, the stationmaster changed his mind. Briefly, Joseph wondered why the man's wife, Bernadette's music teacher, hadn't showed up to say goodbye to the girl. He had thought the child and the Englishwoman were such great friends. He of course viewed this absence as his own loss, never thinking of how Bernadette was reacting or how the woman was coping. Mrs. Allenby was suffering a great loss as well, that of losing her secret surrogate child and her protégé, she was at her home tending to her wounded soul. He instead, felt a faint pang at not having had one last glimpse at the redhead whose body he had violated so often in his mind, without ever having said more than a couple of words to her in the whole nine years he lived in town. A moment of self pity possessed him -- but it was just that, a moment, no more.

Then the engine of the Tin Lizzy was shuddering painfully to life with terrific grinding and coughing sounds. The doors were clanking shut, the relatives were waving and yelling, although only with a fraction of the emotional zeal they displayed at the departure of the women, and he and the boy were at last in motion, rolling in their gold colored metal shell down by the hard packed stockyard, out into the open land, where it seemed immediately that they were shrunk down to the size of a crawling insect, fleeing, like all others, before the coming of the winter wind. They had not traveled, backfiring and jerking along unevenly, for much more than a few miles when Jean-Paul spotted the first snowflake. By then, only the tops of the great grain elevators could be seen far behind along the parallel track of the road, scarcely more than tiny arrowheads bedded in on the horizon. Then they too, were gone. Only the telegraph poles along the train track remained as evidence that mankind could build things up right in this land -- and then it seemed that what had been built was a long row of crucifixes waiting only for victims to be nailed to them.

"Oh Mon Pere, will we get caught in a blizzard?" Jean-Paul demanded excitedly.

"Who knows, eh?"

"If we do, will we build a fire?"

"But yes, of course!"

"And hunt for buffalo?"

"Well, maybe we will find a cow."

Jean-Paul was quite unable to sit still. He quivered with excitement. Joseph was so pleased with himself, and with the world, with life, with his son, his car, his whole family, so pleased with having escaped from Father Benoit, out of the reach of crazy half breeds and pushy Mounties alike, out of the town he had hated since the day he arrived, that it seemed to him he was taking part in a dream. There were moments as he drove when he seriously wondered about waking up.

Otherwise, he felt blessed.

"There's nothing to worry about from the weather yet," he told his son with complete confidence. "This road, it's not just a path like it seems. There is another path here too, you see. It just goes along and just goes along and just goes along. Sometimes it makes a turn but most of it just goes straight to where a man is going, eh! You understand, little soldier of Jesus. The path of life, I call it. Sometimes you know you are following it but other times you know you're not. Right now, we are following the real path, so don't worry about this road here, boy, it will stay open. It is just the physical part of it all. It has to let us through because we're on the real path. Do you know what I mean?"

Jean Paul's young brain whirled, trying to keep up with his father. His eyes strained.

"I only see one road, Mon Pere." He complained.

"You don't see the other with your eyes. It's invisible."

"Oh."

Joseph smiled serenely.

"But, Mon Pere, how do you see it?"

Very seriously, keeping his eyes fixed on the two dirt ruts running as straight as the train track in front of him, Joseph confided.

"Sometimes I pray, my son. Sometimes ---an Angel comes and whispers in my ear."

The boy stared open-mouthed at his father, feeling so much more reverence than ever before that his mouth was left hanging open and for several moments, he could think of nothing to say. He always loved it when he could be alone with Mon Pere. On those occasions, rare as they were, Joseph opened up and talked to the child as he talked to no other human being. He unburdened himself of all his beliefs, his experience, his philosophy. He allowed himself to speak to the boy as he would have liked to speak to other adults. The problem was that no adult ever listened to him quite as intently, nor accepted what he said with such automatic and complete agreement. Neither did any adult -- except, sometimes, Augustine -- treated him with such respect and honour. The most compelling reason for Joseph to expound so nakedly before his son, however, was none of these. It was instead Joseph's impression that the boy understood what he was saying. The same could not be said for anyone else on earth.

"When we get to Saint Boniface, I'll show you the Basilica." Joseph promised.

Jean-Paul finally found his voice.

"What does an Angel look like?" Mon Pere.

"You can't see them. They are invisible too".

"What do they say?"

"They don't talk. They make things happen at certain times. They are like ghosts and sometimes they scare you a little. But they are always truly kind. They never hurt you. They make sure you do not trip over anything or do anything that might make you get into trouble, eh? For example, here, I'll give you an example. This road, eh? If the Angels did not want us to drive along here, they'd do something about it, wouldn't they? Of course, they would! They might make one of our tires go flat. Or make the engine go wrong. Or put some mud in the way so we couldn't go forward. They do that to keep us safe that's why they would do it. But if they want us to go through right now, today, they'll keep the snow away, they'll keep the road open. We are incredibly lucky, you know, my son. Not everybody is born Catholic, you know."

Although the words seemed clear enough as his father uttered them, Jean-Paul had little hope of remembering much of any of it. He was more interested in the sights unfolding around him than he was in another of his father's fascinating but largely incomprehensible talks. What struck him most forcefully was the fact that instead of blustering loudly and talking about himself as though he were someone else, always saying "Labouchere thinks this or that," his father for a change, thankfully just referred to himself as "I," like everybody else. That in itself made the boy happy. Now, at least he knew whom he was sitting with. His father. Not someone who talked a lot about his father but was not him.

The sky remained a heavy grey nothingness all through the day as they putted and wobbled eastward, travelling at an average of 20 to 22 mph. From the horizon downward white flakes could be seen drifting silently to rest against the black stubble and disappear, or else merge in dun coloured wheat fields. The flakes struck the windshield like tiny soft white insects with shells and only water inside. Even though each flake died within a fraction of a second of touching the ground, by noon it was clear that the sky had already begun to win its battle to bury the earth alive. There were vast sweeps of plowed open soil that were dusted with silver, wet and mostly transparent, as fragile as the thinnest glass, but thickening in the distance, turning what had just an hour ago been a checkerboard into the mirror of the overcast sky, flawed by tiny clumps of bush, the odd tree or tattered lines of fence post, but substantially, a single great shroud.

By the time they reach Headingley, stopped at the fuel pump, added water to the radiator, and pushed onto the gravel road, leaving the mud ruts behind from now until reaching the city, Jean-Paul was having to keep wiping the inside of the windshield with a handkerchief, to clear away the condensation from their breath. Joseph kept his left hand on the wheel, crouching forward to peer through the blurred glass, his right hand steadily cranking the handle of the single windshield wiper. On either side of the road there was a ditch filled with cattails. Steam rose from the water as the air cooled above it. Behind them, the clouds had become dark, snowflakes were thicker, and their tires left marks in the white mantle that had settled over the gravel. During the journey from Agassiz to Headingley, they had not passed a single vehicle. But now a car could be seen moving ahead of them far down the road. And another coming towards them. And less than five minutes later, yet another. The road was narrow enough that Joseph had to bear to the right, with the wheels on the passenger side sliding perilously close to the ditch, and the driver coming from the other direction had to lurch to the side himself, both machines slowing to a crawl as they maneuvered past each other. But in Jean-Paul's eyes the amazing part was that they managed to pass at all while remaining on the road at the same time. Joseph exchanged waves and broad grins with the other drivers.

Jean-Paul had long since stopped counting the grain elevators as they poked up over the horizon, and grew larger and larger, then went by in a blur, and dropped behind. Now he concentrated on counting cars that passed him coming out from the city. By late afternoon, after they had been on the road for close to five hours, he had counted no less than thirty-two motor cars, eight trucks, and a bus.

The boy's first glimpse of the city left him startled and confused. All there was at first was smoke. A grey cowl that reminded him of the fields after they had been burned. There was nothing to see ahead on the land, only a turbulence in the lower reaches of the sky, as though something huge had been wrecked and scorched and now lay smoldering, ruined, flattened. Out of his confusion of smoke and steam and cloud there emerged a locomotive, hurtling toward them on the track that had run beside the road all the way from Agassiz. It seemed to Jean-Paul the train must be fleeing from some disaster, so urgent was its headlong motion. Attention gripped him, based on a fear that the city had been destroyed and they had come too late.

But then the houses began to thicken, and the gravel road widened. There were too many cars moving about on the roads that began to intercept regularly for him to keep count any longer. He saw his first electric streetcar, his first factory, his first row of lofty incinerator towers and his first horse racing track all within minutes of each other. Impressions began to pile up and overlap. He twisted his head this way and that, frantically trying to absorb everything while Joseph negotiated the unfamiliar traffic. Huge buildings loomed ahead, rising on either side of what had become a wide expanse of flattened stones with rails for the streetcars bedded in them. The building stood higher than anything the boy had ever seen, with row upon row of windows – Twelve rows, in fact, of window built above window, yet, immense as the structures were, great brick chimneys rose even higher, belching out whole cloud formations that raced beneath the scudding overcast. Whirling snowflakes stood out vividly against the cliffs of brick and glass that rose on every side. The iron wheels of the streetcar clanged. Motor cars backfired. Truck engines roared. There were sidewalks as wide as streets back in Agassiz, and they were filled with an incredible long crowd of people, everyone in motion. The air was thick with yells and cries and muttering noises, like a river in flood. Horses hooves made distant plunking sounds on the cobbles and the wheels of carriages clattered loudly.

Jean Paul knew, from what his father had already told him, that they had not yet arrived in Saint Boniface. Rather they were passing through Winnipeg, the city which had been built on the west side of the Red River, the area where most of the factories stood, along with the huge Eaton's and Hudson's Bay Department stores, restaurants, warehouses, with a sprawling train yard so vast that a bridge which had once spanned the Nile River had been dismantled, shipped to this city on the edge of the Great Western Canadian plain, and reassembled to allow automobile traffic over the width of the train yard. Jean-Paul caught one brief glimpse of a structure greater than all the others, something his father called the "Legislature," a stone building with pillars and a dome with a glint of gold at its top. Then they were through the clamor and jangle, past the biggest of the buildings, and headed out across an iron bridge over a River at least four times the width of the Assiniboine back home. And a sign, in both French and English was greeting them:

Welcome Bienvenue
To
Saint Boniface

Immediately, one structure stood out. It reared above the tree-line along the river, pale in the silent fall of snow, its twin Roman-Byzantine steeples each as large as a great temple itself, yet they were only crowns on the tremendous limestone edifice beneath them. Jean-Paul squealed with excitement, more impressed by the Basilica than by anything he had seen yet, even though the building was neither as large as some of the department stores they'd already passed nor as tall as the fluted incinerators from which smoke was still belching behind them. The Basilica, he knew, was the largest cathedral in all the West, and from here an Archbishop ruled all the Catholics in fully half of Canada. What Jean-Paul wanted so badly to see and hear, however, were the famous sixteen hundred-pound bells, which he had been told about in catechism.

"Can we go there now, Mon Pere?"

"No. Will go to your grandmothers. That is where your mother and sisters will be. Then tomorrow, we'll all go to High Mass."

The boy tore his eyes away from the magnificent steeples to look down, almost giddy from the height, at the grey river moving sluggishly beneath them. It was the biggest body of water he had ever seen, and it frightened him to be out above the middle of it. The bridge was so long he was afraid it might break in half at any moment, but Mon Pere was smiling serenely. Then Jean-Paul remembered about the angels and how they were taking care of everything.

Once the car was safely over the bridge, Joseph pulled over to the edge of the road, slipped the gear into neutral, and climbed out stiffly. The ground was coated with almost an inch of damp and clinging snow. Jean-Paul hopped out beside him. Joseph was staring back across the river at the silhouette outline of the city through which he had just passed.

"Thank God we're back on French soil," he said.

"Are we going to live here forever, Mon Pere?"

"Except for going back to Québec, there's no place else. Everything else, except for this one blessed city, is owned by les Anglais. So, we'll stay here, yes. I don't wish to live among them any longer. Here we have all your mother's people and I have my brother, Emile, the priest I told you about. And soon I'll have a business, eh? Why should I go anywhere else? This is where I met your mother and married her and this is where I should have stayed, except that I wanted to do everything on my own. Well it's done now. I have enough money to get us going. We're going to live here forever, Jean-Paul!"

They climbed back in the car and putt-putt-putted slowly past the Basilica, past block after block of houses built so close together that a man standing between them could touch both at once. In Agassiz, the houses had been much, much further apart. Dimly, Jean-Paul wondered if he was going to like living so close to other people.

"There's your grandmother's house!"

Joseph had barely stopped the machine before there was an eruption of bodies through the front door of the narrow two-story brick house as his daughters and their cousins leapt forward, all calling at once. For an instant, he was puzzled by the girl's frenzy -- after all, it had only been six hours ago that they'd been together at the train station. Maybe they'd been worried by the snow, thinking he would have trouble getting through. Then he understood what they were babbling so excitedly about. One word came through. Baby! Augustine was in labor.

"When did it start?"

"Oh Mon Pere, when we were on the train!" Bernadette cried. "The conductor said there was nothing to worry about because we'd be here so soon, but Ma Mere was hurting! She's still hurting! Auntie Flo is with her, and the lady next door, and Grande Ma Mere. Uncle Charlie's gone for le docteur, but she cries out for Mon Pere! Oh, I'm scared!"

Joseph was up the stairs, into the house, into the bedroom within seconds, arriving just in time to see Augustine double up on the bed in the midst of a particularly painful contraction, a hiss of pain breaking through her clenched teeth, her sister and mother perched protectively but helplessly on either side of her. They had already changed her into her nightgown.

"How long now?" Joseph demanded.

Florence looked up, shrugged.

"Maybe soon, maybe not. Her contractions are ten minutes apart, very regular though."

A groan burst forth from Augustine. She opened her eyes, gasping, and saw her husband.

"Oh Joseph, stay!"

Joseph looked wildly at Grande Ma Mere for guidance. She nodded. "For a few minutes, it's alright."

Augustine's blue eyes were wet from crying and she was breathing heavily. Joseph dared not look at anything except her eyes, for he had already noticed a spot of blood on the sheets and a stain on the front of her nightgown. He felt a touch of revulsion, of helpless terror. The last birth, Monica's, had been difficult, he knew, as bad as the first. This one might be like that too. Augustine's face was chalky, and her eyes had that frightened, distant look he remembered from the other deliveries. It was as if she was trapped somewhere out of his reach, threatened by some monstrous beast -- or did she have the expression of somebody locked in a torture chamber?

"Oh, Joseph."

"Augustine, my love."

He held her hand fiercely.

Another contraction seized her.

"Oh, Mon Dieu! Mon Dieu! Mon Dieu! Sweat broke out on her forehead. Her hand was clammy. She made a guttural noise, almost a squeal, followed by a helpless string of gasps that went "ah, ah, ah, ah, ah, ah." The seizure held fast, bending and twisting her cruelly. Her eyes held his for only the first few seconds, then her lips closed in a grimace that contorted her entire face, and although she clung to his hand like someone drowning, he had a sense of her falling away from him, falling down a long cliff into some bottomless pit, and the anguished animal grunting sound that came out of her seemed like the voice of some other creature, anyone or anything but his beloved, gentle Augustine.

"Joseph!" his mother-in-law snaps, "Get out now! Leave!" The old woman bent urgently over her daughter and slapped her face lightly. "Don't be silly," she scolded, "the more it hurts now, the better later. Don't fight it, don't fight it. Let it happen!"

Joseph left the room, feeling weak. Augustine had begun to wail hysterically the moment the contraction was over. She did not even seem to notice as he pulled his hand away from hers, so lost was she in her own suffering. A glimpse of her deathly white face, slippery with sweat and tears and now even drool was enough to propel him out the door, leaving his hands trembling and his heart pounding. It seemed he had scarcely moved away down the hall when a scream split the air, as though a branding iron had been jammed into his wife's tender flesh. It was all he could do not to run -- whether back into the bedroom or out to the front door he could not say. Both impulses were upon him at once. Baby Monica was crying in the front room. Bernadette, Teresa and Cecile were sniffling, horrified by their mother's cries. Little Jean-Paul stood in the corner still bundled in the scarf and mitts and boots and coat he had worn during the long drive, his eyes wide, as though not quite understanding what was happening. Joseph's three nephews were similarly stricken by a paralysis that kept them glued in their positions on the sofa. His niece, Yvette, only a child herself, was feebly trying to console Bernadette, Teresa and Cecile, leaving the baby alone to howl, almost in harmony with her mother in the other room.

Finding his voice, Joseph said:

"Come on, get dressed. I'm taking you all for a ride over to your Aunt Marie's until this is over."

Within a matter of minutes, impelled by a mutual desire to escape from the range of Augustine's screams, the children had thrown on winter clothes, and were colliding in the front alleyway, whispering and crying and grunting from the effort of pulling on their boots. Just as he was in the process of herding them through the door, he discovered with a shock that Bernadette was glaring at him furiously. She was no longer crying. Her jaw was set, and her brows were deeply furrowed. She was looking straight at him, and her eyes were slits. Before he quite realized what had happened, Joseph had looked guiltily away. It was the first time one of his children had ever stared him down. He resisted an impulse to swat her. All he wanted to do right now was get these kids and himself out of the house and over to Marie's place. There was nothing any of them could do for Augustine now. Briefly, he wondered. Why is Bernadette looking at me that way? Does she blame me for her mother's pain? Probably. It did not cross his mind that there might have been more to it. It did not matter. Yet there was something disturbing about the little girl's expression. It was a look that he had never seen on her mother's face. Never. Not once. It was as if she was someone other than the daughter of Augustine Labrochere. I don't like that look, Joseph thought.

The next moment he realized that he was hungry. And that Marie would put some sort of supper together. Escaping from the house where Augustine was being tortured was such a relief that, quite without being aware of it, he hummed an old song as he sat behind the steering wheel, waiting for the children to settle themselves into the car, young Yvette holding Monica, and Bernadette squeezed into a corner, still glaring at him.

"Why was Ma Mere making that noise?" Jean-Paul demanded, his chin quivering and his face streaked with tears.

"Having babies hurts," Joseph said abstractly, starting the engine, thinking ahead to the meal Marie would happily prepare for them.

It was not until ten minutes after five the next morning, after ten hours of labour, that Augustine finally delivered her seventh child, the sixth to be, counted among the living. Another girl.

The shadow that passed over Joseph's face when he heard the news was gone within seconds, but during its brief stay it revealed the features of a man who was bitterly disappointed. A fifth daughter?

"Well," he said, and it was his only direct comment, "c'est la vie."

Stark blue shadows edged the multi form lumps of snow so brilliantly that it might have been that the atmosphere had frozen, leaving an airlessness that allowed perfect vision. Everything stood out with extraordinary detail, as though the oxygen itself had been transformed into crystals that lay like a glittering skin across the whole earth. The sky flared with the first fires of twilight. The snow fields became suffused with a blue-purple colour, a void into which it seemed the skeletons of trees were sinking, rather than being a vastness out of which they rose. For the eye, it was ecstasy. There was nothing to fog the prism through which pure light was leaping out of the western sky.

Joseph closed the glass door of the shop, having to jerk it hard against the crust of ice on the bottom sill, turning the key, and stepping back several paces on the sidewalk. He looked at the right and left to make sure no one was watching him, then allowed himself the inexpressible luxury of staring hard at the flowing black letters on the big display window beside the door.

LABOUCHERE CO. (LTEE) LTD.
Vetements Pour Hommes – Men's Shop

He was located on Rue Provencher, the main thoroughfare, in the block opposite City Hall. He was only three blocks away from the Basilica, and close to Provencher St. Bridge, which led across the river to Winnipeg, which meant that In addition to his local customers, he got many of the English speaking shoppers who ventured across the bridge to look for cheaper prices. An excellent location from all points of view, but especially from the point of view on the steps of City Hall. No one coming out from there could fail to see the name **LABOUCHERE** printed in letters fourteen inches high.

Joseph sighed, expelling a cloud of steam. It looks so beautiful, his name, right out there where everybody could see it. And if anyone spotted him standing in front of his shop like this, he could always pretend to be studying the display mannequin in the window, rather than admiring his own sign.

"You have done well, Labouchere," he told himself.

In the years since arriving with his family in Saint Boniface, he had gone into a partnership with Augustine's brother Jacques, who had been in the men's clothing business ever since he was a teenager. What Joseph lacked in experience in tailoring he made up in knowledge about how to keep books, do inventory, and plan ahead. Then, last November, Jacque had been offered a job with one of the big Department stores across the River. Joseph had finally succeeded in selling off the house back in Agassiz, so he had the cash on hand to buy out half of Jacques's share of the store, with a promise to pay the rest over a five years, and still have enough left to hire a competent tailor while Joseph himself concentrated on the selling and purchasing side of things. He far preferred it to barbering, or running a grocery store or a pool hall, and there were other investment properties he had an eye on. "Labouchere," he muttered exultantly, "you are going to be one of the big men in the city."

He did a sudden about-face, almost slipping in the process on the ice, and looked across the street at the three-story red brick City Hall, with its limestone foundations and bell tower reaching into the brilliant gold sky.

The crest of the city was clearly visible from where he stood. It was a colorful shield whose surface was divided into scenes depicting an anchor and a star, representing hope and charity, three crosses, representing the community's three founding bishops, two open books representing the Old and New Testament, several fleur-de-lis's, representing distant origins in France, two downward pointed arrows, indicating the acceptance of Christianity and civilization by the Indians, and a Pelican stabbing itself with its beak to draw blood to feed its young, which was a heraldic way of saying that there are some for whom no sacrifice for others is too great. Below the shield was the motto, Salus a Cruce, and above was a white lamb carrying a cross. Joseph's favorite part of the crest was the Pelican stabbing itself. A good touch, he thought. That was the way public officials should be. That was how he himself would behave once he got elected.

Bundled in his coonskin coat, with a beaver hat, mitts and earmuffs made of rabbit fur, Joseph could easily have been taken for some kind of bear, shaggy and bulky. With a huge homemade woollen scarf wound around his neck and over his chin, and the beaver hat pulled low to protect his forehead from the wind, there was little of him showing except mouth, nose and eyes. His feet were swallowed in great black galoshes. When he moved, it was with unavoidable awkwardness. But it was worth the weight and the discomfort, for deep inside all this shielding, a body was pleasantly warm. Outside, it was 34 degrees below, with the wind at 15 mph, gusting, the radio said 20. When you added the wind chill factor, you had a mean temperature around 50 below, and every breath paradoxically filled the lungs with a burning sensation. Joseph was glad the wind was from the west, for his direction lay southward. Ultimately, he was heading home, towards the very end of Rue Provencher, past the railway tracks that had once marked the town limit. Normally, he would have taken the streetcar, the idea of driving his McLaughlin D 43 in this kind of weather being completely out of the question. But today he had a visit to make, important enough to have motivated him to send the tailor home and shut the store down early. The visit was to see his brother, Emile. It was to ask a religious question.

Emile was two years older than Joseph. He had been a priest for close to twenty years and it was generally understood that when the new church in Norwood opened, which shouldn't be much more than a year or two more, it was Reverend Father Emile Labouchere who would become the new parish priest. He was still young enough that he might become a Bishop yet.

Emile regularly turned up at family functions, except of course when his duties kept him at the church, or out in the community. Every once in a while, he disappeared down East on mysterious business which some said involved bringing messages from Bishop Tachereau, the man who ruled the Basilica, to Archbishop de la Broquerie himself in Montreal.

Emile and Joseph were the only Labouchere's to have traveled as far West as Manitoba. Of the fifteen brothers and sisters who had been born back in Dorval, Québec, only nine had survived. Of the six sisters, two had stayed in the hometown and married, two married and moved to Montreal, and another two, Graziella and Andree, had become nuns. Of the three brothers, the fates of only two were known, the priest and Joseph. The youngest brother, Alexandre, had gotten into trouble when he was seventeen, accused of stealing a horse. He could have gone to jail for ten years easily, maybe more. So, his father had given him money and told him to run to the United States and never come back.

That was in the early 1900s. Since then, no one had heard anything from him. So far as he had any way of knowing, Joseph was the only one of his immediate family to be passing the name Labouchere on to future generations -- and then, just barely. For, In addition to the girl that Augustine had delivered the day they'd moved to Saint Boniface, whom they'd named Bilou, she had also, on the last day of this December, given birth to yet another girl, Loretta, leaving Joseph with six daughters and one son. Surely this next one due in April, just another two months -- had to be a boy. Surely.

Reaching the rectory behind the Basilica and climbing up the back steps clinging to the handrail lest he slip on the fine dust of ground up ice which remained despite vigorous shovelling by altar boys, Joseph's mind turned back to the question at hand. What to do about the business of the sinner, Letellier, and this latest ruling by the Judicial Committee, which threatened to violate the sanctity of holy ground around the Basilica itself.

Since making the big move to the city, Joseph had gotten into the habit of consulting his older brother frequently. Emilie's advice was generally more practical than priestly, which was a relief after the young idiot Benoit in Agassiz. And of course, Joseph could talk to Emile, so long as they were in private, as he could talk to no other priest. It had been Emile who had suggested that he entertain the thought of running for City Council in the future.

"It might be that you could be mayor, someday, Joseph," he said, almost wistfully.

"And if you were Bishop," Joseph began, but Emile cut him off there.

"That's not something we can talk about because talking about it -- and he winked -- is one way to make sure it never happens."

Joseph just nodded solemnly, honoured that his brother, even though a priest, would still confide in him. So, it was true. Emile had ambitions too. Yes, if their father could see them now, eh? Or in a few years, better yet. Maybe they would get the old man out here from Québec someday -- it was a thing they talked about often, but never seemed to get around to doing. Joseph felt remarkably close to his brother Emile.

Emile himself had often said: "Joseph, it is you, not me, who should have been a priest. You are the one who might be a saint someday, eh? Not me. I shall just go on being an administrator of souls. Mostly it is a dull business, my brother. One soul is much the same as another."

One of the nuns let Joseph into the rectory kitchen. He unburdened himself of the coonskin coat, the hat, earmuffs, mitts, scarf and galoshes, pausing after it was all removed to wipe the steam off his glasses, blow his nose, and delicately pick away the bits of icicles that had already formed in his mustache. He exchanged murmured pleasantries with the nun, waited while she hauled his furry pile of outer garments down the hallway to hang them up, then followed her down another hallway into the sector of the building that contained the private quarters of the priests. At the door in the southwest corner, she knocked.

"Reverend Father. Your brother is here."

"Come in, Joseph."

The room was appropriately spare. On the table there was a pyramid inkwell and sand blotter. A narrow iron bed and two maple chairs accounted for the rest of the furnishings. Pale cream Victorian wallpaper and bare hardwood floors were equally austere. A radiator rattled faintly on the wall beside the closet. There was not even a chest of drawers. The only decoration, apart from an amateur painting of Christ, was a deep frame with a glass covering and that contained a display of small bunches of human hair, some of it blonde or white, but mostly various shades of brown and black. The site was not uncommon -- French families made a point of shearing off a little of everybody's hair and putting it together in some display or other. Joseph knew, without looking, that the display in the frame over Emile's desk contained locks from all their brothers and sisters, alive or dead, their mother and father, and even their grandparents on both sides of the family.

Joseph had never quite been able to get over the twinge of resentment he felt whenever he saw the heirloom. Rightfully, he felt it should be his. But the old man had chosen to pass it along to Emile, and it would be utterly inappropriate to even hint that such a treasure should be displayed in a family home rather than being locked away in the cell of a lonely priest.

And then, again, maybe Emile had a greater need for it.

Emile was sitting by the window, watching the sunset across the river. The priest was much heavier than his brother, his paunch was noticeable, and his features had soft, almost flaccid contours, a characteristic Joseph ungenerously assumed to be the result of years of having one's meals spiced with saltpetre.

"Well, little brother, you're off work early today," Emile said cheerfully.

He did not get up. His voice was a baritone, much deeper than Joseph's. His eyes, which were the same shade of dark oak, sparkled in the sunset as if a hot coal had been plated in the pupils.

Joseph helped himself to another chair, pulling it into the middle of the room, opposite his brother.

"I sent Gabriel home. I'm going over to the hotel after to talk with a few of the boys from the chamber." He paused, "about Letellier, eh!"

"Yes," said Emile. "My guess is a lot of people are talking about

Letellier today, isn't that the case?" He rolled his eyes heavenward, his way of indicating that Bishop Tachereau himself could definitely be counted among them.

"Everyone who comes into the store today, they have one thing to talk about, eh? Even the high and mighty Alderman Audette decides to step across the street `just to say hello'. Joyal the constable --you know the one -- he walks by without even looking in through the window –"

"What did Audette have to say?"

"Audette? Well nothing." He just says to me, "Monsieur Labouchere, I would be interested to know what some of the clergy, not just the Bishop, think of this."

And so, I say to him, "Monsieur Alderman, I would be delighted to know myself."

He says back, "If you see your brother in the near future, give him my regards. And my regards, of course to the Bishop!"

Emile smiled.

"Did anyone else stop by?"

"A couple of dozen. It was a good morning, although business fell off in the afternoon."

"Did you see Paul Lemure?" Emile prodded mildly.

"Ah yes, Lemure! Metis, eh? You do not see many of them in town, do you. Not like back in Agassiz. Yes Lemure. He did stop by. Yes. I am trying to remember what he had to say. I was not paying much attention. Not too many savages come into my store eh. Ha!"

"Joseph," said Emile sternly, ``don't make a joke of it. "What did Lemure say?"

"He said -- he said, ah! I remember! He said to give his greetings to you if I saw you soon -- and -something else. Something odd. I should have written it down, I guess. I did not realize it was important, eh!"

"You should have" -- just concentrate, Joseph," said Emile, closing his eyes as though praying.

Joseph furrowed his brow and rubbed his forehead nervously.

"Ah yes, it was -- he said, uh, 'Remember Batoche'. Could that be it?"

Emile smiled again.

"Yes, that would be it."

"It's a message, eh? From the -- half-breeds?" Joseph was startled. "You mean that you are involved with them in all this.?"

Emile took a deep slow breath.

"Yes Joseph. The church says they are her children, my children, eh. You do not need to bother with that. But you do need to get it clearly in your mind that they are the only ones whose courage you can be sure about, because they have already lost everything. Joseph, they were the majority here up until yours and my lifetime. They were the ones who forced the first government into existence on the prairies, before you and I were born, brother. They were the ones who carried the fight against the Orange Lodge and les Canadiens."

"Joseph, what Paul Lemure was telling you to tell me was that the Metis people are still with us, and he was telling you so that I would be able to get the word to Tachereau, who has to know before he decides what to do."

Emile paused; his face slightly flushed. He fingered the crucifix dangling from a chain down the front of his simple black soutane and fixed his eyes intensely on his brother. It irritated Emile to realize that Joseph was so naive, although that was not the real problem. Naivety could be cured easily enough by a little exposure to reality. Even Joseph's prejudices could be overcome by a good scolding every once in a while. The fear was that Joseph might prove to be stupid. There was nothing that could be done about that.

"Paul Lemure was passing a message along, alright, Joseph. And you see, it could not pass to the Bishop directly because he must avoid being seen as anything other than a man of the cloth. The same applies to me, my brother. That's why you, your store, that's the place for the messages to pass back and forth. In between City Council and I and from me to the Bishop, you understand. Alderman Audette stops by, eh! He understands it. I would have hoped that without me having to spell it out that you would have understood too, eh!"

Joseph was dazzled. To have so quickly become the link between great forces --

"I – I did understand, I just did not think any of it was so urgent."

"Oh, Joseph, you did not understand, but that is neither here nor there, eh? I had not told you, and until now there has not been much urgency. I was waiting for you to see for yourself. Maybe," he added kindly, "with a little bit more time you would have had the flash go off in your head, eh? Ha, ha!"

Joseph laughed weakly, his mind still whirling with the thought of being a part of the mysterious alliance he had known must exist in opposition to the will of the Orangeman, English, Protestants, and Canadiens, but whose centre he had never been able to locate. Now it turned out, through Emile's handiwork, his own clothing store, halfway between City Hall and the Basilica, was a secret place for passing messages back and forth that were not intended to be public. Joseph realized belatedly he had clearly disappointed his brother.

"I will have to think about all this," said Joseph slowly.

"What's there to think about?"

"There is responsibility involved, eh?"

"Joseph, of course there is. But you want to be on council, is that not true? You will need to know more people than you know now, many more people. For them, Joseph, you become the voice that speaks to them from the Bishop. That is not to be sneezed at, my little brother. Right away, they start treating you with respect, eh?"

"I see." And Joseph did. His heart seemed to slightly change position, as if he were being set on a whole new course. Yes, he could see clearly now.

"My dearest Emile, I do not know what to say. I am slow, eh? But I learn."

The enormity of the favour his brother had done for him registered. Joseph reached out for his brother's hand and took it in both of his, his head bowed with sudden emotion. Firmly, Emile gripped his two palms and squeezed. His eyes were closed, and he muttered something in Latin, then released Joseph's hands and said:

"When they try to bring that Letellier's body across the bridge, they will be met by the biggest force to oppose them since the rebellion. He said it almost in a whisper."

Joseph's skin was immediately pebbled with goosebumps.

"Oh, Sacre Bleu!"

"Joseph, I'm telling you that Letellier will not be buried in holy ground!"

"My sweet Christ, I am glad to hear it!"

"Letellier, Letellier, Letellier, even the name is beginning to hurt my ears," said Emile. "A turd on a turd, eh?" Joseph, I must admit there are moments when I think it would have been better if the Bishop had left well enough alone –"

Joseph nodded, astonished again that his brother would confide in him so. He was otherwise completely unaware of the priestly practice of criticizing the Bishop at every turn.

It was true, what Emile said. Everyone knew it. The Bishop should never have been so uncontrollably angry about Letellier's stupid little pamphlet of verse, which had been published some four or five years ago. True, it had depicted the Bishop himself as "the last Buffalo" and described the great Basilica as a "Sunday marketplace," but that was nothing worse than the sort of things the communists and atheists were always saying anyway. Perhaps it was that Letellier was the husband of one of Bishop Tachereau's own nieces, lived in Saint Boniface, published the pamphlet in French, and had the nerve to hand it out personally as people were coming out of church. Whatever the reason is, known only of course to the Bishop, he had demanded Letellier's excommunication -- and got it. Letellier had been forced to leave the city, moving across the river to Winnipeg, where his children would not be beaten up on school grounds and he himself wouldn't be mocked and threatened every time he walked down the street. Letellier's wife, it was rumoured, had personally gone to see her uncle to try to prevent the excommunication, but had left the Bishop's office in tears, and had never been seen on Saint Boniface soil again. Relatives who wanted to visit the Letelliers from then on had been forced to travel to the Winnipeg side of the river.

"If only the idiot hadn't died!" rumbled Emile, shaking his head.

Joseph shook his head in sympathy, not with the fact that Letellier had died so soon after his excommunication, but in sympathy with the awkward time of his death, from the church's point of view. It was eerie to begin with, the man collapsing from tuberculosis within less than a month of the news of his having been formally excommunicated. A superstitious shudder had gone through the community like mild earth tremor. Poor Letellier! No sooner had he been barred from entry to heaven, but he had been struck down, seemingly as surely as if by lightning. Bishop Tachereau's stature among Catholics in Saint Boniface had jumped several notches, but it was not the way the church would have liked. In the new century, the objective was not to leave the impression that mere bishops could fling deadly bolts at will. All in all, Letellier's untimely death had proved a general embarrassment. One which turned into something approaching panic when it was learned that Letellier's wife was demanding that the man be buried in a plot that the family owned on the grounds of the Basilica itself.

"I remember," said Emile with a wry chuckle, "how appalled the Bishop was. It was not just that such a thing was being done, but that his own niece was doing it. And doing it to him, eh? The fact that he could not even control the members of his own family did not exactly make him look like the material from which Cardinals are made, let me tell you. Poor Tachereau! I remember him saying, and everyone laughed -- we were in his office, eh?" -- he said, "When she was little, she used to sit on my knee, and even then she used to worry me, because almost every time she did, she wet herself all over my robes. I should have known. But otherwise, you know, it is embarrassing for him."

"Worse than embarrassing now," said Joseph grimly.

"Yes. Much worse."

The Bishop had immediately announced that there would be no burial of an excommunicate in consecrated ground. At any previous point in history, that should have been enough to settle the matter. But now it was far from enough. The Letellier woman had hired lawyers and taken the matter to the Capitol in Ottawa. The case had been shuffled into the hands of a special Judicial Committee, which had taken almost a year to reach a conclusion. In the meantime, Letellier's body had been interred in a Protestant Cemetery in Winnipeg.

The Judicial Committee's ruling had just been published in Ottawa and its contents telegraphed westward to Manitoba. According to the committee, burial in a Christian Cemetery was a civil right that could not be denied on grounds of death while excommunicated.

"I still cannot believe they would do it," Joseph offered.

"They invented a new law," growled Emile. "There is nothing new in that. They do it over a bottle of port every day. But believe me, it is law now. They will drive Letellier's coffin into the ground like a knife into the body of the church. It cannot, and will not, be allowed."

Joseph waited a few moments for his brother's wrath to subside.

Emile drew a deep breath and folded his hands into a praying position.

"The Bishop has, of course, not had time to receive guidance from Rome."

"The Pope himself, then, knows of this?"

"Rest assured, little brother."

Joseph's mouth dropped open for several seconds before he recovered himself.

"The Pope is, of course, infallible," Emile said slowly looking at Joseph very evenly. "But sometimes, as during the rebellion, the truth of a situation does not get to the Pope, and so it is difficult, even impossible, for him to use his infallible wisdom. After all, he has the whole world to watch out for, while we are only a tiny outpost in the middle of nowhere, and our Bishop, while a great and generous man, does not himself possess the divine gift of inability to be wrong, eh? Do you understand?"

"I think so," said Joseph uncertainly.

"If you are my eyes and ears and tongue in the community, my dear brother, we may do great things together. And what we must do now, whether the Bishop finds the courage or not, is make sure that those who do possess the courage are on hand to act to prevent Letellier from being buried here. That is what we must do, you and I, Joseph. And since I cannot speak openly, you must be my voice among the people."

"So, I am to say to them, 'No burial,' am I?" Joseph asked.

"Yes, Joseph."

"I guess this will mean trouble."

"It is trouble already."

"Hm."

Emile laid his hand on Joseph's shoulder.

"This too is God's will, Joseph."

In the kitchen, the nun helped Joseph bundle himself back into his furs, scarf, galoshes and mitts.

"Watch the steps," she warned as he descended carefully into the silver and blue world of winter night, with its shadows from the lanterns along the sidewalk. The shadows were etched with precision by a blinding third-quarter moon. The wind lazily scuffled powder over steeply scalloped drifts.

Joseph's mind was spinning with a bewildering array of new information about politics, about Emile's importance in the scheme of things, about Letellier, and Alderman Audette, about the half-breed Lemur, about Bishop Tachereau, but most of all, about the discovery of his own unique position of stature. Labouchere, you are on your way! He exalted. Good old Emile, connecting you like this right up to the highest levels, eh? Now you go down to the hotel and you tell the boys what's what. No burial. Remember Batoche.

He hurried toward the Marion Hotel, feeling excited and full of importance. The hinges of the door were encased in ice. They squealed loudly as he pushed his way into the warmth and bright light. His glasses immediately fogged, and he had to pause to clean them before proceeding.

He felt vaguely uncomfortable in this atmosphere of laughter, clinking glasses and suds spilled on the floor where it mingled with the sawdust and melted snow from men's boots. But he overcame the feeling and quickly found a seat in a rough circle of more than a dozen men who had pulled their chairs together around three of the round little beer tables, covered now entirely by glasses of foaming draft.

Cigar and cigarette smoke were so thick that the men playing billiards at the far end of the beer parlor were faint colour-rinsed shapes under the glare of lights.

Any nostalgic feelings Joseph might have had for his own pool hall in Agassiz were lost in the electricity of the mood that now seized him, seated at the very heart of the Marion Hotel, counted as one among the members of the Chamber of Commerce, on a first name basis with them all, exchanging handshakes with several other men whom he had not met before who had pulled their chairs over into the growing circle.

There was only one subject: Letellier.

Jacques Saint-Pierre, the Chamber's secretary, was defiant.

"We should destroy the bridge!"

"What bridge? What bridge?"

"The Provencher Bridge! The Norwood Bridge! The railway bridges! All of them!"

There was a general roar of approval, but no one was taking the idea seriously. For one thing, destroying the great stone and iron girder bridges would be no minor task.

"It is an idea, I will admit," Charles Deschamps said. He was portly, wore mutton chops, owned a small meat packing plant, and was not known for wild ideas. Tonight, though, even Deschamps was feeling a bit crazy.

"When will they try to bury him?" demanded Roland Michel, the jeweler.

Saint-Pierre was first with the answer.

"Not until they can organize a show of strength enough to make us sit up and take notice, eh? A month or two. Maybe three. They know they have us by the short hairs. They are in no hurry now."

"They will send the army in?" asked Rigaud de Vaudreuil, a thin, pipe-smoking administrator from the stockyards, who also owned an appliance shop over on Rue Dubuc.

There was much shrugging, but no one seemed to know the answer. Then came a ragged bark of laughter from the end of the line of tables and chairs nearest the door. It was Leon Beaujeu, the lawyer, with a cynical expression on his face. He bent forward suddenly and went through the motions of a man savagely hammering someone into the ground, then gave a vicious push at an imaginary object.

"Whatever happens, gentlemen, you can be sure the bastards in Ottawa are going to nail your balls to a stump and push you over backwards."

Beaujeu coughed out cigarette smoke.

"They have put three long hard years of work, careful and expensive work, into baiting this trap, gentlemen. Anyone so stupid as to step into it can blame no one but themselves if they get chopped in half, eh? I'm telling you, you are fools if you do not think the army will be here to guard that coffin and make sure it gets buried, and they will come in force, I'm damn sure of it. Sacre bleu! Can't you see? They will bring gatling guns, just like they did at Batoche?"

"Remember Batoche!" said Joseph suddenly.

All eyes around the table jerks toward him.

The lawyer Beaujeu looked surprised.

"I did not think you had those kinds of opinions, Labouchere." He nodded approvingly and raised his glass.

"Remember Batoche!" he cried.

The men all hoisted their glasses, but it was done more in solemnity than boisterousness, because the truth was that they all did, indeed, remember Batoché. The crushing of the Red River rebellion had been completed more than a generation ago, and while the gatling guns had long since been replaced by weapons developed in the Great War, they remained a potent symbol of the ruthlessness of the central Canadian government when confronted by open insurrection. To remember Batoche -- aloud --- was still a radical act for a French Catholic, especially in Manitoba.

"No burial for the traitor!" Joseph cried, lifting his glass high again.

"NO BURIAL!" the men roared.

Going to High Mass was the major event of the week.

It began at eight in the morning, when Augustine started issuing orders to Bernadette and Teresa and the roundup of the rest of the children got underway. There was always last-minute ironing and stitching to be done, shoes to be polished, and, of course, all of the girls, right down to little BIlou and baby Loretta, had to have their hair curled. When all were finished with and the sobbing and whining had ended, it was Bernadette's turn to attend to Augustine's own thick tresses. Since no one could eat before going to confession the children were inevitably irritable and troublesome, except for the three smallest, including Monica, who was still too young to attend Catechism, and therefore too young to be taken to Mass. Cecile was attending Mass for the first time this year, and Jean-Paul was more trouble than all the girls together, including the babies. As soon as he was dressed, Augustine ordered him outside. It made no difference whether it was raining or snowing, he was just too much of a distraction while she was trying to get the girls ready.

The new Labouchere house was very much like the old one in Agassiz, except that it was larger, it had two gables instead of one, and there were three extra bedrooms. Otherwise, a trellis ran along the front inside verandas just as one had in the old place. There was no proper basement, just a root cellar which could be entered through an outside door. There was a single light bulb down there, but when it was off, the cellar was so dark the children could not tell if their eyes were opened or closed. It was a favorite place for hiding. As before, there was a chicken coop and a vegetable garden in the backyard. A thick hedge guarded the front yard.

Joseph had picked the place partly because it looked so similar to their family's old home. We will not need to feel homesick, eh?" But also, he picked it because it was the only house yet to have been built to the east of the train track. There were farms, but between them and the new Labouchere house there was at least a mile of open field. Looking westward, Joseph could take in the view of Saint Boniface and the skyline of Winnipeg rising beyond. But by turning around he could look out over a stretch of land that was basically untouched. His brother Emile had commented that it was one of Joseph's peculiarities that he should have a taste for isolated locations. The problem with it was that the children were cut off somewhat from others their age. The nearest house on the city side of the tracks was a block away. It was perhaps inevitable that the Labouchere's should gain a reputation of being unsociable.

A game that the children often played was to close their eyes, hold hands, and pretend that they had been transported by magic back to Agassiz, upon opening their eyes, facing East, it was easy to imagine that they really had returned. Or that they had never really moved to Saint Boniface at all.

At 9 30, the hustle of preparations took a leap in the direction of chaos with the arrival of Andre and his sister Jeanette and their brood of six children, three of which were dropped off to be taken care of by Bernadette, Teresa and Cecile while the rest of the family attended the 10:00 o'clock Mass. As soon as they were out of church, Andre and Jeanette and the kids would hurry back to Augustine's and take over the babysitting operation while the Labouchere's in their turn set out for the Basilica.

Now, because it was winter and the car was up on blocks beside the house, the Laboucheres waited for the streetcar. Jean-Paul took up watch just outside the front hedge, watching the streetcar as it sat at the end of the line, less than a mile to the East, waiting for the moment to begin its clattering, rattling, steel on steel run down Rue Provencher to the bridge and across into Winnipeg, getting lost there among the twelve story canyons of brick and billowing clouds pouring night and day from the incinerators.

In the distance, the streetcar looked like an insect. The bell mounted like a nose, the two panel front windows like compound eyes, an antenna-like trolley clinging to a web slung from pole to pole, and the grillwork of the scuppers mounted front and back like a slack open jaw. It was painted bright orange.

"It's coming." yelled Jean-Paul. Buttoning up their coats, the Laboucheres plunged from the warmth of the house into the arctic harshness of the last Sunday in February. Augustine moved cautiously, clinging to Joseph's arm. She only had a little over a month to go before her ninth delivery, and her face showed the strain. Bernadette hovered protectively just a step behind her mother while Teresa kept an eye on Cecile, and Jean-Paul fended for himself. He absolutely refused to be commanded by any of his sisters.

Augustine bore the lurching, hurtling motion of the streetcar stoically, but by the time they reached their stop, and began the three-block hike to church, she had to stop to get her breath.

"Shouldn't we take her home, Mon Pere?" Bernadette urged.

Joseph shook his head. "She'll be alright, won't you, ma chere?" Augustine nodded weakly, trying to smile.

And after just a couple of minutes, she began to move again, Joseph on one side and Bernadette on the other. Bernadette was already almost as tall as her mother. In the last couple of years, she had shot up swiftly, although she had not filled out like Teresa. Jean-Paul called her "Boney "and her aunts worried incessantly that she didn't eat enough. It was partly true. She seemed largely indifferent to food, whereas everyone else in the family ate with great enthusiasm. Her face had lost much of its roundness. The seriousness of her expression had not changed in the least.

Going to church normally excited her. She loved the tremendous vibrations of the organ, the crystal quality of the choir and she remained in awe of the great altar, the mysterious Latin chants, the solemnity of the ceremony, the vastness of the Basilica itself. But today she was worried about Ma Mere. Augustine had not been herself for several weeks. There was a strained look on her face, a slight roundness around her eyes. Thinking back, Bernadette could not remember her mother being anything other than cheerful through all the other ordeals, but now she was withdrawn, self absorbed. She had been irritable that morning and had complained while Bernadette did her hair. It was so unusual to hear her mother complain about anything that Bernadette had been startled into tears. Poor Ma Mere! By now, Bernadette's head reached a tentative conclusion that there was something more to having babies than special prayers. It involved Ma Mere and Mon Pere doing something to each other, although, try as she might, Bernadette could not imagine what. Often enough, when he was small, she had studied the little pee pee between Jean-Paul's legs, and she knew that she herself had no such thing. She knew, too, that there were boys and girls in the neighborhood who played dirty with each other in the bushes behind Archibald's field, but she had remained aloof from such things. Her piety was far too strong. Besides, if she did do something like that, she would have to confess it before going to Communion, and the thought of having to make such a confession was too painful to bear. Bernadette's knowledge ended there. About the only thing which she was certain was that when Ma Mere began to swell up with a baby inside her, it was somehow Mon Pere's fault.

Why did he keep doing it?

Surely, they didn't need any more babies. Eight was enough. And look at poor Ma Mere now, feeling pain already and trying to hide it, looking so tired, even haunted. Vaguely, Bernadette knew about something called "The revenge of the Cradle," a plan put forward by the clergy in Québec after the British had defeated the French at the Plains of Abraham, making new France into a colony of hated English. At that juncture in Canada's history, there were roughly equal numbers of French and British living in the new country. Said the priests: "If we can't defeat the enemy in battle, we will overwhelm them with sheer numbers." The conquered peasants, urged on by men who could have no children themselves, set about having the largest families possible. All the French society on the new continent organized itself into a deliberate program of population expansion. The French empire might have been crushed and its name erased from maps of North America, but on the narrow farms and habitants, in the town and villages and parishes along the great Saint Lawrence River, five generations of French women had made war by making love, carrying on a battle that their husbands had long ago lost. Not since the Union Jack was raised over the old Fort at Quebec City, in 1760, had the war to out-populate the conquering invader paused -- yet the priests of the time had not counted on the waves of immigrants from all over Europe, but mostly from the British Isles, who were to arrive over the next century and a half, effortlessly outnumbering even the overflowing cradles of Québec.

The Revenge of the Cradle? Bernadette had no firm opinion whether it had been a good idea or a bad one, but one thing was clear -- it had failed. Saint Boniface itself was proof of it. When the first French settlers had reached the junction of the Red and the Assiniboine Rivers, a generation after the fall of New France, they too were under priestly orders to multiply as quickly as possible. Yet today, it was the English speaking city on the west side of the Red River that sprawled from horizon to horizon, and by comparison, the French St Boniface was not much larger than any of a dozen municipalities which had sprung up around Winnipeg, giving it a total population of a quarter of a million people. Even though having started the race to expand across the Prairie at roughly the same time, the French had lagged far behind. St Boniface had retained its own language and religion but was now surrounded on all sides by les anglaise or others who took English as their second tongue. There were fewer than thirty- thousand Frenchmen and their families within the enclave. The bells of the Basilica were already ringing when the Laboucheres reached the front gates and joined the thickening stream of people making their way along the wide block long sidewalk leading to the massive archway that was this cathedral's entrance. It reached almost all the way to the top of the building, where ornate spires began their jagged leap into the sky. Between them, in the centre of the facade above the arch, a giant statue of Saint Peter had been carved, sitting on a throne that was at least twenty feet high. Above him towered a stone cross, and beneath, framed deep within the arch itself, a traceried circular window with a diameter equal to ten men standing on each other shoulders. Beneath the front window, there was a balcony and beneath that, three archways with pillars at the top of a flight of stone steps. In school, Bernadette had studied about the trilobites which had lived in the long ago ocean that had filled all the space, whose shell-like bodies left white fossil impressions in the otherwise uniform grey of the stones out of which the Basilica had been blasted, chipped, chiseled, carved and sanded into it's Gothic Majesty. There was something effortless about the flow of the lines, as if the rock had originally been soft enough to mold, and some said that was almost true. The material out of which the immense edifice had been shaped was called Tindal stone, after the town twenty miles away where the great blocks had been quarried. It was much softer than granite.

The church's bells were almost deafening by the time the family reached the entrance. Every child in Saint Boniface knew the story of their long voyage from England, where they had been built in 1840. Weighing 1600 pounds, they were delayed by a strike and did not reach the prairies until 1843. A fire destroyed the original cathedral in which they were mounted, and they were damaged so badly they had to be sent back to England for repairs. In 1862, they were sent out from England again, only to be driven ashore in Newfoundland by a storm. From there they were sent to the United States, but the cost of over land transportation proved to be too much, and the bells were sent back to England to be re shipped through Hudson's Bay, in the centre of northern Canada and brought down from there by boat. Finally arriving in 1864, after crossing the Atlantic five times.

Bernadette noticed that her mother cringed as the tremendous sound descending from directly above.

"Are you sure you're alright?" Ma Mere.

"I am. But I don't think I shall be able to do much kneeling!"

As relative newcomers, the Laboucheres sat close to the back of the cathedral, but in a pew, which was the same every Sunday in recognition of the regularity of attendance. In due course, they would move forward as old-time parishioners either died or became infirm or moved away. They could have sat much closer to the front by attaching themselves to the numerous groupings consisting of Augustine's various brothers, sisters, uncles, aunts, cousins, or of course her mother. But it was Joseph's insistence that they sit separately, as Laboucheres not merely as in- laws under the umbrella of her family. He did not want to be swallowed up as he put it, by the large Lagimodiere family. On any given Sunday, Augustine was liable to have a dozen brothers and sisters present in the congregation, plus a dozen of their spouses, and, depending on how many children had colds or measles or mumps at the time, anywhere from three or four dozen nephews and nieces, the largest concentration of which were seated with her mother in the third and fourth rows to the left of the aisle, indicating how long the larger Lagimodiere family had lived in the parish. In all, the church could sit eight hundred and fifty people at a time. On special occasions, like Midnight Mass or Easter or Christmas, the capacity was never enough. As many as twelve hundred people would crowd their way in, kneeling on the floor of the outer aisles and even in the foyer, backed right up to the front doors.

Inside the Basilica, Bernadette always experienced a feeling of sublime security. There could be no safer possible place in the world. Not only was there the security of numbers, there was the security of knowing there were virtually no strangers among the crowd. Everyone was related to dozens of others present, or else were neighbors or work together, or saw each other during the week. The tremendous stone walls were like a fortress. The oak doors, once closed, could hold even polar bears at bay. And it was not just the warmth of being protected from harm in the world outside, it was, more importantly, the relief of knowing that here not even the creatures who crept into her dreams could reach her.

It was the altar that commanded Bernadette's attention. It was the richest looking thing she had ever seen, with its acolyte candlesticks, incense box and spoon and burner, the holy water vessel, the canon tables, chalice, cruets and holy water font, glistening in gold. She understood almost nothing of the ceremony, since the catechism books said little about it, and while she had long since memorized the responses that the congregation made in deep many throated rumbles to the incantations from the priest, it was all in Latin, and she really had no idea what it meant. She knew when to kneel, when to stand, when to sit, and when to slip out of the pew and line up for her turn in the confessional booth prior to communion. Once in the booth, she knew how to wait on her knees until the priest had opened the grillwork and lowered his bowed head toward her. "Bless me father, for I have sinned. It has been a week since my last confession –" Seldom could she think of many sins to confess, and generally had to settle for admitting to having wished that her brother and sister would fall out of a tree or forgetting to say her prayers or not paying attention in catechism class.

The family had just lined itself up to enter the confessional booth when Augustine fainted. Her head struck the floor with a terrible thunk and her hat flopped loose. It happened so quickly that nobody caught her, although Joseph was immediately on his knees beside her, and several men and women were clustering around. Cecile started to cry. Teresa quickly slapped a hand over her mouth, responding to the dictum that no matter what happened during Mass, no one should make any unusual noise. Within minutes,

Augustine was being deftly carried into a room off to the side, where a nun attended to her immediately. Despite her concern, Bernadette found herself blushing furiously as she remained in the lineup, with Teresa, Cecille and Jean-Paul, each of them clutching their rosaries. Ma Mere's huge belly had wobbled as she was carried away, and it had looked almost funny. At least one woman, watching, had tittered, and a couple men had smiled knowingly.

Joseph had disappeared into the side room with his wife. When he emerged, his face was chalky. He hurried over to Bernadette and bent down to whisper in her ear, thrusting some coins into her palm. Make sure you all get home as soon as Mass is over. Your mother is sick. The nun is arranging for a car. I'll go home with her.

"Mon Pere, can't I---"

"No! Stay here. One of your aunts will come with us." He hurried away.

Bernadette stood there, petrified. Sick? What did he mean, sick? She shivered with a rush of rage that followed the initial embarrassment. Why should she be left here with the children when her mother needed help. How could she be a little Angel to her mother if Mon Pere kept telling her to do all the wrong things. She wanted to break away from the lineup, run to the door of the room into which they have taken Ma Mere and rushed to her side. But no, Mon Pere had said stay, and that was what she had to do.

When it was finally her turn in the confessional booth, she said the Act of Contrition, but said it quickly, and did not admit that the paramount thought in her mind was, I wish Mon Pere would be so sick he'd die. She was furious with him, not just for treating her once again like a child, but for not listening to her on the way to church when she said that Ma Mere should be taken home then. Why didn't he ever listen to her? What was wrong with him? Why did she have to have him as a father?

But the only words that passed her lip were the traditional ones: "Oh my God, I am heartily sorry for having offended Thee and I detest all my sins, because I dread the loss of heaven and the pain of hell, but most of all because they offend Thee, my God, who art all-good and deserving of all my love –"

Grande Ma Mere Lagimodiere moved in right away to be with Augustine twenty-four hours a day. Of the seventeen children the old woman had born, six of them had died before reaching maturity and one daughter, Birgitta, had died delivering her own child. Yet Grande Ma Mere did not trust doctors and would not allow nurses into the house -- or any of her children's houses, if she could help it -- unless they were Catholics, and certainly not if they were English or any other kind of foreigner. Formerly, in Saint Boniface, it was no trouble to find doctors as well as nurses who were both French and Catholic.

Augustine was almost a precise replica of her mother, but all similarity seemed to have been used up there. Whereas Augustine seldom spoke, her mother chattered without pause. It was easy to suspect that Augustine had found as a child that she could never get a word in edgewise and so had abandoned the territory of communication to her mother. For her part, Germaine Lagimodiere did not seem to recognize a need for anyone else to talk, except to answer direct questions. There were periods when the old woman slipped into silence, but there was not much point talking to her then since she took no notice of anyone around her. At sixty years of age, Germaine displayed almost as much physical strength as Augustine herself. She was buxom, short, silver haired and generally impatient.

She quickly had Bernadette, Teresa, Cecile and even Jean-Paul on the hop. Taking over between them all the functions Ma Mere had previously performed. Her favorite instrument of persuasion was a broom.

When Jean-Paul balked at helping with the dishes, she whacked his bottom without hesitation.

Bernadette burst out laughing. It was not that the broom had hurt her brother so much, it was more a question of what it did to his dignity. His face turned bright red. He looked desperately at his father, expecting him to overrule Grande Ma Mere, but Joseph merely cleared his throat, as though to cover up a laugh, and turned his attention back to the paper he was reading.

His pride wounded, a sulky Jean-Paul took the dish towel thrust into his hands by Grande Ma Mere and joined Cecile at the sink. The task of feeding the family had been handed over entirely to Bernadette, and the care of the babies became Teresa's preserve. This, on top of all their normal chores.

"You must pull your weight now," Grande Ma Mere Lagimodiere nagged. "Do not talk back. And get to bed early! The last thing your poor mother needs now is a lot of noise. I want you all to tiptoe. Teresa, you bathe the little ones in the kitchen. Jean-Paul, I want the ice scraped off the front porch. Bernadette, we will have the bedtime snacks early tonight, then I want you all to kiss your mother goodnight and scoot!"

Life under Grande Ma Mere's rule was not much fun. She had no tolerance for bickering between the children and was especially hard on Jean-Pau, who was accustomed to getting away with much. The girls loved it when the old woman grabbed for the broom. She had expert aim. For the first time that they could remember, their brother seemed thoroughly cowed. Once, shortly after she moved in, he had bolted through the door when she came after him. Calmly, the old woman slammed and locked the door, and ordered Bernadette to do the same at the front. It was about twenty-five below outside. She waited half an hour before letting the boy back in. By then, his hands and face were pale blue, and he was shivering so badly his teeth rattled. His nose was running, but the phlegm had frozen to his upper lip.

Joseph made no move to interfere at all.

It was not that he approved of the old lady's manner of handling the children, but he knew better than to fight her. Germaine Lagimodiere had dominated everyone of her children, and when they married, managed to dominate their spouses. It was only natural that she would dominate her grandchildren too. Her husband had been the only one she made no attempt to order about, but he had been dead ten years now. It had been the strain, some joked, of resisting Germaine's fierce will that killed him.

Even if he had the energy to resist his mother-in-law's method of running the house, Joseph would not have argued with her. She was too valuable. Anyone with an eye on public office in Saint Boniface had to keep in close touch with his natural allies. In Joseph's case these were, first of all, Augustine's huge family. Grande Ma Mere Lagimodiere could report in voluminous detail about every child and adult in the nexus of all her sons and daughters, nieces, nephews, sisters, brothers, aunts, uncles, grandchildren, cousins, second cousins and the invisible army of all these other's immediate and distant relatives. Only a fraction of her tribe lived in Saint Boniface, and some she had not seen for forty-five years, but her memory of their life stories right up to the latest echo of a rumor was as thorough and accurate as any of the indexing systems of the new City Library. If Joseph wanted to know anything at all about any of these people, most of whom were basically strangers to him, all he had to do was ask the old lady and she would supply him with the answers. If he was to become a successful politician, this was exactly the kind of information he would need in order to be able to create the impression that he was deeply interested in all these kin, not just interested in their votes.

Ah yes, between brother Emile and Grande Ma Mere, how can you lose, Labouchere? Your luck is incredibly good, eh?

The only thing wrong in the entire world, it seemed, was this business of Augustine being sick. She hadn't been so good during the last two pregnancies, either he reflected. But she was strong and he was lucky, they could have prayers right from the Bishop if they wanted, and there were even doctors and nurses, trained nurses, nearby, not to mention Grande Ma Mere and the stream of sisters and sisters in-law who passed through the front door every day, making inquiries. It wasn't like being out in Agassiz, where the best you could hope for was an experienced midwife.

Every afternoon, as soon as he got home from work, Joseph went straight to the bedroom, eased himself onto the bed in a sitting position and took his wife's hand.

Her blue eyes were still bright and clear. Even though her head was propped up on pillows, the lump of her womb rose higher than her face. She seemed to be looking up at him as though buried under a mound of sand. Her face was strained, and she looked bewildered, as if she couldn't believe she was actually confined to bed instead of carrying on as usual, as she had always done right up to the last day. When he bent over to kiss her, she rose too quickly. Their teeth clapped together, and his nose bumped against her cheek bone.

"Oh, my lover, how are you today?" he asked, taking her chin between his fingers and kissing her gently.

She shook her head so that her hair, unbraided, rustled on the pillow, and she struggled up into something closer to a sitting position.

"I feel like a turtle, upside down, a big turtle, that's what I feel like! A big green turtle. This is so silly, Joseph. I should be up. I will just get lazy here."

He patted her hand.

"Ma chere, there is nothing for you to do. It is all being done. You just have to rest -- how are your legs?"

She looked away, pouting.

"Still swollen, eh?"

She nodded.

Her legs had been swollen for at least a week prior to the day she collapsed in church, but Augustine had mentioned nothing about it. It had only been after Joseph and Sister Elzire had gotten her home to bed that the swelling in her legs had been noticed.

"And look at that!" Sister Elzire had demanded. "A varicose vein if I ever saw one!"

Conscious by then, Augustine had been furious. It was plain

that she still did not like any reference at all to the condition of her legs, and, by implication, the vein.

Knowing why she was still brooding, Joseph said patiently. "There is no shame, ma chere. It is your badge of motherhood."

"Oh Joseph, sometimes when I don't want to talk to you about something could you just for once not talk about it!"

Joseph stiffened.

"Oh Joseph, I am sorry. I do not like lying here like this, Joseph."

"Helplessly," he said.

"Well, it is not just your mother saying you have to stay put, you know, it is the docteur too, and I have asked Emile about it, but he says if the doctor says to stay in bed, you owe it to the child to do what he says, eh? You cannot argue with that, can you. Besides, it will be over soon. Just another ---"

"Another month!" Augustine burst out disgustedly, visibly appalled at the thought of spending that much time in bed.

"Oh well, it might be sooner," he said lamely.

Augustine clamped her teeth together and looked toward the wall. Joseph looked at her curiously. Expecting to see some sort of physical change in her features. But no, the two front top teeth still overlap, setting both at minor odd angles in the gum, legs and belly bloated, with a painful vein spreading in clots down her left ankle, her face was still as fine and as childlike as the day he first saw her.

"You are as beautiful as the moment I first met you, ma chere." Joseph said tenderly, kissing her hand. He looked her directly in the eyes so she would have to look back at him. When she did, her first peek was wary, oddly frightened, as though she was afraid, she might see that he was lying. But when he made no attempt to justify himself or convince her, instead letting her look as deeply into his eyes as she wanted, hiding nothing, she sighed heavily -- with relief or sadness, he could not really tell. A simple tear gathered in the corner of her left eye. He leaned over, absorbed it with his tongue and hugged her.

They were silent for several minutes, hugging each other tightly.

A shudder passed through Augustine's immense frame, but she did not cry as he had expected she would. They muttered "I love you." to each other repeatedly and squeezed each other's shoulders and ribs.

Joseph kissed her firmly and tousled her hair.

"Ah, Joseph, how do you ever put up with me?" She laid back, relaxed, her smile playing with its customary ease. The sparkle in her eyes had never gone away, but it glistened more beautifully than ever now it had been washed. Augustine had a faint glow, as though she had been bathed herself, and she had. For as Joseph stared at her, she knew it was with mute admiration. He had never stopped praising her. He had never stopped marveling aloud at her beauty.

"The light of your soul is in your eyes, ma chere," he said.

Augustine was happy.

No one could ever have convinced her that Joseph was anything other than her greatest admirer, her worshipper, her lover, more than that, in some ways her father. She loved Joseph as a man and as the head of the family, but she often loved him best when he was fatherly, when he told her what to do, when he came to protect her. There was nothing in the Catechism that said there was anything wrong with sometimes feeling like your husband's daughter or treating him a bit as if he were your own father. The feeling was good. Joseph liked it too. Sometimes he would push his forefinger against her nose, and say, with a wicked gleam in his eye. "My little girl" --- and she would adopt an expression that was both innocent and lecherous, lick her lower lip, and say, "Come here, papa... "Then they would laugh at each other.

February was always the worst month of the Canadian winter. Even though the days had begun to lengthen, there was still far more darkness than light and everyone had been cooped up indoors for so long there was a crankiness in the air that could almost be calculated by looking at the thermometer.

The cold had a weakening effect. It drained the spirit as well as the body. There were plenty of people with bright red cheeks, who shovelled snow from their sidewalks with vigor, and genuinely appeared to be stimulated by the snow and ice. But for everyone of these, there were many others who were getting over there fourth or fifth cold of the season, or a bout with flu or pneumonia or frostbite or any one of the of a dozen ailments of the stomach and bowels that resulted from the kinds of abrupt and radical changes in temperature that the prairie people routinely endured every year.

For everyone, the sparkle of the sunlight on the great dunes of snow was a jolt to behold. The snow had by then drifted into smoothly flanked hills so large it seemed a dinosaur might have fallen over on its side and been covered up. It was common for icicles on the side of a five-storey apartment block to reach from the rooftop to the ground in a single gleaming fang. And everyone agreed that the sunset exploding in slow motion above the blinding sheets of the fields had to be the most incredible phenomenon in the world. And yes, it was invigorating in the extreme -- except taxing in the extreme.

By the end of February, exhaustion had set in. Every kind of work was twice as difficult in the winter as summer. Merely to avoid not slipping on the ice demanded concentration. Leg muscles protested at the labor of sloughing through snow drifts that had sprung up overnight across freshly plowed roads. Backs and arms ached from shovelling. The whole body had grown numb from taking off three layers of clothes and putting them back on again -- how many millions of times. There was a point every winter where it seemed that the cold had lasted too long, that night had permanently overwhelmed the day, that an Ice Age had indeed sneaked back out of the north, seized all the territory it had surrendered long ago, and would now remain for a thousand years. Who could prove that summer would ever really come again? When this point was reached -- a hopeless feeling that gripped almost everybody at one time or another -- A fatalism set in that kept everybody going. They gave up looking forward to anything except endless ice, endless snow,

perhaps endless night. A mood of pessimism and gloom prevailed --
only to be wiped away at the first touch of March's breath.

Suddenly, everybody was hurrying, impatient, full of irrational
laughter. Objectively, not much had changed. Certainly, the drifts
had not melted by an inch nor had the ice on the river uttered a
single creaking noise. The sunset still came by suppertime. Yet the
body knew. That slight downward adjustment of temperature was
all that was needed to rekindle the dream of a golden age of summer,
with green and yellow and all those colors whose memories were dim
after a month of nothing but whiteness under the blue of the sky.

Shut away in the downstairs bedroom, Augustine had little sense
of the quickening pulse of March. Rather, for the first time in her
life, she was filled with the lethargy that grew with each passing day.
The swelling in her legs expanded to include her arms and fingers,
which became so puffy that using plenty of soap, her mother had to
work on her engagement and wedding rings to free them. She wore
them after that on a string around her neck, but she wept when they
finally came off, as much for self loathing as pain. Her face, too,
began to take on that horrifying puffiness.

During her other pregnancies she had moments of fear and
plenty of pain but never had she been turned into anything so
monstrous as she now felt herself to be. Although the emotion was
almost completely new to her, Augustine now experienced prolonged
periods of self-pity. She fingered her rosary and passed the long hours
of isolation by praying. How many times she muttered the Lord's
Prayer, the Angelical Salvation and the Apostles Creed, she could
not begin to guess -- but it did no good. At least, the swelling did
not go down.

Doctor Gendreau came once a week to administer something
he called a Benedict Solution to check her condition. "You have
toxemia, Madam Labouchere. That means your blood pressure is

up and I am afraid there is sugar and protein in your urine. You are retaining fluids. We shall have to put you on salt restrictions. But other than that, the only treatment is bed rest."

"Will this hurt the baby?"

The doctor hesitated.

"Well, I do not think so. But we will see. If your blood pressure gets much higher or the toxemia increases, we will have to induce it."

"Induce?"

"Make it come faster, Madame. Instead of waiting for your full term, maybe when the baby is eight and a half months, when it is viable, as we say, we will bring it on then, you have never had any trouble before though, have you?"

"No, no." Augustine assured him, embarrassed at the thought of causing 'trouble' during a delivery.

But after he had gone, she found herself feeling frightened. He was a nice man, that Rene Gendreau, but he was like all doctors -- they lie to your face if they feel like it. Toxaemia? Induce the baby? What was all this nonsense?

Afterward, Grande Ma Mere Lagimodiere crept into the room. She entered furtively, as if afraid the doctor might return any moment. She still did not like the idea of a doctor coming so often. It was a bad omen. She absolutely refused to be in the room when he was in attendance.

"What does Gendreau say?" She demanded.

Augustine told her.

"Huh! Devils talk! No one makes a baby come earlier than it wants unless they are trying to kill it.

"Ma Mere!" Augustine was genuinely scared. "Was that what the doctor was up to?"

"You cannot tell, the old woman said firmly. "Besides," she sniffed, "in my time everything was left to God's Will and that's the way it should be. Some of these children that the doctor brings into the world, well, Sacre Bleu, my dear Jesus, it is easy to see some of them should have been stillborn, eh? There is no faith in God's wisdom anymore. Lord knows what He's doing when he weeds the garden. What can a doctor know? Or any of us?"

Augustine's brother-in-law visited her at least as often as a doctor, but the presence of the Reverend Father Emile Labouchere had an opposite effect on her. Whereas Doctor Gendreau seemed always to be full of gloom and use strange words like "glucosuria" and "increasing proteinuria" -- words intended, she was sure, to hide a terrible truth -- the priest was relaxed and treated her as though she was a normal human being instead of some loathsome stricken monster, which was what she felt like.

He was also more honest.

"Have you talked to the doctor, Emile?"

"I have."

"And what does he say to you.?"

Emile took her hand gently and asked:

"Has Joseph talked to you about this yet?"

Augustine shook her head, for she was sure that Joseph knew more than he had told her.

The priest hesitated, just as the doctor had done, but for a different reason. It was not that he believed there was ever anything to be gained from lying to a patient or a victim, especially not for a priest. His hesitation, rather, was to allow time for a flash of anger at his brother to pass through his system, discharging itself before he spoke, lest it creeps into his tone of voice. Damn that Joseph!

Emile had to admit his younger brother was a disappointment in more ways than one.

It was not just that he was slightly loose in the head and that he was a blabbermouth who could not even be trusted to carry a message to the right person without spilling its contents all over town, but when it came to dealing with his own wife, he was a coward. A coward. Or merely too stupid to realize her situation.

Emile knew that the doctor had spelled it out clearly to Joseph because he himself had talked separately with both men. Yet was Joseph any worse than Rene Gendreau? Emile sighed and shifted his position. All the incredibly difficult tasks got left to the priest to do, he mused. But that is maybe as it should be, eh?

"Augustine, as it turns out, you are what they call prediabetic. Do you know what that means?"

Her eyes were riveted on his, suddenly very alert. So, it was true. The doctor and Joseph had been hiding something.

"Am I going to die?"

Emile smiled as reassuringly as he could, yet the smile was unavoidably bleak. Damn! He liked this stubby little woman. She did not say much but she was no fool and she didn't waste time with nonessentials.

"No, no, no, it doesn't mean that. It means that you might get diabetes in the future, and then -- well, it's hard to say. There is not too much to be done about it, except pray. But that is, only if you get it. With a bit of good sense and luck, you won't get it at all and then there is nothing to worry about."

"Dr. Gendreau said they might -- induce the baby. Am I going to lose it?"

"There is no more danger in that than there is in any birth, I think. You will have to go to the hospital."

Augustine was no longer looking at her brother in law, she was staring through the window at the blinding white and blue world beyond, distorted by the frost on the pain, and somehow remote, as if she was looking at a picture on the wall of a different land, a different age. It seemed so far away. She hardly felt like part of it. Lying here, swollen like a toad, with the incubus child inside her moving sluggishly as if it too were bloated by sickness, she felt only half human any longer. The rest of her seemed to have turned back into some kind of leech. Looking down at this strange unknown body, she had a taste of panic. Of course, she could not see her legs or feet and perhaps, with a varicose vein, that was just as well. The disgusting spectacle was safely hidden behind the tremendous bulge of her womb, itself traced with brown stretch marks that made her want to weep when she thought back to the small unmarked belly that had once, so long ago, been hers. And the bosoms, as she called them, which had once rose miraculously in the air now hung like blubbery pouches, marked with small brown scars of their own. Worst of all was the weight which pulled at all her limbs, pinned her to the bed so surely that it was only with enormous effort and help from at least one other person that she could even make it to the floor to squat over the porcelain bedpan. While squatting, she trembled from the effort of fighting against gravity that seemed twice as strong as ever.

"Am I going to die, Emile?" She asked again, this time in a tone that demanded the straight facts.

"Augustine, of course we are all going to die –"

"Do not fence with me! Is this diabetes going to kill me?"

"It could -- if you get it." He shrugged. "You're more prone to it now than other people. He looked her in the eyes directly. Do not worry too much about it. Just do as the doctor says and you will probably be fine."

"I'm not so sure I would not welcome it," she said.

Emile started to correct her, to warn her that it was a sin to harbor such a thought. But stopped himself.

Instead, wearily, he said: "I understand how you feel."

"I doubt that, Emile. I doubt that very much. You should be me for a while. You should be a woman and see –" she, too, stopped herself, alarmed by the words coming out of her mouth. She had been on the verge of saying, "you don't even know what it's like to be a man, let alone a woman. How can you understand anything?" Yet her brother- in-law or not, even if he insisted on a first name relationship with family, Emile Labouchere was still Holy Father and Augustine's lifetime of training to respect such a one held her tongue in check now.

Death! At the moment, she longed for it. Could it be so terrible compared to this. But then she thought of the children and the look that would be on their little faces at the funeral, and all her instincts rose up against the dark, intruding notion of release from life. So long as one of the children lived, she was bound to the world, no matter how awful every moment became. She stared at the priest and was filled with astonishment that he could exist. It was hard enough for her to guess what kept men at their toil. She knew what it was that kept women alive, that was their children. The whole purpose of women's existence was to be found right there, in the force of her feelings for her children. But priests? For that matter, nuns? Without children to forge a meaning out of the vague stuff of their lives, why didn't they just lie down in a snowbank one night and pass on directly to heaven. That was the place they all seemed to be mostly concerned about, not life on earth at all.

Yet she could easily imagine Joseph having become a priest too. She did not think for a moment that he felt anything towards the children even close to the feeling she herself knew all the time. Except for Jean-Paul, perhaps, but Augustine had always sensed that it was not the boy that Joseph loved so much, it was rather something of himself that Joseph saw in him and loved. For she knew that Joseph loved himself more than anyone else on earth. She had never blamed him for it before, so long as he continued to love her second best. But now she wondered. Why had it been left to Emile to tell her about this pre-diabetes business? Could Joseph not bring himself to do it? And, if not, was it because of love or was it because he did not care enough?

"Emile," she said, struggling to rearrange her wobbly torso in a more comfortable position, "my head is confused. I am sorry. I didn't mean to speak to you the way I did. I appreciate you talking to me about the truth. I wish -- I just wish it had been Joseph."

"So, do I," said Emile stonily.

Sensing that she had pushed the boundaries of her privileged position as the priest's sister-in-law, she tried to back away by making light chatter. But nothing would pass through her lips. She felt too bitter, too heavy, too ugly, too lost.

Emile patted her hand and kissed her on the forehead.

"I must go. Vespers, you know. But do not worry, Augustine.

You will be fine. Your work is not done in the world, yet. Eh?" He nodded toward the mound.

With Ma Mere confined to her bed and Grande Ma Mere running the house with unemotional efficiency, the children turned to Bernadette to comfort them. Even Jean-Paul wanted her to stay and read stories at night. Bilou whimpered if she was not allowed to sit next to her oldest sister at supper.

Monica and Cecile, who looked so much alike despite the year between them that few aunts and uncles could ever get their names straight, now eagerly sought Bernadette's help on every little matter from washing the linoleum to darning socks. In the past, they had expressed a mutual disinterest in anything the oldest girl had to say. But the removal of Ma Mere from the centre of activity had pulled away the single pillar upon which their rebelliousness had been based. Most surprisingly of all, Teresa dropped her usual attitude of spite, and for the first time that Bernadette could remember, actively cooperated.

In the normal course of events, the Labouchere children were divided into five distinct camps. The babies, Loretta and Bilou, whose needs were too basic to be dissimilar and who seemed to do much of their crying and screaming as a team, the second team of Monica and Cecile, the look-alikes, Jean-Paul, who lived a virtually independent existence, mostly outside somewhere playing hockey or lacrosse or exploring with his friends, Teresa who usually stayed at her mother's side, and Bernadette who stayed mostly to herself, watching what was going on around her with far more attentiveness than any of the younger siblings.

But Ma Mere's virtual absence changed all that. The five separate camps were united, at least inside the house, into a single unit with Bernadette at its head.

Grande Ma Mere's only objective in life seems to be to keep them all busy. She kissed them perfunctorily on the cheek before they went to bed at night, but it was left to the older girls to organize the getting-to-bed operation. It was then, when they were alone, that they could express all their laments and complaints and comfort one another.

Bernadette now found herself in the evening in the unusual situation of sometimes having to put her arms around chubby Teresa, hugging her and wiping tears from her eyes. Until then, the two of them had never done anything but fight. Bernadette was surprised by the tenderness she suddenly felt towards her old arch enemy. Poor Teresa, she was so worried about Ma Mere. And even if she was fat and always used to be so horrible, Bernadette did not have the heart any longer to laugh at her and call her names.

It was Bernadette who suggested to the other children that they get together after the babies were in bed and say the rosary aloud to pray for Ma Mere to get better. On their knees, led by Bernadette, Teresa, Jean-Paul, Cecile and Monica muttered their way through the Lord's Prayer, Angelical Salutations and the Apostles Creed. The door to the bedroom was slightly ajar, and each of the children was perfectly aware that Grande Ma Mere and Mon Pere and once even the Reverend Father Emile were standing quietly in the hallway listening. The morning after the first night they tried this, they were allowed into Ma Mere's downstairs room to see her even before breakfast. Weeping, she had hugged them one by one. "Your Papa says you are all praying for me. Oh, my children, I love you." The children had wept in her arms and they crowded onto the bed around her all trying to hug and be hugged at once.

Blushing with pleasure, Bernadette overheard the Reverend Father Uncle Emile tell Mon Pere:

"That Bernadette, she is a real little mother. Intelligent, too. I can tell by the gleam in her eyes, eh? She is good in school, I bet."

It was true. Bernadette had taken instantly to learning. She had a bright, quick mind, and although none of the Sisters of the Precious Blood Parish Church treated her with any degree of respect that her old piano teacher, Mrs. Allenby, had shown, they nevertheless displayed an appreciation for her ability to grasp a subject. And nowhere had that ability shown itself faster than in her very first days at school, when she had grasped the essential fact of life in the classroom. Power was vested purely in the hands of the nuns. Little boys were stripped of it. But girls, if they were careful not to be silly and lucky enough to be able to understand what the nuns were saying, could become important, getting to sit at the front of the room and having their work held up as an example to the others, that they would do well to copy. In her five years at school, first at the Sacred Cross Mission in Agassiz, and now at Precious Blood, Bernadette wasted no time fighting with the stiff, starched Sisters whose rule was enforced by a yardstick that made a swish that could be heard right across the classroom before the loud clap was connected with the open palm.

Bernadette had passed through the Catholic school system all the way to grade five with the unusual distinction of never once having been whacked or strapped. There were only a handful of girls she knew who could make such a claim, and of course, no boys. In fact, she loved school and did not mind at all that the nuns wielded their yardsticks almost as often as they did their chalk. The moments she did not like it in school were those when the nuns were out of the room and the boys began firing their peashooters and hurling straws with gum stuck on the end at the ceiling. The entire class had been known to have to stay as much as three hours after school until someone confessed to one crime or another and was sent to Father Begin to be strapped.

Otherwise, Bernadette loved nothing better than to stick her face between the pages of a book. It was far better than helping Ma Mere with the housework. Bernadette looked forward to the classes at Precious Blood in the way that most other children look forward to recess or holidays. In Agassiz, she had been cut off from the other boys and girls her age by virtue of not being good enough at English. Now, though they spoke French around her, she was still the latecomer. Most of the others had been in the same classroom with each other since the first day of school and tended to snub her at first as a "country kid". Then, when she began to demonstrate marked superiority in lessons and was promoted by the nuns to the front row, she found herself further isolated

It was fine with her. Most of the other girls squealed too much, said things that were even dumber than the things Teresa said, and of course the boys were dangerous little animals who filled her with contempt. She secretly exalted every time one of them got a taste of the yardstick. If it were not for the danger of having her hair pulled or being pushed down or snowballed or splashed by the packs of boys that ran around wildly in the schoolyard before classes, she would not have bothered to stand in a group with the other girls at all. As it was, she did so just for protection, and had grown quite used to being called "snotty". She would stand, slightly apart from the other girls, or her back pressed against the wrought iron bars that surrounded the school ground, while snowballs whistled through the air, alert and wary least one should hit her, somehow maintaining a stance that suggested a visitor rather than an inmate of the brick and iron cage that contained them.

Rather than feeling lonely, Bernadette savored her isolation. She considered herself a tragic figure, a young woman whose chance to be a great concert pianist had been dashed by an uncaring father. Her loss set her apart. None of the others had ever been a protege. There was no one with whom she could share her secret tragedy but so far this had not bothered her. Her intent was to suffer in silence. And instead of complaining, to bend over backwards at home being a little saint. No one would notice her suffering and saintliness, of course, except the Virgin Mary, and when it came time to die and go to heaven, Bernadette was absolutely certain that a grand piano would be waiting for her, and Mon Pere might even get sent to purgatory for having treated her so thoughtlessly.

If she could not be a pianist in this life, she could at least be a martyr and she would enjoy the martyrdom. It kept alive the sense that she was special, which the piano -- or was it Mrs. Allenby? -- had given her a sense that she wasn't ordinary. Everything else in life conspired to make her as much like the other girls around her as possible, even though she thought they were brainless and that the school grounds at lunch time were as noisy and silly as chicken coops in the backyard. Often, when she was looking at one of her peers in the eye, pretending to listen to what they were saying, she was actually thinking, exultantly, I am smarter than you. Humiliated by being struck by a snowball and made to cry, the worst thing she could think to call her assailant was "Stupid".

It was a word she had often used to describe Teresa and which she threw out at Jean-Paul, time and again, but with no effect. Teresa took the insult seriously enough so that she considered it legitimate grounds for revenge. Jean-Paul carried on with whatever he was doing. The truth was that Bernadette didn't really think Jean-Paul was all that stupid, compared to the kids at school, at any rate. Maybe it was because he stood out already. First, he was almost always the smallest boy attached to any team or gang. He had more freckles than anyone else in the neighborhood. He was eager to prove he could run as fast as anyone and would challenge any boy, no matter what age or how large, to an arm wrestle. His arm was thin but surprisingly strong. His nickname quickly became "Dynamite Jean."

At lacrosse or on the ice rink or the baseball field, "Dynamite Jean" was never picked first, because of his size, but as soon as the obvious first choices, the boys who weighed the most or had the longest legs or stood the tallest had been picked, "Dynamite Jean" came next. He was a popular choice because he darted about so quickly, he was hard to catch up with or stop and he never seemed to run out of wind.

From the Basilica to the Saint Boniface hospital was only a five-minute walk; from the hospital to the Provencher Bridge was only seven minutes; and from the hospital to Joseph's clothing store, across from City Hall, no more than ten. The physical closeness of the cathedral, hospital, bridge and City Hall was matched by the intimacy of their origins.

The hospital and the church grew out of the rocks at the same time. Both of them founded by the Sisters of Charity, otherwise known as the Grey Nuns, who arrived at the forks of the Red and Assiniboine rivers in 1844, having traveled by canoe from Montreal, a journey that involved no less than eighty portages, wading through muskeg, assailed by mosquitoes and black flies. It took forty-nine days to travel from the largest French city on the continent to the smallest new settlement. In those days, there were no bridges, only steam driven ferries and shallow bottomed Red River barges.

Thirty years were to pass before the first locomotive would arrive from the east. When a bridge was finally built, it would be named after a Bishop and when enough people had settled on the east bank to decide to give themselves a name other than the Red River Forks, they would name their community after a saint. It was not just that the church had left its imprint on Saint Boniface, rather it had shaped the place from its very beginning. The first white couple to emerge from the eastern Canadian woods and wander out onto the flattened ocean bottom were French. It was here, at the Forks, that they settled, on soil now covered by a seven-storey hospital, only a stone's throw away from the cathedral which stood in place of the original missionaries' house.

It was Augustine's first visit to the hospital as a patient, her first visit to any hospital in such a role. She clenched her teeth and prayed. At least there were Holy Water fonts and crucifixes in each room and there were as many nuns as nurses. Priests pattered back and forth in the hallways, everyone was French, everyone was Catholic. Joseph was the only ten minutes away. Emile was only five minutes away. Two of the nuns and one of the nurses were cousins. She had dozens of aunts and sisters who lived within walking distance.

Still, she felt more alone than she could remember ever feeling before. Most of her other babies had been born in the same bed where they had been conceived, the only exception being Bilou, conceived in Agassiz and born within hours of arriving in Saint Boniface. The one that would soon begin its violent journey out from her body would be the first to emerge into the porcelain and tile sterility of an operating room, under the glare of blinding lights, surrounded by strangers. When Augustine learned that not even her own mother would be allowed in during the delivery, she wept.

It was April 10. Normally, she would expect to wait another two weeks before her labor began, but Dr. Gendreau had insisted that she enter the hospital now.

"The cervix is ripe," he said. "If we wait any longer there is a chance you might go into convulsions. As it is, your blood pressure has gone down, and you are retaining far too much fluid."

She hardly needed to be reminded of that. For weeks, she had been keeping her eyes fixed on the ceiling, the walls, the window, anywhere but her body. Yet morbidly she found her gaze creeping back again and again to the puffy arms, the sausage-like fingers. Her eyes were misty half the time and she went through two or three handkerchiefs a day. The only times when she appeared at all like her usual self were when the children paid their daily visits, or when Joseph sat down with her after work.

She had felt frightened at this stage before -- the fear was anything but new, but this time there was an element of horror as well. This change in her body made her feel as though she had contacted some disease. The doctor kept saying it was not a disease, but with a name like toxemia what else could it be? She felt invaded. It was as though the infant straining and kicking inside her had displaced all the liquid normally in her middle parts, forcing it under pressure into her limbs, like filling a pouch with water. Every other child had felt at least that it fitted inside her, hand in glove, taking its place between her heart and intestines as snugly as another organ. But now it was as if she was completely plugged up. Even her pores were sealed, and nothing could escape. As the child grew, it kicked and thrust everything aside, disrupting her whole body from head to toe. It did not really feel like her child. In her melancholy, Augustine frequently dwelled on the notion that the fetus was not a child at all. Its movements were too jerky, too twitchy, too inconsiderate.

Once she had blurted aloud to her mother, "they have put an animal inside me!"

On the way down to the hospital, with Joseph driving through the April slush so cautiously one would have thought that the road was pure ice, Augustine had said:

"I think this one just might be a boy, Joseph."

"Oh well, we do not get our hopes up yet, cher."

"But it feels different, more like with Louis and Jean-Paul than with the girls."

"Oh well, we shall see."

Certainly, there was one respect in which the fetus was different than any other she had held within her before. It was huge. The other babies had all been around seven pounds at birth. None had been as large as this one. She dreaded the moment of its delivery because it was almost certain it would be bloated like herself, ugly, diseased.

From the car she was taken in a wheelchair up the elevator to the 6th floor, the maternity ward, and helped out of her clothes into a white gown. She felt ashamed that even a nun should see her body in its present state.

"That's a bad vein you've got there, child" The nun said unhelpfully.

How did the nun feel, looking upon a woman paying the price for the companionship of a man? Was she disgusted? Filled with pity? Did she feel superior? Or was she in fact full of envy? Normally, Augustine's feelings toward nuns were tinged with condescension. She felt vaguely sorry for them -- not sorry in the sense she thought they did that poorly in life, sorry in the way that one felt towards a cripple. Never to hold one's own warm wiggling baby in one's arms, never to have its softness pressed against one's flesh, to watch the process of it discovering of the world, the puzzlement in its eyes, it's first attempts to smile -- Life as a woman without babies was unimaginable to Augustine. Yet now, in her grotesque baby-swollen body, she found herself wondering if the nuns weren't perhaps smarter than she thought. They looked so clean and trim and untroubled, while she felt dishevelled, sweaty, close to panic as the thought of what lay ahead.

Joseph and Grande Ma Mere Lagimodiere were in the corridor when the nun, accompanied by a nurse who looked to be hardly more than a child, pushed Augustine by on a bed mounted on rubber wheels heading towards the operating room.

Augustine's lips felt dry and her hands were trembling. Joseph leaned over to kiss her on the forehead while her mother squeezed her hand. The old lady clutched her rosary, muttering either a prayer or a curse, it was hard to tell from her expression. She was furious at this madness of her daughter being taken away into a locked-up room to have the baby forced out of her body, and she had fought to the last minute to ignore the doctor's orders. But her son-in-law had gone along with the doctor, appalled by the deathly pallor of his wife's face and the stench of her breath, and not entirely sure that his mother-in-law's warnings about hospitals weren't true. He tried to make a joke.

"Your mother tells me she's going to stand by the door to the room there until they come out with the baby and then she's going to follow the nurse to where they take them afterwards and then stand guard to make sure no one switches babies around, eh? Ha, Ha."

Augustine tried to smile but failed. Grande Ma Mere fixed a stern glare on Joseph and kept on muttering her prayers -- or curses. Then the nun and the nurse had the bed in motion again, and the doors to the operating room were swinging open. Augustine squeezed her eyes shut, afraid to look. She had never been in a chamber such as this before.

Doctor Gendreau was in his late sixties, a thin, drab man whose favorite grey suit hung on his frame as if discarded. He bore a perennial expression of tiredness. Life had been searing him down for so long that he could no longer be bothered to muster so much as a change of expression in response to its ceaseless demands. In his white gown and mask, his voice muffled, his eyes seemed even more mournful than usual. He didn't believe in wasting what breath remained in his fragile rib cage, so he went directly to work. Augustine was rolled onto the operating table with deft movements by the two nuns and two nurses in attendance. Desperately she filled her head with the sound of Hail Mary's and Our Fathers. A single glance at doctor Gendreu's face convinced her that there was nothing to be learned by watching him. The nurses and nuns were careful not to look at her directly. Rather they studied her body like some sort of cow at an auction, discussing its condition among themselves in muted voices. It was as though none of them was aware that inside the body there was a human being -- two human beings. Augustine cringed at the site of an array of stainless-steel cutting tools, both large and small, on the nearby trolley. They glittered under the rays of the huge overhead light.

Her body was rigid, and she clutched the sides of the table. Surely this was a mistake? Any second now Joseph would come through the door and push them all aside, Wheeling her away, taking her home.

How could she even be sure that the man behind the mask was Gendreau. There was a crucifix on the wall above the tray with its fancy meat cutting equipment. She stared at it over the heads of the nuns, thankful that the plaster of paris Christ was pure white rather than being one of those painted ones that always bled.

The nurses were near the end of their shift. Their legs hurt from hurrying up and down the long hallways. Their feet were sore. One of them had missed her lunch break and was ravenously hungry. Doctor Gendreau had already done five operations.

The nuns alone seemed unhurried, and it was them that Augustine turned her eyes imploringly, wishing that one of them at least would look back at her directly, instead of glancing at her furtively, then looking away. It was as though they felt guilty or ashamed. Were they secretly in a plot to murder the baby?

How did she know they were really nuns? She had never seen

them before. And that nurse -- so young. Just a child. What could she possibly know about having babies?

Without warning, the older nun clamped a cotton rag across her mouth and nose and lifted a bottle high over her face, allowing a few drops to spill down onto the rug. Instinctively, Augustine squirmed to free herself, grasping at the nun's cold bony hand.

"No, no, daughter," the nuns said together. One of them seized her left arm and firmly pinned it to the table. The young nurse grabbed the other, and though Augustine tossed her head and made a muffled protest, the rag remained clamped firmly over her lower face. She tried not to breathe for a moment but was finally forced to gasp for air. The sting of the ether burned the lining of her nose and made her gag, then choke, then set her to coughing harshly. She could not believe what was happening to her. What were they doing? Why was Doctor Gendreau allowing this? It was outrageous. She started to cry from anger, shame, humiliation, and then, with horror, realized that the remaining nurse was pulling up her gown and lashing leather straps around her thighs.

Through all this, the doctor stood to the side, his hands dangling idly in front of him. He was staring into space, his mind off somewhere else. Her sudden burst of panicky struggle triggered a string of spasms in the baby, setting elbows and knees to stabbing painfully against the organs around it. Then her stomach gave a strange whooshing sideways kind of lurch and it felt for a second as the half of her head had been sheared away. Everything came back into place, but instead of there being two nuns and two nurses hovering above her, struggling to hold her down, there were eight. Or was it ten? Or was it a small crowd? Astonished, Augustine stopped struggling and stared ahead, blinking and squinting as much in wonder as confusion.

Voices were disembodied. Even when she could make out someone's mouth moving, it seemed that the voice came from somewhere else, and it bloomed more than it should, like a voice of a person ten feet tall.

"We do not have to use the arm straps!"

For a long moment, Augustine was a little girl again, back on her grandparents' farm in Saint Norbert, playing with her sisters in the barn with the new litter of cats, all of them black as coal. Rays of afternoon sun fell in narrow dusty shafts through the cracks in the roof and the hay smelled so rich that it left her giddy with happiness at the pure joy of being alive. The kittens made the tiniest sounds she had ever heard, complaining each time their mother dragged her delicate tongue across their fur, or took their necks in her teeth, holding them without moving for minutes at a time. How sly and aware of every little detail the cat had seemed, and how she closed her eyes and purred while the fuzzy little balls butted and wiggled at her teats, climbing on top of each other --

Then pain stabbed at the very centre of her being. Her body jerked wildly. The doctor had slipped a foot-long stainless-steel hook into her vagina, through the cervix, and had nicked the membrane of the womb.

"More ether!"

"Did that get it?"

"I think so. Oh hell, look at the amniotic fluid?"

"It is black, doctor."

"I know that, Miss Patenaude. It is full of meconium. It should be clearer. We have got a problem of fetal distress here —"

The pain was gone as quickly as it came, but Augustine could not stop shivering in fear of its return. Nor could she stop coughing as the ether seeped into her lungs.

"OK, that is enough. Let us see what happens."

The mask was removed from her face and the nuns and nurses stepped away. An image came to remind her of a Christmas turkey left on a table, the dinner guests standing around, waiting for the signal to begin to feast. She felt cold, then hot. Dizzy. Fever. Her arms were free, but she had no idea of what to do with them.

Scarcely a minute or two had passed before she felt a familiar spasm. The first contraction. Whatever Doctor Gendreau had done, it worked. Labor had begun.

"OK, that is it," said the doctor.

Promptly, her legs were unstrapped, and she was rolled back onto the bed with wheels. Before she quite realized what was happening, the same nun and nurse were pushing her out of the operating room and down the hall. Both Joseph and her mother were hurrying along beside her, but the nun would not slow down.

"There is still a long time to go." she announced. "You can wait for her in the other room,"

Thirteen hours of labor lay ahead, a labor that seemed curiously unreal to Augustine. Never having had either before, she remained in a dreamy state, forgetting from time to time where she was or even who she was. Breathtaking knots of agony formed time and again in her flesh. For a long period, she controlled her desire to scream. But in the final four hours, she no longer cared. Never had a delivery taken so long. Maybe some others -- the first, yes, the first one for sure -- had been as painful, but if so, she had forgotten just how much it hurt. Her body felt nowhere as strong as it used to. But then she remembered how her father had forced her to lift him off the ground when she was yet only a child to impress his guests -- and a surge of pride went through her, Of course she was strong enough! When, at last, they came and took her back into the operating room, she was so exhausted she could hardly lift her arms. Yet they insisted on strapping her arms down as well as her legs, a ripple of rage went through her. Strapdown like this, like an animal that could not be trusted. The one thing it did for her was remove any last trace of a sense of dignity. If they would treat her like this, she would let herself go completely. And so, she screamed and grunted and howled and found a certain bitter relief in not having to pretend to be brave or even human. At the very end she bore down in a vengeful desire to hurl the baby out like a cannonball into Doctor Gendreau's face. She no longer cared whether it was a boy or a girl, or for that matter whether it lived or died, all she wanted was to have it *out... out ...OUT.* She pushed so furiously that blood vessels in her face burst by the hundreds, leaving her cheeks speckled with blue black dots.

The baby was large: Nine pounds, ten ounces. Its eyes were wide open when the nun held it up, wrapped in a blanket. It made a single tiny cry, then lapsed into silence. Its pupils, never before exposed to light, filled its eyes entirely. All Augustine could see were two black holes, glistening in the reflection of the operating room lights, as bottomless as night.

"Oh, give him to me," Augustine gasped.

The nun laughed. "No, no, it is a she."

"Oh shit," said Augustine.

It was the first time she had ever sworn in front of a nun. Unable to stop herself, she began to cry.

Rene Gendreau eyed his patient with much sympathy. He knew that what he had to tell her was going to cause a lot of grief. He looked at Joseph, sitting on the stiff-back wooden chair by the bed, and felt no sympathy either.

Raised a Catholic, the doctor had long since stopped going to church except on social occasions like Easter, Christmas, funerals, christenings, marriages. He did not doubt for a moment that there was a brilliant powerful God behind everything, some entity that was at least as far above puny humans as humans were above bacteria. But not since medical school days had he paid serious attention to anything said by a priest. And if there was one Catholic teaching that the weary, greying general practitioner disputed, it was the prohibition on contraception.

"If you follow the logic," he was fond of saying," then any man who has a wet dream, murders a million babies in his sleep."

He frankly admitted that he found the business of giving birth to be dangerous, messy, torturous -- and a hell of a lot of work and responsibility to boot.

He had delivered more than five hundred of the bleeding little devils and had never lost a mother. It was only partially that he was lucky. The other part was that these peasouper women were tough. It was almost like it was bred into them, as though generations of the Cradle Revenge had made them into highly specialized stock, fit for a steady diet of dumping infants into the world, but not much more.

Rene Gendreau's own wife had been dead nearly twenty years. He had only three children, did not remarry, and never intended to. In his opinion, it was obscene in this day and age to carry on having babies by the dozen. There were other things to do in life. Or there should be. The trouble was no one ever asked for his opinion on the matter. In Saint Boniface, the issue of contraception was a religious issue, not a medical one. It was the priests who gave instructions on this count to the husbands and wives, not the doctors.

Well, for a change, the doctor was going to have his say. And the priest could go hang themselves.

"As far as I can tell, the child is just fine," he was saying, "and your own condition has obviously already begun to improve."

Augustine glared at him but was unable to dispute what he had had to say. The swelling had gone down enough so that within a day or two, she expected to be able to fit her rings back on. The blubbery mass of her belly would take much, much longer, if, indeed, it ever went back down at all. But her breasts were flowing with milk, the baby was taking it without difficulty, and so she had little to complain about. At the thought of ever again being trapped in an operating room, she shuddered, and would not allow Doctor Gendreau to touch the infant. She was still furious with him for the way he had let the nuns and nurses treat her.

For his part, the doctor knew exactly the way Augustine felt toward him. He did not mind in the least. He preferred it. A long time ago he had taken the attitude that gentle persuasion was a time consuming, inefficient way to conduct a delivery. The object was to get both mother and child through it alive. There was no way it could be a picnic -- and, finally, it was Rene Gendreaur's private theory that by deliberately not pampering women in labor, he helped in the long run to discourage them from getting pregnant again.

When they screamed, his general reaction was. "You asked for it, Madame. Don't cry to me."

Now he felt a sour sense of satisfaction. It was clear from the look on her face that this one, at least, had got the message. She was alive. The baby was alive. What more could she ask for? Left to her own devices or the half-baked superstitions of her ignorant mother, she would be dead by now, and so would the child, that was for sure.

"Thank you, doctor," Joseph was saying, looking nervous and ill-at-ease, "with all the troubles there were, it's a miracle eh, that they are alive?"

Doctor Gendreau blinked. He stifled a sarcastic remark.

"Monsieur Labouchere, I asked you up to the hospital tonight, because your wife will be going home tomorrow, and she will be back to normal, more or less, quite soon. I put some stitches in, but she can come back in a week and I shall take them out. You never had stitches before, did you? Madame."

Augustine shook her head solemnly, thinking. Quite a few things happened this time that never happened before, you evil old goat!

"Some doctors do not believe in it. Stitches, that is. They say it just makes it harder the next time. Generally, I think that way myself, but in your case it is different."

He paused, looking at Joseph, making it clear by his tone that what he had to say next was too important merely to be said to the woman.

"Why is that doctor?"

Gendreau did not answer immediately. He savored the suspense. Also, he could tell that the woman had been bitching to her husband about her treatment in the operating room, and the husband was squirming, not able to bring himself to complain directly, but uncomfortable because of the pressure from his wife to do so. Why was it that the authority surrounding a doctor had so much greater effect on men than women? Men were willing to treat a doctor almost like a priest, but women seemed suspicious, and they were quick to criticize. Whatever the reason, it was easier to keep the men in line.

"I will put this as simply as I can, Monsieur. While your wife is not flagrantly diabetic, she should not have another child!"

Their reactions flickered nakedly across their faces, then, in both cases, were masked for good. But in those few seconds, the doctor saw what they truly felt. In Augustine's eyes, a spark of excitement was viable, a wild instant relief.

But Joseph was clearly stricken. It was as though a death sentence had been pronounced. He stood up suddenly and was halfway through the gesture of reaching for his hat to remove it before he checked himself. His mouth worked soundlessly -- and then the moment of befuddlement passed, and he snarled: "What the hell are you saying doctor?"

Augustine sagged into her pillows, flopping on her side, and buried her face in her hands.

Doctor Gendreau remained seated, not certain whether to take Joseph's anger seriously or not. As for the woman, why was she crying? He did not know. He was sure it was the best news she'd heard in a long time. Of course, it meant that Joseph wouldn't get to have his precious second son, but that was the way it was.

"Sit down, sit down, Monsieur," the doctor said irritably. "I'm just telling you what you both have to know. If you like, I shall explain it to your brother too, so he can counsel you on the, uh, spiritual aspects of the situation."

"What is wrong? Why can she not have any more children? She is only in her early thirties. Why my mother –"

"Your mother was not diabetic. Your wife is, Monsieur. If you go ahead and make her pregnant again, I cannot guarantee her survival. As it is, so long as her body does not go through any violent biological changes, that swelling will continue to go down and she will be as good as normal, but she's definitely reached the stage of mild diabetes. If it gets any worse, she is in trouble. And if she has another baby, well, you can almost be sure it will kill her. I cannot make it any clearer, Monsieur. Believe me."

Joseph staggered over to the wall and leaned his forehead against it, balancing on his toes, his hands clasped behind his back. Softly he said: "But doctor how do we ---"

"Not have babies?" Gendreau could not keep the triumph out of his voice. "Well, if you stick strictly to what the church says, you will have to abstain, that is all. But I guess you would have to ask your brother about that, Monsieur Labouchere. If you ever decide not to listen to what he says, he can always ask me. I am quite familiar with contraception."

Joseph made no response. Augustine was curled up, sobbing, beating one's fist against the mattress.

Suddenly, the old doctor felt no satisfaction at all. For a few minutes there, he had looked forward to striking one more blow against superstition, forcing this little bourgeoisie couple to their senses, kicking the ass of the Vatican, getting even for all those years of being ignored by brain washed peasants, smug in their dogmas, following priests around like puppies.

But the blow had landed wrong. Didn't it always. It never seemed that he could find a place to strike that would ever have any kind of effect, except, like now, to squeeze a bit more anguish into the world. For the most part, Doctor Gendreau's cynicism more than balanced his sense of sadness of life, but for the moment the best he could manage was a neutral feeling.

Tiredly, he got up and shuffled to the door.

"It will be feeding time soon, Madam Labouchere,' he said softly. "They will be bringing the baby in. Monsieur, if you are listening, I have only one thing to add that you must remember. Your wife's life is in your hands. Either you learn to control your urges, or she quite probably will die. I do not say that lightly. Do you hear me?"

Joseph's forehead was still pressed fiercely against the plaster wall and his hands were still clenched behind his back. He had made no move to comfort his sobbing wife. Nor did he make any effort to answer.

Doctor Gendreau took a deep breath, preparing himself to yell at the man, but changed his mind. What is the point? Either they would understand --- or ---

The moment he left the room, Augustine rolled over on her back and whispered:

"Joseph!"

He ignored her. she could see that his body was quivering. For a moment she had, indeed, felt a surge of relief at the thought of not having to go through the hell she just been through again, but then the meaning of it stuck. She would lose Joseph. It was not that he would run away, she was sure of that. It was that she would not be able to possess him again. What would they do? Sleep in separate beds? Separate rooms? Never to ---Oh no!

"Joseph!"

Slowly, he straightened. When he turned to face her, his expression was impassive. Not even after all the years together could she read anything from the arrangement of his features. He might be waiting for a streetcar for all she could tell. And that was the most frightening part of it, for Joseph's face was usually an open book. Somehow, for the first time she could remember, he had managed, in the midst of an emotional situation, to clamp a wax mask over his soul, to hide his inner turmoil completely.

"Joseph!"

"It is alright, ma chere!" He sat beside her," looked at her briefly -- nothing to read in his eyes either -- and folded his arms gently around her shoulders, pulling her head against his chest, kissing her hair. He rubbed her back. "I love you, ma chere. It does not matter -- about the other. I love you, that is all."

"Joseph, am I going to lose you?"

He grunted and it sounded negative, but she could not really tell.

Ma Mere came home from the hospital a changed woman. She held the infant as if she were doing penance. There were momentary bursts of motherly squealing and squeezing, but after a few seconds Augustine's expression would sober, she would almost seem to correct herself, and she would handle the child more or less, impersonally.

Augustine had felt this way once before, when she had been in mourning for her first-born son. Now she was in mourning for a son who would never be born at all. She mourned also because the happiest marriage in the world -- her own -- was shattered at his core.

"Ma Mere," Bernadette asked, "why are you not happy? The baby is fine. You are getting better. Mon Pere seems ---happy." She paused there, not certain if happy was the right word. She meant that Joseph seemed far away in his head, not really in the same room as the rest of them, but at least he showed no sign of a bad mood. He must, she concluded, be, therefore happy.

Her mother looked at her sadly, and said, "It will get better, little petunia. Do not worry. Being sick like that and having a baby at the same time, it is hard on you, eh?

"It is just taking me awhile to get over it. I will be alright soon". She forced a fragile smile, and then looked quickly away.

The baby was named Jacqueline at Grande Ma Mere suggestion, after one of Augustine's cousins. No one at home was enthusiastic about the name but no one pressed forcibly for any other. It did not seem to matter. Joseph himself paid little attention to it. This was only to be expected. The desire for another boy had been palatable, on top of the general worry about Augustine's health, the children had held their breath, fearing a calamity. The calamity was now occupying the bassinet from which Loretta had been moved, suffering the same displacement that each of the others, in their turn, had known at about the same tender age. Loretta had been luckier than the others for she had remained the baby of the family for close to two years before falling to the position of merely second youngest.

Only Grande Ma Mere reacted to the girl with any good grace at all. She could not have cared less whether it was a girl or a boy.

From her vantage point as the oldest child, Bernadette looked down on her newest sister, lying there emitting squall after squall that did not seem to impress anyone around her. She felt sorry for the lonely little thing -- but there were moments when there was no one around, when she wanted to pinch it as hard as she could.

The new arrival was unwelcome. How different it would have been, Bernadette thought, if it had a pee pee between its legs. All that fuss over such a silly little thing. It seemed to have made the difference between a life that presumably would have gone as before, only more so, and a life that now seemed changed beyond recognition. The unshakable harmony that had existed between her parents, and interplay that she had never seen fluctuate for so much as a single day, had for some unfathomable reason vanished. The only reason Bernadette could see for the stunning change was that the stupid baby had come out another girl instead of a boy, and absolutely no one wanted another girl. But there had been girl after girl before, and while the level of disappointment had risen steadily as each new arrival proved to be devoid of that special rubbery little toy, it had not affected the way Ma Mere's eyes sparkle when Mon Pere came into the room for that particular smile he displayed only for her. Often enough, Bernadette had envied her mother that smile.

And now it is gone.

Why? It could not just be the baby, for Ma Mere was still young and there would be more babies, wouldn't there?

But when she asked this question, Ma Mere kept her attention rigidly fixed on her laundry and said only, "stop chattering about babies!"

Eagerly, the children had been waiting for the word that Grande Ma Mere would move back to her own home, but it did not happen. The old woman announced her intentions to stay until Augustine was back to normal. Bernadette whispered to Teresa, "that means she's going to stay forever."

Teresa covered her eyes with her hands in horror.

A month had passed since Augustine's return from the hospital and although she limped toward the end of the day and still wore a bandage around her varicose vein, she had lost most of the extra weight she gained and should have been capable of running the house again. But she showed no sign of being interested. Instead, she seemed willing to re-enter what had once been her own domain as nothing more than one more of Grande Ma Mere's work slaves. The children were appalled.

Jean-Paul whispered in the dark one night after the lights were out, "If she stays, I'm running away."

Monica cried hopelessly. Grand Ma Mere's broom had become the most hated object in her life. And because Monica was crying, Cecile cried too. Soon, they were all crying. It was not just because their grandmother was staying.

There was also the sense of the loss of something invisible but basic to their well being. There was an intuition that Ma Mere had been hurt worse than she showed.

If the new baby cried in its bassinet, let it cry. Somehow, this was all its fault. The one thing the children all agreed on was that they did not like the new arrival. It was pure bad luck.

It was the presence of Grande Ma Mere and the new baby that the children believed accounted for their father's absence from the house so much of the time now. Mon Pere was hardly home a single evening of the week. And when he did come home, it was almost always after children had been marched off to bed and the lights turned out. They could hear him talking downstairs, always about affairs they did not understand. Ma Mere hardly ever did anything more than murmur a vague response.

He can't stand Grande Ma Mere anymore than we can, Teresa theorized. He hates the new baby, I know it. And him and the Ma Mere hardly talk to each other.

But by far the most ominous sign of some secret fissure in the firmament of their world was that it was Grande Ma Mere who slept with Ma Mere and the baby. Joseph slept in the parlor on the settee. Surely such a state of affairs couldn't last.

Yet no one had heard even a single harsh word exchanged between the two parents. It was maddening to know that something terrible had happened, but without knowing anything of what it was. Grande Ma Mere Lagimodiere herself did not know the truth. She knew only that her daughter had some kind of sickness and she guessed that Joseph didn't want to contact it, a sickness to do with a woman's insides. She guessed it would pass. It did not occur to her to ask the doctor what it was all about. Augustine's description of what it had been like in the operating room had only confirmed her suspicions about the medical profession, she had no wish to mingle with devils unnecessarily.

If Joseph seemed happy to his oldest daughter, it was because everything made sense to him.

Not since the night in the hospital when he had been told never to touch his beloved Augustine again had he entertained any doubts about the God given orderliness of life. He did not expect that life would be sweet forever, but what he did expect was that it would be arranged in some meaningful pattern. At the moment that was exactly how it seemed. He would not have dreamed to try to explain it to anyone, not even Emile. He doubted that he could "explain" it to himself. All he knew was that he felt a calm certainty that everything was being taken care of. Maybe this was what was meant by the word "serenity". Each day, it seemed to him, there was some new evidence of the invisible hand of God was at work behind the scenes.

PART FIVE

THE BRIDGE

1931

Just one day after the session at the hospital, Joseph had been approached by Jacques Saint-Pierre, the Chamber of Commerce secretary, and invited to attend a meeting designed to deal with the Letellier affair.

Stepping into the parlor at Charles Deschamps' place had been like stepping on stage, acting a part in a play. Every pair of eyes in the room had riveted on him, as though the twenty odd men gathered there had been waiting for no one else.

The lawyer, Leon Beaujeu, was there. Immediately, he said: "Monsieur Labouchere, for some time now you have been saying things like "Remember Batoche" and "No burial for the traitor in sacred ground." Until now, no one wanted to press you too hard because of your wife's condition, and by the way, congratulations on the birth of your new daughter. But the time is getting close, Monsieur, and we expect that an attempt will be made shortly to bury Letellier's body on this side of the river. Some of us have been getting the distinct impression that you, yourself, have the intention of taking some action to try to stop this from happening.

"They will have to bury me before they bury Letellier," Joseph said.

Immediately, the room exploded in applause and cheers.

"Good for you, Labouchere!"

"We are with you!"

"Spoken like a Frenchman!"

"No burial!"

"NO BURIAL!"

When the noise had died down, it was Beaujeu who asked:

"Well and good, Monsieur. There is no one here who does not admire such a sentiment. Yet I still have no idea what steps you will take to prevent them from doing what they want. Remember, they will probably send in troops, Mounties, a strong force."

"I will meet them at the foot of the bridge and stop them there."

In the clamor that followed, with men jumping to their feet in a rush to be the next to pledge to go to the bridge only Joseph seemed unaffected. The thought of being martyred bothered him not at all. God's hand had to be at work here.

By the time the meeting broke up, everyone present was committed to going to the bridge. No one, including Joseph, had any clear idea of what would happen when they got there, but it no longer seemed to matter. What counted was that they would be there.

Bernadette could remember the days, back in Agassiz, when it seemed her father was the most important man in town, when the Labouchere name was the most famous, and everyone treated Joseph with respect, now it seemed that something of the sort was happening all over again in Saint Boniface, but in a different way.

Whereas, in Agassiz, it had all been very muted, very polite, now there was something frightening about Mon Pere's sudden fame. Bernadette did not like the look of the hulking, frowning men who came to pick Mon Pere up in the evening to take him to another meeting. She did not like the way that the Reverend Father uncle Emile drew Joseph away for huddled conversations at the end of the porch, out of everyone's hearing. She especially did not like the way Mon Pere seemed hardly to see Ma Mere any longer. And poor Ma Mere, her eyes were bleak as she bent resignedly over the new baby, feeding it milk, but milk alone. Just what the connection was between her father's importance and the baby at mama's breast, Bernadette could not imagine, yet it was just since the baby was born that life in the Labouchere home had done such a violent flip-flop. Grande Ma Mere seemed indifferent, secure in the unopposed tyranny she wielded. That was perhaps the worst part of it all. Having Grande Ma Mere take over the house, with Ma Mere sitting off blankly in a corner, weak and exhausted looking, completely submissive to her mother's will, and Mon Pere, well, he might as well have deserted us, thought Bernadette. He doesn't even play with Jean-Paul anymore.

Sundays were strange. At mass, people all over the church peered at Joseph and his family furtively. Children actually pointed their fingers, and while most of them just stared stupidly, a few stuck out their tongues. After mass, a little bit of space opened up between the Labouchere's and those around them. Men by the dozen greeted Joseph by name. Others tipped their hats at him, and they made comments like: "A fine thing you're doing, Labouchere!" "Bless you, my brother!" "I'll be there, too, Joseph!" "Hey, Joe! It's good!" Or: "Remember Batoche?" "No burial!" "To the bridge!" It was all very mysterious. What burial? What bridge? What Batoche? What was this fine thing that Mon Pere was doing? Once, she nerved herself to ask.

"Mon Pere, what are you doing that all the men talked to you about?"

He would look at her directly. "It is not for little girls to worry about," he said.

Bernadette boiled.

But it was hopeless to pursue the matter. She decided instead to ask Ma Mere if she might follow along to one of these meetings that took Joseph away almost every night, to see for herself what was going on.

"Your uncle Bert works at the stockyard," Augustine snapped. "Do you ask to go watch him kill pigs?"

Even the Reverend Father uncle Emile was closed mouthed.

"It's politics, my child," was all he would say, and found in a way that was meant to remind her that he was a priest as well as an uncle.

"What is politics, Ma Mere?"

It is a man's thing -- for elections -- or wars. She shuddered. Bernadette did not know for certain whether she should be angry with Mon Pere or whether she should pray for him. He seemed to have gone into one of his moods again. Only this time it was not wearing off. His face was slightly flushed. His hands, Bernadette noticed, trembled all the time. Not much, but it left an impression that her father was as fragile as a leaf. In fact, the veins of his hands reminded her exactly of that. His eyes were frequently blood-shot, and he seemed on the edge of a cold, but at the same time he was full of energy. He could scarcely sit still at the supper table, and he tended to eat at least twice as fast as his usual speed. For a change, he reminded her of Jean-Paul. Certainly, father was every bit as jittery and energetic as his son. Mon Pere was not steadfastly somber either. He had moments of laughter that went on much, much longer than normal, and while he seemed to enjoy it, he always ended up having to take off his glasses and wipe his eyes. And the laughter would seem to drain him for sometimes as much as half an hour afterwards. It was uncomfortable being around him. Sometimes it was scary.

Poor Mon Pere. He was being dragged away out into the big dangerous world, and he was so small, as men went, and he trembled -- whether from fatigue or excitement, she could not tell. She had always worried that something might happen to him. For, as much as she told herself she hated him, for ruining her chances to become a pianist, she also could not imagine life without him around, and she knew that Ma Mere would go into mourning and never come out. So she was bound to pray for his safety every night even though her last conscious thought before sleep might be an image of her father shrunk down to the size of a doll that she could spank as long and as hard as she liked.

Of the children, only Jean-Paul defended his father outright.

"Mon Pere only does what the Angels tell him to do," he shouted at the girls, "You do not know anything. I know. Because he told me, that is why!"

At school, the Labouchere girls found themselves often enough standing together, something they had never done before. Most of the other girls somehow seemed embarrassed to be near them. And "Dynamite Jean" found himself starting to have fights on a regular basis. It began when the big, curly-haired Laurent Trombley suddenly yelled at him, in the middle of a lacrosse game. "Your father is a girouette!" It was a word that was too sophisticated for Jean-Paul. It meant an agitator whose reputation seldom lasted overnight, a man with few principles or policies, a weathercock who would swing with any change in the wind of popular favour. Jean-Paul did not need to understand the word, however, to know that his father was being insulted.

He lost the fight but made a good showing. His face reddened and he drilled the Trombley boy with his fists, elbows, knees, feet, even batting with his head. It took the bigger boy nearly five minutes to pin Jean-Paul down solidly enough to start pummeling him and by that time the jostling circle of other boys had been pleased by Dynamite-Jean's performance. "Let him up," they shouted. The moment Trombley let go, however, Jean-Paul solely punched him in the eye. The fight went on for another five minutes before the Labouchere boy could be pinned down again. This time, Trombley pummeled him properly.

"Girouette! Girouette!" The word haunted them at the school grounds and on the way to and from school. Whatever Mon Pere was involved with, it was something that made some people mad at him, yet when the children went out with him to church, there was no sign of anything other than admiration. It was other children who were rude, and then only when there were no adults around, as though they had been privy to the honest opinions expressed only in the privacy of the homes. Out in the public world, no one raised a voice against Joseph. Yet underneath --

"They are jealous," said Jean-Paul, "That's all. They are jealous because our father is so famous and important, and the Angels talk to him."

Bernadette's own real fear was that Mon Pere was somehow making a fool of himself. The boys at school might be jealous, but she was sure that the girls were mostly full of nothing more than contempt. And, again, because she did not know what it was that Mon Pere was doing, she had no way of knowing how much shame to feel. It did not cross your mind to feel pride, for she assumed that everyone knew as well as she did about Mon Pere's moods, his shakiness, his ragged laugh.

Reverend Father Emile Labouchere paused at the train tracks on the eastern edge of town and swiveled on his heels to look at the Seine River. He was glad for the rivers, even if they were dangerous, unpredictable things with a hunger to crawl over the shoulders of the eroded loose clay ravines that normally contained them, spreading out as far as the horizon, converting the prairie for several miles on either side into a delta, as soggy as any flooded rice paddy lands in China., sometimes tearing down bridges, uprooting trees. Every spring there was a tense period where everyone waited to see how high the melted snow would flood. Every spring it was as though the water was responding to a prehistoric impulse to climb skyward, to fill up the whole bowl of plain from the Rocky Mountains to the eastern Canadian shield of ice scoured rock, from the Arctic Ocean to the Gulf of Mexico, to become again the mighty inland sea of bygone ages.

It would be pleasant to stand there, by the tracks, letting one's mind drift back across the millennia, sniffing the rotten cabbage, urine and mulch smell of the river, for a long, long time. But time was something he could not enjoy at all. Events were closing in. The Archbishop had left no room for maneuvering.

Damn His Grace! Emile thought with a bitter, frustrated bolt of anger. If only the old goat had had the brains to keep his nose out of the non-church aspect of this thing. It might have been so easy. But no, the Bishop had started panicking weeks ago, but it was not until this week that the desperate message he was sending to his superiors in Montreal had finally gotten through their thick skulls, and now Montreal was panicking too. The panic, Emile guessed, might not be quite so contagious in Rome, where, surely, cooler heads must prevail. The problem remained that the seasoned diplomats of the Vatican would no more want to get into an open struggle with the Canadian government now than they had a generation ago, when the last rebellion took place.

If only foolish old Bishop Tachereau had not reported what he was hearing from other priests with whom he had contact. After all, if he had turned a deaf ear, there could be no repercussions for him afterwards. He could always claim innocence – and, in truth, for a Bishop, he was innocent indeed. Too damned innocent. Emile moaned almost aloud. His plans had been so well laid. Without the Bishop crying to Montreal, the political forces down East would not have known what they would be running up against. All the meetings which had gone into the planning for the blockade of the bridge had been conducted behind locked doors. Nothing had leaked into the newspapers, and since no one who was English or non-Catholic had attended, it might have been a beautiful surprise. A victory to be relished. To be written into the history books. The day they closed the bridge down and sent the English conquerors, bearing Letellier's cursed coffin with them, back across the river. Let his remains rot in the same ground as theirs, but never among good Catholics. We could have surprised them, outnumbered them, beaten them. We had over one thousand men ready to join Joseph, all of them pledged in Jesus Christ's name to die rather than move aside. The funeral procession coming from the west side of the river would have been stopped, would have been forced to turn back. For the first time in oh so long, Frenchmen might look back at the

English with steady eye contact that came from the only kind of equality there was. Knowing you could win something, not just lose all the time.

All pissed away because the Bishop got wind of the battle that was shaping up and had called for guidance from Montreal, and Montreal had talked to the Vatican, and the Vatican had in turn instructed Montreal to talk to the government of Ottawa, in privacy, of course. And now Ottawa knew. The element of surprise was completely lost.

Who told Tachereau? Emile wondered again. But it was a useless question really, it was impossible to screen Tachereau completely, and so Emile's months of secret planning had been in vain. He had set up all the initial meetings, through old friends such as Leon Beaujeu and Paul Lemur, and had steered his wild eyed brother into their arms, and had kept the Bishop lulled as long as he could with reports that no organized resistance was forming. Now it had all backfired in his face. Emile did not feel remarkably close to a Cardinal's biretta, let alone to the mitre and the cape of a Bishop -- which had seemed almost within grasp not long ago. Father Emile knew that his upward rise within the church was finished, unless -- unless he could somehow demonstrate an ability to wield sufficient control over the forces, he had set in motion to bring them to an immediate halt. The Bishop had not left any doubt about it.

Emile's head still reeled. The only thing he had not expected from the old man was an outburst of anger that was close to physical rage. For a moment he had feared -- hoped -- that the white-haired patriarch was going to suffer a heart attack. Never had Emile seen him in such a state. Purple faced, his fingers opening and closing like claws, and his eyes, so frequently warm and indulgent, although the colour of melting ice, suddenly became as cold as a marksman taking a bead.

Certainly, everyone in Saint Boniface had known that there was going to be a fight at the bridge on the day Lettelier's coffin was moved, and certainly it was true that the Bishop had been kept in the dark, and, of course, your Grace, it might be construed as a sign that you were not in touch with your parishioners, but then is that the task of the Bishop?

Tachereau had not bought this argument for a second. Fixing Emile with his I'm-going- to- pull the -trigger- look, he said, "I trusted you, Father, to keep me informed. It appears you kept me blinded, and that is a profoundly serious departure from your vow of obedience. If this madness about mobs running in the streets is not eliminated, I will hold you fully responsible. Please do not insult my intelligence or my assumptions about your loyalty any further, and do not compound your sin by lying to my face. Just make sure that that march to the bridge, or whatever it is you have cooked up, does not happen. You do not need any further instructions, but for your information, this order comes from Archbishop de la Borquerie himself, and he, in turn, has already implemented instructions from the Curia directly."

Emile had scarcely been able to maintain the neutrality of his expression. The Curia! So that was it. The issue had never gotten as far as the Holy Father.

It was the Vatican bureaucrats, once again, who were deciding the course of events. Secure in Rome, ignorant of the desperation of French Catholics in the northwest, they had a long history of betraying uprisings against the Canadian state. Again, they had demanded passivity when action was needed, submission to a hated authority when a chance existed for successful rebellion. It is not, thought Emile, as though we were going to arm ourselves and cross into Winnipeg, storming the legislature. We were just going to prevent them from burying Letellier, and excommunicate. It was so simple.

He did not know at the moment which emotion was strongest.

Humiliation, frustration, the urge for some first time in years, to walk out on the church and do something himself, as a man, or whether he didn't feel, most of all, a terrible fear that the old Italian men at the Curia might be right. After all, they had been running a universal church, teaching a universal truth, for a long, long time. And there must have been many rebellious priests along the line who would have pitted the church, if they could, against other regimes.

The Bishop's parting shot had found its mark: "My dear Father, you have much humility to learn."

Yes, I am like Joseph that way, Emile thought. We Laboucheres might be too big headed for our own good, eh? One other deep fear filled his heart, the last few weeks had changed Joseph quite remarkably. The little brother Emile had so often thought of as being almost simple-minded, fit only to be a messenger boy, despite his otherwise unaccountable knack of making money as a businessman, had adapted to the role of agitator with ease that left the priest shaking his head, at first in amusement, but lately with some alarm.

Sensing his helplessness, Emile had been considering, during his walk eastward from the Basilica, not telling Joseph the truth of what the Bishop had said. After all, was it worse in the end to fail in the eyes of your Bishop or in the eyes of your brother? Why not simply say to Joseph: Bless you, go ahead? Why not, in fact, join him at the bridge? Why not go further and tell him that the Pope approves? Why not shield him entirely from Bishop Tachereau's cowardice and diplomatic shilly-shallying of the Curia? It came down to a choice between his vow of obedience and the feeling in his stomach that if the church backed down now, when good Frenchmen were finally prepared to make a stand -- good Frenchmen including his own brother -- the very last chance to maintain the power of Catholicism in this corner of the world would be lost. Protestant Englishmen would come to rule all of Canada except for Québec, and Canada, after all, had been a Catholic country from the beginning. It was priests, not Protestants, who opened the pass through the forest bigger than some continents, and who died, tortured by savages, long before British ships arrived with their red coated troops to take what had been won in the name of Christ, not Canterbury.

Yes, yes, yes. But who wants a forty-year-old ex-priest? What do you do, Emile, if the Bishop gives you a choice between being defrocked or sent to a parish probably one or two provinces further west, where nothing but the oblivion of old age awaits you?

Pushing open the gate into the yard, Emile found that his hand was unsteady. And when three of the children, Cecile, Monica and Bilou all rushed toward him, squealing happily, he found that the smile he forced was equally unsteady.

"Where is Papa?" Emile demanded, having to make a conscious effort to temper his voice back to some semblance of gentleness.

"Papa is out by the river," said Cecile.

Emile nodded. He walked swiftly around the house, past the vegetable garden, the chicken coops and outhouse, not wanting to linger lest his sister-in-law decide to come to talk.

Past the outhouse, the crabgrass sprang up knee deep except for a footpath that lead into the trees, mostly poplar, maple and oak. A tire dangled from the nearest oak and there were planks nailed into its branches maybe fifteen feet above the ground. A sandbox and several rusting old toys marked this as the children's area. Beyond, the foliage was thick, and the underbrush composed of brambles, poison oak, nettles, a natural barrier that extended some two hundred feet down a gentle slope that led to the banks of the Seine, whose gurgle could already be heard. A narrow foot beaten path continued down the slope, with sudden gorges and ravines opening unexpectedly at one's feet and enough vines dangling across the tunnel through the leaves that small children would soon give up trying to move toward the sound of the water. Emile himself found it hard work pushing the vines aside and keeping his skirt from snagging on brambles. Swatting at the occasional mosquito, panting slightly, he grasped the narrow trunks of saplings or the branches of bigger trees to steady himself, slowing his descent. It was a relief to leave the scorched flat tableland behind, dropping beneath the surface of a river of leaves that rippled above the clay-coloured water from which all these trees drew their life. Instead of unrelenting dryness, there was a damp and musk that was like a cool drink.

Joseph was standing by the river, watching the torrent flowing swiftly by. The water was some half dozen feet above its normal summer banks, so that there was a zone of trees on either side of the open area. The river proper whose leaves trembled with special vigor, was shaking in the grip of the current. The sound of insects was loud under the green ceiling, and the slobbering, hissing monotone of the river was louder than usual too, carrying as it did the weight of the last flashes of runoff from the fields. Emile was able to get quite close before Joseph heard him coming and turned to see who it was. Joseph's face was radiant.

His eyes were abnormally bright, as though he was running a fever. He looked either mildly sick or excessively healthy or was it both. He had his hands clasped behind his back and his shoulders squared. The posture was uncharacteristically military.

In fact, there was something about him that was entirely out of character. Not just his posture, but the lines on his face were altered. As though they were off centre, or inexplicably as though they had been off centre before and now finally, were lined up as they should be.

Joseph merely stared, and his look reminded Emile of nothing so much as a well-fed owl staring speculatively at a mouse.

When he spoke, he did so hoarsely.

"I walked all last night out across the fields, Emile. I had to climb some fences and -- push through cows and horses, eh? Three-quarter moon." He paused, still staring unblinkingly at the priest. "I felt the earth, Emile. I felt it moving, you know. And I thought such thoughts -- no words. I cannot –" He shook his head, eyes pained. "I just kept walking, eh? Did not get tired. Watch the sun come up -- have not done that for years. Good feeling, Emile! I feel good. Never better." He sighed deeply.

"I look forward to tomorrow, Emile. I have been feeling all this electricity coming up from the ground through my feet into my heart, eh?" And even when the air touches me, it is like what the comb does to your hair. It is all inside me. Tomorrow, I let it out." Another sigh, a shiver.

"Joseph –"

"The birds came out and danced around the moon and then danced around in a circle over my head. The trees, some of them, they tried to grab my arms and legs. But my Angels pushed them away and then told me to stick to the open ground, eh? That's right. The stars are the eyes of God, you know that, too? I never thought that before, but –"

"Joseph!"

"-- now I see that is how he watches us at night, eh?" Those birds, though, Emile, I never saw birds like that before. They were like little rainbows in the moonlight, little—"

"JOSEPH!"

The other man stopped speaking and stared with mild and amused curiosity, inclining his head slightly forward in a display of tolerant condensation. He smiled.

"Yes?"

Emile fought for his breath. With rising horror, he realized that Joseph was not in touch with the ordinary world anymore.

"Joseph, your -- not feeling well."

The smile was mocking.

"Oh, explain to me, please, dear brother, because as I have told you, I never felt better." He held out his left hand, palm downward. There was no quiver at all. "Steady is a rock", Joseph noted, obviously pleased with himself.

Emile glanced briefly at the hand, then fixed his eyes back on Joseph's, trying to meet them without flinching away. It was hard. There was a glint almost of cruelty there, something he had never detected in his brother before.

"If I didn't know you, Joseph, I would say you were a pretty sinister character. I'm not talking about your damned hand! I'm talking about --Emile jabbed a forefinger at his temple ---up here!"

Joseph appeared astonished for a moment. His mouth dropped open. Then he threw his head back and laughed. And laughed. And laughed. It was an unpleasant laugh, loud, barking, animal like yet textured with an unmistakable tone of superiority and contempt.

"Joseph, what is happening to you? Joseph? I want to know! Let me help! Let me "--

Joseph stopped laughing and sneered.

"Help me? Help me for what? God talks to me, Emile. Why is that Emile? Should you not be the one he talks to. You wear the cloth, eh? But you have no ears. It is me he talks to. You should be the one to listen to me. That is how it should be. Like those others do, eh? If Labouchere says he goes to the bridge, every man in town stands up and says he will go to the bridge too. I do not have to tell them God talks to me, Emile. They know it. I know it. What is wrong with you, Emile? How can you help me? I need to help you, that is what."

Not once had Joseph's remorseless eyes let go of his brothers. But now he looked away, his jaw muscles twitching.

"Joseph –"

"Rainbows, Emile. The birds around the moon were like rainbows. Little things. Beautiful things."

"The Bishop talked to me today, Joseph. Joseph? Are you interested in knowing what is going to happen tomorrow?"

He nodded warily.

"The Bishop told him that the government knows there is going to be a big demonstration, but they do not care. They have special coaches arriving in Winnipeg today from Toronto. Troops, Joseph. Five coaches full of troops. Veterans, Joseph. They will supplement the Winnipeg regiment. I do not know how many troops that is, Joseph, but it is more than a thousand. All of them with guns –"

He paused. There was something else, rumors of a "special coffin" which had been manufactured in eastern Canada and shipped westward along with the soldiers, a coffin that was going to defy any and all efforts to block or remove it. But not even old Tachereau had known what the secret of the coffin was. It sounded almost supernatural. Emile found that he did not want to mention anything about it, and before he could make up his mind whether to succeed or not, Joseph started talking again. His voice was weary.

"Emile, it does not matter to me if there are a million soldiers, and it does not matter to me if I am the only one against them. I am going to stop them. You have got to have faith. It is like at the walls of Jericho." That thought brought a boyish smile to Joseph slips. "Yes, that is it. The walls of Jericho!"

Emile took a couple of steps backward, the better to appraise his brother who had gotten so completely out of control in such a short time.

By God, he might be just what this community needs, someone to go up against the Canadian army and spit in its face. By God -- the priest brought his thoughts up short. I am getting caught again. It is infectious. Whatever this madness is that Joseph has. It makes me want to run in a mob too.

"Joseph, I have to tell you something."

Emile licked his lips, knowing he had come to the point where he must serve one master or another. Who will it be? His own wild impulses to egg Joseph on? The bishops direct order to tell him to stop.

At the last minute, though, it was neither of these considerations. It was the thought of being banished to a dusty little parish somewhere out there in the great nothingness of the west.

"Joseph, as your brother I am speaking now. Nothing else."

He said it with all the sincerity he could focus. "Joseph, will you listen to me as Emile, as the brother you have always known, who has always helped you. Joseph? Will you?"

Joseph was still wary, but his eyes cleared, a softness crept into his expression. A small affectionate smile formed. He nodded sheepishly.

"Joseph, I beg you not to do it. I made a mistake, Joseph, encouraging you, encouraging the others. I did it on my own authority, no one else is. It was wrong. It is hard to say this, Joseph, but I must. I lack humility. I was headstrong. Joseph, I have sinned in my way, and -- and -- it's like this, my dear little brother, if you go ahead with this, I will be sent away, I will not be here to guide you or the family any longer. You will lose me. I will lose you. Please, as a favour to me, if you believe that I have ever helped you at all, do not go, Joseph, just do not go. Please. For me. For my sake."

Joseph's face was completely blank for a full minute. Emile said nothing, just remained standing on the path, shoulders hunched forward, his face set to express as much pleading as he could muster, eyebrows lifted in a position of vulnerability, weakness, coaxing.

For the moment Joseph came out of his trance, Emile knew he had failed. Instead of the solemn nod of agreement which he had always been able to extract in the past when he put his mind to it, Emile found himself extracting a slow, firm shake of head. It was a calm gesture, fully conscious.

Then Joseph turned his head, pucker his lips, and spat noisily. The wad of saliva landed on a thick coil of barbed vines poised a foot above the ground. Emile found himself staring, hypnotized, at the saliva. He had no need to look at Joseph anymore. The discussion was over.

Actually, it was a relief to stare at the ground. He heard the crunch of Joseph's shoes, and out of the corner of his eyes saw Joseph's shadow withdraw, knew that his brother was stalking angrily up the path, and while Emile thought for a moment it might be worth calling him back, a pervasive lethargy kept the priests attention fixed on the spot of earth where Joseph spit had landed. The truth was Emile was glad not to have to struggle any longer.

Eventually, he raised his eyes to look at the river. His mind felt remarkably clear. He saw everything as though events and people were lined up on the shelf in front of him. It was pleasant here by the river. The solitude, now that Joseph was gone, was like an ointment. The smells were overly rich. A marsh-like stench that came from the soggy ground just above the high watermark, mixed with a dankness of cellars, the essence of manure covered farmland through which melted snow had been leached before joining the tide, a hint of dead things, of invisible drowned animals beneath the swirling grey soup, odors so strong they gave rise to the kind of embarrassment that came from standing too close to an outhouse. Of the fear that the smell might cling to you. For a moment, Emile did not care. He felt intoxicated. After several minutes of deadpan staring at the water, his eyes not quite focused, he found tears on his cheeks.

For the first time in decades, Emile found himself troubled by a certain word, a word whose possible meaning once had had the power to render him sleepless for whole nights at a time but which, over the years, he had thought he'd successfully put aside. The word was: emasculation.

Since the day before, wagons from out of town had begun to appear parked on the side streets of Rue Provencher, most of them within a three-block radius of City Hall, where the march was due to start at noon. By 11:00 a.m. small clusters of men could be seen up and down the street, most of them on the south side where they could stay in the shade. The biggest cluster by far was gathered opposite City Hall, outside Joseph's clothing store. A gritty dust stirred in the clay along the edges of the boardwalk. The heat was like a smithy's forge, enough to make a bear-headed man faint after a few minutes in the open. Men's vests were stained with sweat. Most of them had their waist jackets thrown over their shoulders. There was a great deal of spitting in the dust. Planks creaked under boots and shoes and the moccasins of the large contingent of Metis who stuck mostly to themselves in a knot halfway between City Hall and the Provencher Bridge, as though intent on being closest to the centre of the confrontation. Several of them had large hunting knives slung loosely from their belts or strapped to their thighs. Only a few white men -- the lawyer, Leon Beaujeu, was one -- bothered or dared to approach them, and then only for brief, whispered conferences.

Perched safely on the roof of her father's store, with a view all the way down to the foot of the bridge, Bernadette stared in fascination at the Metis. It seemed to her that they looked like pirates, some of them with bright red sashes, buffalo hunter hats, moccasins tied all the way up to their knees, like the old time Coeur de Bois who were their ancestors. Above all, their dusky skin and high cheekbones made the whites of their eyes stand out strikingly. By contrast, the four- and five-men groups of Frenchmen lounging along the street in a futile attempt to look casual or dressed mostly as though it was Sunday, even though Sunday wasn't until tomorrow. In their best suits, with their shoes and boots polished, their shirts starched and their celluloid collars clean. Had she not known that there was some terribly serious purpose behind what was to come, she would have naturally assumed that the men were all getting ready for a parade.

Since 9:00 o'clock, the stores and shops along Rue Provencher had been opened, and so women flowed back and forth along the boardwalk, doing their regular Saturday morning shopping. Many of them seemed angry with the men who were lingering in their way. But whereas on an ordinary Saturday there was a steady stream of men and women walking or driving across the bridge from the Winnipeg side of the river, today there was hardly any traffic on the bridge at all. Even from three blocks away, Bernadette could see that the bridge was vacant, a great black iron rib that made her think, for some unaccountable reason, of an altar before Mass. The streetcar rolled back and forth, it's bell ringing, and there were a few passengers, but nothing like the usual overflow of shoppers and visitors. The bridge intended to link the French and English communities was suddenly nothing much more than a buffer zone.

The smells of a hot early June Saturday in downtown St. Boniface were as ever. The cold breath of Monsieur Lapiere's freezer, with its tingling hint of immense beef carcasses; the reek coming from the brownish slime drooling from sewer outlets; another identifiable odor that emerged from nearby chimneys; something like the smell of burnt mattresses; garbage fermenting in the back lanes; faraway traces of beets being refined into sugar; tar somewhere, bubbling in the heat; horse turds baking on the cobbles; the delightful tang of vegetables in there open bins just three doors down from Mon Pere's shop; the teasing perfume of carbon monoxide coming from the autos as they passed, whiffs of sap bleeding from the fresh planks piled up in Guay's Lumber Yard; rubber tires on hot stones; potato chips frying nearby; and something else, a human smell that rose from where men were gathering in larger and larger groups, as surely as from flower patches. A leather and tobacco and sweat and shaving lather smell, stronger than usual, as though singed by electric sparks from the passing streetcars, yes, an unmistakable whiff of whiskey soaking into the sweaty flesh.

At 11:35 it seemed to Bernadette that some sort of convulsive movement occurred all up and down the street. She hadn't seen any signal being given, but the men who up until now had been keeping their distance as groups, one from the other, suddenly all began to drift toward the wide street space in front of City Hall.

The street filled up with men, more men than Bernadette had ever seen in one place at one time, hundreds of men, no, more than hundreds. She tried to count, using a forefinger, but it was impossible. They were all in motion. Ten of them over there, coming from around the side of City Hall. Six or seven or eight just turning onto Rue Provencher, coming from the direction of the Basilica. A dozen, easily, emerging from the shade of the lumberyard office. Five men coming from Lapiere's where they had been keeping cool in the walk-in freezer. Another fifteen, maybe two dozen, detaching themselves from the wooden benches outside the Marion Hotel, and a steady trickle of men came two or three and four at a time, stepping out slowly from the beer parlor itself, and moving uncertainly in the blinding light of approaching noon.

The biggest single group that Bernadette could make out was still the Metis, enough of them to fill two or three whole streetcars, well, maybe one streetcar, if they all stood up and squeezed close together. Up the street, towards home, automobiles, mostly Fords and Chevys, were still pulling up to the boardwalk, disgorging as many as six men at a time. In heavy booted rhythm, they clumped and banged along the boardwalk, bearing directly to where a single block of men was congealing. Already, the number of men standing in front of the red brick City Hall was so great that they were spread back from the grey stone steps of the building right across the street to the jammed open glass door of Mon Pere's shop. Any streetcar attempting to push through the middle would have had to run over several dozen bodies.

By 11:45, the streetcar which normally would be passing through on its scheduled run from the terminal at the end of Rue Provencher, was stopped two blocks east of City Hall, its driver having refused to risk pushing any further because of the men resolutely standing in his way. The streetcar due from the western side of the river had failed to appear, presumably delayed by the army troops known to be moving in formation from the downtown Winnipeg Protestant Cemetery where Letellier had been buried until now.

Since dawn, runners had been darting back and forth across the bridge, bringing reports of the movements of the Mounted Police and the troops, including not only the newly arrived trainload of veterans from Ontario, sent, everyone assumed, by the Orange Lodges but also the entire local regiment, known as the Lord Strathcona Horse, mostly veterans themselves of the Great War. Bernadette could make out the voices of the men directly below her well enough to have followed the morning's development step by step. By 8:00 a.m., she knew, like everyone else, that the traitor's coffin had been hoisted onto a truck an hour before and placed inside yet another coffin, a coffin such as no one had ever seen before.

It was reported to weigh several tons. Some said three tons. Some said five. Instead of being fashioned out of wood, it had been crudely but powerfully constructed out of scrap iron with great chunks of concrete cemented together. The large winch mounted on the back of the flatbed truck had not been enough to pull the thing up a ramp, some thirty soldiers had strained at ropes slung tautly around pulleys fixed to nearby trees. Obviously, the English had thought ahead, realizing that even if they succeeded in bullying their way through to the Basilica Cemetery and burying Letellier, his coffin could not be expected to long remain in the ground. It would only have been a matter of time before angry Frenchman came with their shovels at night to remove him. Now, they would need much more than shovels. They would need heavy equipment and teams of construction workers to hoist the iron-weighted hulk, and any idea of simply opening the lid and stealing the body was thwarted too: the lid was reported to have been welded into place. Torches would be needed to cut it open.

The news about the coffin at first had a chilling effect. It was as though the men had heard the sound of a giant footstep in the distance. There could be no doubt any longer that les Anglaise were taking this business seriously. The number of troops, too, was a surprise. Somehow, everyone seemed to know all at once that there were precisely twelve hundred soldiers massing on the other side of the bridge. Yet no one knew how many men there were on this side. Estimates placed the figure perhaps two thousand, not counting the women and children crowding along the boardwalk, mostly still in the shade, watching as the men assembled in the street, But Bernadette could hear the men directly below her arguing about the number.

"There will be three thousand of us by noon!"

"That is a Hill of beans! Watch, I'll bet there are not five hundred here who will go all the way."

Sneered another man: "Five hundred, see if there are five!"

"We will all go," said another man calmly. But in his calmness, this man was an exception.

Mostly, the men were nervous, prickly with the heat. They talked animatedly among themselves. There were outbursts of harsh laughter and men shouted each other's names across the heads of those around them. The only spectacle Bernadette had ever witnessed which came close to this was the annual lacrosse championship match, played in October in the field next to the stockyards, when everybody in the city came to watch. There was always a horrible worry that the Saint Boniface team might not win, but it was nothing like this. Thankful that she was safe on a rooftop, removed from the dangers of the street, Bernadette felt her small stomach churning furiously, and she was afraid she was going to be sick. In her imagination, the great coffin on the other side of the river loomed as large as a building, and she could vividly see some gigantic mummy emerging and starting to walk stiff legged across the bridge. Down below, it seemed to Bernadette that most of the men's faces were drawn and pale, and their eyes flickered toward the bridge uneasily, as though they, too, were imagining some supernatural horror. Bernadette had noticed that when the rumors about the coffin reached their ears for the first time, most of the men automatically crossed themselves. The news about the large number of troops was sobering, and should by rights have elicited a stronger response, since troops had the power to hurt, and the coffin had no power at all. Yet it was definitely the coffin that captured everyone's attention.

As noon approached and the crowd thickened in front of City Hall, the mood of almost superstitious dread passed. The men had been packed close together long enough by then to feel a certain invincibility. The yells were more boisterous. There was more laughter. Pride took the place of anxiety.

Someone cried: "If they go to all this trouble, they must be afraid of us, eh?"

A wave of approval broke. So, the English were making a big deal of this. It made everyone feel especially important. A sense of history dimly glimmered in every man's mind, big history or small, who could say. But it was true that outside of Québec, where riots against conscription had flared repeatedly during the Great War, there had been no French uprising for over a generation, and no one could remember a time when the church and state had been pitted against one another. The presence of the large band of Metis would itself normally have signified something of a moment, for not since the Red River rebellion had the half breeds aligned themselves so openly with Frenchmen against the English. It brought back memories, in the minds of the very old men present, of a time when it was the French and the Metis who controlled the River passes to the West, with all of English Canada contained in the East, held back by a barrier of muskeg and white-water streams through which few men other than the tough bush wise Coeur de Bois had found a way. The memories were painful, contrasting as they did with the present in which the English had burst through all the barriers, stabbing inland from the north, as well as the south, over running the entire northwest, decimating some Metis along the way, outflanking and encircling the French -- and now they would push right into the heart of the last French Kingdom on the plains in order to impose their own laws over those of the church. Physical fear there might be of the troops, and suspicious fear there might be of the already legendary coffin but pulsating beneath these emotions was an anger that was lifetimes old. Every man present had been retreating before the English all his life. His father, too, had spent his whole life retreating. And his grandfather and his great grandfather before him. Once, there had been a great new world empire, now it was dust. Dust as dry as the gritty powder that filled their mouths while they waited.

The lawyer, Beaujeu, mounted the steps just before noon. The crowd cheered him.

"Brothers, countrymen! We all know why we are here. We are here to make a stand. We are here to defend the sacred soil of our Basilica. I say: No burial for Letellier! It is too bad our mayor cannot be here" -- there was general laughter because it was common knowledge that Beaujeu himself coveted the mayor's chair, and Beaujeu flashed a grin and a wink in response to the guffaws. But then his voice became serious again.

"Brothers, there is one among us who has pledged to stand in the path of the monstrous casket the Protestants are going to try to stuff down our throats today. That one is Joe Labouchere, a good family man, eh? This is a father and a Catholic and a Frenchman!

And he is going to stand there at the bridge, and he says if they bury Letellier, they will bury Joe Labouchere too."

Beaujeu paused. Then: "Is he going to stand alone?"

The "NON!" that rose from the street came in one thunderclap trailing away in echoes that repeated themselves. "Non, non, non, non. And when the ripples of sound had died away, Beaujeu yelled:

"Are we going to stand with him?"

The "OUI" that came back was a roar greater than the negation that preceded it.

Now there was a commotion below where Bernadette was perched. Men began to file grim-facedly out of Mon Pere's shop, cutting with purpose through the crowd. After a dozen of them had pushed their way outside, Mon Pere appeared. Bernadette could not make out his face from above, just his familiar grey Sunday hat. She was startled at how short her father seemed among the other man, and held her breath for a moment, afraid that Mon Pere would not be able to make his way through the press of bodies. For an instant, Bernadette was reminded of the view she could get by perching on top of the fence at the stockyards, watching the cattle milling about. Then the confusion ended, and Mon Pere was out on the street, surrounded by a half a dozen men who were clearing a path. It was like watching a magnetic chip being pushed slowly through scraps of metal in a classroom experiment, for as soon as Mon Pere was safely through the centre of the crowd, they flowed smoothly into position behind him and began to move like a slow river westward towards the bridge.

The goal was to arrive in mass at the foot of the bridge just at the moment the troops arrived at the other side. The thinking behind such timing had originally been Emile Labouchere's. It would give the military a chance to back away, if they chose, without being already committed to the bridge, where it would be impossible to turn around. Somewhere, alarm bells would be ringing to the masters in Ottawa. A long enough pause might lead to a political decision to withdraw, rather than risk violence along racial, linguistic and religious lines. The uneasy balance between the powerful English and the French blocks in eastern Canada had always quavered on the verge of civil war, and once already, handfuls of squabbling language groups on the prairies had come close to triggering the generalized conflict that everyone feared.

Joseph was walking in the middle of the streetcar tracks which ran down the middle of the street. Ahead of him, the cobbles were empty, except for a few boys running along the edge of the pavement. The boardwalks on either side were lined with spectators whose faces, seemed to Joseph, were studiously blank. On either side of him, Frenchman and Metis had fallen in line, marching shoulder to shoulder, at least a dozen abreast on either side. The bridge was only a block away now and still there was no sign of the army.

Joseph's mouth was so dry that he had to keep gulping and his heart fluttered like a newly captured bird. He had dressed for the occasion in his best clothes and had polished his shoes obsessively. It was a shame to see that they were already powdered with dust.

Since the hour before dawn when he had awoken, Joseph had spent almost every minute praying. From time to time his concentration had been interrupted by the need to dress or cross a street or unlock a door or exchange a few words with the dozens upon dozens of men who had greeted him or else crowded into the shop to shake his hand. But he had entered into no conversations, had not paid more than a few minutes attention to what anyone said. Like the old Regina music box at home, the prayers played over and over again in his head as he fingered the rosary cupped in his left hand:

"I believe in God, the Father Almighty, Creator of Heaven and Earth -- Our Father, who are in heaven, hallowed be Thy name -- Hail Mary, full of Grace-- the Lord is with the -- Glory be to the Father, and to the Son, and to the Holy Spirit -- Oh Jesus, forgive us our sins, save us from the fires of hell -- I believe in God, the Father Almighty –"

Except for the prayers, he was sure his legs would already have collapsed. Except for the prayers, he was sure he would never have managed to make himself walk from the house to the shop this morning. Except for the prayers, he could not imagine being here. This way, he did not have to speak, and that was best, for he was afraid his voice would betray the turmoil in his chest and stomach.

An impulse to sniff the air seized him and his eyes darted this way and that, taking in the sights of the familiar storefronts, the green rim of trees along the river, and the spires of the Basilica rising above the shops on the left. It was odd, after all those meetings he had attended, that the men he should find flanking him on either side were strangers whom he had never seen before. Oh, there were plenty of familiar faces and voices nearby, but the Metis on his left were unknown, and the white man on his right must have come from out of town. It did not matter. Joseph felt alone with his prayers, and alone with the tension of knowing that he still did not know what he was going to do when the army started coming across the bridge. He was waiting for the Holy Ghost to whisper in his ear, and so far, the Holy Ghost had remained silent.

Then they were at the bridge.

Joseph stopped. Not knowing what else to do, he folded his arm across his chest and looked straight ahead while the men behind him and beside him grudgingly slowed and stopped, as though having difficulty overcoming their impulse to keep moving. There were scattered yells such as:

"Let's take the bridge!"

And: "On to Winnipeg!"

"Keep going! Keep going!"

But there were authoritative shouts in reply, "No! Here.! Stand here! NO BURIAL! NO BURIAL! NO BURIAL!"

By the hundreds, the men took up the chant. Exercising their lungs seemed to compensate for the exercise their legs demanded.

"NO BURIAL! NO BURIAL!"

Directly ahead, Joseph could see nothing except the pavement of the bridge stretching away roughly three hundred yards to the other side of the river. Iron trestles lifted higher than a man's head on either side of the wooden walkways flanking the pavement. The span was wide enough for automobiles to pass on both sides of the tracks, a dozen men could easily march abreast across it.

Right now, it was empty. It was impossible to see what was happening on the other side because the road took a sharp bend on the west bank and the view was obscured both by warehouses and trees along the river, many of which could be seen standing in water that had risen several feet over the embankment.

The crowd quieted quickly, each man straining to hear some signal from the other side, the sound of a trumpet or drum perhaps. But the only evident noise was the swish and the gargle of the late spring water gnawing at the clay that restrained it from spreading everywhere. In the trees, the colonies of birds could be heard, mostly robins and sparrows, but a crow cawed from the other bank, dogs barked, a meadowlark sang out unexpectedly, and a dazzling white cloud of pigeons exploded from under the bridge, like a burst bag of feathers.

Across the river, where the pencil thin obelisks of the incinerator towers stood, smoke lifted like thickly muscled arms, bright white, smudging to grey, blurring into a pastel cowl that lay beyond the outlines of the buildings. Above, the sky was a gigantic lens of sparkling blue nothingness so brilliant that the unshielded eye could stand it for only a few seconds. Spots danced wildly. Impurities more in the instruments of vision than in the atmosphere itself, for it seemed impossible that such a vast and open arch could ever seriously be tarnished with dirt. For all the smokestacks, the sky remained as it might have been at the beginning of time. The faint grey smudge that lay over the city was somehow gentle, comforting, like a veil.

"Maybe they will not come," someone said.

"Shut up idiot," someone else growled.

Joseph became aware of a harsh breathing, almost panting. He stiffened, embarrassed, thinking it was a sound he was making himself. Then he realized that it was coming from all around him. He did not want to look to either side, partially because he did not want to have any man see through the window into his soul where they might spot the fear he was barely keeping from overwhelming him, partially because he wanted the strangers beside him to remain what they were, but mostly out of a sense that if he looked directly at anyone else, the prayers which he had stored up in his head, concentrated into a ball of pure virtue and good grace, would somehow leak away, like water pressure being lowered because of a tap that had been turned on. So long as he could maintain a balance where the world as it existed at the moment, only contained two essential forces -- himself and whatever demon's gang moved onto the bridge -- then he was doing what was right. When the moment came, he would be in touch with the Holy Ghost, and nothing could go wrong.

Joseph had always wanted to be at the very centre of the largest crowd imaginable, but now that he was there, he found the presence of the others was merely a distraction. He allowed himself to see nothing but the empty bridge, heat waves rippling across its surface, and he allowed himself to think nothing but: "Glory be to the Father, and to the Son, and to the Holy Spirit –"

The small figure of a man appeared on the far side, waving his arms over his head -- the signal that the procession from Winnipeg was in motion.

"They are coming!" Somebody close to Joseph yelled. Like an echo in reverse, growing louder the further it traveled, the cry went back through the mass of humanity filling up the entire intersection and overflowing onto Avenue Tache and back at least a full block on Rue Provencher. Immediately, the chant began again:

"NO BURIAL! NO BURIAL! NO BURIAL!"

The noise sent a vibration through the cobbles -- or was that a distant trembling caused by the movement of soldiers and trucks on the other side.

The man who had signaled was running now, retreating from

whatever was about to come around the corner and out onto the bridge. At first there was nothing more than a flash of red. Then it was a line of red. Red above black. Mounties on their horses. It was the kind of procession Joseph had seen pictures of when the King had passed through Quebec City. Then, as now, there had been no outburst of patriotism or loyalty, rather, a silence that invited the noises of the natural world to fill in the gap in human communication. As the red line swung from the corner it had negotiated onto the bridge itself, presenting an unbroken wall of red jacketed riders astride horses that were filled with furious energy, a long drawn out sigh went through the crowd gathered on the east bank. Mounties again, eh! It was an old, old story. The Metis knew it well enough. The French knew it. The Mounties were still remembered by Englishmen as the tough no-nonsense heroes who had ridden one by one into Indian camps on the plains, including the camp of Sitting Bull himself, and said, "Lay down your arms!" Forcing whole nations to bow before them. Yet in the minds of those against whom the Northwest Mounted Police had been used to crush opposition, the sight of that line of redcoats elicited no feeling except hatred. The red of their jackets matched perfectly the red that everyone present knew had been worn by the conquering army at the original battle which had lost New France to the British Empire.

It was impossible to make out anything more than the boots of the soldiers coming in the wake of the horses, although, after several minutes, the black hood of the trunk bearing Letellier's coffin could be seen. A vague shudder seized the bridge. The rhythmic trump of boots, the clop-clop of hooves, the rumble of a heavy engine, the tinkle of metal fasteners and brass buttons in collision -- other than that, a strange quietness in which the guzzling sounds of the river could still be clearly heard.

Thought Joseph fiercely: "Oh Jesus, forgive us our sins, save us from the fires of Hell, lead our souls to Heaven especially those who are most in need of your mercy –"

The slight tremor on the bridge seemed to resonate through

his body. He had been braced to hold himself steady, an impulse to flee. But, instead, he experienced the sensation that his insides had hardened. He felt ponderous, weighted down, welded to the cobbles. Exultantly, the thought broke through his prayers. "You poor bastards, I've got you now!"

For not only did the sight of the oncoming Mounties fail to fill him with the physical terror he had expected it to, it had the opposite effect. He felt like a giant. The redcoats and the booted boys marching along behind were reduced, in his field of vision, to mere insects. He could swap them aside at will. His heart seemed to roll about. His face grew hot. He made a noise like someone climbing into water that is either too hot or too cold. He wanted to growl, to bark, to make snarling noises, to bound forward and start clawing at them. He did not think of himself as a man standing in the street, backed up by a crowd, rather, there was just himself, a single gargantuan creature, part beast, part man.

What he did next seemed so natural it was as though the idea had been there in his mind all along. Keeping his arms folded over his chest, he turned around one hundred and eighty degrees and stared into the face of the man directly behind him, who proved to be none other than Alderman Audette. For several seconds, the Alderman's mouth was slack. He blinked stupidly, unable to grasp what Joseph was doing, and kept looking up at the line of Mounties already halfway across the bridge. All around Joseph there were confused movements, startled oaths, exclamations of concern, even a touch of panic. What the hell was the little bugger up to? Audette watched Joseph's eyes but did not get back so much as a flicker of recognition. Audette might as well have been invisible.

Then it dawned on the politician that there was a good maneuver here. Of course, put your backs to them. It combined everything. It was very Christian, a turning of the cheek, and it made the enemy come to you as though from behind, like a sneak thief, yet it said that your opinion of them was so low you were ready to fart in their faces, it was a grand gesture, like a matador putting his back to a bull. It gave the Mounties no chance to try to win an eyeball-to-eyeball contest of wills, where they would have the advantage by virtue of their weapons and horses. Yes, it was the right thing to do! The instant he saw the beauty of it, Audette whirled around as Joseph had done.

At the sight of the wily old Alderman also putting his back to the soldiers, the men in the immediate vicinity quickly followed suit. If Audette would do it then it must make sense. It had appeal, it had flair, it was something only a brave man would do, yes and at that moment every man was there to prove how brave he was. Ah, a shrewd one, that Labouchere!

The Metis caught on to the idea as quickly as the Frenchman, and within an amazing short period -- a matter of minutes --the entire crowd had performed what look like an expertly drilled maneuver, almost military in precision, with the result that everyone was looking to the east, with the Basilica on the right. Out on the bridge, the first line of Mounties abruptly found themselves bearing down on a crowd that had its backs to them, as though ignoring their existence. It was disconcerting. They had never run into that before.

The Mounties are stopped.

The horses. The troops. The truck. Everything came to a noisy, clattering, boot-clicking-in-unison-halt. Orders were yelled in English. There was a span of silence that seemed to stretch for minutes, but which was probably only a matter of seconds. Then one of the Mounties rode forward a couple of horse lengths and stopped. He yelled something out slowly, in a surprisingly high-pitched voice. It seemed the voice was actually pleading. The Mountie was still speaking when someone yelled:

"Mange d' la merde!"

It was a great burst of excited high-strung laughter and more rude shouts. Several men started to turn around, to face the envy, but there were savage commands from the frontlines:

"Standstill! Don't look back! Do not turn your head! Look away!"

"NO BURIAL! NO BURIAL! NO BURIAL!"

Somebody with a bull voice yelled:

"If you bury him, you will have to bury us all."

"NO BURIAL! NO BURIAL! NO BURIAL!"

Although individuals could be seen looking over their shoulders, unable to resist the urge to see their adversary, most of the crowd remained rigidly fixed in a position with their backs to the bridge. The Mounties made one last attempt to communicate but were drowned out in a steady chanting.

"NO BURIAL! NO BURIAL! NO BURIAL!"

He shrugged, swung his horse around and fell back to his own frontline.

What followed had an almost leisurely air, either as though it had been rehearsed or as though it was simply the natural thing to happen. At a single command, the Mounties swung their horses to the left and right, lining themselves up single file beside the trestles, like an honour guard, leaving enough room in the middle for the troops to pass on formation. It was like a gateway of red being swung open to reveal the faces of the waiting khaki-clad soldiers, their rifles held in both hands at an angle, their helmets covered with nets.

Joseph could hear the sounds behind them as clearly as anyone. He could feel the tremors passing through the cobbles. He heard the, in English – "FORWARD MARCH!" -- felt the impact of all those soldiers' boots striking the bridge at once, heard the sound of the gears being changed and the engine of the truck bearing the coffin revving up, felt and heard all this like blows already landing on his body. His shoulders constricted. His windpipe seemed clogged. He started to tremble. I am growing weak, he thought numbly. I must not. The prayers he had been uttering over and over again were going too fast, they were overlapping, filling his skull with a jumble of phrases, nothing coherent. He squeezed his beads and found that even his fingertips were slippery with sweat. He clamped his teeth together instinctively, aware that, around him, other men were twisting and writhing, unable to hold still as the tramping of boots grew louder and its rhythm faltered not a bit. The soldiers were coming on as though no one stood in their way. There was not even a hint of uncertainty. Surely, they would not -- but they did.

In the final seconds before the first row of soldiers waded into the crowd, using the rifle butts, the men around Joseph whirled to try to defend themselves with their hands. There were shouts, curses, then the first howl of pain. Joseph alone remained with his back turned, arms folded across his chest, right to the very instant when the butt of the Handfield-Martini British Army rifle impacted with perfect aim against the base of his spine and a cracking sensation blazed through his whole being. He crashed into Alderman Audette's shoulder and before he could even begin to fall, the second blow landed on the back of his neck, snapping his head one way while the left side of his jaw seemed to leap out another direction. Half of the teeth in his mouth seemed to dissolve. His eyes felt like they had all popped out. All he could see was a glimpse of Audette's terrified face and a splash of blood and puke appearing on the alderman's jacket. Joseph's mind was a chaos of lightning bolts. His body was one huge spasm. Strong hands seized both of his arms, pinioning him, actually lifting him into the air, spinning him around. Before he could grab for breath, another rifle butt caught him in the stomach, driving anything that was left in him up through his throat into his mouth, already spilling over with blood and bits of tooth so that he was convinced he was choking to death. His eyes were closed. He felt himself falling, smacking against the cobbles with his forehead, elbows and knees. Then a hard tip boot connected with the side of his head so that it seemed, to his failing consciousness, that his skull was cracked like an egg. He was only dimly aware as one more boot and one more rifle butt came down simultaneously on the front and back of his rib cage as he thrashed on his side, curled up gagging, his hands clawing the air, unable to choose which too clutch, still unable to breath. Somehow, that was the worst part. Then he was hurled aside, landing on his back.

"Mon Pere! Mon Pere!" Bernadette screamed from the rooftop,

but it was a tiny sound, lost in the pandemonium. It seemed that the khaki uniforms had plunged forward like a wooden spoon into warm butter. The first line of civilians had simply vanished from view. The second line likewise went down within less than a minute. The third line had already broken and was struggling wildly to escape. It was impossible. Most of the men down in the street could not see for themselves what was happening, so they balked at running. But as the third and fourth lines of resistance were also chopped down and flung to the side, bleeding and roaring with pain, it became clear to everyone that there was no stopping the assault. Not a single shot was fired. The sound of rifle butts connecting to flesh and bone, the harsh panting of soldiers, the solid grunts they made as they wielded their weapons, the whinnying of the Mounties horses -- somehow like a maniacal laugh -- the yelping and snarling of the men being beaten, the screaming of women spectators, the sound of feet breaking into a run on the boardwalk and cobbles, their noises alone were enough to create all the panic that was needed for the soldiers to clear a path for the black truck that was advancing steadily across the bridge, bearing Letellier's massive cast iron coffin steadily towards the Basilica grounds.

Through her tears, Bernadette saw only a blurred picture. The tremendous tide of brown and black hats was breaking up like a jigsaw puzzle hurled against a wall. The blunt khaki wedge exercised a right turn, and was bearing, unopposed, down Ave Tache, with a seemingly effortless flow of more soldiers pouring off the bridge like nothing so much as brown ants bearing the shell of a beetle. People fled by the hundreds before them, dazed by the fury of the attack.

The truck came off the bridge bearing its heavy burden, flanked on either side by soldiers. The coffin had a certain elegance. It was a brute, densely packed implacable. Rocks were flying through the air. A few bricks. One man even threw shoes. But all bounced harmlessly off the coffin's bulk. The helmeted soldiers paid no attention at all.

Doctor Rene Gendreau had not had a day like this in his life. The nearest nightmare he could recall was the influenza epidemic of 1918. Victims were overflowing into the hallway on the first and second stories of the hospital. Any way he looked at it, he was dealing with the aftermath of a disaster. man-made or natural, what was the difference?

In the last fourteen hours he had set more bones and treated more fractured jaws than he had seen in the last five years altogether. The miracle to him was that no one was dead and that, somehow everyone had escaped concussions. Miracle? He hated the word. Yet, how else to explain the lack of loss of life. He had not been at the scene himself, but from all reports -- and no reports were more eloquent than the mute testimony of the bludgeoned, blackened flesh and ruptured organs that lay before him -- the level of violence had been what you would have expected on a battlefield. There were only three soldiers among the forty or fifty men who had been brought to the hospital for treatment and two of those were suffering from knife wounds. One Metis had been brought in with an eyeball knocked so far back into his head, squashed like a piece of vegetable, that there was nothing to do but scrape the remains away and clean the wound.

Doctor Gendreau did not know whose side deserved the greater weight of blame, since anybody but a fool knew that the armies were not to be messed with, and armies themselves were not supposed to mess with anybody except another army. Weakly, angrily, the aging doctor had gone about his work, making no effort to minimize pain or give comfort to his patients except in the basic way of trying to save their mangled limbs, making sure that none of them got any infections. As the hours wore on, he became increasingly brutal, reminding himself that if the only way to discourage women from having more children was to make childbirth as unpleasant as possible, so it must be if troublemakers were to be discouraged from causing anymore trouble. The victims gasped and wept and whimpered in his grasp. Some became enraged. He ignored their cries steadfastly as a cowboy applying a branding iron to a calf. It was the craziest business that he ever heard of grown men without guns trying to stop an army. And all over some minor pamphleteer whose only genius lay in his knowing when to die to cause the maximum nuisance. The stupidity of human beings overwhelmed him. But this had happened so often in the past that he no longer felt anything except withering contempt.

All in all, it was a foul and useless business. The troops had dug a hole in the cemetery at the Basilica, hoisted the coffin on a crane, lowered it, and packed soil back in. No priest had been found who would perform the ceremony, so the body went into the earth excommunicate anyway. Afterwards, Tachereau had announced that the soil containing the coffin was no longer to be considered consecrated. There were threats from a dozen lawyers of civil actions against the military and the Government of Canada. But it would all bog down in the courts, doctor Gendreau knew. It had been for nothing. Unless you counted the psychological effect of Frenchmen once again being bashed and kicked aside by English-speaking soldiers. There were rumors of riots in Québec, attacks on non-French stores and shops in Saint Boniface by people who had witnessed the scene at the bridge. It was reported that charges of assault with a deadly weapon should be laid against some of the half breeds who had been involved. It was likewise reported that the Premier of the province wanted to meet with the Mayor of Saint Boniface to prevent this unhappy affair from becoming a source of division between the two great founding peoples, meaning the English and the French. In the English language papers, Dr. Gendreau was fairly certain, there would be lengthy accounts the next day that would talk about the army being provoked and about the attempts of the Mounties to settle things peacefully being thwarted by a handful of Indians, anarchists and extremist French nationalist. Oh yes, he could see it coming from a mile away. Well, what did anyone expect? Lettelier's body had been buried, fifty men were beaten into pulpwood, the army had filed back across the bridge, and the supremacy of the state had been convincingly established over that of the church. Rene Gendreau had not had any sympathy for the church for a long, long time, but there was nothing in the behavior of the government or its bully boys in the last day to inspire him either. They all seem somehow to have sunk to the lowest level possible at the same time.

There was one patient whose condition caused the doctor to chuckle. It was a cold, remorseless chuckle, the kind of bitterly ironic sound he had first learned to make back in medical school, at a time in his life when it was considered good sport to steal cadavers from the morgue and leave them, lavishly dressed, sitting on a chair in the hallway where the night watchman, a poor Kraut, would run into them on his rounds with his lantern. Doctor Gendreau had learned this chuckle, he supposed, as a defensive covering. Whatever the reason, it welled up in him now at the site of this poor particular patient, the bourgeoisie little man who owned the clothing shop on Provencher.

Doctor Gendreau got the impression, from the conversations around him, that this Labouchere fellow had been some kind of ringleader. Well, if that was the case, he had paid for it. But that was not what drew the bitter laugh. Rather, it was the recollection that not long ago, the doctor had told this man to avoid impregnating his wife. Well there was a lot less chance of him doing that now. After the beating he'd gotten, he'd be lucky to walk, let alone -- Oh, sure, he would probably be able to get around in six months or so, but he'd have to use canes to balance himself. His jaw would never be straight again. He'd be lucky if he could make the muscles of his mouth work well enough to talk.

Why the hell would a man put himself into a situation where that sort of thing could happen to him. People did not really seem to realize how easy it was to wreck a human body, did they?

"Well, Monsieur Labouchere, you know now," the doctor muttered.

PART SIX

VANCOUVER – BRITISH COLUMBIA

1979

By the time the diaphanous morning fog got burned off, the Point Atkinson Lighthouse, which they had heard grunting out its warning for an hour now, was a beam on the port, maybe a mile away, and the fluted pastel apartment blocks of the West End lay dead ahead, pressing like driftwood against deep shadowed Stanley Park's southern flank, while the Lions Gate Bridge soared across the first narrows to the North Shore, like a fantastic brooch. On the starboard, the great meringue tidal flat of Spanish Banks lay like exposed, sodden flesh. The fog had only lifted to a low ceiling of cloud, the kind that came in from the ocean and piled up against mountains and stayed there forever. This was not any better than Rupert, Bernadette thought sourly. No chance of seeing the Lions, let alone Baker. She could only make out the lower slopes of Mount Seymour, scarred by roads and lifts and now – Mon Dieu! There were *houses* up there, just below the clouds. She aimed the binoculars, amazed. But pulled away quickly. It made her dizzy, just to think of living up there. She scanned Ambleside and the stone walkway around the park and Kitsilano for signs of life, but the beaches were deserted, the parks as empty as before the white man came, as though the inhabitants had vanished underground. This was the rain coast at its worst; leaden, soggy, sky the colour of solder and the sun so furtive people had to keep their lights on in their homes all day long.

While she could contemplate it with some calmness from this

distance, Bernadette avoided aiming her binoculars at the mighty steel pylons of the Lions Gate Bridge, one leg now beginning to disappear behind the park's great fir and cedar shoulder. Her eyes were getting sore, and just the most fleeting memory of being up there was enough to leave her dry mouth, her heart shifting gears. She had foolishly allowed Linda and David to drive her across it once, with her eyes closed and her ears covered, but halfway across -- like Lot's wife -- she hadn't been able to prevent herself from taking a peak, and her body went as numb and senseless as a statue: actual paralysis brought on by pure, unadulterated terror. Stifling a shriek, she could not stop a dog-like wine escaping her lips, because this was higher than any building she'd ever been on, the whole thing was shaking in the wind as a bus the size of a seiner crashed by, nearly ramming them, setting the whole bridge bouncing like a giant spring, and all this weight couldn't possibly stay up -- it defied logic. She really thought they were going to fall from the bridge, or it was going to fall over, or crumble beneath them, or maybe even flipped them into the air. She wanted to be *anywhere* on earth except where she was. If there was one thing she could not stand, truth be known, it was heights.

Bernadette shivered, pocketing the binoculars, slipping her dark glasses back on, and tightening the scarf around her neck in a gesture of resolve, despite her gloom. She'd finished up in the galley, including scouring the stove with salt, and had nothing more to do, so she climbed up to the bow, gripping the guy-line that ran up to the top of the radio pole. Young Rene scrambled gleefully by, bouncing bumpers and tires over the side, happy the trip was coming to an end. He still had a long way to go to get home, little prairie dog that he was. Doug Moore lounged on the flying bridge, plucking away with his lips as he relished his snooze, while Jim handled the wheel from inside, trying to get through to the marine operator.

"Hello, Vancouver, hello Vancouver, this is the *Mary Boehm*. Do yuh copy?" He been trying for the last half hour, but traffic was heavy, and maybe it was because they were too *close*, and the radio waves were having trouble bouncing back from the satellites (most likely some bubble-gum chewer was just asleep now at the switch), he wasn't having much luck, and it was making him jumpy. "Goddamn government slack-ass dummies," he growled. Nobody was inclined to go near him.

Bernadette did not feel much like talking anyway. She had been uneasy since awakening from a dream which had left her emotions in turmoil. In the dream, she had been on board a boat that looked like a Chinese junk. She could not understand the strange symbol painted on the sails. But she was certain they said something important. She had become aware that there were two figures standing near the bow. The sea rolled away to the horizon all around without a trace of land. The sky looked ragged and empty as though a major storm had just blasted through. It was a scene that took her breath away with a menacing beauty. The men at the bow both wore monks' cowls. She heard them talking but did not understand the language. Abruptly, one of them vanished into thin air. The other turned around and removed his cowl. It was an ancient Oriental man who was either blind or who could not see her for some reason. He acted as though he was all alone on the boat. She tried to speak to him, but he did not hear. She felt panicky. She reached for him. He vanished. She was left alone, feeling like the sky; torn apart, shredded.

Jim finally got through on the radio phone to someone at the dry dock where he was supposed to be taking the boat. Whoever it was answered, nobody had told him anything about the *Mary Boehm* being booked up on the ways today. Nobody around just yet you know, either.

"Better tie up in False Creek till somebody figures out what to do," the voice at the other end crackled disinterestedly.

"Roger," was all Jim said, until he clicked the mike off, and let loose with a stream of obscenities and invective that had the Indian boy falling down on the deck hooting, and sent Doug scuttling down to the engine room to get out of the way. Poor Jim. One thing after another. Now there would be docking fees. In the old days, of course, Mary would have made good and sure the ways were booked, but Jim obviously forgot to double check, like you had to do with these days. This was the coast, after all. Of course, this meant Linda and David and the baby would be on their way to the address she had given them to pick her up, and there was no point trying to call them now. They'd just have to figure it out -- although she could easily see this turning into hours of confusion. If only they hadn't insisted on meeting her. She would have been happy to get a taxi. But no, they were already thinking of her as an old lady. She shouldn't have given in. She should have said, "No, I'll get to your place on my own." (John used to say, once you lose your initiative, you're finished). Indeed, and now there would be chaos while they thrashed around looking for her or calling up the marine operator to find out why the *Mary Boehm* was late. Was it missing at sea? Call the Coast Guard! David was sweet, and she genuinely liked him, but he had done too many drugs, she suspected. He got flustered easily -- the very opposite of what you would expect. As for Linda, she would use any little foul up with the boat as an argument about why Mom should move to the city. Once she got her mind fixed on something, you had to practically run away from her if you didn't want to just give up and do it her way. God knew that if Bernadette were to move into this town, she would have her zealously well-intentioned, loving, overprotective daughter running her life, or trying to. And they would fight over it. David said it was because Linda was a Taurus, and Bernadette was a Scorpio. And, yes, there did seem to be something to astrology, superstitious twaddle that she officially believed it to be. Despite her vow, decades ago -- not long after Ma Mere's death, in fact -- to ignore everything except scientific truth, Bernadette had been unable to avoid noticing that, by and large, peoples character tended to match their Zodiac signs. Take Jim, the Leo, up there in the wheelhouse, pacing and growling.

It was flat calm in English Bay, with at least two dozen freighters at anchor, either waiting for the slowpokes at Customs to clear them or for yet another teamsters strike to end. There was still a trace of fog on the water, enough so that as they approached a freighter, it grew from a grey silhouette and turned into something huge and real, every detail, down to the peanut butter jars used to shield light bulbs, bits of food stuck to the barnacles below the bilge, a broken porthole stuffed with a blanket, the sweat of dew enhancing all the colours, making even the grey and rust sparkle, while the other vessels were mostly ghostly, then, like a steel iceberg, it faded astern, and another ship became the only real one in the world. A few forlorn deckhands, desperate for distraction, stared down at them, but did not bother to wave. Poor devils.

Jim weaved his way through the towering freighters impatiently, passing close between the lines of a couple of anchored sawdust barges in his haste to catch the tide going into False Creek. The water peeled cleanly open around the rusty strip of iron on the bow, white underside folding with a hiss on top of the surface blue. Jim did not slow down until they were closing in on the gas barge in the shadow of Burrard Bridge, a shadow so big, so deep, Bernadette felt the temperature dropped several degrees. The tide was awfully low, Bernadette noticed with a twinge of alarm. It was a wonder the *Mary Boehm* hadn't grounded. Another few feet and she probably would. Which explained why Jim was rushing. If they didn't make the train bridge, where you only drew something like eight feet at low tide, they wouldn't be able to get through and would have to wait a couple of hours. Nobody wanted that. The closer you got to the end of a boat trip, the more everybody wanted to get ashore.

Down this low in the channel, there was a constant sizzle in the air, bubbles coming up from clams, the faint gnashing of the beaks of barnacles, a crackling sound resulting from some chemical change in the salt deposited on the slimy bull kelp fronds by the departing sea. There was an immense moaning, whining, thunder echoing among the steel girders holding the giant structure, the dreadful sound of cars and buses and trucks moving across the sky directly *above* (this was almost as terrifying as being *up* there. Well, no. Nothing *near* as bad) the bridge made more noises than a boat, for the sake of Jesus, creaking and shuddering as though it might come apart any second, depositing an avalanche of asphalt and steel and cement and cars on their heads. She was enormously relieved when they finally got out from under the shadow, cleared the narrow wooden chute under the little train bridge -- with at least a *foot* to spare and a tight little grin on Jim Boehm's face -- and turned into Fisherman's Wharf. Oddly enough, in here, the water was choppier than it had been out in the Bay, a rogue vortex of wind whipping down from the Coastal Range, gusting from Chinatown, setting torn flags flapping.

All of the boats ahead had that end-of-the-season look. Slime-covered Steveston gillnetters not much larger than a rowboats had their nets piled up in incredible tangles beside looming ninety-foot long liners with all the latest radar gear, squat halibut seiners with TV antennas, medium-sized crab boats and sail-rigged trawlers, two big D.F.O patrol vessels, and a minesweeper converted into a yacht, flying an American flag, must have waited too long to head south, and now its owner was afraid, and you couldn't blame him. The decks of most of the boats looked like they were covered with grey nail polish from years of fish scales being crushed under gumboots. The white-washed wheelhouses were rust-splotched, the paint peeled off in great scabs. The masts swung back and forth like the rifle stocks of hundreds of hunters all trying to get a bead on a flock of passing ducks at the same time, each taking aim at a different bird, each adjusting and readjusting its aim.

Now Bernadette was engulfed by the smells of the harbor, diesel fumes, paint, fish, a trace of rotting seaweed, a hint of sewers, coffee brewing and someone's galley. Riggings clacked against mast poles in the wind. In the water, everything was turned upside down and chipped into millions of jigsaw pieces, things came apart, wavered, came back together again.

As the *Mary Boehm* approached the dock, the pilings loomed ahead, their long thin stems sheathed in stockings of barnacles.

It was like coming up to the mouth of a dripping cavern. To her astonishment, she caught sight of a psychedelic painted Volks van turning into the parking lot. The kids! Her heart skipped joyously, and all her previous negative thoughts were flushed back into the dark parts of her mind. How wonderful. She was almost as pleased that they had had the brains to figure out how to find her as she was to the fact that they were here.

By the time the old packer bumped heavily against the pilings, squashing a swath of barnacles into yoke, David had managed to get out of the van and run to dockside, which was a good thing because there was no one else around and Rene was too green to risk him trying to scramble up a ladder before the lines were tied. David got to the dock quite amazingly -- at exactly the right moment to catch the bow line, so that, so far, everything looked rather organized. But the look on David's face – utter astonishment that he had actually caught something -- was hilarious. He was so like Linda, well intentioned as all get-out, but not mechanical or athletic in the least. He stood there, thrilled with himself, like a kid who just caught a football, in his sandals and flared paisley jeans and Mexican vest, wearing a headband, no less, his long jet black hair blowing in front of his eyes so he could hardly see, and yelled; "What now?"

Incredulous, Jim shouted, "Put it around the cleat, yah dummy!"

David's expression turned to near panic. Brushing frantically at his hair, he looked around, he did not move. The *Mary Boehm* was starting to drift away, and Doug was having to let out the line.

"The cleat!" Jim roared. "*The cleat!*"

"What's a cleat?" David yelled back, anguished.

Jim was thunderstruck. To no one in particular, he said. "He don't know what a goddamn cleat is!"

Standing near the bow, little Rene had removed his headphones and was following all this with delight, a huge, toothy grin on his face, eyes sparkling. Oh yes, such stuff to tell when he got home!

"Over there, over there!" Shouted the engineer.

Young David finally saw where he was pointing and hauled the heavy rope toward something that looked to him like a miniature Henry Moore sculpture bolted to the edge of the wharf. Once there, he stopped, panting, and stared in dismay, totally unable to comprehend how to connect the hoop of rope in his hands to the eggshell shape of the cleat (What's this, he thought, an ancient Rubik's Cube, shouldn't have smoked that joint on the way over. Should've known something like this was bound to happen) still, this was an emergency, lives could be at stake, and he knew how to override the THC in his brain, a supreme act focus, a little yoga breathing. It's a puzzle. Concentrate. It only took a moment, in all, for him to figure it out, but a moment is a long time in a docking manoeuvre. Jim was already gunning the engine forward to slow their drift away in the tide, which was probably moving at four knots, Bernadette suddenly realized. Mon Dieu, couldn't that crazy boy speed it up. The moment the concept finally clicked for David, he performed deftly enough, although he slipped in his excitement and fell with a thud on his butt before managing to thread the line through the eye of the cleat and loop it around one end of the strange metal art object. Wow, he thought. What a thing. Swaying proudly to his feet and dusting off his stinging bottom, he looked up, expecting applause.

Instead, the big, grizzled old grease monkey at the wheel on the upper deck was shouting:

"Christ's sake don't just stand there like a log! Get the next line! *That* way!"

Normally, David would have told anybody speaking to him in a tone of voice like that to get stuffed, but he had a cultural weakness for elderly types. Besides, he'd heard about this old seadog. Supposed to be quite a salty character. Besides, this stoned, David was inclined to go with the flow, see what happened. Obediently, he jogged along the dock as the boat's big rear end swung slowly in. But the old engineer threw short and the steering lines splashed uselessly into the wake. It took three more tries. Twice, David got there an instant too late, puffing, and the line snaked back into the water.

"Goddamn hippie," Jim growled.

Bernadette heard that. "Watch what you say, Jim Boehm," she warned. "That's my son-in-law."

By now, she noticed out of the corner of her eye, Rene had fallen down on the deck, clutching his gut, kicking his legs, hardly able to breathe from convulsive laughter. As he stopped by, looking for the spring line, Doug swatted the boy on the back of the head. "Watch it." The kid kept giggling.

Jim was silent for a moment., "Hm," was all he said.

Bernadette gave him a fierce, challenging look. "Anything wrong?"

"Nah, course not Bern. Jus' didn't know Linda married a Jap."

The word stung. But Jim had meant no offence by it. It was a descriptive word to him, not derogatory. She had known him long enough to *know* that he didn't give a damn about a man's skin colour, just how hard he worked and whether he knew what he was doing and could be trusted or not. He'd hired every kind of man in his time -- and fired every kind of man. Indians, Japanese, Chinese, Irishman, Italians, and Slavs. It made no difference. Knowing this, she checked her automatic response, which was testy: "He's a Canadian." No point lecturing the old salt, it's too late for that, he can't change his habits of thought.

Instead she said, proudly. "His grandparents came from Hiroshima prefecture."

Jim's eyebrows went up. "The place they bombed?"

"We bombed, Jim." She primly said.

"Hm." He got busy with the wheel, not wanting to get into *that* can of worms, knowing how Bern felt about the war.

"His ancestors were samurai," she added.

Jim rubbed his chin and looked at the silly flower-power idiot on the dock, waving now. Why wasn't he out somewhere protesting?

"Yeah, well, I don't see no sword."

It was Bernadette's turn to laugh. No, she couldn't imagine young David with the sword either. It just was not his style.

"He ain't one of them pacifist, is he?" Jim asked.

"Absolutely!"

This time, the old skipper snorted derisively, and turned his attention back to the business of landing the boat.

"Grab the spring line, ya dummy!' he yelled at David.

By now Linda had arrived at dockside with the baby in her arms, sheltered by a red umbrella, and Bernadette found her attention completely riveted. She waved eagerly, jumped up and down. There he was! The little shining Buddha: chubby-cheeked, golden-skinned, narrow-eyed and glistening black hair. Linda held up one of his hands and waved it as he stared gravely down at the boat, taking it all in calmly. No sign of recognition, but then how could that be. He was only a week old when she had last held him. Look at that! Her heart began to thrash too much, and she had to tell herself to be composed. But like the bebe: serene, curious, confident in his universe. So she slowed her waving hand down and just stared, taking a couple of minutes to soak in the sight of the little miracle in front of his eyes before getting around to taking a good look at her daughter, wrapped in some kind of fatigue jacket and blue jeans, her hair back in a long ponytail, wearing hiking boots -- looking rather military except that she had some flowers pinned in her hair. Bernadette could tell immediately from her daughter's distraught look that there was bad news.

The old bugger got away from me, was her first thought. She locked it out. One step at a time. She was *not* going to be denied this. And it could not be that bad -- otherwise Linda would be far more stricken. Her look conveyed bad news, but not the worse.

Because of the low tide, they were now tied up against a dock that was higher than the wheelhouse. The only way ashore was up a rusting old pipe ladder with some two dozen rungs.

Bernadette took one look at the ladder, turned to Jim, and said, "You're going to have to get the dory in the water, Jim, and take me over to a proper dock."

"Ah, I could help you up, Bern. Hell, I could carry you on my back!".

"If you think I'm going up that ladder –"

"Hell, the clinkers all banged up, Bern."

Linda's anxious voice echoed from above: "Mom you can't come up '*that*'!"

"Don't you worry, there's no way on God's green earth –Jim!"

Outnumbered, he grumbled "Awright, awright, don't hen-peck me to death."

Knowing how much more work was involved. "Doug, slack off the boom. Gonna have to put the clinker down."

"Ain't no lifejackets left!" Doug tried.

"Shuddup!"

One last time, the Indian boy fell against the bulwark, giggling uncontrollably. Jim shook his fist at him, "Smart-Alec!"

It took nearly twenty minutes to get the moss-greened old dory in the water, between the boom lines being tangled, a bent buckle, a frayed strap that had to be duct taped, something Jim did sullenly, while Doug and Rene bucketed out the saltwater washed in when they nearly went up on the rocks at Lasqueti. *There* was a story Bernadette sure wasn't going to tell when Linda was round. The poor little hen would have a fit. "Mom, it's too dangerous!" Those would be her words. Mon Dieu, *Life* was dangerous! It was dangerous to drive in that psychedelic van of theirs, she was sure! But you don't stand still. You move. You have to. Sooner or later, you fall -- there was also something sad about the end of a trip on a boat. As the menfolk struggled to free the dinghy -- Jim fuming, Doug spitting snoose vehemently, and little Rene having the brains to look serious indeed this close to the skipper – a long sigh went through her. The boy was the only one having fun. Is that what life did to you? Beat the sense of fun into the ground, piling up responsibilities and debts and schedules and obligations and duties until you couldn't even appreciate the *fun* of a docking anymore? For a moment she was absorbed in what she called her 'Sadness of Life' feeling. When she sensed that underneath everything, including the beauty, there was a bottomless sadness to living, a totally doomed enterprise, with the same ending for everyone: being cancelled, wiped out, completely erased, like a spot-on-glass. And here they all were -- except for the kid -- locked into one unhappy space or another -- Jim because he was going to have to pay docking fees while he waited for the ways to open up, and Doug because he wasn't quite blotto yet, and herself, seething because her plan -- her awful, cruel and perfectly just plan -- might be in jeopardy. And what did it all really matter? A shudder of helplessness passed through her -- and was gone. She took a deep breath and lifted her chin. John would approve. Well, would *probably* approve. That was what had been so wonderful about him. She really never knew until something happened how he would react. He was so much his own man. Old John, she thought. He was so strong. And he said he loved her because *she* was tough. It was the greatest compliment he could give her. Not that she was beautiful or gifted, but tough as nails. Well, she was not going to weaken now.

The boy was sitting at the bow, backpack over his shoulder, headphones on, listening to something.

She had to poke him to get his attention. "What about you?" she demanded. "Need a lift?"

"Nah, I'm OK, Granny." He tapped his wallet. "Got a phone number." He slipped the headphones back on and looked away. He wasn't as happy as she had thought. Troubled by something, too. All that giggling -- probably just nerves.

By the time Doug and Jim managed to paddle the dinghy over to the boat launch ramp, Bernadette could clamber out and walk up the grooves intended to offer car wheels traction, and at less of an angle than normal stairs, it had begun to rain. The cement ramp turned slippery, the Burrard Bridge immediately became a grey silhouette, and the noise of the traffic was muffled. Seagulls settled on pilings to complain loudly. David almost lost his footing in those damn silly sandals hurrying down the ramp to grab his mother-in-law's arm. It was quite unnecessary, since Jim hadn't let go of her right arm for a second since he'd started helping her over the side, and he was determined to walk her safely to the top before he let go.

Didn't need this young jackass gumming up the works. If anything is going to go wrong, it's him falling on his face and dragging them all in. That was Bernadette's concern, too, but it would be an insult to reject help. Gamely, she picked her way up the grooves, trying to keep her balance, both hands pinioned by men of distinctly unequal weight, David slipping, Jim plodding, while little Rene marched up behind, in case she somehow got dropped. Jim had hold of her suitcase. When David reached for it, he held it away.

"What, and have you drop her stuff?"

"David," Bernadette interceded, "this is my good friend Jim Boehm. Jim, this is my son-in-law David Tanaka." Jim grunted, keeping his eyes on where his feet were going.

"Fine by me, Captain," David said politely, although she could tell from his tone that his super hi-fi radar, as he called it, had registered the old man as a racist, and any further hope of communication was probably over. His attention snapped to Bernadette. He kissed her forehead.

"Any adventures, Mother?"

"Nah. Flat calm all the way."

Jim grunted in agreement, but his eyes twinkled in appreciation that she had given the right coast-wise answer. Rene mostly stifled a laugh, nothing Linda would have noticed, although David's ears perked up.

"Is there some element of the story missing here?" he taunted playfully.

"None that's any of your business." It took the longest time to get up the ramp. Silence. The rain. The gulls. Shoes and gumboots on cement. Heavy breathing.

At the top, the proud, radiant, triumphant new mother was waiting with the bebe: the very peak moment of evolution! For a moment, everything felt like a dream. Bernadette was moving slow motion, it seemed, as she reached for him, Linda beaming nervously as she offered him, but not letting go until Bernadette realized just how heavy he was. His head pulled back to regard her with mild curiosity, as he would anyone new swimming into site. A tiny frown took shape just below the glossy hair. She was careful not to rush the contact. Let him see her, maybe even sniff her, hear her voice as she babbled endearments at him, almost whimpering with ecstasy. And then, when his slight stiffening ended, with her arms around him, holding him bottom and back, and Linda finally letting go of his armpits, and he could feel himself being held aloft by her alone, his dark intense gaze suddenly softened, and the sweet, most perfect smiles seized his lips, his apple cheeks pulled back, he lifted a chubby little hand, made a sound like "Ga", and grabbed her eyeglasses. And they all broke into delighted laughter. Maybe I *will* move to town, Bernadette thought in the midst of surging emotions. Oh, so beautiful! So soft! Oh -- and so strong! She tickled his belly and he squealed happily, kicking and waving her glasses, which Linda tried to retrieve. "Say, Hi Grandma! Hi, grandma." But "Ga" was the best they got. And more squeals.

Good lungs, Bernadette laughed joyously. What rapture. Yet in the midst of it she found herself, even though she had sworn she would never do such a thing, looking for traces of Stephen in the baby's face. Not that it should be there. Stephen would have been his uncle, but it *might* be. No. Not a trace. Not only of Stephen, or Laverne, for that matter, or even herself -- the Japanese genes had dominated completely. David's face was there, and probably his father's -- and grandfathers. Little samurai! In some ways, this was *more* than the usual miracle. For look what her own blood had metamorphosed into: not a copy, something different – unpredictable! -- and yet an extension of *her* every bit as much. He would be easy to worship. Was *this* worshiping? No, this was stronger than any worshiping she could remember having done. She had wondered if a grandchild would be the same thing as your own child, but no it wasn't. If anything, it was *more* precious because you could not hold it as tightly as your own.

She turned to show the prize to young Rene, but the kid had slipped. She could see him pushing his way into a telephone booth on the other side of the parking lot. Not missing a beat, she showed the infant to Jim, who made funny faces at him and endured the little finger poking at his nose and eyes as old men are supposed to, but made the mistake of saying, "Ah so."

David bristled immediately. "I see you spreak my ranguage," he snapped in and exaggerating stereotyped accent.

"I see you speak mine," Jim growled back, eyeballing him.

Blinking Jim out of his life, David shifted his attention away to the bebe and held out a finger for him to grab. "Heyyyy...."

"My, isn't this ending on a charming note?" Bernadette said icily, angry with both of them. Men! She grabbed her suitcase from Jim's hand, transferring it to David, who took it with a grunt of satisfaction. Jim rubbed his jaw unhappily. Bernadette gave him a quick peck on the cheek with a touch of her fingers on the back of his neck, a few seconds frozen like that, just to let him know they were still friends, long enough for him to get his arm around her and squeeze her once with longing. She drew quickly away. Otherwise, she would cry. Such a great stout-hearted old gentleman in his own honourable way, not easy to understand and not much caring whether he was understood or not. She knew he'd meant nothing by saying "Ah so." It was a reflex. An effort, really, to communicate. David was too damned prickly, and didn't she smell marijuana on him? But she did not have time or energy to stand around in the rain, trying to make them like each other. "Go," she said to Jim with a firm wave. "I'll call when I get back."

With a perfunctory nod to Linda, ignoring David -- studiously involved with the baby -- the old fisherman put his back to them, and crunched down the ramp to where Doug was waiting, hunched in his yellow rain jacket, hood pulled forward, not looking up at anybody. Poor old booze hound, it was not a life, just going back and forth on a boat, and he had no one, no family -- no precious, radiant, drooling jewel like *this* little one to call his own! She had to yell Doug's name three times before he responded. She waved, showing off the baby. All the engineer managed was a vague salute, a sad little smile. Then Jim was clambering heavily into the boat, keeping his back to her, and the two old farts paddled grimly back across the rain pelted harbor. As they neared the *Mary Boehm*, the bilge pump coughed out a stream of oil, which spread out, breaking into fragments that swilled and leapt in slow motion patterns. David stared, mesmerized, by the spectacle of the slick spreading out in the rain-veiled light. What should have been dark, glowed. What should have been shiny was almost transparent. Faint purple film with traces of bronze and gold an emerald. Flows of silver dissolving into cobalt. Every movement of the water as the ancient dingy with the two men passed through transformed not just the shadows and shapes but the colours, shifting in them. A kind of magic two-dimensional fire seemed to be undulating out of the fish boat's hull. His artist's eye dilated with pleasure, until the reality of what it was clicked in.

"Ought to report the old bastard," David muttered, coming out of it.

"Don't you dare! He's got enough trouble!"

"Just kidding, mother. How *are* you?"

"Group hug," smiled Linda urgently. With the bebe between them, they hugged, and the baby twisted his little head around, laughing, looking up delightedly at each of their faces, grabbing again at Bernadette's glasses, the raindrops beating and running over his seamless, perfect skin -- copper one moment when the red umbrella swung overhead, purple when the blue umbrella was about.

Spoiling the mood, Linda admonished her husband, "You shouldn't have landed on him so hard."

"He deserved it," he replied laconically, proud of something.

Wait. So *that* was how they saw that little exchange at the top of the ramp! Bernadette was astonished that Linda hadn't perceived how big Jim Boehm, in fact, had backed little David Tanaka off real quick, not vice versa. And now David was acting like he hadn't noticed what had really happened. Such bullshit! What world were these two living in? Mon Dieu, in most circumstances Jim would have thrown somebody like David off the dock in a minute for so much as *hinting* he was some kind of redneck. Hell, he was one of the first guys to hire an Indian on the whole West Coast. Redneck he might look like, but he wasn't dumb! Oh contraire! He saw a lot more of what was going on around him than most men she knew -- including this young smart-ass her daughter was so proud of for his supposed moral triumph over the old seadog. Is this what came from living in the city? Jesus Lord.

No! Moving down here and getting involved in all this nonsense -- out of the question! Maybe they could send the baby up to *her*. In her adult life, Bernadette had prided herself on her liberal attitudes. More than attitudes: beliefs, central to the way she tried to make sense of the world. One such belief had been the assumption that her children would be smarter than her, more highly evolved. Stephen certainly hadn't proved that, had he. Super sensitive, but, he did not have enough time on this plain to display his intellect fully to himself or to her. It pained her too deeply to think of his passing. The hurt was ever present. Better to not go there. And if there was one thing that grieved her more about Linda than anything else, it was the fact that the girl just did not seem to know how to use her brain to its capacity. It was a brain in there. Bernadette saw glimpses of it. But what she got back were mostly anguished looks of one kind or another, so the smart part of the child (still a child, yes!) was afraid to come out and compete. She let emotions sweep her back and forth, and poured far too much energy into details, getting bogged down in them. One thing the baby would get was a lot of attention. (Phew! Someday, he will run away from it, and come to me for a while. I'll be there---)

In a cluster, arms around each other, the rain so heavy now the ribs of the umbrellas stood out, they scurried across the wharf towards David's distinct, ridiculous, red, blue, white, green, yellow and black 67 Volks van, its windows covered with Hindu style curtains. In the rain, you could make the mistake of thinking that the paint itself was running, but, no, that was the way it was intended. Apparently had to be on drugs to paint like this. Uh-huh. She could believe it. But the colours were bright and cheerful, and while she was glad no one from Rupert was around to see her climb into this rig, she had to admit it had a certain cheeky charm. You could say that about it. She never minded eccentric people before, why start now? She just didn't expect them to be her own family.

"Lorene called, Mom," Linda said in a strained voice.

"Yes?" Trying to keep the impatience out.

"He's fading faster than they thought."

"How long?"

Deep sigh. (Speak!) "Could be just the next twenty-four hours."

Fear! A ripple went through her whole body; physical fear, as though an animal had jumped out of the bush at her -- because she knew immediately what this meant. She stumbled in the first rush of vertigo.

David caught one arm, Linda the other. "Oh, Mom. You poor soul." Comforting arms, genuine tears against her neck, the bebe tugging her hair. David crowded in protectively, the umbrellas colliding. "We are here for you," he blathered, "you can stay with us, you're coming home with us, Mother." He thought she was grief stricken, but it was terror that left her limp. She saw no way around what she was going to have to do. Except give up, and that was out of the question.

"All very wonderful," Bernadette rasped, straightening herself and fending them off, along with the fear. "But that just means we won't be going to Montreal by train, doesn't it?"

The two young adults stared at her in shock, they started jabbering at once, their umbrellas being shaken emphatically –" Mother!" "Mom!" David let Linda go: "What are you talking about? You would have to *fly*, Mom! On a jet. *Way* up in the air (arms moving in a steep arc), got it?" Thirty-six *thousand* feet, Mother! --- "You'll have a heart attack, for God's sake!" ---"We can't possibly countenance that kind of behavior!"---"A lot of good you'll be to *him* (holding up the Buddha) if you die of a heart attack."--- "You're upset"---"Mom, you can't afford it anyway! You don't even know if you can get the train tickets refunded."

"I sold the two lots up in Desolation Sound."

"You *what*? Oh my God!"

"The water frontage? Not the water frontage!"

"Mom! How could you?"

"Another ten years, if you just could have waited!"

"I'm going." She poured every trick of body language and facial expressions and eye contact and sheer will she knew, drawing on the residue of her once mighty power over this girl. "And you and the baby are coming with me!"

Linda went rigid and instinctively pulled the bebe closer to her breast. "What, take him on a jet? Are you crazy?"

Bernadette said, as evenly as she could, "You have to come with me, sweetheart. And *he* must come too! Please. I don't ask you for anything, not a thing, no hand-outs, eh? But I'm asking you this. Sweetheart. The three of us. We'll –" she gulped, -- fly. You know how scared I am. I can't do this alone, Linda. I need you."

By now the girl should have wavered, but the bebe was in her arms. *He* gave her the power to resist. She had always been stubborn, but now she was unassailable, a full mother in her own right, not to be forced into anything that wasn't in the best interest of the little holy creature she and she alone truly represented. Bernadette knew all the tricks of motherhood. Now she would have to learn the tricks of grand motherhood, and surely the basic one was how to re-subdue your daughter.

"There may be an inheritance involved".

The look that flickered between Linda and her husband was birdlike in its swiftness, both instantly alert. Hippies they might pretend to be, they still obviously understood the value of a buck. So, they weren't complete idiots, even if they looked like it. Linda's expression went from genuine motherly indignance to total mercantile interest with a single blink. The art of Japanese facial nuances did not seem to have rubbed off on her, nor was it very much in evidence in her third generation Canadian-born husband of good Hiroshima stock, whose attention had also been captured entirely.

"Could we get out of the rain, for God's sake?" Bernadette pleaded, sensing the right moment (And before anybody sees me).

The van, it turned out, was parked just a few yards down from the row of phone booths. In the nearest stood Rene Whatever-his-last-name-was, holding a phone to his head, not saying anything. Looking blank. She veered off while David and Linda raced with the baby for the shelter and banged on the glass window. Rene looked up and flashed her a peace sign.

"You all right?" she yelled over the rain. "Did you get through to anybody? He pointed out the receiver, making a face like an idiot. "So, you're getting picked up?" She insisted.

"Yeh yeh yeh. Thanks." He turned his back to her.

There was something wrong, and she knew it. He hadn't got through to anybody. She ought to go back and get him. But he wasn't going anywhere by the looks of it, and, meanwhile, there was plenty enough on her plate to deal with. Next thing she knew, she was at the van's side. Still holding the blue umbrella, David fumbled with the handles two fold open the two side doors, revealing an improbable over-decorated interior that, at first glance, made you think of a bordello, but since that couldn't possibly be what they intended, it must have been modelled after a fairy tale, a place where elves would live -- burning a lot of incense. Bernadette had to grin, shaking her head. It was bizarre and outlandish, and still rather embarrassing, because adults should not have anything to do with a setup like this, but she had to hand it to the kids, they had created something quite extraordinary in here. She'd seen the outside paint job before, a year ago, but the interior hadn't been fixed up like this yet, now it contained a bed that became a foldout table, with room for two people to sit on each side, cupboards, sink, fridge, an propane cooker, Afghan rug on the floor, the ceiling covered with a collage of pictures cut from magazines, making no sense that she could immediately grasp. It was like being in a little sawed-off submarine done up in rococo style, or like an opulent chamber -- well, barely more than a closet -- in a mad Bavarian kings castle. And the great wonder, which would have caused the Kings to go mad (if they weren't already) with envy, was the fact that this luxurious, even decadent little boudoir was mounted on axles and had wheels and a motor and could go practically anywhere.

While they settled themselves inside, Bernadette, Linda and Paul in the back, David squeezed behind the wheel, the windows steamed up, and David turned the engine on, activating little fans that blow warm air at the glass. A heater kicked in at floor level.

"This will take a minute to clear up," he said, turning around in his driver seat, trying to sound casual. "Are we talking about who I think we're talking about?"

Of course, they all knew the family legend of Joe the Mouth Labouchere, who was actually included in Manitoba high school textbooks, although he hardly got a mention in historical histories. They also knew -- hadn't Mom told them a thousand times -- that several years after his wife's death, alienated from his daughters, he had moved to Québec, marrying a nurse – Lorene -- and not having anything more to do with any of his family west of the Québec border. Through his political connections, and his own business acumen, he had -- rumor held -- amassed something of a fortune, probably not that big, but substantial. It was always assumed that when he passed on, the wealth would go to his Québec relatives, who were around to influence him, if he needed any influence. He had banned his children so long before -- even if they were adults by the time he did it -- that he might not actually remember them, depending on how ravaged he was by age. In his late eighties now! But Mom had suddenly opened the door on another possibility entirely. Age of Aquarius notwithstanding, they could use some money. David had another year before he got his degree. If things didn't change, soon enough they'd be *living* in the van, not just camping in it.

"Let's not play games, Mom," Linda nearly shrill. "Are you saying there's money in this for – who? Who for? You? Us?"

Bernadette took hold of the baby's soft miniature chin.

"This little guy."

Bernadette screamed to herself. Don't do this! Once you start lying, you risk everything. When they find out you've lied, they will never trust you again. This is reckless. Sooner or later, it will come out that there was no inheritance in the works, that she had told them a bold-faced lie, all to further her own obscure cause, and she might end up forfeiting everything that remained of her life which was of any substantial value to her, the kids, and the bebe. They could get truly angry about this; she knew perfectly well. But surely, they would understand someday. She just had to keep the truth away from them long enough. She had to do it. She would argue that it was particularly rational, but then, was life? This was going to get her in trouble, no doubt about it, unless she could lay out her basic total lie in convincing detail, and stick to it, riding things out. Never change the story --- One of John's famous admonitions. No matter what. Mon Dieu, that man taught her a lot. 'Don't be afraid to lie. *They* ain't.' Another John-ism.

"Mom!" Linda looked deadly serious." You're not just fucking with our brains, are you?"

"Don't talk like that to your mother!" Bernadette barked.

"Oh Christ, spare me the third person stuff. Just tell me exactly what you're saying."

Bernadette composed herself and lied with a vengeance. "I'm saying the message I got from Lorene was that the evil old bugger wanted to leave something for his great grandson, the sexist pig that he is, but he wanted to see him in person before he died. I am not saying this is *good* or *wonderful.* Same as ever! Does not trust anybody! Especially me!" Bernadette said this with what she thought was just the right mix of exasperation and indignance (I can do that too, sweetheart) to convey her contempt from Mon Pere's tricks. But she had over-acted just a bit, and Linda's hiding brain was peeking out.

"Mom, I don't believe this. This is bullshit!"

"It's not, and what have you got to lose? I'm saying, take a trip with me and the baby to Montreal so I can show off his great grandson to the very old man who's dying, my dying father and your dying Grandfather, what could be wrong with that? Never mind about the money, for the sake of Jesus!"

"Can the Jesus shit, Mom! You only got religious when you're trying to manipulate people!".

David, dismayed. "You can't talk to your mother that way!"

"It's fuckin true!"

Bernadette decided on a new tactic: "She's right. I do." She bowed her head slightly towards her daughter. Linda's look of victory was warming to behold, nothing wrong with that girl. Don't be so driven to win! Bernadette successfully resisted a smirk, fairly sure that this next gambit would work.

"But you know what?" She looked at David directly in the eye, screening out Linda for a moment. "Maybe this time it *is* a religious issue. It's not just Catholicism that talks about forgiveness, is it?"

"Every religion, I think. Every philosophy." This, of course, was where David liked the discussion to be. At *his* level, as he would say.

"Good, because I worry this is just a leftover Catholic habit of mine, I haven't been able to get rid of. But if everybody has an opinion, that is OK? Mine is that I must forgive."

Linda's jaw dropped. "Mom, cut the –"

David brought his hand down in a chopping motion, his face hardening. So! He was more dominating, between them, than you would think from the surface appearance. She noticed her daughter, for all her feminist talk, shut up the moment her man basically snapped his finger.

Linda had the sense to quiet down, her eyes on David, but not because she feared him in any way, this was the one area where she accepted him -- the moral and ecclesiastical -- as the leader, even a teacher, at least in the sense, as the Theosophists said, that, *No man is your friend. No man is your enemy. All alike are your teachers.* She supposed, taken to its extreme, that could even apply to old Mom here. So, she hesitated, in difference to both her husband and her mother, and had a brief, unhappy thought that perhaps some behavior transcended cultures throughout the ages. Either that or she was just oppressed. Why couldn't she tell them what to do? Because, together, they overpowered her, and ---moreover she knew from reading Fritz Perls and R.D. Laing -- they were conspiring at some atavistic level to control her – *And*, through her, the baby! There was a gestalt, sort of like a group psycho-monster, at work, but she couldn't say any of this, of course, without sounding like a paranoid basket-case. (Even if it was true.)

"You want to *forgive* your Dad?" David inquired, in a tone that reminded Bernadette of the way priests used to speak to her through the screen in the confessional booth. Where did he learn to talk like that? "Is that what you're saying? To somehow forgive him?"

"Yes! How many times do I have to say it?"

"But you're afraid of heights! I can't believe you're willing to climb in on a plane, after all these years of refusing to, just so you can rush to your father's side, a man you have always told us was a really bad piece of human shit, so you can forgive him! This doesn't compute. What are we dealing with here -- the Mother Teresa of False Creek?"

He laughed but looked at her piercingly. The clatter of rain on the van's tin roof had eased up and the windows were almost clear. The light caught his eye a certain way. He was on to her. On to the fact that something was wrong. No fool, this one, despite the fruitcake look. He had grown out of that. Good for her daughter that she landed one who was not completely brain dead, especially nowadays, with all the drugs and radiation from TV sets. So, she had to ratchet her story up a notch.

"David, you and me, we've yapped a bit about mystical stuff a few times, and I've agreed with you that, even if I don't believe in God, I admit something still seems to be going on. I don't know what. And then you talk about all the ancient wisdom from Two-Humps-Camel-Land—"

"Tibet," David said. He and Linda both laughed, gently but with superiority. ('Let them think they are smarter': John again.)

"Tibetan Buddhism! Something about karma. Do you believe in that stuff?"

David paused. "Well, karma is not just a Buddhist idea –"

"But it means if you do something bad, something bad comes back to you?"

"Well, it's more cause and effect, not just eye for an eye."

"But if you forgive somebody you wind up being able to forgive yourself."

"I've never heard it put quite that way, but it has a ring." He was being oh so coy with her. "That actually sounds more like a Laingian Knot." He looked over to Linda to see if she caught that. She nodded admiringly at the profundity of his words.

Bernadette caught her breath. This was going nowhere. So much for trying to talk mumbo jumbo.

"Look," she said, letting her voice rise, "I've hated my father almost all my life, and here's my last chance to make my peace with him. It's important to me, OK?" Bernadette kept her eyes fixed on David's, leaned forward, and spoke with all the passion she could summon: "If I don't do this now, I'll be haunted the rest of my life by the fact that *I didn't* take the chance to see if we could forgive each other before he was gone –"

David intruded: "So it's not just you are forgiving him now, it's you and him forgiving each other, hm?"

"That would be a miracle! That's the best I can hope for out of this. But it is not just me involved, of course. I don't really matter except he knows I can get in the way of him seeing the one person he wants to see most in the whole world, his one and only great grandson. Or I can bring him to his side. That's how I can forgive him his trespasses, by sharing this -- gift of life -- with him."

But she had overplayed it again. A little too lyrical. Their suspicions came back -- particularly Linda -- knowing how vociferously *anti*-religious her mother usually was, and how she had been that way for as long as anyone could remember. Why the sudden conversion?

Softly, trying to be highly intelligent, David said. "I thought forgiving trespasses was something only priests or God could do?"

But he had overplayed it too, and Linda snapped at him: "What kind of sexist shit is that?"

Bernadette left them to squabble for a minute about the fine points of female liberation, glad that her daughter could carry the argument, even if she were making a fuss, as usual, over details, missing the substance. Fortunately, her radical blither blather had successfully deflected David from penetrating into the hollowness of Bernadette's theological case.

"Don't be ridiculous," the older woman finally said, allowing her anger and frustration to get into her voice. "I'm trying to do the right thing by my dying father, and you're opposing that."

Again, at the same time, their expressions changed. They were suddenly shamefaced. Kids again.

"Mom, I'm sorry," Linda whispered, leaning forward and clutching her around the shoulders, the baby squeezed between so that he protested with a squeal.

"OK, Mother," sighed David. "The nearest travel agent. Or straight to the airport?"

Bernadette groaned. "Airport"

The rain was shaping up to be the kind that lasts for days and weeks. After tapering slightly, it had trickled again. As David cranked the van into gear, Bernadette pulled open the curtains to see if young Rene was ready to accept a lift to wherever he was going. He would get a kick out of seeing the inside of a real hippie van. More to talk about when he got home. But the booth where she last saw him was empty and the phone was back on the receiver.

"David, can you circle around, look for him?"

They drove the length of the wharf, paused at the top of each floating dock to look and see if the kid had wandered down there to look at the boats, but the docks were uninhabited. Nobody came out into the rain unless they had to. The decks of the boat were just as empty, and the parking lot, now that they were gone;

abandoned. The storage sheds were locked. A plague might as well have come. David patiently idled the engine, allowing Bernadette to peer through her binoculars, even though they both knew it was useless. The only sounds were the splattering of rain sluicing down through troughs and pipes, the echoing of a streetcar over the bridge, the screeching of bumpers, the piercing shrieks of gulls. Uncovered, the old clinker dinghy was tied up beside the *Mary Boehm*, filling up with water again, and the lights were on in the galley, Jim and Doug settling in for the long haul. Even though it was only mid-afternoon, the day was being bled away, rinsed away, flushed. Drains gurgled and bilges sloshed. She focused on a cormorant perched on a wobbling piling, followed a muskrat sleuthing across the tide flat, a dog rummaging in some garbage, but no trace of the boy. The wind off False Creek rattled the van, making it yaw on its springs. He was gone. Just like that. Surely, if he were in trouble, he would go back to the boat. Jim would not be able to just toss him out without calling somebody, like the relatives up in Rupert who had arranged to put him on the boat in the first place. Jim was not that kind of man. But if the boy had no intention of going back to anyone or anywhere, he would not be showing up at the boat. And there wasn't much chance, on his own, he'd ever find his way back to Portage la Prairie, either. Not once the lure of downtown hit him. She feared he would pass through Skid Road, which was where he might be heading straight for right now, find some brothers, and learn about the streets. Well, she pegged him for a runaway right from the start. Just waiting for his chance. Had probably thought getting to a reserve on the northwest coast was pretty good after Portage, but now, after a while up there, the city lights must look awfully bright, and he sure wasn't interested in going back to where he'd got away from. He was out there somewhere in the rain, climbing toward that grey bridge with the lights coming on, probably about to have the time of his life, even if it killed him.

PART SEVEN

A TREE ON SIDE THE SEINE RIVER, ST. BONIFACE

1934

The chunks of the ice left behind when the river retreated were coated with a film of streaked black soil washed up from the parishes to the south, some from as far away as North Dakota. They lay at awkward angles, like wrecks, melting quickly because there was no leafy canopy to shield them from the Prairie sun. The trees immediately along the river's edge had been submerged all through June in opaque clayish water and had sprouted no leaves. The underbrush lay flat and covered with a crust of dried clay. Elsewhere, Bernadette knew, there were places where the water had spread out as much as ten miles from its banks. Here, behind the house, the Seine had risen thirty feet, but had been contained almost completely within the ravine. The water had crept up to within a couple of feet of the back-porch steps, but it stopped there. Except for the one thing that went wrong, the flood would have passed the Laboucheres by without damage. The house, it seemed, stood on a slight rise of land that no one had really noticed before. Water had entirely covered the fields to the east and had oozed silently out onto the road in front of them. But it was only a couple of inches deep and could be driven through without a problem.

There had been talk of building a dike along the train tracks to the West, which would have left the Labouchere house just outside the perimeter of the city's defences. There had been a lot of grim laughter about that -- leaving the mayor's house out in the water on the wrong side of the dike, but Joe himself had not said anything about it and hadn't seemed concerned, although it was worth noting that the dike, in fact, never got built. Who could tell whether Joe Labouchere had had a hand in that? Would not put it past him. But of course, then the business of his boy disappearing had happened, and no one made jokes anymore.

A month after the peak of the flood, everything below the Seine River's high-water mark was coated with slime, baked on the surface, although still cold to the touch, and like sticky wet gum underneath. The squirrels had not returned from whatever places they had run to hide. There were no traces of rabbits, gophers or garter snakes. The only animal life Bernadette spotted as she picked her way in an agony of terror and disgust down the slippery embankment was a rat gliding with horrible quietness into the murk of the river, leaving hardly a ripple.

Her legs trembled. Her feet kept sinking into the grey mulch past her ankles, up to within a few inches of the tops of the old fashioned many buttoned shoes Ma Mere insisted she wear, even though Bernadette burned with embarrassment at being seen in such granny clothes. The snickers of the other girls, with their sleek ankle length laced footwear, was unbearable. All the more so because she herself had been so rude to them all along, and especially since the day Mon Pere got elected. He was not a girouette any longer, was he? Despite herself, she had felt a surge of pride in her father. She still hated him for everything at home – Ma Mere's eternal mood of misery, the need for all of them to wait on him hand and foot, his absolute indifference to anything that was happening to anyone in the family except himself, the endless business of having to help him dress, help him up from sitting or lying down until he could steady himself with his canes, help him through the doors, down the stairs, into cars, out of cars, into the pew at church, out of the pew, back onto the steps, into the bathtub, out, on an on and on. And almost never a word of thanks. It had fallen to Bernadette, naturally, to become Ma Mere's assistant, and it had fallen to Ma Mere, just as naturally, to become Mon Pere's full-time servant. True, the burden had eased slightly over the years, as Joseph recovered to the point where, today, he was only a quarter as helpless as the first year after they brought him home from the hospital. He'd been in a wheelchair, then hadn't he? It took some time before he'd been able to walk unaided except for the canes into meeting halls to make the speeches that everyone loved so much they came from miles away to hear. Mon Pere was so inspiring, wasn't he? At least that was the word she had heard used. Well, they should see him at home, she thought bitterly. He sits there like a Pharaoh, eh? On his throne. And all he does is talk, talk, talk, all that boring stuff about politics and what he thinks about this and what he thinks about that, and the worst part is that every time someone comes over to visit, they sit there, just as silent as the rest of us, while Mon Pere goes on an on and on. When he got beat up there at the bridge, something must have come loose. He talks now more than Grande Ma Mere, and for some reason everyone seems to listen to him. Some reason. Oh, yes. Because he is a hero. And the Mayor on top of it. He is happy. It was worth it. Now nobody can tell him to shut up. Yet, despite all that, a queer thrill, enormously powerful, had passed through Bernadette's body when the word reached the house that evening that Mayor Huot had been defeated by Joseph Labouchere by a margin of several thousand votes. A *sweep* was the word they had used. And hadn't Mon Pere grinned? Well, she had grinned too. Ma Mere had wept with joy -- or maybe it was not joy. None of the children had been able to tell for sure.

How long had it been now since there had been even a peep of laughter in the Labouchere house? Well, certainly not since the third of June, the day Jean-Paul went missing.

That was the phrase they still used around the house -- went missing. Gone missing. Missing. Sometimes they just said 'went" or occasionally only referred to him as "gone". No one ever said anything about him being dead or drowned. He was just missing and since nobody had been found, he was, indeed, just missing. Except it was the end of the first week in August and Jean-Paul had been missing, especially during a flood that had only seen the waters fall back to their ordinary summertime levels within a week or so.

For all we know he is dead, Bernadette thought. But no one wants to be the first to say it. We all still carry on as though he is going to walk in through the back door, dirty and hungry, any minute, full of stories about his adventures. It's not going to happen. The thought sank through her mind like a weight plunging to the bottom. It's not going to happen. We're all kidding ourselves. Not even doing that, really. We're just not facing it. No one can face it.

She suddenly stopped and her shoulders began to heave. She cried with the racking; gasping forced that suggested a release She had not experienced before. Yet not a single one of the last forty-four days had passed without her breaking down crying several times during the agonizing periods between sleep. If it wasn't she who triggered it, it was one of the other girls, or Mere or Grande Ma Mere. Mon Pere himself had not cried once in front of anyone, unless it was Ma Mere in the privacy of their bedroom, but what he did do was stare a lot into the air. If there was nothing else to be grateful for in the whole world, there was this one thing. Mom Pere had finally shut his mouth. He hobbled around in the backyard a lot by himself and offered no comfort to either his wife or his daughters, but neither did he ask for any. He just withdrew into himself. If she could, Bernadette would have blamed him for what happened to Jean-Paul, and there were moments when, yes, she could see it was all Mon Pere's fault for moving them in from Agassiz to here, otherwise Jean-Paul would never have been near the Seine at the time of the flood, but Bernadette was already a little too old for that notion to stick for any length of time. That was too far back. Much too far back. Or was it? Who could you blame? You could not blame God. How could you blame Jean-Paul himself?

Oh surely there had to be some way to go back in time to the day before it happened, to just go back that one day, and lock Jean-Paul in his room, surround him with people to watch him, and sit tight until the next day had passed, and then let him out, so that he'd be here now. Oh, how could it have happened? How could have been allowed to?

As she cried, hands covering her eyes, she saw again the long thin line of men, most of them wearing hip waders, sloughing through the rain along the edge of the water. Men. Hundreds of men, including the entire police force, sloshing through the mud, some of them up to their waists in the dangerous bogs along the racing great torrent, probing with sticks at every half submerged dead hog or calf or dog. Priests and nuns, too, had fanned out along the river, their dark robes making them look from the distance like birds of prey. In the middle of this small army of searchers, Ma Mere herself had crashed through the water, a wordless scream lodged in her throat, panting, floundering, cursing as she had never cursed, tearing her hands on brambles, glimpsing her child one thousand times in her imagination, and at least twice throwing herself headlong into the torrent, even though she couldn't swim, thinking she spotted a small boy just below the surface. She had been like a wild animal in pain and finally two of her brothers had caught her and dragged her home, while she wailed and thrashed in their arms. Mon Pere had struggled to join the search, but his canes had sunk in the muck and he pitched face first into the shallow cream coloured water that filled the backyard. Bernadette remembered seeing him start crawling, his glasses dangling from one ear, while he made gagging sounds. Then he, too, was dragged inside.

It had poured all that day of the search, and the river was speckled, its gurglings and slushings muted in a great *HISSSSSS* of rain. Men yelled back and forth through the leafless trees, grunting, panting, their boots making popping sounds as they pulled them with effort to free them of the mud. Branches and twigs crackled as the men crashed heavily through the underbrush. By the time darkness fell, there hadn't been a man present whose face didn't register his belief that the boy was gone and that he would probably not come back up to the surface for days, by which time he would either be snagged underwater or his remains would have been carried miles downstream. From the tracks in the mud, the police said they were pretty certain he had crossed the field east of the house, following a plateau that was just high enough so that it had taken the shape of a peninsula. When it fell off finally into the swollen river, it did so abruptly. There, by an Oak that had long ago been shattered by lightning and whose tree trunk arched over the water, the tracks the police had been following ended. They guessed he tried to climb out over the flood stream and must have slipped. By then, he would have been too far from the house for anyone to hear his cries for help.

It had been too wet for hounds to determine that the tracks were Jean-Paul's, for sure, and there was no proof that whatever boy had got to the shattered Oak to climb it hadn't simply climbed down into the water at the very edge of the stream and waded away. He had been wearing rubber boots, after all.

Yep, for all the 'ifs', Bernadette had dimly realized all along that the search was not really a search. It had been a dark and necessary ritual, a chance for the whole community to close in around one of the most famous members, around the whole remaining Labouchere family, so that individual grief might become community grief. Each man in the search party took on part of the loss, scrambling through the bush as though it was his own child he sought, and each of the women who worked day and night for close to a week to keep the food and dry clothes available had become the child's mother, absorbing some small part of her pain, diffusing it, spreading it around, sharing it. Bernadette was a long way from understanding yet what it was that made people struggle on so far beyond the point where there was any hope at all. In part, she guessed, it was practice. All those people who had come around to help, she was sure they were preparing themselves for the day when they too must face such loss. They were here to get the feel of it, maybe so they would be that much more able to cope with the situation when their own turn came. In part, it was not so different from the thrill of the hunt, whether for an animal or a criminal. Everyone stood the chance of being the one to find him, to be loved by everyone for having done it.

But there was something more. A demonstration, an expurgating of secret guilt that everyone felt for having been so undeservedly spared themselves.

Bernadette remembered the police chief, Andre Joyal, dragging himself exhaustedly into the kitchen at the end of the sixth day, the great grey chest of water locked shut behind him, revealing nothing. "We can only help him by praying now," Joyal had said.

Oh, they had prayed. The whole family had prayed. The relatives prayed. The whole city prayed. Hundreds and hundreds of candles had been lit, not only at the Basilica, but in the churches in surrounding parishes, where Joe Labouchere was still a legend for his attempt to hold back the Canadian Army at the Provencher bridge. Bernadette could not count how many times she had heard people saying, "Isn't that a bitch?" "Poor Joe. Of all people. He did not deserve that, God's will, eh? But how can you understand that?" For a while, the only subject that Joseph and Augustine Labouchere could talk about was their son who was missing, and Ma Mere would break down crying every time. Mon Pere looked almost watery, as though he was going to dissolve and fade away any moment. His voice was shaky and faint. He seemed to have lost all his strength. And mostly he stared. Bernadette noticed after a while that when either he or Ma Mere mentioned Jean-Paul's name, the other adults present became embarrassed and looked away. Sometimes, if the talk went on too long, they got up rather rudely and hurriedly made some excuse to leave. Sometimes she heard people talking in English, which she had been studying at school and knew well enough to pick up most of the inflections. English, she had long ago discovered, was a language that many French adults used to communicate sensitive subjects among themselves without the children knowing what they were talking about. It had been partially because of this awareness that she had plunged so eagerly into her English language studies, although there were plenty of other reasons. Thus, she overheard uncle Robert say to Aunt Bernice, in English: "They are carrying on too long, these two," meaning Mon Pere and Ma Mere. Surprisingly,

Aunt Bernice had replied, "I think so. I'm sick of it." Yet, in French, and when Mon Pere and Ma Mere were around, the uncle and aunt were nothing but tenderly sympathetic. The more she began to understand about adults, the more confused Bernadette got. They were always saying different things to different people and different things again when they were alone. It was almost as though you couldn't believe anything they said.

The praying had not stopped. Even up until the night before, Bernadette had said her own prayers over and over again. She had arrived at a decision. Specifically, she had turned her prayers to the Virgin Mary, asking that this be made the day that Jean-Paul either came home or else his body was found, because the waiting and not knowing couldn't go on any longer. It was worse than anything she could imagine, worse even, she suspected, then knowing once and for all that he was dead

DEAD. DEAD. DEAD. The word haunted her. She found her breath coming in an uneasy gasp. It was not just the thought that her brother was dead. For, ever since leaving the lush August crabgrass and blackberry bushes behind, descending into the grotto-like ravine behind the house, she had had the feeling normally associated with entering a cemetery. Everything was the colour of wasp's nests and cocoons and rain-soaked rags. Trees whose soil had been leached away by the spring torrent creaked as they staggered in the breeze, held upright by nothing more than a fistful of roots desperately seeking to grip in the slippery paste that was all that was left behind in the wake of the flood. Many of these weakened trees bore extra burdens of debris deposited high on their branches making them as wobbly as overloaded ships. The wreckage of chicken coops, tires, a broken wooden chair, two by fours escaped from the lumberyard, a perfectly good wash tub, even part of a bridge pontoon -- anything that the river had been able to carry away.

Bleakly, she wondered if the pain would ever go away. She didn't think so. She guessed that she would feel this awful emptiness forever until she died. She guessed that nothing would ever be the same and that the best part of her life was over. The only relief she had been able to find so far was in the recital of her beads. Aloud, now, she tried to pray, to ward off the fear that crept into her limbs.

"Hu-hu hail MMM Mary, fu-fu-full of grace, the Lord is w-w-w-with thee, bl-bl-bl-bl—"

Her voice was scarcely much more than a whisper yet hearing herself say it -- please come home --- made matters worse. She knew it was futile, that her prayers would not be answered this time, at least not the way she wanted them answered.

The horror was so overwhelming that for several moments she remained rooted up to her ankles in slime, wishing that God would just make her vanish -- and then a lingering child thought occurred that sustained her: A miracle would happen, like the miracle of Lourdes, a flaming bush or an angel, or even just a deep voice speaking through the spectral trees, and Jean-Paul would come running toward her, and they would go home, hand in hand, and the whole family would celebrate Mass together, and from all over St Boniface everyone would gather at the Basilica, maybe the Pope would come from Rome to kneel before the child, Saint Bernadette, whose faith and prayer had restored the lost brother to life, and even a snarling dog that belonged to Dolbeaus down the street would wag its tail at her ---

If the dream was fragile, it was at least warm and comforting, and there was nothing in her experience yet that ruled it out absolutely. Sniffling and wiping her nose and eyes, she started walking again, feeling a bit of hope she had felt in the morning, when she made up her mind to go looking for Jean-Paul herself. In her mind's eye she scarcely saw the bones of the tree around her nor the death-sheet soiled ground.

In fact, as she stumbled along, cheeks streaked with tears, lower lip trembling, Bernadette smiled to herself, fully convinced for the moment that the fantasy was real. Jean-Paul's hand was warm in hers. God walked with them -- she could tell from the passing impressions of sunbeams moving through the wire-thin branches, just like the coloured pictures in the Catechism books that showed the Saints or Jesus or Mary standing with their heads bowed in a golden shaft of light from Heaven. For the first time since the accident, Bernadette was momentarily joyous, her pale face almost radiant. There was a slight spring to her step, quite unconscious.

By the time she remembered where she was again what she was supposed to be doing, she had covered nearly half a mile of snaking, looping riverbank, so close to the eastern edge of town that she began to get nervous, thinking about coyotes.

It was an area that had been searched dozens of times by hundreds of men. Dead leaves rustled slightly on the ground, despite their film of dried clay. The trees creaked more often. The gurgling of the river sounded much louder. The ravine had widened and sloped more gently back up to the tabletop of the grassy plains all around. The dead underbrush was thicker, too, and even though the nettle stalks were waterlogged and sagged close to the ground, their thorns still pricked at her skirt. Somehow, despite her best attempts to stay clean, grey splotches of mud had splattered as much as halfway up her knees.

She was out of breath from the desperately difficult business of trying not to fall on her face while thrashing through the slippery mud. She was suddenly aware how far, already, she was from home.

It had taken all her courage just to come down into this haunted place. She suddenly felt frightened. At the back of her neck she got that shiver she always got when nightmares started, and she wanted right away to wake up but could not. It wasn't just that the thought of coyotes -- or wolves -- that started her heart pounding again, it was also the sharp memory of the dream she'd been having almost every night for a week -- that Jean-Paul was in Purgatory and he was screaming in panic for her to come and get him out. She learned how to wake up from that nightmare, at least. Quickly. It was too violent, too savage, too adult for her. She squeezed her eyes tight and refused with all her will to even – allow – the – thought—to – occur.

It was the most painful thought of all. No one had said

anything, neither her parents nor uncles or aunts or priests or the nuns, but Bernadette was not at all sure herself that Jean-Paul had automatically gone to Heaven.

And this place here, where the ground looked like the leftover grime at the bottom of a wash tub, and the trees all seemed to be kind of sick and soggy and rotten, and the stink of the river was just exactly like everybody in the world had been sick in it. This was probably just like Purgatory. It seemed so much like her dream, she jerked her head over her ears, terrified that at any second, she would hear Jean-Paul's high pitch screams.

But there was only the gargling of the river, the faint hiss of pie-sized whirlpools forming along the savagely eroded banks, the plock of some object either falling or diving into the water. Sparrows darted like animated leaves. A robin called querulously, searching for a lost nest. A young poplar leaned out, trembling, almost horizontal over the current. So narrow was the Seine that the poplar reached more than halfway to the other side, yet on the surface of the water there was no hint of a reflection, only a blurred shadow on the thick mud soup swirling below.

Bernadette made a supreme effort to get back to the bliss of her prayer-fantasy. And after a few minutes, the nightmare passed from her mind. She felt again the presence of the Holy Virgin, the certainty that her prayers would be answered. For, as far as she knew, prayers were as substantial as locomotives or threshing machines. They were even like arithmetic. If you committed a small sin, you had to say a small number of Hail Mary's and Our Fathers. For a bigger sin, a bigger number. She was not quite sure how many prayers equal how many sins. That was something only the priest really knew. And while she had a clear idea of the difference between venial sin, which didn't deprive the soul of sanctifying grace, and mortal sin, like killing, which did, she understood that there were some sins which needed more than just Hail Marys and Our Fathers -- they needed Confession and Communion and Absolution and sometimes you had to light candles and go to early Mass all during the week as well as High Mass and Catechism on Sunday. But in the end, it was always the same -- just like putting the washing through the wringer. The soul came out pure and clean again.

Already, Bernadette was feeling better, prepared to step into the role of small saint.

Yet Purgatory -- surely God would not have sent Jean-Paul to Purgatory, not unless he had done something that no one else knew. He had sneaked away from the yard, against Ma Mere's orders, and he was bad in church, nothing that could not be fixed with a few Hail Marys.

But there was a dark hole in her knowledge of the arithmetic of prayer. She knew that once you were Baptized, you were Baptized, but all it guaranteed was that you would not go to Hell. To get to Heaven, she was fairly sure, you had to have Last Communion, which, of course, Jean-Paul had not had.

The tension of not knowing where her brother's soul had gone had left its mark upon her. Until that summer, her aunts and uncles had always described her as flighty. She giggled too much. She liked to roll her dark chestnut eyes in an exaggerated expression. And flutter her eyelashes at boys, tilting their head to one side mockingly, even though she felt a terrific indifference towards them. She was a couple of inches taller than the girls in her class, and so thin that her ribs stood out, the only one of the Labouchere girls who was not plump.

Her complexion had always been pale, but now the skin of her face was almost translucent. Fine blue and purple veins could be seen in the cheeks that had lost their childhood puffiness, allowing the high knobs of her cheekbones to emerge, giving her an appearance strikingly like that of a plains Metis.

Once, she had overheard her Aunt Jeanine joke that there must have been "an Indian in the woodpile" somewhere back in the families long past history in Québec, where all the Laboucheres, until Mon Pere and uncle Emile had lived. She was not quite sure what an Indian "in the woodpile" meant, but when she asked her father, he snorted angrily. "That's dirty talk," he said. "Stop it!" That had not answered her question, but there were so many other French families in Saint Boniface with bone structure like hers that she assumed it had something to do with having been Québécois for so long.

And besides, for years now it had not mattered what anyone thought of her -- whether she was too skinny, or too silly or too Metis -- not since Mon Pere had become Mayor. At school, she had been free, during lunch time and after classes, to be as snobbish as she liked, and she had revelled in it, learning to turn her small nose up in a way that she knew infuriated the girls with whom she did not wish to talk.

But now Bernadette felt neither snobbish nor sassy and had not been flighty since that day. She had even worried -- desperately, at night -- that her own sins, venial though they were, might have had something to do with what had happened. It was, in part, in the genuine hope of making penance for the smart-alec she had been, that she had forced herself to come down into this grey oozing ditch, this kind of Station of the Cross by the river, this doorway into Purgatory and death.

That there was death all around her, she knew. It was the main reason -- apart from the fact that Jean-Paul had disappeared and they didn't want any other little boys or girls disappearing -- that the nuns and health nurses alike had warned the children not to venture below the high water line for the duration of the summer. Fear of diseases with strange names that came from decaying animal bodies. And fear, above all, of malaria from the mosquitoes.

Yet mosquitoes had so far turned out to be hardly any problem. It was not just that Bernadette was covered entirely, despite the heat, in thick woolen stockings and long sleeves, her neck protected by a high lace collar and her dark hair deliberately swept down so it covered as much of her head as possible. It was, rather, that there were few mosquitoes in the air. The rare one that tried to approach her skin was easily, automatically dealt with. The fiercely surging flood tide of June had wrecked worse havoc among the mosquitoes than any other creature, engulfing and obliterating any traces of the quiet back eddies, the scummy ditches and green-weed blanketed ponds where they normally bred.

But flies. As if to make up for the loss of mosquitoes, there were more huge black flies than she could ever remember seeing. And they behaved differently. They seem to be ignoring her, concentrating in dozens of droning, buzzing clusters, hovering in constant motion above tiny anthills on the ground.

Except that they were not anthills.

They were little bumps covered with moving ants, with a shudder, she remembered the bloated dead pig she had seen being swept past when the flood was cresting. Belly up, it had gone sailing slowly by, with a horde of flies darting above it.

Carefully, she avoided looking directly at the little mounds where the ants were swarming, and the flies were making a sound almost like grease sizzling in a pan. She most definitely did not want to see what was below, whether it was dead catfish or a squirrel or a bird or whatever.

She failed to realize that just in the act of not running headlong from that place -- in forcing herself to come to the river's edge to begin with -- she had displayed far less squeamishness than most of her aunts, and possibly even her mother, and less fearlessness than many of the boys her own age.

But she had reached her limit.

She knew that if she turned now and headed up the slope to the clear open prairie above the ravine, she would be within running distance of the road that led past the packing house and lumber yard to her home. The grey spooky trees with their dead things and flies would be behind her. The pious certainty she'd felt when she started her search had worn itself out just controlling the terror she experienced every time a twig cracked, or a branch shifted position.

This was no place for a Miracle of Lourdes to happen. It was too smelly, too filthy, too scary.

She had taken no more than a dozen careful steps uphill, almost tiptoeing, to the extent that it was possible in the dank sludge without falling flat, and was feeling proud of herself for not looking back over her shoulder for fear of ghosts or coyotes, feeling proud that she hadn't started running like a baby, when her eyes roved upward, seeking a trail to the top of the slope, and instead she saw the doll sitting in the tree.

For close to a minute, she stared, amazed. A stick-limbed doll with a blue jacket and shoes, caught on a branch. Waterlogged, like everything in this awful place. But intact. And her first thought was that maybe she could get a stick and reach up and dislodge it and take it home and fix it. The head was caved in like a baked apple and was hard to make out because there were flies buzzing around it too. But it could all be scrubbed and disinfected and repainted. She spotted a little plaster-of Paris hand.

It was only maybe ten or twelve feet up the tree, caught there just like all the other junk she had seen.

From the first instant, she had probably recognized the bluejacket, but some part of her did not want the recognition to occur. Unlike the other dead things she had averted her eyes from, she looked at this intensely, eagerly, curiously, even greedily, thinking how nice it would be to fix it up for one of her little sisters, and so she was off guard and the picture that leapt into her senses was far from indistinct. It was, finally, grotesquely detailed.

What she had taken to be cracks in the plaster-of Paris were lines of ants marching single file. There were no eyes, only dark open passages where streams of insects converged in slow motion turmoil. The skin of the face had been replaced by a fine scaly covering of lice that quivered as though each single pore pushed out a single murky teardrop, a little blob of solder that trembled on the edge of falling away. Yellowish teeth could be seen -- the beginning of a lopsided grin. The curly brown ringlets were flattened against the skull, matted with bits of twigs and moss. From one ear a big black beetle was emerging.

Now, finally, she knew what it meant for the soul to be taken away. The body was neither hanging in the tree nor even snagged, like the other garbage she had seen. Instead, it sat -- as though waiting, maybe even hiding, ashamed of what it had become.

Desperately, she covered her eyes, but it was too late. The thing inside her mind. When she screamed, it was as much because she knew she would never be able to chase it out, as it was because the thing in the tree was her brother.

The police chief drove Mayor Laboucheres home, helping him from the car, and then up the steps up to the front door. Joseph wielded his canes absentmindedly, making it more difficult for Joyal to help him than if he had simply tucked them under his arms and let himself be carried. But that would never do. There was Joseph's pride. And there was the respect that the men like Joyal felt towards him. It was alright to help le petit maire but not alright to lift him entirely, unless it was on your shoulders at a rally, so people could see him.

The chief constable had expected the house to be swarming with relatives, the woman already in black, with preparations for Requiem Mass fully underway. Instead, he thought for a moment the house was empty. Then he saw a shape moving behind the curtained oval door window. It was Madame Labouchere.

Francois Joyal had the feeling that he was a delivery boy again, as he had been in his childhood, only instead of delivering potatoes or coal, he was delivering a sleepwalker. Mayor Labouchere had stared straight ahead all the way home, saying nothing. He stood in front of his own front door the same way, balanced between his canes, withered, silent, vacant. His hands were trembling. The policeman was still holding him by the elbow, almost as though he was delivering a prisoner.

"It never rains but it pours, eh? Joe." The chief said, aching for the moment when Madame Labouchere would take the Mayor off his hands.

The woman opening the door was wearing a grey shirt waist dress, her hair disheveled -- in contrast to the severe netted bun she usually wore. Her eyes were red. Her cheeks were wet. She clutched a soaked handkerchief and a black bead rosary in one hand. The other let go of the doorknob and flew to her lips as her eyes fixed on her husband's face.

Stricken as she had looked when the door opened, she looked twice as stricken now. It just took a second, but in that time, Augustine's pain seemed to double. Francois Joyal had to turn his face away. The site of men suffering scarcely made him flinch, but with women it was different. He had no stomach for it. He bowed automatically, and stood back, hat in hand, not daring to look at Madame Labouchere's bewildered, torn features. My, he thought, Joe is lucky. A woman like that who sees your pain even in the midst of her own, that is one strong woman to have to take care of him. Joe was in good hands. Amen.

He hurried down the steps to the waiting black car. God damn, why do things like this have to happen to such people as that, eh? A good man. A good woman. As the car pulled away, the policeman caught a glimpse of the Mayor and his wife, still on the porch. She had her arms around him. Then he saw Joseph canes drop. One of them clattered down into the front yard. Madam Labouchere was carrying her husband into the house, holding him in a bear hug.

Joseph was only vaguely aware of being home. In his mind's eye, he was seeing scenes from distant moments in his life, one forming after another in no order whatsoever. Daydreaming would have been the word that most people would have used to describe his state, but to Augustine it was something more like Joseph being sucked into a void, the doorway to his inner world closed tight behind him.

This might be the time he will not come back, she thought.

She gripped him as you might a man dangling over a cliff or someone half-drowned in the water. She felt him gasping for air, grunting from the pain he must be causing his back, but did not lessen the pressure. She had been bracing herself for over an hour for the moment when Joseph would be brought home to her. She knew that if there was ever a time when he might turn into a permanent daydreamer, it was now. She had lost her only son already. She did not want to lose her husband too. And it would be worse, having his body here, if his mind were not around.

"Oh Joseph, oh Joseph, Joseph, Joseph, Joseph, please, please, please, hear me, Joseph, don't go away, please don't go away! I need you, Joseph! I need you! Joseph, oh my poor wounded Joseph!"

She placed him tenderly on the settee, then settled on her knees on the floor, her arms around his shoulders, face pressed against his chest. She squeezed him again, then lifted her face to look at his. Her hands cupped his head, forcing it downward so she could look directly into his eyes.

There seemed to be no spark of recognition. Or rather, there was, and then there was not. It was like someone coming up for air, then vanishing.

"Oh Joseph!" she cried once more. Then, without quite realizing what she was doing, she slapped him across the left cheek so hard that his glasses were knocked half off his face and a bright red welt appeared.

He looked at her, dazed and startled. The recognition came flooding back.

"Augustine?"

"I'm here," she gasped. "And you, Joseph Labouchere, are you still here too?".

"They found ---"

"Yes, I know."

A spasm passed through Joseph's body, but no tears welled up in his eyes. His chin quivered. He opened his mouth to say something, then shut it. He tried to look away, but Augustine was sitting beside him now, his face clasped in her palms, forcing him to maintain eye contact.

Desperately, his eyes pulled away, sweeping the room. He seemed not to feel the sting that must be in his cheek.

"Where is everybody?" he asked.

"At Florence's."

"Why aren't they here?"

"I asked Flo to take the girls and tell everyone to keep away and leave us alone until eight."

"Eight?"

"The Requiem is at nine."

"Shouldn't we "--

Augustine shook her head.

"No. I want us to be alone."

She took a deep breath, planning on explaining what she had been thinking and feeling since the moment when the Chief Constable had arrived at the front door with the news that Bernadette had found Jean-Paul's body. But the words would not come. Instead, she buried her face into Joseph's neck, and clutched him again as tightly as a drowned man, except this time it was Augustine who felt like she was going under. How long had it been now since she hadn't been afraid to close her eyes lest she become overwhelmed by the sensation of sinking beneath water. In the days since Jean-Paul's disappearance, she must have drowned ten thousand times in her mind herself. Now the feeling swept over her again, possibly more forcefully than ever before. Just for a moment, she wanted Joseph to hold her, to lend strength. Finally, he did fold his arms around her and squeeze. Hard.

He did it more in surprise than anything else. Not since the day at the Bridge had he held Augustine and pressed her to him like this. He had, of course, not dared. But surely even if they could not share love, they could at least share grief? How long had it been? Years without holding his beloved in his arms. Oh, how good it felt, the physical reality of her. The strength in her arms and shoulders. They were silent, pressed against each other, frozen into an awkward position side by side on the settee.

Oddly, neither of them cried.

Joseph felt rinsed out, spent, emptied. There had been no thought that the boy might have somehow escaped from the river. Yet until today, there had been some small part of Joseph's awareness which had held back from a complete acceptance of the fact son was dead. Now even this last stubborn resisting hope was gone. Joseph found himself thankful for the familiar jabbing agony in his spine. At least, with each pulsation of pain his mind was swept clean of any thoughts.

For her part, Augustine had known in her heart by the end of the first day of searching that Jean-Paul was gone forever. Whereas Joseph had resisted his grief, she had allowed herself to be pitched into a frenzy of hysteria, wailing and beating her head with her fist, even smashing her forehead against the wall -- all to no avail, except that after a few days, it was as though a great knot had worked its way through her body, and twisting every muscle into a hard lump along the way, then releasing everything. After that, all she felt was a limpness and lethargy that reminded her of when she had been all swallowed up during the pregnancy for Jacqueline. There had never been any question that the only thing to do was to behave as you did when you had a terrible wound -- grit your teeth, endure, wait for the pain to change to numbness, and when it came, be thankful for the numbness, even though it was like paralysis. A kind of little death itself. The arrival of Chief Joyal with the news about the body had caused her no fresh pain, except for the knowledge that it was Bernadette who had found him.

Silence reigned for five, six minutes.

Finally, Joseph was able to ask:

"How did it happen? Finding – it?"

"You don't know?"

"Francois didn't say. I didn't ask. He told me Michel identified it. I didn't have to go. He paused. I didn't want to see it unless I had to. Francois said it was not far along the Seine, a place where they had looked before. That it was -- in a tree.? Eh?"

Augustine straightened, letting her hands fall into Joseph's. It was her turn to look away.

"It was Bernadette who found him."

"Oh, Christ almighty!"

Joseph discovered, to his amazement, that he had several spasms of emotion left in reserve. They came now and seized him so that his head collapsed feebly into his palms and he moaned. Not Bernadette! That his daughter should have to have been the one to see what Jean-Paul must have looked like by now, something that Joseph himself shrank away from, was -- well, one more blow. Emerging dry-eyed back into the world, but feeling even more helpless than before, all he managed to ask was:

"Is she alright?"

"She was hysterical. I guess she'll have bad dreams. She is with Michel and Lorene. Doctor Gendreau went over and gave her some medicine. He said it would be wrong to try to make her go to the Requiem. She's too -- she was screaming a lot, Joseph." Augustine had to stop and gulp to keep control of her voice. "Joseph. She told me something you should know."

"Hm?"

"She told me that she had a dream where Jean-Paul was calling her from Purgatory." Augustine spoke rapidly, afraid that if she paused at all, she wouldn't be able to get started again. "She knew she wasn't supposed to go down by the river, because of the germs but, but the dream was so strong she did anyway. She walked right to the spot where Jean-Paul was, Joseph." Augustine's voice began to break then. "You know how many men went over that area, Joseph. A dozen times. But no one saw except her. She went to exactly the place, Joseph! She said she was called! Jean-Paul called her and so -- so – help—me—God—I—believe—her!"

Augustine broke down completely then.

When she recovered her breath, she said:

"It was a miracle, Joseph."

Then she sobbed with the fullness that caused Joseph to

straighten painfully, lift his arms and let them settle around her shoulders. She kept on sobbing and gasping, her body swaying back and forth. He rocked with her; his face pressed against her shoulder. And at the touch of softness he had not contacted for so long, some barrier way down deep inside him came apart at last with its almost physical sensation of dismemberment and he too was swept by grief. Together, they rocked and wept. Augustine pressed against him, desperate for an embrace that might shelter her soul from the unrelenting horror of living and of death.

It did not occur to Joseph to seek a rational explanation for what his wife had said, such as that Bernadette was so much shorter than a grown man that she might have been able to view things from a different angle.

He took the report at face value. That his oldest daughter should have been the vehicle of Divine Intervention neither surprised nor frightened him. It was a cruel intervention, to be sure, but all of God's actions seemed to have a cruel edge, like a knife. This was, if anything, a cleansing knowledge. It meant that they had not been abandoned and that his will was still being served.

When the storm of feeling had exhausted itself and she could manage a few words again, Augustine said:

"Sister Patricia thinks maybe because he hadn't been buried or had last communion, maybe he was in Purgatory. By finding him, Bernadette released him. Now he can go to Heaven. Oh Joseph!"

Joseph's heart should have leapt at such a thought. Instead, the idea of his son being released from Purgatory hardly registered. He was too busy being astonished by a bizarre discovery. There was a weak but definite stirring in his groin. A flush of shame -- a genuine shock -- hit him. Under the circumstances, it was disgusting. Utterly disgusting. What kind of monster am I? Joseph wondered. Yet it had been so long since he had done anything more than peck Augustine on the cheek, and then only when there was someone else present. He slept in the same room as his wife, but on a single bed against the north wall.

Since he was a cripple everyone had assumed that the damage was worse than it appeared, that it was not just his ability to walk which had been affected. In fact, there was nothing wrong with his apparatus at all.

She had tried perhaps a dozen times over the years to approach him, but had done so awkwardly, unable to make up her mind whether she did him more honour by leaving him alone. When his only response was to flinch away, her unsubtle groping quickly ended. She blushed deeply and retreated, mumbling apologies. In the years before the incident at the Bridge, she would never have been so timid, Joseph reflected. But since the Bridge, she had displayed a complete breakdown in confidence. There were two subjects they never talked about, his condition and her condition. Now, he supposed, there would be a third taboo subject; Jean-Paul. That is how it would be. He knew he had to think now to recall the name of his first son, the one who had died before Bernadette was born. Louis, of course. But there was a pause nowadays. The memory was dim -- would it be that way with Jean-Paul someday? There was so much more to remember --- Oh, Augustine, Joseph wanted to say, I know you have tried to comfort me, have wanted to do sinful things to me when I can do nothing for you, unless you would have me pervert myself or go against the will of the Church, God's will, eh? I am like a priest now, really. God has made it so I cannot be a man for you without putting your life in danger, and everyone thinks I cannot be a man for you because of a great sacrifice that I didn't make, so there is an excuse, a reason, eh? It is so perfect it must be God's work, ma chere? Let me believe that, eh? If I did not believe that I would want to die even more than I do already.

But none of these thoughts were put to words. Joseph said, instead:

"Augustine, stop!"

He expected her to back away without a struggle. The moment was too grim for anything else except misery.

Yet she did not move.

She remained with her arms locked around his neck. And there was an expression on her face that was -- that reminded him of -- that increased the feeling -- that made him weak -- sent a rolling hollow feeling through his lower stomach -- an urgent tingling between his legs. Her blue eyes were searching his face. She seemed dangerous somehow. Hungry. He was suddenly acutely aware of her tremendous strength -- strength greater than his own, he knew. He had never in his life been afraid of a woman, and certainly never his wife. But suddenly, he was. It was a kind of fear that only made the tingling worse, that filled up his forehead with the smell of her, made him abruptly aware that the house was, indeed, deserted except for the two of them. He realized that he had come to depend on the presence of others to restrain her. And to act as a check on her himself, too, of course. But now there was no one around. There was just the veil of knowledge that Jean-Paul's body had just been found, and at such a time, a sense of decency ---

"Augustine," he croaked. "Leave me be. Please."

Her breath was laboured, and she tilted her head slightly to one side, a coy habit she used to have. Well, still had, obviously. Her hair cascaded over her shoulders. Her lips parted just so slightly, and the pointed pink tip of her tongue appeared. There was a serious, intense expression on her face, as though she was contemplating something very practical, like trying to remember a recipe. Except that in those eyes, there was that hint of luxury.

How dare she. A surge of indignance began to gather in his chest. He started to struggle, to push her away. But then her face moved swiftly up to his, she looked into his eyes from only a few inches away, and then those perfect lips brushed delicately against his.

Joseph was struck dumb.

He tried not to groan. But did. He tried in a panic to stifle the buzz of excitement that was already swelling his member, so long held dormant, but failed. Alarm bells rang a futile warning through his head. His body was already trembling. Even if she had not been holding him in a grip that made it impossible for him to pull away, he could not have done so. Already her lips were pressed against his, her tongue was pushing into his mouth. She was holding his face in her hands like a cantaloupe, as though she had begun a process of devouring him, except that instead of an insect-like stab, she was devouring him in softness and wetness, not with her teeth, but with lip muscles that had a life of their own. From deep down in her throat came a whispering sound.

"Augustine!" He gasped." We can't "---

All she said was:

"You'll have your son, Joseph. I swear to you!"

"But you can't –"

"I can!"

He did not know which emotion was stronger -- the lust or the fear. There was danger. He knew it. There was a sense of being high up on a steep mountain face with a wind tearing at him.

Augustine was aflame with something more than a craving for sex. Joseph sensed his last bit of resistance collapsing, and, dimly, the thought of dragging himself through the depths of his mind that this was something he could not deny her. A sadness welled up in him alongside the lust. He had been the martyr for so long and had stood away from her, above her, perhaps now it was her turn. Maybe all either one of them sought was the release of the "little death" as it was called in French. Maybe this was Augustine's way of forcing them both to go on struggling. Maybe -- many things. His brain wanted badly to stop working. And now this woman was making it possible. The promise of a few minutes of blissful mindlessness stood out like a light on the mountain side, and whatever it was that was driving Augustine to do this thing was something that emanated from the bottom of her being. It still frightened him. He could detect a trace of the serpent, of the witch. Here, surely, was forbidden fruit. How did he know that the years of refusing her had not let some poison into her system? How did he know that this was not some act of revenge? Come to think of it, what did he know about his wife anyway? Almost nothing, he thought. She had become a stranger.

278 | *Robert Hunter*

It was his last coherent thought.

Then he was aware of being picked up and carried into the master bedroom, of being lowered onto the spool bed where he lay helplessly while she struggled his pants free, his underwear, his shirt, incongruously leaving him naked except for his socks. Neither of them attempted to say a word.

As Augustine removed her garments, he had the dizzying feeling of being a decadent Roman whose slave had just come into the chamber. Then she was crawling over him, bringing her slackly opened mouth down on his, her passage soaking wet, and smooth as silk. She's crazy, Joseph thought. I'm taking advantage of a crazy woman. God forgive me. I want to do this so badly. I can't help It. The more she is like a dumb creature with no mind, the more I want to do this. Only fleetingly, as the final convulsions began to seize him, did the danger alarms ring again. He struggled for a moment to withdraw, but she locked her legs fiercely around the backs of his thighs and buried her fingers like claws in his thin buttocks, arching her body so that she pressed sweating against him, retaining his shaft to his fullest depth inside, holding him so tightly that he could not have broken away even if he had been able to muster the will to try. He was pinioned. Never had he had such an experience before. Only when he had completely spent himself and the seeds had soaked in did Augustine relax her grip at all.

Afterwards they lay on the bed together, staring at the ceiling, holding hands lightly. For the moment, Joseph chose to forget that he was a cripple and to try to forget what the doctor had said would happen to Augustine if those seeds were to ripen within her. He wanted to trust her rather than the doctor. He was content to believe that, as a woman, she knew what she was doing with her body better than anyone else on earth. He did not want to think about the risks they had taken. He only wanted to think about the promise.

Augustine whispered:

"I wanted to do it now, my lover, you know, while his soul is still close to us here, eh? He did not really go far away, did he? When he called out to Bernadette, I knew he was still somewhere around, so maybe now we have captured him again. We are giving him another chance, Joseph. He has come back to me. I am sure."

Joseph looked over carefully and saw that her eyes were wet, but a tremulous smile was playing up on her lips. For the first time in many years, since back before the time she was carrying Jacqueline, she seemed happy.

Joseph could find nothing to say. Unaccountably, he felt a pang of envy --for Augustine was embarked on a dangerous journey and this time it would be his turn to stand by and watch. She was -- there was only one word for it:

Radiant. A light shone out from inside her.

The months that followed were a turmoil of differing emotions. The smaller girls, Jacqueline, Loretta, and Cecile recovered swiftly. They still broke into tears at odd moments of the day, to be sure, and Monica developed a terror of the river and would not even go into the backyard because from there you could still see the yellow line of dead grass and scrub which was the high watermark that the flood had reached. Cecile was less genuinely frightened but as usual imitated her look-alike sister. Yet by the time August was a month behind, and as the days reached the middle of October, an outsider would not have been able to tell, from watching the girls at play, that tragedy had just cut its way through the middle of their lives. Teresa took longer to recover. Of the girls, she had been closest to Jean-Paul, possibly because to her had fallen most of the task of babysitting him in his infancy and through the first years of learning to walk and talk. It was Bernadette whom everyone worried about most, for even as much as two months after discovering her little brothers' body, she still woke regularly in the night, screaming hysterically. At first Augustine got up every time and silently raced to her daughters' side, holding her and soothing her and singing old French-Canadian songs in her ear. When the waking did not cease, Augustine sent Grande Ma Mere to sleep in Bernadette's bed, in the room with Teresa, and took the girl into the bed beside her. Augustine herself showed no sign of ever experiencing a single moment of impatience. She cradled Bernadette like an infant again.

"It is all good, my flower," she whispered, over and over again. "It was God's will. You released your brother. He loves you more than anyone for that. It was God's will, my sweet little Angel. God's will."

The girl was just beginning to show signs of having learned to push aside the image that continued to haunt her when she woke one morning to feel an uncomfortable itchiness between her legs. The sunlight was just beginning to peek through the curtains, and she could hear the soft breathing of her mother in the bed beside her. Thoughtlessly, Bernadette reached under her nightgown and scratched herself. It took a few moments for it to register that something was wrong. There was something slippery all over her skin. At first, she thought. Oh, I've got the runs. A feeling of shame overwhelmed her, and her nose started sniffing automatically with the telltale odor. But no. There was a smell, but it was something she couldn't identify. She became alarmed and jerked her right hand away from down there, held it up from the covers, and as her fingers emerged with blood on them, she immediately assumed she was dying. The scream that came from her throat was so much louder and shriller than her regular nightmare screams, that both Augustine and Joseph made gasping sounds themselves.

It had never occurred to Augustine to warn her daughter what to expect about this time of her life.

"It is alright, my flower. I shall get a towel. You will be alright. That is just nature, eh? You are a woman now, my little one, that is all. It happened to me. It happens to all your aunts. It just lasts a few days, then goes away for a month. It is no big thing."

But in Bernadette's mind there was a direct connection between the lingering picture of Jean-Paul's lopsided death grin and the insects coming in and out of his head, and her own blood-soaked hand emerging from between her thighs. As a little girl, as soon as she learned that little boys had pee-pees and she had wondered why all the food and stuff in her tummy didn't just fall down on the ground from that little slotted hole just below the bump where her legs came together. She could see how, in Jean-Paul's case, it could not fall because the pee-pee hole was too small. But with herself and her sisters it was different. Often, she had jumped up and down with the purpose of seeing if anything would spill.

In the first few seconds after the discovery of the blood between her legs, she had the feeling that the rupture had at last happened, and everything would flow out of her if she dared to stand, even her lungs and heart. She would be left as hollow as Jean-Paul had been. Later, when Ma Mere got around to explaining that it was blood, somehow, that made it possible for babies to be born, Bernadette nodded solemnly, but didn't believe a word of it. The blood related to death, not life. She knew it. She could not fathom why her mother didn't understand.

By this time, Augustine was lying when she used the present tense to talk about her, saying "it happens to me." For, in fact, she was overdue then, and was positive from all the signs that she was once again truly pregnant. It was strange, she thought, that I was always the one in the house to be experiencing the monthly's, now Bernadette is the only one, because I have stopped, astute as she was at perceiving the thoughts behind the mask of her daughters faces, Augustine this one time missed completely the interpretation that Bernadette had placed upon the beginning of fertility.

Augustine's own emotions had a terrible double-sided quality to them. The loss of Jean-Paul was still an immense wound inside her, like an actual physical hole. She could never pin down its location, but it was there all right, as though a tooth had been removed. A bloody and jagged gap. Yet rooted firmly in one spot in the middle of her being, there was another presence. No one around her could see it or sense it yet. She alone knew of its arrival. A secret thrill went through her, for again, here was an intimacy greater even than the intimate moment with Joseph himself. In the past, the internal liaison with the tiny thing within, not much more than a fat earthworm, had been feeble until at least three or four months. This time, from the moment of Joseph's ejaculation, she felt the sweet bloom of life coming out of nowhere into the middle of her flesh. An invasion, but always a strange one, for it was as if Joseph had shrunk himself down to a needlepoint, then turned himself inside out and started growing all over again. For Augustine. The single most astonishing thing about reproduction wasn't that Joseph could do that, but rather than a man could create a girl instead of just being able to create a boy. She saw her role basically as being as passive as the garden itself. It was the biggest mystery of sex. How a male could put his own seed into the ground -- like planting a carrot, eh? -- only to have a creature the opposite of himself emerge, sands penis. A carrot begetting a squash. Like that.

The wound and the new life stirring in her womb seemed balanced. One shrank. The other grew. She knew that a point would come where each would be equal to the size of the other, and then the wound would stop shrinking and would remain constant for the rest of her life. It would never go away entirely. The other. Well, the other would grow to any size, to be the biggest person in her life, even. Who knew? It was somewhere ahead where no one could say.

She felt fear.

She remembered, all too well, the pangs of Jacqueline's birth -- the hideous swelling, the varicose veins, the ordeal of the hospital, the long trial of hanging suspended in nothingness, obese, useless, utterly dependent, fingers like fat sausages. Her heart thumped rapidly at the thought of having to go through that again. But she had no less vivid memory of the last years of her banishment from the centre of family existence. With Joseph withdrawn into his own pain and bitterness -- Oh, she knew how bitter he felt about what happened, even though he was careful never to say anything about it -- she had been left with a task that was not much more important than being a chimney sweep. She tended to the children; it was true. But that was just for something to do. The children, in all, had been capable of taking care of themselves. They did not even really need Grande Ma Mere. She, Augustine, had lived like a ghost on the edge of existence. The worst part of it had been the fact that there was no one against whom she could rail. Often, she had felt upheaval of anger directed against Joseph for getting himself into the situation he was in. Times when she did not want to help him down the stairs anymore. Times when she did not want to dress him again, forbidden, as she was, to fondle him or excite him or play with him anymore. Yet Joseph had been like a saint. Never once did he complain about not being able to make love. A saint. A great man. There lay the source of anger she would like to direct at him. Why couldn't he just lower himself a bit and they could go back to being like a little boy and little girl again, playing. It would be better than nothing. But no Joseph would have to be fanatical about it. Ah, yes. And anger would have been nice. But she was denied even that. For, of course, Joseph was forcing them into living like priests and nuns, not for his own sake, but for hers. And what argument could there be against that. Augustine felt empty-handed, unable to find any target to strike -- unless it was God.

The fear of what lay ahead was tempered by the knowledge that she was no longer a ghost. She was flesh and blood again. Her body moved about at the centre of Joseph's attention. And God knew it had been a long time since he had noticed her. She had felt during all that time like something discarded. It was the feeling, maybe, that her own mother felt -- that all old women felt. Especially, she guessed, the old maids whose flesh had failed to extend itself outward and whose entire life was left contained in a single frail container of their aging bodies.

She did not believe for a moment that what Doctor Gendreau had said about her dying if she became pregnant was true. The torturer, she thought, he only said that to ruin our lives. He hates us. He only goes to church to keep his patience from going to other doctors. He is a devil. Augustine felt strong, still. The last time had been hideous, yes, but like all other pregnancies, sooner or later, it was over, and the pain and suffering were done with. All that remained was that pink little jewel. That is how it would be this time. Just the same as all the others.

And Joseph will have a purpose in life once more, she reminded herself. Yes, Joseph will have a reason to live and to stay here and not drift off into daydream land like it looked he was doing for a while there. At heart, Augustine felt proud of herself in those first few months, not only for having forced Joseph back into being deeply involved in her and her life, but for having found a way to save him from becoming too strange. Pride. And confidence. A sense of having got back in control of events. It was wonderful.

It was easy, too. No one other than Joseph -- and the doctor, of course -- knew that there was any serious prohibition on her becoming pregnant again. As for her age, she was not considered too old, at least not in Saint Boniface, where women were still used to the idea of bearing children until nature herself finally said non.

To the girls she said:

"Do not cry, my flowers. You lost one brother, but now you are going to have another. Start thinking of a name for him."

To Joseph, she said:

"It is God's will. There is nothing for you to worry about. The Labouchere name will go on, my lover. I know."

Only Grande Ma Mere thought to ask:

"Why now? Why was there such a wait? Tell me what is going on, my daughter."

Augustine averted her eyes.

"There is nothing, Joseph just found himself again."

"Right after his son drowns. I have never heard of such a sing. Sacre bleu!" Her tone of voice became conspiratorial. Her expression became frankly admiring. "I think you were smarter than I thought, daughter. No one tells me these things, and who am I after all but the mother of more children than any of my daughters or sons have ever had. But I tell you, I do not know what you and your husband thought you are doing for a long while there, but it seems to me Joseph just thought his thing was good for going to the bathroom, that was all, eh? Well, it is not an ornament, so I am glad he is not using it like that anymore." Her eyebrows popped up as Augustine blushed. "Do not think I could talk that way, eh?" the old woman demanded. She cackled. "Oh, your father used to have a few drinks, he would tell me all the jokes the men told to him, eh? Then he would forget that he told me. But I remember -- of course, I would never tell you!"

Augustine waited until she was beginning to show a bulge before she said anything to anyone other than her daughters and mother. Then, one Sunday morning coming out of the Basilica after High Mass -- it was a few days before Halloween, and yellow leaves were beginning to drift across the wide stone steps -- she saw Doctor Gendreau coming toward her. There was nothing in his expression yet to indicate that he suspected anything was amiss. Rather, he looked as if he had some minor social enquiry to make. He was about ten strides away when his eyes widened, then narrowed. Augustine saw his lips move as he muttered something under his breath, then he marched over to her side, completely ignoring Joseph, who was braced on his canes, talking to Alderman Odette. As Mayor, Joseph did not have to notice anyone he didn't want to, so he kept his attention fixed on his aging political ally. A dozen other men were hovering nearby, waiting their turn to get to say their piece.

Planting himself at Augustine shoulder, the doctor asked in an icy whisper:

"Is it true, what I observe about yourself?"

She thought for an instant of fencing with him, trying to delay the inevitable, but the look he threw at her was too harshly demanding, too furious. Suddenly, she felt girlish, as though she had been caught by an adult who towered over her. Angry with herself for letting him intimidate her, she pouted. And lowered her head guiltily.

"Madame" -- he started to speak, but took a deep breath instead, his head jerking as though he had been slapped. "Oh, my dear Christ."

Augustine had been anticipating this moment for quite some time. She had planned to be defiant, to sneer at him, to tell him in front of everyone that she had seen through his awful joke, maybe even to tell him the truth. That Jean-Paul would live again. She had, indeed, looked forward to the chance to humiliate and reject le docteur, but now, instead of triumph, she felt infuriatingly like a child caught stealing from the collection plate. And she had to admit to herself that she was also glad that the old monster had appeared. During the last week, she had begun to feel -- sick. she tried to pretend it was her imagination. She ignored it. She busied herself. But it brushed against her, light as a down feather at first. Like something eating her.

Doctor Gendreau let his breath out slowly. His glaring eyes leapt to Joseph, standing in profile not four feet away, but Mayor Labouchere did not look away from the face of the Alderman in front of him for so much as a fraction of a second. The doctor knew that his presence was felt, and that he was being studiously ignored.

Quickly he scanned Madame Laboucheres features. Sure enough, the signs were there. He could tell by the traces of puffiness that framed her face. The toxemia had begun. The mild bulge in her waist told him the infant had to be at least three months gone, too late for an abortion, even if he could talk her into it. It would have had to be done secretly, of course. The priests who run the hospital would never, under any circumstances, permit such an operation. That had not stopped Rene Gendreau in the past, nor would it have stopped him now. Except that it was already too late. Inwardly, the doctor groaned.

He forced a completely artificial smile, effectively enough so that anyone watching -- and they were standing, after all, in the midst of a crowd -- would think he was merely exchanging pleasantry with the Mayor's wife.

Caught off guard, Augustine had a few seconds of fantastic

relief. The doctor was going to say everything was alright and he had been joking.

Instead, he hissed at her.

"It is a rotten way to die, Madame Labouchere, messy, too."

With that, he turned and walked quickly away.

Teresa caught the stricken expression on her mother's face.

"Ma Mere! What is the matter? What did he say?"

"That man is a monster," she growled, grinding her teeth. But her voice was shaky. And she knew that Joseph had been monitoring the brief exchange with his ears, and now he flashed a look at her, to see how she was reacting. He was alert enough to see right away that she had not dominated the situation. The doctor had got the best of her. Which could only mean the worst.

As they were driving home, Joseph kept his glance fixed on the trees and the houses and the people they passed, never once looking at her. Even as she helped him out through the door, she on one side, Teresa on the other, until he could brace his canes against the sidewalk, she averted his eyes. She could tell from the way he trembled that he was barely containing his rage. As soon as he was placed on the chesterfield, he ordered the girls to go to their rooms. Grande Ma Mere too. Augustine slumped on the settee across the room. Joseph spoke in a shouted whisper.

"I thought you said —"

"Joseph." Her voice was weary. "Do not berate me. I am not so strong now. Do not make it more difficult, eh?"

Joseph's face was livid.

"My God, woman, do you realize what this means? My God, my God ----"

He wept.

As she had known she would have to from the very moment she saw him at church, Augustine made an appointment to see Rene

Gendreau. She did not look forward to it in the least and she was prepared to dismiss everything he had to say. Yet she could no longer deny that the sickness had returned. At the end of the day her legs felt as though she had hiked across miles of fields, even though she had confined herself to the house all day and stayed downstairs. Her body felt weaker than at any time she could remember.

Doctor Gendreau's attitude when she finally went to the office, was surprisingly calm, almost sympathetic.

"Madame Labouchere, we have a serious problem," he said. "There is sugar and protein in your urine. You are starting to retain fluid. Your blood pressure is up. As I warned you, in your pre- diabetic condition, the effect of a birth on your body will be traumatic. The big danger is convulsions. Of course, I will put you on salt restrictions, and bedrest has to begin immediately. And when the baby is viable, we shall induce, as before. With much, much luck, you might survive the delivery. Madame. If we somehow manage to squeak through though, the next big danger is that your diabetes will probably become flagrant. There is talk of a treatment being developed in the East, but I have no evidence of it." He paused and looked at her quizzically. "Do you mind if I ask, Madame, who's bright idea this was? Yours, or your husbands?"

"Mon Dieu! That is not for you to ask, doctor".

He shrugged.

"It does not matter. You did not believe me, did you."

"No!"

"Ah, there is no hesitation. Even in these straits, you are still proud of your ignorance." A look of weariness crossed his face and the tiniest spark of compassion. "Well, Madame, I will do everything I can to help, but that is not much. Unlike-- others -- I am no miracle worker."

Augustine's voice sounded childlike in her ears.

"Docteur? The baby?"

"Hum. It has a better chance than you, Madame."

He shook his head. He was grim faced, worried. Then his face cleared. "However, it is all will power, eh? We will make a good show, will we not. But I would urge your family to pray for you, Madame."

Overcome by her newfound confusion and despair she asked a question she had never asked anyone before.

"Will it really do any good, doctor?"

He looked back at her evenly.

"Ninety-nine percent of the time, no. But sometimes I cannot think of any other way to explain what happens." He added softly. "I say try everything, Madame. Light candles. Shout the rosary. Get everyone to kneel. It might make a difference. I cannot say it will not."

After she had left, he thought:

That is the extent of my poverty, eh? Here I am, a doctor, and I do not dare tell this woman that chanting and magical rituals will not work because you never can tell. Certainly, pop up and down around the fire, beat drums, swallow ducks' eggs -- anything, anything, to avoid the darkness. Funny, is it not. They swear all their lives they believe in Heaven but when it comes time to go there, they are all afraid. That poor female is afraid to. Damn it, I should have cut Joe Leboucheres pecker off while I had a chance after that idiotic business at the Bridge. It is too late now.

It was somehow dirty, having a baby now, Bernadette thought. Maybe it served Ma Mere right, getting sick again. If her and Mon Pere could go along all that time without making babies, why couldn't they wait any longer. Bernadette knew by then that there was more to making babies than saying prayers. It was something like going to the bathroom, only a man and a woman did it together with their clothes off. Whatever it was, it was Mon Pere's fault -- that was for sure.

Bernadette found that she was allowed a new intimacy with her mother, now that she was -- a woman. The words sounded strange because she still felt like a young girl. The slightest bumps had begun on her chest, but her ribs still showed, her legs were straight, and her disinterest in boys had not been affected at all. Stomach cramps and blood, as though from a terrible cut -- it didn't make her feel womanly. As for having babies, the thought filled her with a burst of fear. Oh no. Oh no.

The only nice part about it was having Ma Mere talk to her almost as though she were a grown up. Between that and continuing to sleep with her, Bernadette felt herself coming so close into contact with her mother that it seemed, for dreamy moments at a time, that she was a baby again herself. At night, she snuggled against Ma Mere's ample back. It would have been quite heavenly except that Ma Mere was so edgy that she jumped at every little sound, her voice tended to tremble at unexpected moments, and mostly, all she did was say her beads. Over and over and over and over and over ---

After school, the girls and Grand Ma Mere would gather in the bedroom on their knees on the floor around the bed, taking out their own rosary's, and they would pray aloud together.

On Sundays, everyone of Augustine's sisters and brothers and their husbands and wives and children lit candles for her at the Basilica. Perhaps one hundred other people, who had never met her but were aware that the Mayor's wife was having another baby, and she was sick, also dropped coins into the little metal box in front of the candles and lit them one by one. They blazed prettily. After church, dozens of relatives would crowd into the house, going into the bedroom in twos and threes to hold Augustine's hand, hug her, and talk. Grande Ma Mere presided over these functions exactly like the Mother Superior at school, leading visitors into the bedroom, then inviting them to leave when Augustine showed signs of fatigue. Grande Ma Mere fussed over her daughter as she had never before done.

It was Joseph's attitude that baffled and enraged Bernadette. He stayed in the kitchen with the uncles and the older cousins, pouring himself one glass of Scotch whiskey after another. By the time the family members had departed, usually late Sunday afternoon, his voice would be slurring. His last act would be to have one of his brothers-in-law help him to the chesterfield, where he would pass out until supper. He would wake up in a foul mood. All evening he would be grouchy. Everyone, even Grande Ma Mere, would tiptoe around him. Promptly at ten o'clock, he would order Bernadette and Teresa to help him to his feet and into the master bedroom. Whoever had been sitting with Ma Mere would have to leave. Once he had been lowered onto his own single bed, it was Bernadette's task to remove his shirt and undershirt, his slippers, trousers, and socks. She had to tug the night shirt down over his head. From there he could swing his legs upon the bed himself. All she had to do was drop the covers over him. Then she could retreat to the bathroom to change into her night shift herself, creeping back into the bedroom, crawling beside Ma Mere, turning the electric light out. All she heard her mother and father say to each other across the darkened room was: "Bon soir." After then, they were silent.

A nurse was brought in to help. Until Ma Mere's sickness, it had been she who helped Joseph in and out of the bathroom, but now she was bedridden, and Grande Ma Mere was not quite strong enough. Any number of relatives could have been called in, but Joseph insisted that he would rather have professional help. Maybe he meant simply that he wanted the best care for Augustine and himself, but maybe he also meant he did not want some no nosy sister-in-law taking him to the bathroom, gossiping afterwards.

Whatever the reason, the nurse was welcomed by everyone partially because she was remembered as the girl, who had lived in the big brown house that was in the first block opposite the Convent, who went away to Toronto to study nursing. Now she was back, and this was her first job. Her name was Lorene Nadeau. She was only twenty-one years old, plump, friendly -- the first bright ray of light to enter the Labouchere home in memory. She was strong-willed enough not to be deflected from her duties by Grande Ma Mere, attentive to Ma Mere, like a doting niece, like an older sister to the girls, especially Bernadette, and she treated Mon Pere with a crisp businesslike air, more as though she was a secretary than a nurse. She wore her uniform at all times, her light brown hair in a bun, and she hummed cheerfully as she worked.

Grande Ma Mere was still suspicious of anyone who had anything to do with the medical profession, and the children were overawed at first, but Ma Mere took to the nurse immediately. They sat and chattered by the hour when the children were in school and Joseph was at the office. After he got home, however, Lorene's attention shifted to le petite Maire. She treated him like a baby -- whisking him off for his bath or to the toilet. It was arranged so that the young nurse would never have to see Monsieur Labouchere without any clothes at all, since he would either be expertly draped in a towel or a nightshirt. Her job mainly was to assist him in the process of sitting down and getting up or climbing in or out of the bath, an intimacy no one had experienced until then except Ma Mere. No one questioned it, however. It was all a professional thing. And Ma Mere was happy to have Lorene around during the days to talk too. At supper, the girls found they had another adult female with whom to talk.

Twice a week, Doctor Gendreau arrived. His visits were short. He nodded grimly to whatever else happened to be around, asking the young nurse a few clipped questions, seldom made any comment other than, "Hmph," and left without giving any assurances at all. He refused to attend in the evenings or on the weekends when there was a chance Mayor Labouchere would be at home. The doctor seemed unwilling to so much as talk to the other man. And for his part, Joseph showed no eagerness to have anything to do with the doctor. It was as though the one did not exist for the other. And now that there was a nurse she could act as an intermediary, conveying the doctor's scant pronouncements to the husband without Joseph or Rene Gendreau having to come face to face.

During January and February, there was a dull grinding sense to life, typical of the deep winter months, but accentuated in the Labouchere house by Augustine's increasing feebleness and disorientation. The toxemia was worse than the time before. By the beginning of March, her face was almost unrecognizable. She looked obese. There was an unhealthy pallor in her flesh. Try as they might, none of the children could avoid feeling repugnant when they looked at their mother's body. It was as though she had been doing nothing all her life except lying in bed, eating chocolate eclairs and being waited on hand and foot. The image was so ludicrous, compared to the kind of life Ma Mere had always really lived, working her fingers to the bone morning to night, that Teresa couldn't help making a joke about it. "Ma Mere," she said, "you look like a Roman Empress." Teresa had been studying about Rome. But instead of laughing, Augustine made a wailing noise, flopped over on her side, and buried her face in the pillows, refusing to turn around to talk to anyone for hours. Afterwards, the nurse gave them all a lecture on being careful what they said to their mother.

Around their father, of course, they had to be careful as always. More so, Joseph had a strained, menacing quality about him these days. It was, of course, probably just concern about Ma Mere. But there seemed to be more to it. For if it were just worry about her health, he would have been more tender, more sympathetic. As it was, he hardly spoke to her at all. He seemed to be holding himself back from any kind of contact with her. Bernadette guessed that it was shame which made him behave that way.

During the last weeks before Augustine went into the hospital, she lay in her bed staring through the window by the hour, not even saying her beads.

She is despondent, the nurse said. There is nothing much we can do, except respect her wish to be alone. She doesn't feel attractive, you understand.

Oddly, it was at this very time that Mon Pere suddenly got over his abiding anger, whatever its cause. To the nurse's pleasure and the girl's astonishment, Joseph announced after supper. "I'm going to sit with my wife. Do not disturb me."

Once he was on his feet, he shuffled off to the doorway of the master bedroom. He tapped lightly with one of his canes. There was a muffled response. He pushed the door open clumsily, then disappeared inside.

There was only a little light on by the nightstand. Augustine's face was half in shadow. One eye glinted. The other eye could barely be seen. She stirred without curiosity under the covers, a huge, unfamiliar body.

"Oh Joseph, do not look at me," she said, reaching for the string of the lamp.

"No, do not do that," he said. His voice was calm. He looked neither fierce nor angry. He hobbled to the edge of the bed. "Help me," he grunted. Augustine reached out automatically to hold him up by the elbow while he swiveled into position to drop onto the bed, but she miscalculated her own weight and tumbled sideways. Caught in the act of allowing her weight to shift toward her, Joseph lost his balance too. He fell on top of her. For a few seconds they lay there awkwardly, helpless, frustrated, angry. Then Joseph started laughing. It was a feeble laugh, but a laugh, nevertheless. After a pause, Augustine joined him. It had been a long time since the two of them had laughed together. "What a pair we are, eh? Ma chere?"

Augustine wiggled free, allowing Joseph to settle onto the mattress beside her. He let his canes drop on the floor.

"What are you doing here?" she asked.

"I came to hold you." He turned sideways and put his arms around her. "You are still my lover, even if I am useless and selfish and --- things like that. I love you, ma chere. You know," Joseph said.

After a moment, Augustine said: "Yes."

"I am afraid of losing you," Joseph said. "I have always been afraid of losing you. I do not see what I would do if you were not here. So, I have come to stay with you. I want you to be convinced to stay."

"Oh, Joseph, for a while there I was mad at you too. I thought -- I thought –"

"I know what you thought, ma chere. But it is not true. I love you."

At 11:00 o'clock, Bernadette and nurse Lorene opened the bedroom door and cautiously peeked in. They had been silent for hours. Joseph and Augustine were lying on the bed in each others' arms, with him still fully dressed, even wearing his shoes. Silently, the nurse removed them while Bernadette fetched blankets from the other bed and laid them gently over her father. For a moment, it was impossible to hate him. His arms were wrapped around his wife whose face wore a look of happiness that no one had seen there since they could remember. By now she weighed more than he did. In sleep, their faces looked relaxed. Their foreheads were pressed lightly together. Briefly, Bernadette had a feeling about the way her parents must have been at one time -- like two children who were the best of friends. And, somehow, this brought a lump to the girls' throat that talk of something as mysterious as love could never have done. Babes in the wood -- that was what Ma Mere and Mon Pere looked like together in the small circle of light from the bedside lamp. Bernadette had no more idea now of what made adults come and go, to be together and be apart, than before, but she was enormously glad for her mother's sake that Mon Pere had gotten over whatever it was that had made him so still and cold.

Afterwards, the nurse said.

"It will be easier for your mother now that they are on good terms again. She needed that."

It was May 2nd when Augustine went into the Saint Boniface hospital for the second time in her life. Bloated, pale, weak, she barely managed a smile to the children, assembled in the parlor, as she was taken out to the waiting car on a collapsible bed with wheels, two strangers acting as attendants, nurse Lorene giving them urgent whispered orders. Grande Ma Mere hovered at her side protectively. Mon Pere stood on the veranda, dressed in his Sunday best, his face drawn. Jacqueline and Loretta sniffled, but Bernadette and Teresa set an example, so that Cecile, at least, didn't cry. There were three brave little faces, controlling their tears, because, as Bernadette had put it, "We help Ma Mere that way."

It was hard to believe that this was a birth. In fact, it was hardly ever referred to as such. Instead, everyone talked about Ma Mere's disease. It was more like a growth that everyone hoped would be successfully removed. Like a bad tooth. And then the swelling would go down and Ma Mere would be alright. As for the baby within, it had barely been discussed. Of course, it had been years since the last one and the smaller girls were curious to see what one was like. Bernadette and Teresa felt more adult about it. It was Ma Mere's health that concerned them. As for another baby, they shrugged. Who cared? Bernadette was tempted, time and again, to blurt out her thoughts that the whole business was Mon Pere's fault and that Ma Mere, being hauled off in a stretcher, was nothing less than the victim of his lust.

All the way to the hospital, Augustine kept her eyes shut. She did not want to look out the window at familiar houses and streets. She did not want to look for well known faces. She wanted no one to see her. She had hoped that by not looking, she could pretend that she was still at home, dreaming. For the truth was that the hospital filled her with terror. She expected Doctor Gendreau to behave as he had the last time, except probably worse. She fully expected the nurses and the nuns to try to choke her with ether again. And she felt drained, quite incapable of mustering the strength she knew would be required to jettison the huge creature inside her. She had never been heavier and of course she had never been older. It was true, she thought dully, it gets harder as you get older. We just are not as strong. As for the infant, it seemed bigger than any she'd had before. Bigger, even, then Louis.

There was one good thing about getting this close to the main ordeal, she told herself. At least my silly nature is not dredging up doubts and confusion and bad thoughts. She felt surprisingly peaceful.

A feeling gripped her that she had been right in what she had done. To have made herself pregnant again was neither frivolous nor adolescent, as the doctor tried to suggest. And it had not been unwise and suicidal, as Joseph had feared. No. It was the right thing to do and she had known it immediately. The doubts that followed were weaknesses, that was all. For here at last she was on the familiar ground of pain in her body and nothing for the mind to do but endure it as best it could.

The car stopped and she was wheeled into the hospital. She kept her eyes shut, clutching the rosary, letting a tiny smile play on her lips, mocking herself for worrying so much, and she prayed. When Doctor Gendreau appeared, he came to her side and squeezed her left hand comfortably.

"What is this? Are you getting soft in your old age?" She demanded.

The old doctor nodded without comment. There was no point in telling her that his practice of making mothers uncomfortable during delivery, in the hope of hammering some senses about having babies into their brain-washed Catholic heads, was useless in this situation, because he knew, for sure, that whether she lived or died, Augustine would bear no more children than this one. Her body simply would not stand for it. He was astonished that she had endured as well as she had to this point. Now, of course, the trouble would begin. Since there was no lesson to be taught, he saw no point in making things any worse for this woman than they were going to be anyway.

Well, it was bad enough. Her blood pressure was rising. The toxemia was pre-eclamptic, which meant the convulsions would happen anytime.

"I'm afraid, Madame Labouchere," he said, "we are going to have to give you some very painful injections. Nurse, magnesium sulfate. We shall give her two half-ounce shots and see if that does any good."

Her body twitched and tried to pull away and her lips drew back from her teeth. She gasped. But controlled the urge to cry out. It took a long time for the needle to be fully emptied into her arm, and then she thought the arm would never work again. It screamed silently from elbow to shoulder.

Augustine found she was sweating already. She could not help remembering the stories she'd been told when she was small about the missionaries Brebeuf and Lalemont and what the Iroqois had done to them with flame and red-hot iron.

"We will have to wait now," the doctor said. "We cannot induce yet. I shall be back, Madam Labouchere. Please try to rest. If it gets too bad, we shall give you ether, but I would rather wait."

It was pathetic how graceful the woman seemed for even that small concession. Rene Gendreau had thought this thought a thousand times before, but he did so once again with the special certainty that came every time a situation like this developed: Thank God I am a man!

He was back in Augustine's room soon, called by a frantic nurse.

"Doctor Gendreau, something is wrong! She is convulsing!" But it was not convulsions, it was merely her first contractions. A reaction to the magnesium sulfate? Might be. Whatever, there was no need to induce, just to keep a careful eye on her. Technically, she was a week early.

"I do not like this," he muttered. "Nothing is working as it should." He had had enough operations go wrong on him to have developed a sense of when things were going well and when they were not. This was not one of the good times.

The labour lasted only six hours. Augustine tried to stay calm, but she found herself too full of fear and excitement to stop from losing control of her breathing, getting herself twisted in knots that she knew she could avoid if she could keep her senses. Yet from the first hour, she was convinced it was going to be a boy. There was something familiar about the fierceness of the pain, the way her muscles seemed to work.

Yet every other time, she had known some affinity with the thing inside, like a beast swallowed alive, thrashing around in an attempt to escape its predator's gut. This time -- nothing. Quite possibly it was her imagination -- or a fever or exhaustion or the stuff from the needle -- but she was absolutely certain it was a boy. It brooded silently in the neck of her passage, a sulky brute of a boy, she was certain, selfish, gasping, deadly, but she felt tenderness toward him already. Oh, how she would love him and bathe him and tickle him and powder him and kiss him and hug him and hug him. -- Joseph would be in heaven. Life would be wonderful again. Everyone would be happy. It would all be worth it. The excitement was like a tonic. It helped almost as much as the ether they were giving her regularly now as the contractions came faster and faster.

She was strapped down on the table, her arms left free to hold onto the nurse who flanked her on both sides, while a third crouched between her legs alongside Doctor Gendreau. The nurse on her left kept wiping her forehead and assuring her that she was doing well. "You are fine, you are fine. That was good. You are doing very well." But the one down with the doctor just kept yelling --- "Push! Push! Push harder! Come on, lazy bones, you can do better than that!" The third nurse anxiously scanned the blood pressure cup tied tightly around Augustine's arm. Suddenly, the doctor gave a shout.

"Damn, damn! It's a breach! My God, and a big one. Alright, better get more ether. And the forceps. And the tray. It is going to be an episiotomy, I'm afraid."

Augustine caught the desperate undercurrent in his voice. Wildly she looked to the nurse on her left for some kind of assurance, but the nurse was pale and tense. She barely managed to say. "He's going to have to open up your passage to get the forceps in."

They gave her as much ether as they dared but it was nowhere near enough to cancel much more than a portion of her pain. Everything else was naked nerve endings, slashed open. The infant came out in a rush of dark blood, feet first, is blue limbs thrashing briefly, but its head -- the widest part -- got caught in mid pelvis. Augustine's body fought uselessly to eject it, then stiffened, horribly aware that the forceps have been plunged into her middle. The doctor grunted and heaved, pulling so hard that his thin arms trembled. Augustine alternated between being in the operating room and being somewhere in the sky, watching moving checkerboards that rose and fell like waves. Then back, caught in the buildup of another futile contraction, like being hurled again and again at a brick wall. Minutes passed, while the only sound, beside Augustine screams, was the hissing and panting of the doctor and the nurse who was trying to help him, while the other two held Augustine's arms. She writhed. They tugged. It was like waiting for a bone to break. Augustine overheard the doctor gasp to the nun, "Can you baptize?" And she answered, "Yes." "Get the holy water then," he said. He gave a final heave, and the great stone snagged in the cup of Augustine's pelvis came free. But five minutes had passed since its feet thrust out, and although Rene slapped it stingingly, again and again, he knew it was too elongated. There was no heartbeat. The rubbery softness of the form was stiffening already. He noted, as he handed the bloody thing to the nurse that it was, indeed, the boy that Madam Labouchere had predicted. It must weigh at least ten pounds, he thought.

But he no longer cared about the baby. It was beyond help. His concern now was for the woman. She had a retained placenta -- it would not separate from the side of the womb. Now that the passage had been unplugged, blood was pouring out copiously. There was only one thing to do at this stage, and that was to reach into the womb with his hand and claw at the placenta with his fingers. He had never run into this situation before. Words from the medical text leapt to mind. Placenta accerta. Described as "extremely adherent." He scraped frantically while blood splashed all over his gown and onto his mask.

"Blood pressure dropping!"

He drew his arm back out of the slippery mess, not certain whether all of the placenta had come loose, but suddenly aware that it probably did not matter any longer. The womb itself was atonic. It was not contracting. The woman lay open, like a gutted turkey, while the blood poured out of her in an unbelievable tide.

Weakly, she asked.

"Is it a boy? Please, is it a boy?"

The nurse who was trying to mop the woman's forehead looked at Doctor Gendreau pleadingly.

He tugged his mask down for a moment and said hoarsely:

"It's alright, Madame Labouchere. You have your baby boy."

All three nurses exchanged looks, then nodded at each other. It was best this way. They knew as well as a doctor that it was almost over, and there was nothing more they could do.

A minute later, Augustine went into shock. Her face, already pale, abruptly took on a wax like quality. Her heartbeat became rapid and weak in response to the blood loss. Her hands become clammy and cold. Her eyelids sagged shut.

There was a small shudder. Her heart stopped entirely. For a moment, there was silence in the room. Then the nun brought the holy water to Augustine's side, and chanted the incarnation that was necessary so that the soul of the dead might enter heaven.

Rene Gendreau stood up exhaustedly, peeling his gloves away and throwing them on the floor where they splashed in a thick puddle of blood. There was nothing much to be satisfied with. He had lost both mother and child. And undiagnosed breech -- with dangers of convulsions even to begin with. Who could have done anything? Yet --there was one small thing. One exceedingly small thing. At least in death, Augustine's lips wore a smile of triumph. She thought she had won.

PART EIGHT

ARRIVAL MONTREAL, QUEBEC

1979

It had not been as terrible as Bernadette expected, climbing on board the gigantic jetliner, a 747 they called it. Made her think of a big, fat eel. Parked there on the vast slab of concrete that ran all the way to the ocean's edge, it bulged metal roof standing as tall as some apartment buildings, it looked too unbelievable huge and heavy to ever lift into the air anyway. She had never seen one up close. Mon Dieu, is this what the human race has been doing while I've been away in a fishing port? The thing was bigger than some freighters! Going aboard had been so fascinating, in fact, she momentarily forgot her terror. What a nice, clean smell! Look at the carpets, the strange way the metal was moulded – could they *do* that? – the fancy fold-back lounge chairs. All the buttons and lights! What is this? She thought giddily. Have I lived into the future? Tomorrow-Land? It was like something on the cover of one of those old pulp science-fiction magazines her Stephen had collected as a boy. Even the stewardesses' outfits – there were Space Cadets, like Stephen had clipped from the back of corn flakes boxes! Linda had explained to the ticket-clerk that this was her mother's first flight and was assured they knew how to deal with "white-knuckle" passengers. And what about the baby? Did they have earplugs? Candies? Gravol? Bernadette marvelled: they were certainly well-trained, these air-people. A sweet young French-Canadian girl escorted them out through the metal accordion-thing sticking out from the terminal and attached like some sort of sucker pad to the side of the plane, and sat her in the aisle in the very middle between the wings, so there would be less chance of her seeing the ground, with little Paul beside her, a whole seat to himself even though they weren't paying for him because he was so small. Linda perched herself nervously in the window seat, yanking the blind down.

"Mom," she lectured, "if you freak out, he'll freak out too. Please don't be overdramatic, okay? No matter what! It's all psychological." Bernadette gasped at her daughter's appalling insensitivity but had to agree with her reasoning. That was a good idea: worry about the bebe, not herself. Yes, couldn't frighten the little tyke, could she? "If you blow this, you know," Linda added implacable, "I'm sure as hell not letting you take him in to see an old dying man hooked up to a goddamn machine."

Linda was angry because she sensed something wrong with her mother's story – this flight of forgiveness to her alienated father's side, this showing-off of the one and only great-grandson. The old man had been a bigot, hadn't he? Did she want to expose her child, at this tender age, to such vibes? What was Mom's real game? Did she want to shove her little Japanese-looking grandchild in the xenophobic old Frenchman's face, rub it in, get even somehow? Don't even *go* there, Linda told herself. That would be – her lip curled – *using* her baby as a pawn in a dysfunctional Oedipal relationship! Not even Mom would *dare*! Well, she'd be watching. At the first sign of anything twisted, she was outta there with the baby. Karma, my ass! And even if it *was* karma, this wasn't the kind of karma she wanted anything to do with, or have Paul have anything to do with ("Here you are," she could hear David saying patiently, "being paranoid again. Look for the Divine in everything.") Yeh, sure! How could she have said no anyway? David had fallen for it, hook, line and sinker, and he was the guru-in-training who read the I Ching and knew how to do Yoga and meditate and all that, even if his marks were barely average. Still, the nagging doubt: when had Mom suddenly got all hot and bothered about something as esoteric as forgiveness? Of course, she was getting old and maybe her perspective was changing (Was *that* the "Divine"?) As for this inheritance story – shit, that was the kicker. It was *just* possible…

Bernadette came close to crying during the take-off, when the entire plane felt like it was shaking apart, the engine noise became a high-pitched wail louder than anything she had thought possible, and it seemed, if nothing else, the overhead baggage compartments must surely burst open. But the bebe started howling and convulsing when the air pressure dropped, his face turning purple. Linda cradled his head and kissed and caressed and patted him, and Bernadette, in her rush of concern for the child, completely forgot her own near panic. Mon Dieu, supposing he choked. It would be *her* fault! How could she have done this, drag the little angel into this…this… this *hell*!? Mon Dieu, who was the one with no brains? I've killed him! Come on, Sweet One! Breathe! Her awful fear was still there, urgent and consuming, but it had found a new focus. Pressed back in their seats, mother and daughter now had one mutual purpose in their lives: to get the baby to take a breath. Oh, thank God! And another. It was Linda who was doing better at staying calm. Finally, the engine's terrible whine eased off and the extra gravity lifted. It was almost as though they were *gliding*! Immediately, the little angel stopped crying. He looked around, the tears drying on his cheeks, and a mischievous look came over his face. With a happy gurgle, he grabbed Bernadette's dark glasses. Both women laughed wildly with relief, and Linda, having seen the look of genuine anguish on her mother's face when the baby had seemed to be choking, leaned over lovingly and kissed her on the forehead. "You'll make a great granny, Mom," she whispered.

A rare moment. Bernadette was so relieved – at *everything* – she couldn't contain a few tears of her own and several deep gasps. Linda stroked her hair. "You'll be alright." For the first time that Bernadette could remember, her daughter had become the Pillar of Strength. Well! Wasn't that amazing? And Bernadette found, even more amazingly, she didn't object; she felt no urge to resist, to take back over. A new stage, she thought. But then added, stubbornly: I am just vulnerable right now.

The red light pinged off overhead and the NO SMOKING sign went dead. Linda dug immediately into her purse and pulled out a package of cigarettes, a lighter and a small cotton-batten-filled prescription bottle. Shakily, she lit up and twisted the cap. Two pale blue pills fell into her trembling palm.

"I'm an Earth Sign myself," she said sheepishly.

"You? You've never been afraid of heights!"

She grimaced and looked around the place. "Technology, actually. Here, take one. For the nerves. Let it sit under your tongue until it's gone."

"Oh, I don't –"

"Take it, for Christ's sake, Mom. Humour me."

Bernadette meekly obeyed. They were in her daughter's world now – up here, above the earth, the technology place. Listen to her.

The light outside was such a brilliant shining blue, with the wings reflecting light so blindingly, she could not have looked outside into the glare, even if we wanted to. One by one, most of the other window shades clicked down, Linda turned on the overhead lights. Everything else fell into shadow. The muted thunder of the engines became comforting. The bebe kept them absorbed as he climbed like a restless little bear back and forth between their laps, complaining bitterly when Linda insisted on keeping the blind down, pulled magazines and emergency instructions and sick-bags out of their pouches, tried to chew on everything, made repeated efforts to climb over "Ga" to look at the people behind and escape into the aisle, tossed his bottle on the floor, and tried to squirm under the seats. Somewhere over the Rockies, the Valium took effect.

The window blinds were all down by then. Little Paul had drifted off. Soft lighting. A rubber-wheeled tray pushed along. Tinkling sounds. Drinks. Murmured conversations. It was like they were in a cocktail lounge somewhere! For a change, Linda was *listening* to her. And for a change, when she talked, the girl made good, solid sense. This was wondrous! Bernadette could hardly believe it was happening, but she was soon deep into the best conversation she had *ever* had with her daughter. No one subject. They rambled, wandering inevitably into the subject of family, and how strange and sad it was that none of the boys in the Labouchere side of the family in Linda's generation had survived. Of Bernadette's six sisters, all but Loretta and Bilou had had children. Loretta had gone into sisterhood and moved to somewhere in Alberta, teaching at a Catholic school. Bilou had drifted from one affair to another, never marrying, until now it was too late, and maybe as a result she was basically an alcoholic, still living in Winnipeg. Teresa had married a U.S. serviceman after the war, moved to Minneapolis, and had four daughters. Her only son had been stillborn. Cecile was living in Toronto, twice married, with three girls. Monica, also in Toronto, had had one boy, but he broke his skull falling off a highchair; Monica got divorced after that and never had any more children. Jacqueline, who moved with her air force husband to Australia, produced both a son and a daughter, but the boy died at twelve from meningitis. And her own poor Stephen, of course, never made it past twenty-six. It was as though a curse had fallen upon the Labouchere male seed; it meant the sleeping Buddha in Linda's arms was Mon Pere's only direct male descendant.

But then they got off that subject – it was too emotionally dangerous – and Linda started talking about her memories of growing up on the Coast, catching her first salmon, being held up by somebody to take the wheel of a big trawler, staring into a tank filled with King Crabs, all waving their claws helplessly, and she decided then and there that she was going to get involved in animal rights. Bernadette remembered that day, when the thirteen-year-old had come home and announced: "I'm not going to hurt anything again!" And started cooking her own meals after that, mostly macaroni and bread at first. Now, of course, she was a gourmet vegetarian cook. Another new thought: the girl's strength of character had not been evident, somehow until now. Purpose. Consistency. Maybe it was

Bernadette's fault for not noticing. That hidden brain was out in the open suddenly. Mon Dieu, she was becoming an *equal*. A child who had become an adult, just like other adults, like yourself, just as smart or dumb. She had never experienced this before. They hugged and kissed over the sleeping bebe. When the food came, Linda pushed the chicken away with her plastic fork and ate only the broccoli and carrots and peas. Bernadette only nibbled at her salmon. It was too dry, and she wasn't hungry. "Eat, Mom!" Linda spooned some potatoes into her. "Two babies," she giggled. And, again, Bernadette was not stung. After the food was taken away and they were sipping wine from the little bottles – even plastic wine glasses! – Linda said: "Mom? What were your highlights?"

"I don't know about highlights, but I do remember vividly –" And she was off on a stream-of-consciousness about early childhood stuff, her piano teacher, Mrs. Allenby, her chickens, walking out in the fields, the year of the grasshoppers, the Indian boy who saved her, the Great March on the Bridge, being the Mayor's daughter… But here the effect of the wine, the Valium, lack of food, air pressure change, altitude, repressed anxiety – her reminiscences took a turn from high points to low, and she started to teeter on the verge of being maudlin (certainly what she would normally consider maudlin): the years of taking care of an angry crippled father, the flood that took Jean-Paul, the loss of Ma Mere – and how her life seemed to stop, almost, while she carried others on her back, and it took a long time to get going again – not that it ever did, properly.

"And then," she finished stonily, "the bastard ran away."

Linda blew smoke and stared at it.

"You really hate him for that, more than anything, don't you?"

Even in her maudlin fog, Bernadette got instantly wary.

"I don't hate him anymore," she lied. "I've got over it."

"But you did?"

What was to be lost by admitting it?

"Of course! Wouldn't you?"

"You were actually the surrogate mother, weren't you? God,

it wasn't just that you were an abandoned daughter, you were a jilted wife!"

"What kind of garbage are you talking about?"

"Oh Mom, we all play different psychological roles. You were a stand-in for your mother, just like I'm a stand-in for Stephen."

Bernadette froze. No one had even said such a thing to her. Who would dare? What an awful horrendous lie! What an insult. What an accusation! But then, Linda, stricken – and maybe even a little drunk – leaned over and threw her arms around her mother, pressed her face close, and began to sob. "Oh Mom, oh Mom, I'm sorry." It took Bernadette a moment to unfreeze her arms, for the anger to wash away, replaced by a feeling she had almost forgotten: her little girl crying in her arms. They were never closer, she realized with a pang, that when this happened, closer by far than when they were merely laughing together. Sadness *did* triumph over Joy. She forgot the insult. Something about Stephen, about Mon Pere. High school psychology. She shook It away, like a cobweb. The important thing now was to sooth her little girl, to tell her how much she loved her, we all say stupid things, *do* stupid things. It is so hard to grow up. Is it even possible in this world? Poor baby. I love you.

As she was nodding off in the humming, rumbling, tinkling, vibrating cocktail lounge, Bernadette's last uneasy thought was: *Do stupid things? Am I doing a stupid thing?* She began to fear she could see the answer taking shape.

The plane was already banking and lights were pinging on when the stewardess's voice broke into Bernadette's consciousness, speaking in French first because they were in Quebec air space, "Madames et Messieurs...we are beginning our final descent into Montreal." Her stomach whirled. Her hand shot out to grip Linda's arm. It was the same as the feeling when the Ferris wheel had stopped, except that now she was not just trapped at the top, *the whole wheel was keeling over and falling.* The scream was in her throat, but she held it there. The bebe started to cry, but Linda soothed him with the bottle. With him calm, Bernadette's attention shifted back to her own fears. She closed her eyes and found herself praying – in French! But it was all mixed up: Hail Mary, Full of Grace, Hallowed be thy name. Closing her eyes only made things worse because then she could *imagine* the open sky around them. She tried concentrating on the floor, but somebody pulled a blind up and she caught a glimpse of the wing, fading to a silhouette, slashing through streaming fog, little fire truck lights flashing as though this was already an accident. Unperturbed, the bebe pushed away the nipple and regarded her with a small frown of concern – as though it was *his* turn to worry. "Ga!" he yelled and laughed. "Ga!" she yelled back, having to laugh too, the tension breaking, at least enough so she could breathe again. She took his tiny hand, felt how warm he was, saw how serene he was. Satisfied she was okay, he smiled briefly before turning back to his bottle, allowing her to continue to hold his hand while he chug-a-lugged. And she felt some of his calmness flow into her.

It was only when they passed into the terminal itself and were standing on a long moving conveyor belt bumping along a glass and marble and steel corridor that seemed to stretch for miles that Bernadette finally felt steady enough to let go of her daughter's arm. Looking around, she took a deep breath, and, for a moment, she was entranced -- stunned, actually -- by the sheer scale of the building. You could park cathedrals and basilicas in here and still not touch the ceiling. How could so many acres of glass stand upright like that, not supported by anything? And the art! Mon Dieu, the art! Who *paid* for this? Then she saw the end of the conveyor belt coming and didn't know what to do and had to grab for Linda's arm again. "Wait until the very end, then just step off, like an ordinary step," Linda explained, amused. "We're not going as fast as it seems." Angry that no one had warned her and now she was going to look like a ninny, Bernadette tensed herself for the leap, thinking: what is this, a big carnival? Fly the jet plane! Ride the conveyor belt! Now try skidding on the marble floor. Was this all some kind of game? It was like going through a giant pinball machine. Would she ever get to come out the other end? It felt like she had been in motion forever. That stupid pill had left her feeling heavy and sluggish, and almost detached. Which was maybe a good thing, since everything seemed to be falling into place, without her doing much more than keep moving. They were actually in Montreal. She had the baby with her ---

Although now: something completely unexpected. Mon Dieu, there was Lorene herself, waiting for them beside the huge revolving metal disc where the baggage was being claimed. How did she find out they would be here? It would have been so much better to sidestep her and go straight to the hospital. No need for explanations. No need to be scrutinized. Bernadette recognized her right away, of course, despite the blue rinse hair, the wrinkles, the extra weight, the stooped shoulders. The face had not changed at all, except the neck had disappeared. She had always smiled. She was smiling now. Such a gentle soul. Bernadette's argument had never been particularly with her. She remembered that Lorene was just a couple of years older than herself, yet she looks so much older. Surely! They were almost peers and look at her. Ancient. Wizened. Did that come from taking care of an invalid all these years? There had been lots of gossip around Lorene Nadeau's decision to marry Joe Labouchere. Joe must have money, they said, or a cutie like that would not have married him. Bernadette had thought the worst things about Lorene for a long time --- more than thirty years, at least -- but now that she laid eyes on her, and saw that she had become an old woman, the bad thoughts melted away. Mon Dieu, this woman had been -- still was --- a part of her family. Mon Pere's second wife. Her own stepmother. (Did she steal him? If she did, she deserved to be nominated for sainthood, for it liberating all of them from him.)

Saintly or not, Lorene unfortunately had the power to stop them from getting any closer to Mon Pere. At least, she could make it difficult. With one look at the bebe, she would get the picture.

The only question was, would she understand what this would do to the old bugger?

Lorene greeted her in French, of course.

"Bernadette, I knew you would come, I prayed for it. I have been praying for it for months. You have come just in time too. The nurses say he is right at the edge. I told him just an hour ago to hang on, you were coming. I came out here to make sure you did not get lost. The taxi is waiting, we'll take you right to him."

"Merci, Lorene," was all a stunned Bernadette could think to say. (Prayed for me to come? Oh no!)

Her stepmother kissed Bernadette on each cheek, then folded her arms around her neck, and her tears-soaked Bernadette's scarf. "Oh, thank God, thank God. I left so many candles. And that he is still alive, it's a miracle!"

Astonished, Bernadette found herself hugging Lorene. A moment ago, she had cringed at the sight of her. Now here she was, holding the woman up, comforting her. "I'm so happy you came, so happy. And Joseph. You have no idea," cried Lorene. Then her eyes fell upon Linda and the baby.

Switching to English, the blue haired woman said "You must be, Linda, and this is the little one. Another miracle!" She crossed herself. Linda flinched slightly away. (Watch the hocus-pocus, she thought.) Lorene disengaged herself quickly from Bernadette and reached out with frank curiosity to touch the baby.

"Ohhhhh," she moaned, "such a doll!"

"He's going to be a sumo wrestler," Linda said with a grunt, putting the wiggling kicking bundle down. "Paul. Named after Mom's brother," she added, a trifle over eager to establish the little one's pedigree.

Even though clad in an old fashion dress, Lorene creaked down on her knees to touch the baby reverently, beaming with joy. "Paul," she whispered.

"And you must be his step-great-grandmother," Linda said, looking down at the enraptured old woman on her knees before the little guy. Not too shabby a welcome. This was OK so far. Maybe she had been too harsh on Mom, always expecting the worst. Maybe this would actually be some kind of bonding, healing thing. Four generations --well, almost! "What do you want me to call you?" she asked Lorene.

Lorene laughed easily.

"I would like it if you would call me grandmother. I don't hear that very often."

"Okay, Granny."

"Ga!" squealed the namesake.

And the three adults laughed -- Bernadette partially out of relief that Lorene had not reacted at all to the bebe's foreign look. It either meant she didn't think--- calculatingly -- it would have any effect on Mon Pere, or the innocent loving soul that she was, it didn't cross her mind. Bernadette could not help feeling a twinge, though, at how quick her daughter was to suck up to Lorene. ("Granny" yet! That inheritance fib really took!) Here they were, looking like a trio of happy long-lost relatives on the occasion of a family reunion, with people smiling at them and the bebe as they passed. On the surface, that is certainly how it looked, she had to admit. And then a stab of pain. That is how it *should* be! But it was not. All this happy gurgling, it was a charade!

Or was it? For a few minutes, the rapport between the bebe and Lorene and Linda were so infectious even Bernadette felt a warm glow of their joy. Reunion. Reconciliation. Reconnection. This was good. It was a terrible shame it was all going to lead to everyone probably hating each other. Well, not the baby. But then, he was so *aware*, the little one, would he not notice when things went all to merde? Of course! And Linda is going to be furious, if for no other reason than that she will think the inheritance has been shot -- What have I got myself into? Bernadette wondered in agony. Then she told herself angrily. Remember Ma Mere! For God's sake, *she* might still be alive if it were not for the selfish old goat, and his stupid need for sons. He killed her; it was as simple as that. Killed her with his thing! Unless he paid now, he would never pay. This was better. Bernadette felt herself pulling back from the happy little family scene and becoming detached. Enjoy it while you can, she thought harshly to the others. My moment is just coming. There was a certain look on her father's face she was waiting for. Horror! Betrayal! Ultimate defeat! Something like that.

Outside, in the noisy confusing world of large wet snowflakes, early afternoon headlights, slush and wintry gloom, Lorene guided them to a mud splattered taxi. The taxi left them at the entrance of a hospital, a huge stone building with all the lights on inside. The three women climbed out, Linda carrying the child. Lorene insisted on paying, then led them briskly into the lobby where they joined a small crowd waiting its turn to board an elevator. It seemed incongruous to Bernadette that a plaster of Paris Christ should have to hang on a cross between the doors of the two elevators, just above an aluminum ashtray, but there He was. It also seemed undignified to have to herd together like this, as though they were going to a sports event. They were whisked up to the twenty-third floor in three jumps as silent as they were swift. Then out, into a realm of polished floors, the squeak of nuns crepe soles, fluorescent rectangular lamps on the ceiling, steaming meals being trundled past on rubber wheeled trays, a statue of the Virgin Mary on a pedestal at the end of the hall, white uniforms, crucifixes everywhere. Bernadette felt weak, almost weightless, as she followed Lorene down the hall, Linda hurrying along with the baby. A mood of urgency gripped them all. Then they were at a door. Lorene was pushing it open. The foot of the bed came into view, then an array of rubber tubes and plastic bags hanging from a metal coat stand.

She was far from prepared for the sight of him.

He had shrunk. There were only a few threads of colourless hair lying against a freckled skull. His colour was so faint it seemed he must have been powdered with talcum. His mouth was shriveled and on the tray beside the bed she saw a glass with his false teeth in them, covered with motionless bubbles. Elastic tubes climbed down like veins into various parts of his body, most of them mercifully disappearing from view under the covers, but two of them ended loathsomely in needles hanging like fish hooks from his left arm, and one ran up into his left nostril. His nose was covered with a bandage. There were white bristles all over his shrunken chin and hollow cheeks. The sockets around his eyes were fish-scale grey. The eyes themselves were closed. With a shock, she realized that if Lorene had not guided her right to his side, she would have passed him by, so little did this almost insect-like creature resemble the omnipotent Mon Pere she could remember so vividly. Well! So, the memory now was bigger than the man.

Her eyes unexpectedly filled with tears. Mon Dieu, she realized, she had always been proud of him. It was a secret pride, especially to herself, but much as he had ruined hers and so many other lives, he had always been Number One -- at home, at work, in politics. He had been a misguided, intolerant, crazy peasouper with a mean streak but always he had stood apart from the other men. A leader, damn it! And much as she had hated him, she now knew she had admired him, too. Otherwise, why would she be feeling this horrible, writhing sense of *shame*? Shame because he was no longer the giant. Shame because he was more helpless than the baby. Or was it -- this thought nearly panicked her -- shame she was feeling for herself, her *own* shame, not his. Because of what she was doing here. Coming to drive a stake in. To *brand* him. To say: You have lost, Joseph the Mouth Labouchere! Just one male descendant, old bugger, and *look* at him. Do you understand? Everything you stood for, your little French world, swept away --

A quick rush of vertigo hit, and it was not a delayed reaction to the plane trip. Bernadette felt herself standing on the edge of a precipice. I must act, she thought fanatically. This is all wrong. It is not my nature. Or is it? She forced herself to look hard at the old man's face. He *looked* so helpless, but he was still there, wasn't he? Letting go of nothing, and stubborn and unrelenting as ever. It was not that he was losing his grip on life. It was rather that everything was turning to ash and tissue and dust around his fist hold, leaving nothing clinging to nothing. His toothless mouth hung open beneath the hood of bandages over his nose, and his breath was an awful rasp, but he was still unbroken somehow.

Yet!

Every unconscious doubt she had ever had about this undertaking now burst into her awareness. Could it be that there was something deep inside her character that was as unwilling to let go of her anger at everything, just as him? By pushing ahead with this final unforgiving slap in the face was she being *just like* him. Was she being controlled by the dark part of which *was* him? In that case, he would have won. His horrible mean-spiritedness would have triumphed.

But how could she back out now? She couldn't.

Lorene leaned over him and spoke softly. The old creature on the bed stirred and groaned weakly. Linda glided past Bernadette and sat the baby down gingerly on the side of the bed, alert for any sign that he might be alarmed. He sucked on his bottle, eyeing the apparition before him with mild consternation, but no fear. Linda looked more spooked by far than he did. The image came to mind of a lamb being set at the feet of some kind of half-human, half-mechanical monster connected to all those dials and urine bags and transparent water bottles. But the baby was calm. What was that word the kids used? Beatific? Trusting? Of course, we are his family! He can't imagine us hurting him, or maybe even anybody hurting anybody. That kind of innocence. Bernadette held her breath, frozen. I should grab the baby and run from here, she thought, but it would be an admission that she had had a secret, vengeful agenda all along, and Linda might very well never forgive her. It can happen in families; she knew with certainty. How do you break out of it once it happens? And Lorene herself was exerting some kind of strange influence here, as though Bernadette was a part of an agenda, something to do with candles being lit and prayers being answered and a marvelous chance for a deathbed reconciliation; Lorene seemed to be exhibiting almost a zone of lovingness. What world was she living in? She must really think Bernadette was here to pay her respects to her father, not pay him back. To end more than half a life of alienation and heartbreak. She really thought this was about love, not hate. And the strange part was, her presence was making it almost impossible for Bernadette to hang on to her one motivating thread: Ma Mere, I owe this to you! I am doing it for you, more than anyone. She tried to imagine Ma Mere's ghost in the room with them, hoping that would give her strength. But instead, the ghost immediately flew to Joseph's side and kissed him. It was true: Ma Mere had never stopped loving that man more than herself, possibly more than any of the rest of them, including Bernadette herself. She had loved him more than life. Why? What did she see that was so spectacularly invisible to her daughter? God knew there had to be something, for she was too sweet of a soul to have loved a man who was entirely evil. Wasn't she?

Joseph's eyelids fluttered.

It was the moment Bernadette had dreaded and longed-for. Little Paul was squatting on the bed, his knee touching Joseph's hip, staring at him almost mournfully.

"Joseph," Lorene said softly, happily, in French, "Bernadette and your granddaughter Linda are here with the boy. Your great-grandson is here, Joseph." When he didn't respond, she shook his shoulder delicately. "His name is Paul."

The eyes opened. They were grey green and oddly glazed, almost milky. Blinking, Joseph stared straight ahead for a few seconds, then he swiveled his frail skull (a wonder, Bernadette thought, with the neck so thin, he could turn it at all!) And then fixed his eyes on his prodigy for a long moment. Little Paul looked back, sucking nonchalantly on his bottle. The front of the bed had been raised, so their heads were at the same level, oddly equal. Such a contrast. The old man, the colour of a cocoon, the baby a dazzling gold, the old man's eyes filmed, the infants glittering like mica. Joseph's hands, until now were as motionless as the claws of a sleeping bird, twitched and rose and groped and hooked themselves tenderly around the boy. He tried to move the other arm, to grasp his one and only male descendant completely, but it would only lift a few inches before falling back. A shiver went through Joseph's birdcage body. First one tear, then a stream of them poured out of his eyes, he began to sob.

He gasped: "Merci –Mon Dieu."

Both Linda and Lorene closed in on him, Lorene wiping Joseph's tears, Linda hoisting the baby closer to the old man, the better for Joseph to hold him. She reached out and took his other, useless hands.

"Bonjour, Grandpere," she whispered. "I'm your -- granddaughter." And then, to Bernadette's astonishment Linda started weeping uncontrollably. That got Lorene going. The bebe looked around, frowning at them, then shifted his attention to the interesting tube running out of Joseph's nose, and made a grab for it. Linda caught his hand just in time.

"Ga!" he squawked.

"He has your eyes, Joseph," Lorene said, which was patently untrue. But neither Linda nor Bernadette corrected her. It would have ruined whatever spell had been cast.

His translucent, blue-veined hand trembled as he clasped the baby's arm, drew his hand to his mouth, and kissed it fervently.

"bu—bu—boy?"

"Yes," Lorene answered with a gentle smile. "A boy."

A ragged smile twitched along Joseph's lips. A shudder of relief passed through him.

And then he croaked. "Bernadette?" His head moved, but he seemed to not see her -- or had she changed so much she was unrecognizable? Lorene reached out and took Bernadette's hand, tugging her to the bedside. With her other hand, she grasped Joseph's and pulled it over to Bernadette's, joining them. He felt cold and wafer-like, but his fingers closed with surprising strength on her. He tugged her toward him. She moved in a trance -- part of her screaming. No, no, this is all wrong! -- until she bumped against the edge of the bed. She was unable to resist as he pulled her down beside him, squeezed her hand. There was a spring like intensity to his grip, actual desperation. He gasps for breath, managing to control the sobbing.

"Bernadette," he begged in French, clutching her hand like a lifeline, "please -- forgive –" he had to struggle for another breath, and finished painfully: "-- me."

Thunderstruck, Bernadette stared down at him. Linda and Lorene were looking at her expectantly through their tears. The bebe squirmed in his mother's arms, grunting with impatience to be set free.

Her mouth worked as she tried to think what to say. To scream at him: "You old bugger. *Now* you ask to be forgiven. Left it to the last moment, didn't you? You *dare*?" Or to simply say, "Yes." This is been her story all along, after all. It would look like she was merely following through. David and Linda would be proud of her for her compassion. Lorene's prayers would be answered. Maybe even Mon Pere's and Ma Mere's. She had loved him, no matter what. She made her decision and never changed it. But I am being asked to change my decision, and it isn't fair. I have waited for this moment too long. And what is wrong here? Why isn't he stricken by the sight of a Japanese great-grandson?

And then it hit her. She zeroed in on his eyes, which were looking up at her. But not quite at her. She moved her head.

And his eyes did not move.

My God, she realized, he's blind.

She looked at Lorene, pointed to her own eyes, and shook her head questioningly. Lorene sadly shook her head in reply. It was true then!

"Why didn't you---?" Bernadette started to demand.

But Lorene put a finger to her lips and looked at Bernadette imploringly. Some craziness! He doesn't want to admit it! To the end, he doesn't want to let her know the truth. He doesn't want her to know how vulnerable he really is, how utterly helpless. And at the same time -- having been blind those three terrifying months herself -- she felt all her wells of sympathy opening. Not *that* too. My God, this man has really paid.

Just then, a nurse burst in from the hallway and said in French, "I'm sorry, Madames, but children are definitely not allowed on this ward."

"What's she saying?" Linda flared. "She's not telling us to get out?" Why –"

Lorene intervened. "No, please my dear, the rules are extremely strict here. I have an idea. Let us use our heads here. We will wait at the end of the hall. They can bring him out on a wheelchair."

"No," said Bernadette, suddenly feeling very calm, still holding her father's hand. "You leave. I will stay. I would like to be alone with him."

"It's his daughter," Lorene explained to the nurse, who nodded, but put her hands on her hips, waiting for Linda to remove the baby from the room.

"Come," Lorene urged Linda, who leaned over to the old man, kissed him and said softly, "Au revoir, Grandpere." In all her life, Bernadette had never heard the girl utter a word of French. As they left, Bernadette followed, saying: "Give me an hour. I have a whole lifetime to make up for." They nodded solemnly. She closed the door behind them.

She sat and took his hand again. He clutched her but did not turn his head. The only sounds were the ticking of the big clock on the wall, the mild gurgling of liquid through the tubes, muffled car engines and horns, a steam radiator valve hissing, the murmur of nurses – and, of course, Joseph's agonizing rasping. His eyes had closed, as though acknowledging the uselessness of keeping them open. The tears had dried on his cheeks. He sagged back in the bed, waiting.

A thin hint of a smile played on his lips.

She held his hand firmly and leaned over to his ear.

"You old bugger," she said, "you're happy, aren't you?" Your seed's still out there, eh? Well, I could tell you something that would wipe that smile off your face."

"Was he hearing?" He tensed and turned his face toward her.

She paused, uncertain, and looked away, even though she knew now he could not see her. A statue of Jesus was hanging from the cross on the opposite wall. It was a standard plaster crucifix, painted, the blood bright red, the black eyes staring down at her. Did he? Die for our sins? Why? What an idiot! We still sin. Look at us. Look at him! Looked at me! Capable of so much cruelty. Able to inflict so much pain.

She turned back to the old man.

"So, you want me to forgive you?"

He managed to grunt in the affirmative, his hands squeezing hard as another spasm of pain wracked him.

She said bitterly, "You always had a lot of nerve."

She looked back up at the statue. The blood. The thorns. The eyes. Forgive me, Father--

Once a Catholic -- Bernadette cursed, her eyes flooding with tears, emotions boiling up from the fount of her wounded being. In an explosion, the walls of a lifetime crashed. She was a little girl again, and for all wrong he did, he was *Mon Pere*! Huge. Powerful. A man in the world. Towering. Protecting. And now thrown down, almost flattened into nothing.

She laid her head on his chest, wrapped her arms around him, her hands cupping his face like a chalice and pressed her cheek against him.

The pain poured out of her.

"Oh father," she wept, reverting to French. The words that came to her lips totally astonished her. She hardly knew who was speaking, but the voice was undeniably hers, words she could not have imagined, when she set out, ever uttering, let alone having them emerge with such raw feeling. "Father, forgive *me*! All these years! I *hated* you. I *hated* you. But it was not all your fault, was it. It could not have been. You were just caught up like the rest of us in a stupid, cruel world. I did not help you. I went through the motions, but there was no love in it. I was too mad at you. I am so sorry. Father. Father, I love you, please don't die. I've just found you! Of course, of course, I forgive you!"

She looked back at the statue of Jesus and thought it must be the tears in her eyes causing it, there seemed to be a circular rainbow around Him.

It was her oldest reflex, and for a moment anyway, she chose not to fight it. She slowly, with deeply bowed head, made the Sign of the Cross.

Joseph moaned in a pulse of unbearable pain. He was panting now, hacking, his Adams Apple twisting.

And suddenly, she knew what to do.

She saw them so clearly: the Blackfish, breaking the surface together, blowing silver streams of spray, the collective leisurely dive, coming up again, the mighty simultaneous inhaling before another smooth glide of the pod, as one, back into the depths.

She pressed herself against him, clutching her father's hand, and forcing herself to breathe exactly the way he was breathing, matching his jagged, convulsive rhythm. He writhed for several minutes, but sure enough, the rasping broke a bit, and relaxed slightly, caught his breath. That was better. Much better. She adjusted her own breathing to match his new pace. And then, after several minutes had passed, and he grew calmer, she deliberately slowed her breathing down. Slowly. Slowly. In. Out. Slower. Good. It *felt* right. She was so awash in emotions there really wasn't any part of her staying objective or thinking things through. What she was doing felt like an instinct, like the contractions when she had given birth, only this was the opposite. She had pushed outward then. Now she pushed inward against her father's body, melding it with her heartbeat, the rising and falling of her lungs, until it seemed they were almost one body. Breathe. In. Out. Slower. Slower. He shuddered once and started to cough, but she soothed him, and the fit past. Soon he was back to breathing alongside her, not resisting, as though he was driven by some instinct too. Perfectly matched, as though they were gliding through water. Now, slow it down again. Down further. A long, long slow breath in. A long, slow breath out. No hurry to return. A rocking motion almost. A deeper breath, the deepest yet. An exhaling that went out and out like a peaceful tide, came back, out, back, the interlude between each intake getting longer, and as this happened, his grip loosened, a notch at a time, until his hand simply lay in hers, and they were nearly motionless. Bernadette by now was letting her breath go out longer than she had ever done, and it made her slightly giddy, but she felt herself on a pendulum. It was swinging back and forth, and she was simply riding it out, out, out into nothingness, and then ever so slowly, the breath creeping back into her lungs and his, like four vessels being filled at the same moment, taking forever to fill up, and then beginning the journey through the darkness back through and out, out, out-- out. Her eyes closed, like his. Softer breathing. Gentler. So gentle.

Until, like a leaf finally finding its way to the ground, Joseph Labouchere died, thinking *he* had won.

THE END

AFTERWORD

Bob Hunter was a man of legend, who was able to foresee the future and inspire others to do the same. After he died in 2005 there were honours and awards presented in his name. There were also two Parks and several children named after him. His legacy continues.

I hope that this book, one of the few unpublished manuscripts left behind in his collection will be a treasure for those who loved Bob's written works.

I would like to thank some people who have been a great help in getting this book to print.

I thank Brock Silversides for convincing me to place all on Bob's works in the University of Toronto Archives. Brock is a great archivist and a true believer in saving the works of inspirational people for posterity.

I thank my daughter Emily and my son Will for their love and encouragement and editing assistance.

I thank Bob's brother Don for his advice on e-publishing and for his insights into the meat of the book.

I thank my in-law Professor Thomas Hart for his ongoing love of Bob's writings and for the hours put in to documenting what has been preserved of Bob's works in the archives.

I thank Ferdina Juhi Anthony who helped me with all things

technical when doing the transcribing and initial edits of this book. She was very patient with an old luddite.

Thanks also to my Dyment family for sparking the idea of making the production of this book my Covid Project. It helped me immensely to have a project to focus on.

Most of all, thanks to Bob for leaving this treasure behind for me to uncover. While absorbing myself in this project I often felt I was working with Bob again. I am currently trying to write my own story and he continues to inspire me with his depth of feeling in his great writing.

Printed in the United States
By Bookmasters